Impulsive

A novel by Tammy Ellis

Book 1 of the SoulShips series

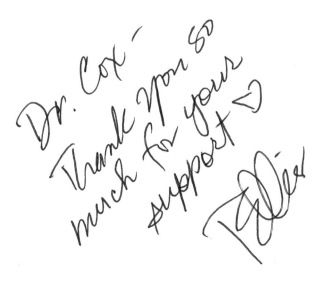

Copyright 2022 © Tammy Ellis

All rights reserved. No part of this publication may be reproduced or distributed in any form or by any means, electronic or mechanical, including photocopying, recording, or by any information storage or retrieval system, without the prior written consent of the author.

ISBN: 978-0-578-39261-5

Dedication

To Marmy. I did it.

Impulsive

Book 1 of the SoulShips series

Chapter 1

Miles Puvi was having doubts. Doubts about his suit. Doubts about his commitment to Sandra. And, probably worst of all, doubts about the wedding.

He was standing in a bedroom he'd never been in before and looking into a chrome-framed wall mirror that reflected his unease. Behind him, he could see his three best friends in various states of assistance. Mara was on the floor with an attitude trying to remember her seamstress skills from high school home economics a decade ago. Sirue was standing in the door frame, focused on his phone, coordinating the last-minute details of the reception. And, Tea was right behind him, fluffing his curly bush of hair that refused to be tamed.

He smoothed the front of his pale-yellow dress shirt and re-adjusted the cuffs for the tenth time. He waved the area beneath his arms, hoping the deodorant held up to its claim. He tilted his chin up to examine his goatee.

"I don't need to shave again, do I?"

"Stop moving, Miles," Tea urged. "No, you look great." She gave him a sincere smile in the reflection of the mirror. "Just let me finish your ha—"

"You're worried about shaving? For real?" Mara quipped from the floor, sucking her index finger after pricking it again.

Miles returned his attention to his hair. He took the pick from Tea to comb and pat his hair into shape.

"Nope, here," Tea grabbed the pick back and pulled him by the arm towards the bed in the center of the room. He sat down and Tea began to style is almost three-inch high tapered bush.

Miles let his gaze fall absently on Tea as she primped him.

"I am nervous as hell," he said, wringing his hands.

From her position on the floor, Mara looked up at her scared friend. She knew he was a wreck. He'd been a wreck since he proposed to Sandra two months ago after knowing her for only three weeks. Mara shook her head and directed her angry energy back at the button she was mending on his gray suit jacket.

His lazy ass should've known this was missing two buttons, she thought to herself. That means he didn't even try it on. It belonged to Sandra's grandfather and was also worn by her father and all her uncles. Miles had time to realize it needed some work, but he never even mentioned the buttons until Mara was on her way to the house. That prompted her to make a quick detour to pick up a cheap sewing kit. Her stitch on the first button was complete and she used her teeth again to tear the white thread. She glared at him and began to unwind another long piece from the spool. *You've known her ass for two months and three weeks, fool, of course you're nervous.* She rolled her eyes dramatically and threaded the needle, not in the mood to repeat the near feud they had almost a week ago.

It was early Saturday morning when Miles called Mara at her apartment. He had just come from Heaven's Gym and, as he'd done every week since they'd met as freshman in college, he dialed Mara's number. Miles would eventually make it around to phoning both Sirue and Tea, but he knew their weekend hibernation habits never allowed them to see sunlight before ten o'clock on Saturdays. Mara was also a gym rat – or fitness freak, as she liked to call herself – so she would either meet him at the gym by seven or they'd meet at the park by sunrise to run. But, this particular Saturday, Miles knew that Mara had a heavy date the night before, so it didn't surprise him one bit that she hadn't reported to the gym.

"Hello, Miles." She answered on the first ring.

"Hey, Mar. I take it you and Steve had some chemistry last night. Where were you this morning, or...do I need to ask?" Miles' phone was in its mount on his dashboard.

Mara chuckled through her grogginess. "Miles, oh my God. He's nice and all…"

"But…"

"Nooooo, no 'but.' *However*, I think he's into his jigsaw puzzles a little too much for my tastes." She stifled a yawn and sat down at her makeshift dining room set which consisted of two creaky, wooden, mismatched chairs she'd found at a yard sale and an oblong cream and blue marbled table. It was a gift from her Aunt Esther who found it while on a garbage run. Owning the E.A.Queden Garbage Company for twenty-five years never stopped her aunt from going on the occasional "run" in one of her trucks. She told Mara it was to keep her grounded and to get on the level of her employees, but Mara knew her frugal aunt did it strictly for the freebies.

"Now, hold up, isn't that the main reason you asked him out?"

"Yeah, I told you how quiet he is at work. One of the only quiet guys there. I thought his interest in puzzles showed a sign of intelligence. Mental acumen," she stated defiantly.

"Dedication and focus." Miles played along.

"Right. A brother into intellectual recreation. Plus, he's tall with perfect teeth. I thought I had it made." Mara propped her feet up on creaky chair number two.

"So…what was wrong with Mr. Jigsaw?"

Mara sighed. "He had pictures on his bedroom walls."

Miles resisted the urge to ask what the hell she was doing in his bedroom on a first date as he maneuvered through the barely occupied streets of Washington, DC.

"Nothing wrong with that," he commented.

"No." She paused. "Pictures of his completed puzzles. I counted fourteen of them. All framed!"

"Oh, nahhh," Miles cracked up.

Mara laughed and could hardly speak. "…and in one of 'em, he's standing next to the puzzle smoking a cigarette."

Miles turned the corner onto his street and struggled to drive while he laughed. "Stop lying."

"Yeah, so it's pretty much over. I mean…we had a lot of sex, but *then* it was pretty much over," Mara played with her fingernails.

Miles' laughter died out, and he fell unusually quiet.

After a few seconds, Mara asked, "What's up?"

He busied himself in the car when he came to a stop sign.

"Miles. Talk." She was never the subtle type. Silence made her uneasy, and she drummed her fingers on the table.

He accelerated and let out a forced sigh. "I'm having second thoughts about Sandra. This wedding might be a mistake."

"Miles! Finally, you came to your senses! We've all been thinking the same thing!" she admitted. "Why don't you call it off and take some time to know each other a little better? You barely know her; I don't even know why you're rushing this shit anyway." Mara was sitting erect in her chair now.

Miles turned into the driveway of the townhouse he shared with Sirue. He put the car into park but left the engine running.

"Damn, you couldn't wait, could you?" The edge in his voice was sudden.

"Huh? Wait for what?"

"You couldn't wait to get that out. Why are y'all trippin' over who I want to marry?"

"Trippin'?" Mara repeated. "Miles, you asked what I thought –"

"No, I didn't." He flattened his tone.

"Well, whatever. You brought it up. I'm trying to keep you from jumping into this penis first."

"What?"

"I'm saying…what other reason would you have to be getting married to Miss Virgin Sandra so soon? Think about it."

"I have thought about it," Miles replied quickly.

"You did not think about it, Miles. Do you even love her?" Mara asked with her hand in the air as if he could see her.

"Do I what? What kind of question is that?" Miles leaned back into his headrest.

"One you can't answer, obviously. I'm waiting." Mara propped her leg up again.

"Yeah, I do, I love her. I wouldn't ask her to be my wife if I didn't."

"But…"

"No, no but. *However*, it just might be too soon, that's all. And what are y'all doing talking about me?" Miles shook his head.

"You know good and well we all talk about each other when one of us makes a stupid decision. Don't act like you don't."

"Oh, now it's a stupid decision. Thank you, again, Mara. You're always so damn easy to talk to." He turned off his phone.

Mara shrugged her shoulders, then rolled her eyes. She shut off her phone. Before the day was over, she called Tea, who confirmed that she was definitely too harsh with Miles. According to Tea, it was a sensitive topic and since Miles rarely expressed his feelings, she should have been more receptive. Mara laid in bed that night, unable to sleep, so she reached for her phone.

"Yo," he answered on the first ring.

"Miles," she said in relief, noticing that he didn't sound sleepy, either. "You know how I shoot off at the mouth."

"Your conscience wouldn't let you sleep, huh?"

"Nope. Can you say 'Don't worry about it' so I can get my beauty rest?" She yawned into her pillow.

"Sure. Don't worry about it," he said.

"Did you talk to Si about it? Or Tea? You know they're nicer than I am," she honestly confessed.

"Yeah, it's cool. I ain't mad at you. At none of y'all, really," he sighed. "I think I was just realizing I had some butterflies. You'll know what I'm talking about when your fast ass finally gets in a committed relationship."

Mara laughed. "Whatever. My prince is gonna be honored to marry this fast ass princess."

"Okay, you're delusional now. Goodnight, princess."

"Bye, jerk."

Mara could feel herself drifting off to dream world, even though the smoke from their earlier conversation still lingered as she closed her eyes.

Back in the impromptu dressing room, Mara resumed sewing the second button.

No one responded to Miles' declaration of nerves.

"Damn. Some friends. No moral support? No words of encouragement?" he asked, looking around the room at each of them.

"No payment for me missing a side teaching gig today?" Sirue countered from across the room, looking up from his phone.

"No band-aids for me poking my finger three times?" Mara added.

Miles rolled his eyes, knowing that was as much consolation as he'd get from those two. He looked up at Tea.

"Tell me I'm not crazy," he said quietly.

"Take a deep breath. It's going to be fine, Miles," she comforted as she finished primping his tapered bush. She took a couple of steps back and put her hands on her hips. "You look very handsome, thanks to me."

Miles inhaled deeply with his eyes closed and loudly exhaled as he stood. He opened his eyes and went to grab the shoes that Sirue held out to him on cue.

"You'll be all right, man," Sirue said unconvincingly, then gave him a half-hug, half-dap. He ended his hold with a few light taps on his back. Although his 6'5" frame slightly towered over Miles' by two inches, he suddenly felt Jurassic in comparison. Maybe his immature decision to marry this woman made Miles appear smaller in his subconscious. "I'll go downstairs and tell them you're on your way."

Miles nodded and Sirue disappeared out of the room. Tea began to busy herself with straightening furniture and anything else out of place.

"Here," Mara held out her hand, and Miles helped her up from the floor. She put the jacket on him, then suddenly grabbed the lapels and made him jump.

"Boy, don't screw this up more than it already is," she hissed through clenched teeth.

He quickly smiled at the double meaning of her warning, because he was sure she wasn't just talking about the old ass blazer. He gently pried her fingers from the fabric.

"Woman, will you just get downstairs? Sandra's brothers are single, go give out your number."

Mara tiptoed and kissed him on the cheek. "You know I already did," she said, then stuck out her tongue. She adjusted her aqua-colored sundress and hummed to herself as she headed out the door. "Tea, I'll save your seat."

"Okay, I'll be right down," Tea answered and smoothed the wrinkles Miles left on the bed sheets. She noticed the needle and thread on the floor took them to the adjoining bathroom. She cut off the lights and walked to the door, expecting Miles to follow.

He stood motionless in the center of the room.

"Tea, my Pops and Aunt Carrie aren't here yet. What if they don't even show up?" he asked in a small whisper.

"Miles, if they told you they're coming, they'll do everything they can to be here. Breathe." She walked towards him and touched both of his arms just above the elbows. He lowered his head to meet her gaze.

"You're going to be fine as long as you're doing what you feel right here," she patted his chest then reached up to hug him.

Miles wrapped his arms around her and inhaled deeply. "You always know how to console me," he said, giving her a squeeze before releasing her.

"Come on, your bride is waiting," she said and grabbed his hand to lead him out of the room.

The stairway was lined with yellow and white lilies, Sandra's favorite flower. Miles and Tea descended, and he was immediately accosted by Sandra's entourage of middle-aged women. They berated him for being so late.

"I know, I'm sorry," was all Tea could hear him utter repeatedly as she turned and walked into the living room, leaving him to the wolves. Three rows of white folding chairs were artfully arranged. The lily motif was exaggerated throughout the room and altar. Tucked in a tight corner was a small white piano. Its player was sitting stoically, presumably awaiting his cue to begin. Tea noticed there were about twice as many guests seated as there were when she'd arrived thirty minutes ago. There was a quiet buzz of whispered conversations as guests looked around the cozy space.

There were no signs to distinguish between the guests of the bride and the guests of the groom. Tea quickly deducted that she, Mara, Sirue, and a few of Miles' line brothers were the sole guests of the groom. Still no sign of his father nor his aunt. She sadly shook her head in disappointment and saw Sirue and Mara sitting in the very last row. She approached and Sirue stood until she sat down between them.

"Hey, y'all. This place got packed fast," Tea whispered.

"I know," Sirue agreed. "And your girl here has been checking out every man with a pulse."

Mara reached over Tea and hit Sirue on the lap. "Shut up and stop sulking because that lady didn't give you the time of day," she whispered loudly.

Tea smirked and looked up at Sirue. "What lady, Si?" she teased.

"Nobody," he said, clearly annoyed.

Mara loudly sucked her teeth. "Boooooy, whatever!"

The older women two rows in front of them turned around with disgust on their faces. One of them put her fingers to her lips and silently shushed her.

Mara looked around dramatically, wondering who they were admonishing. "Um, can I help you?" she asked. Everyone in the room turned to look at her.

"Oh, my goodness, Mara," Tea said, covering her face with her hand. She leaned into Sirue to shield her face even more.

"I don't believe this," Sirue added, taking out his phone and pretending to scroll the blank screen.

The older women simultaneously rolled their eyes and turned back around in their seats, mumbling "no home training" to each other and shaking their heads.

"Mara," Tea whispered.

"Anyway, before the McCleod-Bethune sisters interrupted me...Si was trying to talk to Sandra's friend over there. Miss Lavender Scarf with the matching hat, purse, and shoes," Mara finished.

Sirue and Tea both ignored her. When they didn't respond, Mara rolled her eyes and folded her arms across her chest.

"Where's Miles?" Si asked Tea. He'd seen him come down the stairs, then he appeared to vanish.

"Sandra's family swallowed him whole when they saw him. They took him to a back room somewhere probably to scare the living crap out of him."

Just then, the two bridesmaids and the maid of honor entered all resembling clones of each other. Identical hairstyles, figures, and mannerisms. They walked toward the front of the flora-regaled living room, holding their bouquets in front of them. The pianist in the corner began the processional and the two groomsmen and best man all stood at attention. It was at this moment that Sirue felt the sting of jealousy in his chest. He knew the reasoning behind Miles' decision – or indecision – to allow Sandra's oldest brother to be the best man.

He recalled the conversation they'd had a week ago on Saturday. They were eating a late lunch and Miles had just recanted the argument he'd gotten into with Mara.

"You know she always speaks her mind," Sirue said, while sprinkling more pepper on the baked potato he prepared.

Miles swallowed his bite with as little unnecessary chewing as possible. "Yeah, and she told me that y'all had a little talk about my supposed mistake in getting married. Man, how y'all gonna talk behind my back and not just come out and tell me?" He jabbed three pieces of Romaine lettuce onto his fork.

"Behind your back? Please. Y'all talk about me in my face."

"Yeah, but you do have a lot of issues, my brother," Miles said.

Sirue nodded and they both laughed.

"But, uh...so...I've been meaning to uh...tell you something," Miles cleared his throat and took a long sip of his lemonade. He put the glass down and didn't take his eyes off of it.

Sirue looked at the glass, too, wondering what the hesitation was about. His gaze met his friend's, and he raised his brow indicating for him to proceed.

"Well," Miles tapped the glass. "Sandra's big brother, Ray, is going to Europe for a few years because of his job, and...well..."

"Uh-huh," Sirue urged him on, wondering what it had to do with him.

"And she...well, he asked us if he could be the best man." Miles spat out the sentence so fast he couldn't be sure if he'd said it at all.

Sirue picked up his own glass and took a long sip. He felt the liquid drop to the pit of his stomach. "Can't believe you allowed her to do that, man."

"Si, trust me, we fought about it."

"And she won," Sirue's hand was still on his glass.

Miles was silent, except for his finger tapping the table.

"So, your decision is set in stone?" Sirue asked.

"Yeah, pretty much. I'm sorry, man."

Sirue grunted a response and Miles knew he was going to brood over this one. He was never one to get overtly angry. Every emotion with Sirue was internalized, processed, and stored until a later date and time. Miles actually didn't think it would be such a big deal since no one even believed he should be getting married, anyway.

Sirue stood to clear his plate and Miles followed.

"I mean, check it out. This wedding is all about her and her family, right?" Miles said.

Sirue gave him a quizzical look as he turned on the faucet and soaped the water.

"No, no, get this. I'm letting her do her thing for the wedding, but the reception is all about me. I talked to Tea already, she's handling the food afterwards at the dance hall. I figured you could help her with that. I'm trying to get DJ Toonz from Kazz Beats. You know he's gonna be off the hook, playing Southeast Bangers all night," Miles spoke of his favorite go-go band.

Sirue was washing his dishes and looked over at his best friend. For a minute, he almost felt sorry for Miles. He pretended to intently listen while he surmised that Miles simply couldn't help it. Twenty-five years old and still no real accountability for his actions. Miles always meant well, but for as long as Sirue knew him, he'd always been the type of person who just happened to be in the midst of circumstance. Seemingly oblivious to the gravity of some situations yet could detect someone else being taken for granted a mile away.

"Si, man, you ain't even listening," Miles stated matter-of-factly.

"I hear you. Reception will be off the hook."

Miles continued to play up the festivities while Sirue wondered exactly how awful this fiasco was going to be.

"Do you, Sandra, take Miles to be your lawfully wedded husband? To love and to cherish, in sickness and in health, until death parts you?" Reverend Lawrence asked.

"I do," Sandra's high-pitched voice answered from behind her veil. There was a collective "awwww" from the women in the audience.

"Do you, Miles, take Sandra to be your lawfully wedded wife? To love and to cherish, in sickness and health, until death parts you?"

Miles cleared his throat, opened his mouth, and found himself unable to make a sound. Sandra furrowed her eyebrows and lightly pushed his chest.

"Honey," she insisted.

Reverend Lawrence cleared his throat with exaggeration. "Son, did you hear me?"

Miles looked around at the strangers in the chairs, the lilies surrounding them, the reverend's blank look, and had a few seconds of clarity.

"Aw, shit," Mara said, sitting upright in her seat.

Tea hung her head, closed her eyes, and covered her face in total disbelief.

Sirue checked the time on his phone. *I could have picked up the other teaching gig*, he thought.

Chapter 2

"Have you ever thought: This is the moment I'm going to die? When you have this surreal millisecond of supreme reality? When all your mistakes and all your prejudgments rectify themselves? You know that you won't walk toward some heavenly light because your clarity is your light? That's what happened to me. I couldn't see beyond my clarity. It hit me hard. I knew that if I didn't act on what I was feeling right then that the rest of my life would be this fragile balloon about to burst any second. Everything would be a joke. My own skin would absorb me. That's how I felt up there standing in front of everybody. I knew what I had to do because I felt so relieved that I could die."

Tea, Mara, and Sirue stared at Miles in total confusion. They sat at a table at Pennie's Family Restaurant on a Saturday afternoon – exactly one week after Miles' life-changing epiphany at the altar. It was the first time they'd seen Miles since the wedding. After he took almost sixty seconds to answer Reverend Lawrence's question, Sandra got the point. Before Miles had attempted to speak again, she saw him slowly shaking his head. She shoved him as hard as her devastation could muster. She ran upstairs, lifting her dress as she careened two steps at a time, her aunts following closely behind. Miles had fallen back against an ivory-colored China cabinet but managed to steady himself enough to dodge the first blow that came towards him. The Europe-bound Ray made hard contact with the glass in the cabinet, which left a gushing wound on his right knuckles. He turned and came towards Miles again. Sirue made it there in time to subdue Ray, and Miles stepped to him fast. They were both close enough to feel each other's breath, and Ray struggled to free himself from Sirue's grasp. Miles reluctantly walked away, yanked off her grandfather's jacket, stormed through the living room and out the front door. Tea and Mara were on their way to follow him when Mara accidentally pushed past one of the older women from the front row. The woman cursed at Mara, who immediately retaliated with her own choice language. After five minutes of craziness, Sirue, Tea, and Mara finally made it outside, but Miles was nowhere in sight. He didn't even come home to grab any belongings, nor did he answer his cell. A week later, he called everyone and asked them to meet him at Pennie's.

"Well...say something," Miles insisted. He looked at each of their faces, his finger holding open his journal at the page he'd just finished reading.

Mara felt her jaw hanging open and had to make a conscious effort to close it. She turned to her left and saw that Sirue was also stunned. To her right, Tea was looking at her in confusion. Simultaneously, all three looked at Miles.

"What??" he said, sick of their exchanged glances.

"Uh, Miles. I'm mad you haven't answered my calls or texts in a whole week, then you call us here to listen to your damn diary?" Mara asked, frustrated with the whole production.

"I mean, I know you were going through some things," Tea said softly, "but we never do that to each other. I could barely focus at the salon this week because I was so worried about you."

Sirue rubbed his face. "And you could have told me you just needed some time, man. A text takes like ten seconds. Where the hell have you been?"

Everybody was on edge. No one knew what to expect from Miles from one day to the next. Sometimes, Miles didn't know what to expect from himself. He closed his journal and set it on the table before him. He tapped it and got lost in thought.

"What's going on, man?" Sirue asked with concern.

"Nothing's going on," Miles replied calmly, still staring at his journal. He raised his gaze to meet theirs. "I just had to deal with it my own way, that's all. That was a lot to have on my mind."

"Miles, you did that to yourself," Mara picked up her menu and started to thumb through it.

"But I'm saying…in life, everybody makes unwise decisions. The way the people around you react to you afterwards is the true test of your character," Miles responded.

Everyone got the dumbfounded expression again. Mara dropped the menu and threw her hands up.

"Are you quoting the Qur'an now?" Tea asked.

Miles cracked a smile for the first time. "Naw. I went to my Aunt Carrie's house."

Sirue let out a sigh of relief. "Oh, well damn. That's pretty much the same as a recruitment camp." He reached for his menu. "How'd you get there from Sandra's house?"

Miles shrugged. "The limo driver was out front waiting for us, and I convinced him to drive me to the train station. Slipping him two hundred probably helped."

Tea sucked her teeth. "Well, did she convert you this time?" she asked, referring to his aunt's ongoing quest to bring her only nephew aboard with the Nation of Islam.

"You gonna hold street sessions like Malcolm, bruh?" Mara asked, picking up her menu again.

"No, stop trippin', y'all. I went to a few services with her. The brothers were speaking some truth, though." Miles started to open his journal again, and Sirue and Tea quickly engrossed themselves in the Pennie's Double Burgers on the second page of the menu.

"Listen to what this brother said one night. Brother Abdullah, I think his name was. The theme was destiny, right, and he said: 'You must nourish the faculties of your mind, for they will blossom into the flowers of knowledge that will line your path.' Isn't that—"

"Are you all ready to order?" the waitress politely interrupted.

"YES!" Mara said before she could finish asking. Everyone laughed.

"Y'all aint shit," Miles said, smiling and tossing his journal back onto the table. "I'm trying to share some enlightenment and—"

"Enlighten me on a full stomach, bruh," Mara snapped and ordered her brunch.

After thirty-five minutes of eating and talking, they all walked to the parking lot. They collectively stopped at Sirue's stone gray SUV because his was the first vehicle to arrive at the restaurant, therefore, the closest. He stretched and glanced at his phone.

"Aw, man, I don't believe it's already two thirty," he moaned.

"I know you're not trying to work today," Mara commented, fumbling through her purse for her keys.

"Yeah, just a few hours. There's a new robotic lab I'm creating with Sedrick. It's dope, because it's going to simulate the spread of an experimental virus in a compromised community of specimens. It's for the higher-level microbiology course I've had my eye on and I want to have it written to be approved by Monday," he answered, leaning back on his driver's side door.

Mara was dangling her keys from her hand, arms crossed, staring at Sirue. "And...that's fun to you?"

Tea laughed. "Look at his eyes. They're all glossed over."

"Whatever. In ten years when I run my own biology research company and become paid and published, I'll be doing the laughing when y'all come to –"

"—ask you for a job," they all finished in unison.

"Get a new line, man," Miles teased.

Sirue extended his middle finger at them and opened his door. Miles rubbed his full stomach, which brought into view his journal in his right hand. Tea noticed and grabbed it from him. Sirue started his engine and lowered his window so he could lean out of it. He wouldn't say it, but he was really happy to see his crew together again. Mara came over and leaned on his SUV.

"So, all this week you've been learning about destiny?" Tea questioned Miles, aimlessly thumbing through his cloth-bound journal.

He nodded emphatically. "Yeah, and how every single situation has relevance. I kind of always thought that, I just never knew how to put it into words."

"You didn't seem to be at a loss for words with what you read to us. 'A fragile balloon about to pop'?" Sirue chimed in.

Mara chuckled. "Yes, but his little entry was nice, though. You wrote all that for real?"

Miles nodded again with pride and stroked his goatee.

"You barely made Cs in English," Mara quipped.

"'Cause you and Tea never helped me cheat."

Tea smiled and handed him back the journal. "So, if all situations have relevance, do you think that all relationships have relevance?"

"Yeah, definitely." Miles put his free hand in his jeans pocket and rested against the truck. He squinted at Tea and was pretty sure he knew her next question.

"Even the one you had with Sandra?"

Miles shrugged. "Absolutely. It taught me not to dismiss what I'm feeling."

Mara nodded. "Oooh, I like this new Miles. Don't let the old, annoying one come back."

They all laughed.

"But I really do think everything matters," Miles continued. "Everyone you meet has a purpose in your life. From a cashier to that person who you make eye contact with at a red light."

"Oh, I don't know about all that," Sirue interjected. "Actual relationships matter, not just somebody you glance at."

"Why not?" Miles asked.

"Because then everyone would be connected and your little theory would be bogus," Mara answered for Sirue, who nodded his approval.

Miles raised a finger. "Or would it be? If everybody counts, and we're all connected that could be the purpose the glance serves."

Sirue slowly nodded his head in shocked agreement with his friend. "I see your point, Brother Plato." He held out his fist, which Miles pounded with his own. "I agree with Mara. This Miles can stay. All right, I'm out. We still on for tonight?" Sirue looked over at Mara who was still leaning near his sideview mirror.

She shrugged. "Yeah, I'm going. Tea, you still going past your Granny's house?" She was referring to Tea's great grandmother who recently had hip replacement surgery.

"Yeah," Tea answered sadly.

"She still cussing everybody out?" Miles chuckled.

Tea made a face and nodded. "Yep."

Miles reached over and gave her arm a comforting nudge. "Wait, it's your turn already? Didn't you go two weeks ago? Don't wear yourself out by taking up everybody else's slack," Miles warned with concern.

"I'm taking my aunt's place tonight because it's her anniversary and they want to go out," Tea adjusted her purse on her shoulder and reached out to grab Mara's arm so they could leave, since they rode together.

Miles gave her a scrutinizing look. "Don't let them dump on you."

"I know, you're too young for a breakdown," Sirue joined in.

Tea rolled her eyes, although she was used to them fussing over her by now. They always treated her like she was this timid little bird stuck in a nest somewhere being preyed upon by her evil, selfish family. She knew it was also her short five-foot-three frame that made them so protective, but if she was honest, she loved the security they offered.

"I'll be fine. Come on, Mara," she tugged her arm. "I need to make a few stops before Granny's house."

"Okay, okay," Mara stood up straight and walked over to Miles, hooking her arm in his. She pressed her cheek to his shoulder and looked up at him with a cheesy grin.

Miles squinted down at her. "What?" he asked, putting his hand into his pocket, assuming she wanted something monetary.

"Miiiiiiiles, don't you want to come with me and Si to the Black Café tonight? You're always the life of the party," she said with excitement.

He straightened his face. "You weren't saying that an hour ago."

Tea and Sirue laughed.

"No, no, noooooo, you misunderstood. See, I was just hungry. You really are so much fun to hang out with and vibe with…," Mara jiggled her arm inside of his.

"I'm fun because you want me to pay your way."

"Yep, because I sure as hell won't," Sirue said. "And, Mara, you owe me for the last two times, no three times we went out!"

She gave him an evil eye, then waved him on. "Don't you have to go give robots a disease or something?" she snapped.

He laughed, then put his truck into reverse and drove off.

"Fine, I'll go," Miles said. "I'm in the mood for some jazz."

Mara flashed a quick smile and dislodged her arm. She patted him on the back. "Thanks, buddy," she said dryly, reverting back to her normal tone. "Tea, let's jet. You have stops to make and I want to get my nails done."

"Well, I'm parked on the other side. Bye, beautiful ladies," Miles said, tapping his journal in his hand. "And wait," he paused. "Get your nails done? I thought you were broke."

"See you tonight, Miles!" Mara called over her shoulder.

He grinned and shook his head.

"All right, bye, Miles," Tea said, and he held up his journal to wave goodbye as he turned to walk away.

"I'll be by your place at eight, y'all better be ready," Mara called back to him. He waved his journal in the air again and they parted ways.

Inside of Mara's faded red eighteen-year-old two-door coupe, the static and muted voices from the speakers were as close to music as she could possibly get from her poor excuse for a radio.

Mara sang along to one of her favorite neo-soul singers. "*'Everybody has a mountain to climb'*... sing it, girl!"

Tea was staring out of her window, watching the neighborhood houses move past them. She suddenly reached over and cut off the radio.

"Mara, what do you think about your destiny?" she asked out of nowhere.

"I don't," she quipped, and turned the radio back on.

Tea turned it back off just as quickly. "I'm serious, do you think you have a destiny?"

"I'm about to end *your* destiny if you touch this radio one mo' time."

Tea sucked her teeth. "Girl, please, your cheap radio sounds like a walkie talkie, anyway. Just answer my question."

"Why are you trippin' over what Brother Miles said? You know him – he'll be on some new adventure tomorrow," Mara replied, racing through a yellow light.

"True, he might," Tea agreed, "but I think there's some truth to that, don't you?" She situated her small frame almost completed around to face her friend.

Mara made a left turn at the next corner. "Sure, but it's nothing to get all worked up about. Believing in destiny is just another way to slow you down. I worked my ass off to get into this master's program, you know that whole story. And I'll be damned if I put all this energy into somebody's damn destiny when I'm doing everything myself."

Mara glanced over at Tea, then back at the road.

Tea let out a quiet sigh. She hated when Mara got all fatalistic. She stared at her friend and wondered why it was so hard to get a deep, open conversation going with her sometimes.

"What?" Mara asked, sensing her friend's thoughts. "You think I'm being close-minded?"

"Yep."

"Well, I'm sorry, Tea. I can't be lost in dreamland about stuff. I wouldn't ever get anything done. I leave that dreaming to everyone else. Maybe it was fate that you befriended such a hard ass as me. You need the balance, chica," Mara said and pinched Tea's cheek.

Tea playfully slapped her hand away. "Whatever."

She turned back around in her seat. Mara turned her radio back on, and as they rode along the streets of the nation's capital, Tea wondered how much of their own friendship was really destined to occur.

Chapter 3

Congress Heights was located in southeast, Washington, DC. As far as Tea knew, it wasn't always considered the seedy part of town. She remembered a conversation she had with her Granny since it was her stomping ground. It was originally founded over one hundred years ago with single-family homes in neighborhoods that bordered a psychiatric hospital. She would always be afraid when Granny told her stories of kids playing near the hospital and never coming back home.

Granny also loved to tell her how neighborhoods and neighbors changed since then. Over the last few decades, Congress Heights marked the delineation between the thugs and "not so thugs." Down two more blocks, there were newer rows of multi-family housing inhabited by families who tried to forget they were once surrounded by crime and sirens. Now, instead of two blocks, it took more like twenty blocks to forget the daily drama in Congress Heights. Tea lived in this remote section of southeast with her father, stepmother, and her two younger brothers.

As Tea ascended the four stone steps that led to her front door, she could hear her father and stepmother arguing through closed kitchen windows. She let out a deep sigh and rolled her eyes to herself as she unlocked the bottom lock. The two-beep alarm sounded as she pushed the door open, and before she could get completely inside, she was practically knocked over by Damien and James.

"Tea! Tea!" her brothers called her name in unison.

She closed the door behind her. "Calm down! What?" she asked them, pushing them away enough to give herself some breathing room. Her intuition told her why they were so excited to see her.

"Mommy and Daddy are fighting!" five-year old James said, shoving his two middle fingers in his mouth.

Tea tossed her purse on a nearby table in the foyer and picked him up.

"No, they ain't, they—"

"*Aren't*," Tea corrected ten-year old Damien, and rubbed his head.

"No, they aren't! They just arguin', that's all," he said. He folded his arms across his chest. Tea put her arm around his shoulders and wondered how long they'd had to listen to it this time.

"I tell you what, Day – take James with you down to the basement and play for a while and I'll be down to show you how a real legend plays BattleBlock."

Damien looked up at her and made a face.

"They'll cool down soon, you know how they are." Tea tried to lighten the situation a little and squeezed her little brother's shoulders.

He sucked his teeth. "C'mon, James," he said and took his little brother's hand as Tea put him down.

She watched as they sulked off to the basement steps, and she became even more enraged. She stormed towards the kitchen without trying to calm down first.

"No, you didn't go there!" she heard her stepmother, Anna, yell.

"Yes, I did, and I'll go there again – you are TOO DAMN UNORGANIZED!" her father yelled back, about a decibel louder.

She heard them before she saw them, and slapped her hand down on the counter when she walked in. "I don't believe you can fight like this with them here!" she scolded them between clenched teeth.

Tea's father stopped in mid-sentence. He was sitting at the kitchen table holding a stack of mail and Anna was standing in front of the sink with soapy, dripping yellow gloves, facing him. They both looked at her like she just appeared out of thin air.

"We aren't even fighting, Tea, and I think you need to check your voice level," Anna said, turning back around to finish the dishes.

"*My* voice level? I could hear you outside," she responded, not believing this heifer just tried to correct her. She turned to glare at her father. "And Dad, Damien and James get scared when y'all go back and forth like this."

He turned his attention back to the mail in his hands. "Teacakes, you need to stop babying those boys. They're not as sensitive as you. Plus, they're wired up because we just came back from Anderson's birthday party. Speaking of which," he looked up at the back of his wife. "Anna, Anderson's mother was wondering why you weren't there."

Tea noticed his tone had switched back to condescending and accusatory and didn't know how they ever fell in love.

Anna deliberately dropped a spoon into the sink and turned around with a wet hand on her hip. "And did you tell her why I wasn't there? That every Saturday now I have to tutor some uppity woman's teenage brats to make ends meet? Huh? Did you tell her that or are you too ashamed that your wife has to work one and a half jobs when you're supposed to be some hot shot lawyer—"

"*Supposed* to be? I bust my ass for this family! I pay these goddamn bills!" He slammed the mail onto the table. "And if I remember correctly, my occupation is why you married me in the first place!"

Anna pointed a finger at him. "My mother was right. My whole family was right about you, you selfish –"

"Will you two STOP?! Did you hear what I said about Damien and James?! No wonder they hate leaving Granny's house. I wouldn't want to come back to this either," Tea said, folding her arms across her chest, trying to control her anger.

Both Anna and her father seemed to temporarily concede and went back to ignoring each other. It was one of two extremes with them lately. Tea noticed the change about a year ago, around the time her father left the law firm he helped build. She knew it was a tough move for him, because he worked so hard through law school while she was little, and her mother was still living. He started the business with his lifelong best friend, Peter Johnson. 'Johnson & Racker, Attorneys at Law' was engraved on every pen, pencil, and notepad around the house throughout Tea's high school years. She remembered how happy they were when they got their first lucrative client, which resulted in their most lucrative settlement. Not much longer after that, Tea's mother died giving birth to Damien. Tea picked up a lot of the slack around the house until he met and married Anna. Once James was born, her father started to change. His temperament was awful, and he was increasingly moody with everyone. His business started to decline, until eventually he learned that his partner and friend was not being as honest as he thought. He decided to leave the business and work for the competition, Williams-McDaniels, the most prestigious black-owned corporate law firm in the city. Tea knew her father wasn't happy with the demotion, and it showed in everything he did since.

He broke her out of her reverie and said, "Did Granny call your phone? She called here at the house to see if you were still going over tonight. You know Anna and I are going out with your aunt and uncle for their anniversary."

"I know, Dad, you're all free to go enjoy life," Tea threw up her hands. She walked to the refrigerator and abruptly turned around. "Wait, so who's watching the boys?"

Anna turned her head slowly around to Tea. "Um, we were going to ask...if you don't mind, since you're already going to your nana's house..."

Tea made a face. "It's *Granny*. And sure, why not? How about I go get the neighbor's kids, too?" She slammed the refrigerator door closed and mumbled under her breath. "Why the hell did I go to college again? Why did I even open my own shop? I should have just stayed here and become a nanny." She walked out of the kitchen and felt their eyes following her.

After dropping Tea off at her house, Mara looked at the clock on her dashboard. "Damn," she said to herself when she remembered it had been stuck on three thirty-four for the past week. She pulled her phone from her purse on the passenger seat and convinced herself she had enough time to get a quick run on the treadmill before getting her nails done. She was feeling bloated after eating so much at Pennie's. Tea could scarf down an entire cow plus two pigs and only gain three-fourths of a pound two weeks later. Mara envied Tea's metabolism, but one look in her rear-view mirror reminded her that she had the prettier eyes. They both agreed on that years ago. She ran a finger over her eyebrows and decided she could get those shaped up, too.

Heaven's Gym was a meat market any day of the week. Especially Saturdays. Everybody and their cousins were trying to flex. Mara parked her car too far away for her tastes but didn't have much of a choice. The parking lot looked like a car dealership. She grabbed her gym bag from her back seat and walked inside. By the time she reached the front desk, she was already working up a sweat.

"Damn, that was a long walk," she said to Pierre, the lanky, bespectacled man behind the circular desk in the center of the lobby. He had been trying to ask her out since he gave her the visitor's tour three years ago. All he'd ever received was a half-hearted hello and goodbye. This complete sentence from out of the blue had him flabbergasted. He fumbled the paper clips he was holding and looked up.

"Uh, y-yeah, it's so crazy in here." He pushed his glasses up the bridge of his nose and gave Mara a once-over.

Mara flashed a fake smile, not realizing she even spoke to him. She propped her bag up on the counter and grabbed her laminated ID card from an inside pocket.

"I can get you the…um…the key card that you can um…put on your key ring. Much easier, m-much easier," Pierre stammered, almost too jumbled to be understood.

Mara gave another nondescript smile and tried to scan her card. A red error light blinked.

Before she could try a second time, Pierre grabbed it from her hand, making sure his fingers lingered on top of hers. "I can do that for you."

She snatched it back. "I got it."

"Of course, of course." He held his hand up. "Didn't mean to…you're just so very pretty, Miss Mara."

"Maybe one day when I'm broke, depressed and desperate," she muttered. She swiped the card again and the green light flickered.

"Huh? Wh-what was that?" Pierre moved a little closer, and Mara could smell the breath mints and energy drink on his breath.

"Don't worry about it. Have a good day, Peter," she said and hoisted the gym bag back over her shoulder.

"Pierre," he timidly corrected as she walked off.

Mara looked around to see if she recognized anyone. She usually ran into an average of four familiar faces each time she was at Heaven's. Some she wanted to see and some who just slowed her down. Pierre definitely fit into that category. As she headed to the locker room, she slid the scrunchie off her wrist and pulled her braids into a high bun. Inside the brightly lit room, she found a free bench between a short row of lockers and dropped her bag on it. She quickly changed into her black spandex shorts and a gray Black Lives Matter t-shirt, then locked her belongings away in under five minutes. Mara adjusted her bun in the mirror on her way out and was grateful she allowed Tea to braid her hair a week ago. It was a headache, literally, when she sat for eight hours getting the tiny microbraids put in, but it was definitely a convenience that her best friend was a hair stylist.

Walking back to the main room where the bicycles, stair steppers, and other cardiovascular equipment were kept, Mara found her favorite treadmill occupied. There was a line of people also waiting to sweat off their frustrations, or their lunches. Mara checked her knock-off fitness watch. Five more hours until she promised to meet Miles and Sirue. She grimaced as she mentally recounted her itinerary. She knew she would spend a good hour at the nail salon. She had to hit the grocery store since it was the last day their turkey wings would be on sale. Then, she had to drop off a few overdue library books since she borrowed them using Tea's account, and of course she had to get herself ready. Mara calculated about an hour was free for her to get in a good workout if that damn skinny wench would get off her machine.

She quickly lost patience and although Heaven's was pumping some fire hip hop mixes, she found herself getting agitated. There was nothing worse than having her plans altered by some stranger. She was immediately reminded of Miles and his harangue an hour ago. "So, all these randoms matter in some strange way? Yeah, right," she mused to herself.

She gave up on the treadmill jog and headed towards the weight room, which doubled as the indoor track. She passed a few brothers playing some serious basketball in the glass-enclosed court. They were acting like there were professional scouts in the house. Mara loved everything about basketball and could hold her own on the hardwood, having played the two-guard in high school and for a few years in college. Her five-foot eight-inch stature supported a smooth one hundred forty pounds for the last ten years, and Mara saw to it that any ounce she gained was quickly worked off at any cost. As much as she loved fried turkey wings and greasy fried potatoes, the cost was usually a strenuous workout.

"Ouuuuuch," she said out loud when a mountain of a brother committed a hard foul on the player going for a layup. He ended square on his rear and his goggles sat lopsided on his face. The mountain man helped him up and the other players clowned him for falling the way he did. Mara laughed, too, then caught herself because she realized she was all up in their game.

She decided against going to the court to show off her handling skills because she didn't want to embarrass anyone more than it was necessary, and eventually made it to the weight room. She groaned when she saw that the machines were all being utilized and after a quick once over, she again noticed that she only recognized a few people. There was Sandy, the personal trainer who was obviously bored to death helping an elderly man with his futile attempt to look like a young Adonis. Then there was Lucky Lucas, who always won the fifty-dollar lottery at the liquor store next door and came into the gym to brag about it. He was on the side giving his biceps a workout with the free weights while yapping away to a woman next to him. And the last familiar face was a nameless regular who had lost a lot of weight but didn't talk much to anyone. There were a few brisk walkers on the three-lane track who all seemed to use the inside lane. Mara took off on the outer lane, keeping a steady jogging pace. She managed to clock eight miles in forty-five minutes. She was not pleased with her time, but she admired her own sweaty, medium-brown legs in the mirrored walls as she walked back to the locker room.

When she arrived at her locker, she noticed two women toweling off a few feet away from her. They halted their conversation when Mara approached, simultaneously sized her up, and rolled their eyes as if she'd intruded on some secret, then went back to whispering. Mara stood with her hand on the combination lock and stared at them. She figured she could take the one standing up, who looked as small as Tea, but the one sitting on the bench with the thick, natural hair pulled into two long braids looked like she could cause some damage.

Impulses to say something to the thirty-something women subsided and Mara settled for cutting her eyes at them both. She didn't believe that females this old still started problems. As she opened her locker and toweled her sweat off, she listened to as much of their conversation as she could.

"So, did you get his number?"

"Yes, girl, of course. I took a quick selfie of us both and air dropped it right to him," the short one said.

"Oooh, damn. What if his wife goes through his phone?"

"Shut up," she hit her friend with a towel. "I did not see a ring."

"Okay, just be careful. He could be all the way on the down low. Don't get yourself caught up in what you can't handle. He probably gave his number to like ten women in here." The seated friend dabbed her neck and chest with her own towel.

Mara slightly nodded her head in agreement as she took off her soaking wet shirt and put on the shirt she came in with. She agreed, though it was advice that she rarely took herself.

Then, the sister lost all credibility.

"Sheeeeeeeeeit, 'cause how you gonna get his bag if he got a wife at home? You know bitches be crazy!" Both friends laughed and high-fived each other.

Mara could not get out of there fast enough. Ignorant conversations irritated her. She sped past Pierre and glanced in his direction when he gave her a slight wave.

Chapter 4

Sirue looked down at the designer watch on his wrist. There were few things he despised more than people who didn't follow through. It was ten to eight and there was no sign of Miles, nor had he heard from Mara. Sirue had been styled and ready to go not long after he got back from the biology lab. He and his colleague, Sedrick Gambere, put in a very productive four hours after he left Pennie's. They put the finishing touches on the bio-robotic experiment and were able to run two complete simulations. There was only one major problem with the virus activity that required the expertise of their friend in the engineering department. Once he was able to help them troubleshoot via a video call, Sirue and Sedrick began writing the rough draft of their proposal.

So, Sirue was definitely in the mood to celebrate. When he got home, he put on his favorite mellow jazz album and relaxed while he disinfected the kitchen counters and floors with a pine-scented cleaner. Once everything sparkled to his satisfaction, he enjoyed a long, hot shower. He shaped up his own close fade with the deluxe set of clippers Mara gave him last Christmas after weeks of calling him Jagged Edge. He applied some oil moisturizer, lightly sprayed his cologne, and brushed his teeth once again for good measure.

At five past eight, he was in the living room thumbing through a biochemistry science journal when his phone rang. He yanked it up from the arm of the couch without looking.

"It's about damn time," his baritone barked into the phone.

"Excuse me?" a startled woman's voice replied.

Sirue recognized it immediately and wished he'd let it go to voice mail.

Her name was Teresa Nichols. She was a lady friend he'd been seeing – or rather, trying not to see – off and on for the past year. Sirue had it bad for her when they first shared glances. A twenty-two-year-old undergrad senior majoring in business, but taking time off college to save money as a full-time shift manager at a fast-food taco restaurant. Sirue loved her conversation and the free nachos. He was also very drawn to her strong first impression. She challenged him in almost every debate they had and would rarely back down from an argument. Early on, she explained that her abrasive personality was her defense against her dysfunctional upbringing and being shipped from group home to foster home and back to group homes. Through it all, she succeeded in attaining a full academic scholarship. They dated seriously for a month, both thoroughly enjoying the almost nightly sexcapades. Then, Sirue's job duties required more of his time, and their adventures turned into arguments. The more time he spent working, the more possessive she became. They mutually agreed to call it quits. Or so Sirue thought. Teresa continued to call and come to hear his lectures uninvited. It had been a few weeks since he'd had to endure her fatal attraction, but he knew that a random call like this was waiting in the wings.

"Teresa," Sirue said, not masking his disappointment.

"Damn, good to hear your voice, too," she retorted. Then her voice became liquid sweet. "Anyway, what have you been up to?"

"I thought I was up to changing my number a week ago. How did you get this one?" he questioned, convinced she truly lived up to Mara's nickname for her: double-oh-seven.

"Don't worry about it, I got it." She tried to keep the syrup in her tone, but it was fading fast.

"Yeah, I see. What do you want, Teresa? I'm on my way out."

"Your voice is so damn sexy when you're mad. I just wanted to talk to you, that's all. Can you stop by my apartment? Please?" She begged with lust in her voice.

Sirue could imagine her mouth, pouty lips, naturally wavy brown hair, and lightly tanned skin. He knew she would rock his world. He knew it without a doubt. And the fact that she made it so easy was the same reason he despised himself for wanting her.

"You don't need to be so desperate."

There was silence on the other end. Sirue let out a muffled sigh as he rubbed his face and leaned his head back against the sofa.

"I want your company so I'm desperate?" Her feelings seemed to be genuinely hurt.

He hated to disrespect her, but she never caught his hints.

"Look, Teresa, I'm not trying to –" Sirue heard Miles' keys in the front door, "—hurt your feelings, but don't you have someone else you could call and talk to? It's not a good idea for us...for me to get involved."

Miles walked in with a loud "Woooooo" and clumsily kicked his name brand sneakers off as he did a pee dance then ran down the short hallway to the half-bathroom.

"No, I don't," Teresa stated. "And who's that? Miles? Tell him I said hi. I miss hanging out with y'all."

Sirue thought her voice sounded strange.

"Are you dating? You know, seeing someone?" he asked, ignoring her comment about Miles.

"Is that an offer, Mr. Oseon? I can come drive to you instead, but you'd have to let me do whatever I want."

Sirue rolled his eyes to the ceiling. "Oh, my G—Teresa. That was not an offer. Damn, that was just a question."

"Okay, okay, sorry," Teresa said. "Yeah, I was going out with someone. It...he...didn't work out," she stammered.

He cleared his throat and tried to put an ounce of compassion in his voice. "Teresa, I don't know what happened with him, but I do know that you need to start putting yourself first. You've had a rough time with love, and you have a lot to give, but start with yourself, ok? I'm serious."

After a moment of dead silence, he heard a rustling noise and then Teresa blew her nose directly into her phone. Sirue rolled his eyes again, wondering what he'd done. He had flashbacks of scenes from when they were dating heavily. After a month of seeing each other day in and day out, Teresa started to swing like a gymnast from one emotion to the next. Sitting on the sofa now, listening to her sobbing, he realized her displays of vulnerability are what made it harder to break up with her. Miles broke Sirue's mental concentration and tapped him on the arm, quietly asking who was on the phone. Sirue answered by winding his finger around his ear and Miles gave a nod of comprehension. He walked to the kitchen and Sirue drummed his fingers impatiently on the arm of the sofa.

Teresa blew her nose loudly again. "See, Sirue. I knew you would tell me what I needed to hear. You're so sweet to me," she sniffled. "I just hate how you ignore me sometimes."

"Teresa –"

"No, let me finish." She sniffed. "I call you up because I'm lonely. I don't have any girlfriends. No one at work really fucks with me off the clock." Her sobs increased. "And guys run through me. I found a friend in you, and you want to fucking ignore me? You're such an asshole." Her tone immediately changed like the wind.

"Are you done?" Sirue asked flatly.

Miles laughed out loud and, with a can of cola, plopped down on a nearby ottoman and clicked the big screen to the sports network.

"Sure, I'm done. I'm done with begging for your friendship," she answered.

"Well, I gotta go, ok? Teresa, listen to what I told you and I wish you the best." He ended the call.

"Gotdamn, man," Miles said, taking a sip. "She still giving you the blues?"

"Let's go." Sirue stood up, straightened his slacks, and slowly shook his head in disbelief as he snatched his keys off the coffee table. "Don't want to talk about it."

Miles cut off the television and walked his can to the kitchen. "C'mon, what did she want this –"

"Don't want to talk about it," Sirue repeated, and Miles laughed again.

Once outside, Sirue remembered that they were supposed to be waiting for Mara. Before he could grab his phone to text her, the small red car came around the corner. She parked right behind Sirue's huge SUV and jumped out of her car.

"Damn, y'all were leaving without me?" she asked, smoothing out her peach-colored short sleeved blouse.

Miles glanced at Sirue, then back to her, and stated in a loud whisper, "Si just got a call from the stalker, so you know he's a little stressed."

"Sirue, what hap—"

"Don't want to talk about it. Let's go. I need a drink." He walked over to open the passenger door for Mara, while Miles jumped into the back.

Chapter 5

The Black Café was one of the most popular live band and spoken word venues in the city. It was pancaked between Lou's Barber Shop and Capital City Carry-Out, so parking was always an issue. Especially since Lou's liked to stay open until nine p.m. for the brothers who needed a fresh shape-up before they got their grooves on next door.

Sirue's thoughts were heavy as he found a parking space a few blocks down the street. He double-checked the sign that said the meters were off after six-thirty, then he proceeded to walk two paces ahead of Mara and Miles.

The strong jazz beats hit Mara as soon as they walked through the heavy doors. She swayed to the rhythm and nudged Miles when Sirue paid his cover and walked towards a secluded table without waiting for them.

"Damn. What's up with your boy?" she asked.

"My boy? I've only known him like two months longer than you."

"Exactly, so don't try to pass him off on me."

Miles laughed. He took out his wallet, peeled off two bills, and handed the crisp Jackson and Grant to the young man at the makeshift podium. "Keep the change."

"Oh, okay, baller! I see you," Mara said as they strolled to the table where Sirue was sitting pensively. Leaning forward on his elbows, he was resting his head atop his clasped fists.

Mara dropped her purse dramatically on the table and snapped her fingers in front of his face. He blinked his eyes over to her then looked back down at the small three-man band across the floor. Miles let out a laugh, sat down, and pulled out his phone.

The band finished their song, and the patrons showed their love. The bass player nodded his appreciation and signaled the drummer and horn player to begin a smooth rendition of a well-known 1930s jazz piece. There was a very small dance floor that doubled as the poets' stage located directly in front of the elevated band.

Mara looked sideways at Sirue. She leaned over and stared at him for a good thirty seconds, waiting to reach the point of sheer annoyance.

"What do you want, Mara?" he finally asked, his eyes still on the band.

"For you to get a few drinks and loosen the hell up." She motioned to the waitress. "Excuse me. Can you get us three Long Islands, light on the tea, okay?"

"Sure," she answered, then looked across the table at Miles. "That includes you, right?"

Miles looked up from his phone and saw the waitress looking at him with familiar eyes. Too familiar. Even in the semi-darkness he could recognize her. And she was still fine.

"Hey, Jasmine."

"Hi, Miles. You drinkin' a Long Island, too?" she asked again, fingering the notepad in her apron.

"Uh, yeah. Yeah. How have you been? When did you start working here?"

"About a month ago. Just needed some extra cash."

Miles wanted to say that if she hadn't screwed him over the way she did, she'd never be worrying about money. Instead, he just looked at her.

"All right, your drinks will be right up." Jasmine left before finishing her sentence.

Mara had been following their exchange like it was a tennis match.

"Ohhhhh, I knew she looked familiar," she said.

She glanced at Miles who was engrossed in a text that seemed to have just come through.

He chuckled as he read. "Tea said she'll pay a thousand dollars to anyone who can bring her a can of gasoline and a lighter...and for me to tell you not to forget about the thing y'all are doing tomorrow. And that you need to check your phone."

Mara made a face and suddenly remembered what she knew she was going to forget.

"See, that's why she's my ace. She knows I don't check my texts for shit." Mara slyly kicked Sirue under the table to annoy him further and slid her elbow over to knock his arm off-balance. He lightly kicked her back under the table and she laughed.

"What thing are y'all doing tomorrow?" Miles asked.

"A thing. Our thing. It's a secret. We don't have to tell y'all every damn thing."

"Okay, well I ain't got no bail money," Miles replied.

"Babyyyy, you're rolling in something. I saw your cash at the door. You get a street pharm job you didn't tell us about?"

He sucked his teeth. "You see a brother with some extra change, and it can't be legit? I saaaves mine."

Sirue turned to him and finally broke his silence. "Man, I can't even let you slide with that bullshit. Didn't you order two new pairs of Seven-Ones yesterday?"

Miles squinted across the table. "I can't buy shoes?"

"You have two feet and fifty-eight pairs of shoes."

Miles paused. "That's real specific, man. Like, stalker roommate specific."

They all laughed and Sirue loosened up. When their drinks arrived, it didn't miss Miles that another server brought them. He glanced around for Jasmine, and finally saw her interacting with patrons at another table. He sipped and started wondering what she'd been up to.

About an hour and three drinks later, Mara was at the bar, no longer feeling like being around Miles and Si. She really wished Tea was here so they could scope out the menfolk and get a good conversation going. She loved her talks with Tea, even though lately it was getting tougher for her to open up to her best friend. Mara found herself studying for her marketing classes more than usual and not really confiding in Tea as much. She swirled her stirrer around her ice cubes and started missing her sister-friend. She hoped that this thing tomorrow would help—

"Penny for your thoughts."

Mara didn't jump, but coolly followed the voice with her eyes. To her left was a prince of a man. Medium brown complexion, black-framed designer glasses that fit his face perfectly, freshly shaved, long dreads pulled into a ponytail, smelling like heaven...but where did she know him from?

"Why just a penny?" She looked his face over, searching for more recognizable traits.

His smile displayed perfect teeth that distracted her momentarily. "Well, I wanted to save the rest for the drink I'm going to buy you."

"So, how many women did that line work on tonight?"

Mara went back to studying her drink.

"Including you...let's see, that would be zero. But do you mind if I sit here?"

She shrugged. "I don't own it."

Mara looked at him sidelong as he beckoned for the bartender. She admired his strong jawline and noticed how clean his dreads were. Very neatly tamed. And that sweet close beard was so smooth. And those thick lips. Mara laughed to herself at how she was thirsting for this brother. She glanced at the watered-down alcohol in her glass and moved it forward.

As if on cue, he reached over and handed her glass to the bartender. "You want another of these?"

"No. A chocolate martini, please."

His eyes smiled. "That's an acquired taste." Then, to the barkeep. "Make that two. Thank you."

"So, do I have to guess your name, Mr. Penny for your thoughts?" Mara turned in her stool so that she was facing him. He seemed very interesting. Oddly familiar, and very interesting.

"Andrew Collins. But you can call me Drew." He looked her square in the eyes. "And what can I call you?"

"I'm Mara. No need for last names yet."

He smiled. "You don't play around, do you? Just a straight shooter." He sliced the air with his hand then rested his finger on his temple.

"I guess. I hate games. Why play when we're adults?" Mara loved his eye contact. He didn't seem to have that eye-wandering disorder that afflicted so many men she met.

And she got another whiff of his cologne.

He nodded. "Exactly."

Drew opened his mouth to say something else, but Mara cut in.

"What do you do for a living, Drew?"

"I'm a vice principal at Marshall High, but for fun I play a little ball, ski, play golf, read, travel, you name it."

It was almost as if every word he spoke brought a wider smile to his lips and Mara snuck a peak at those pearly whites each time. There was just something to be said about a man with perfect teeth.

"Oh, okay. I've never been skiing, but I do like ball – maybe one day I'll get to show you some of my Aari McDonald crossovers," Mara did an air dribble through her legs.

"Just don't break my ankles."

At that moment, light applause filled the club and the lights dimmed. Mara turned back around in her stool to check out the stage and joined in the cheers and snaps for the woman walking onto the platform. Wisdom was her name. She'd been the emcee on Saturday nights for as long as Mara had been a regular at the Black Café. She was a short, large afro-donning poetess who could flow like nobody's business and always opened Poets' Night with a new soul-stirring piece. Wisdom started to move to the soft beats provided by the band. A few sprinkled "Get it, girl" and "Work it, sister" accolades got even more applause from everyone.

Mara laughed and started to groove in her seat to the infectious rhythm. Suddenly, the music stopped, and Wisdom walked to the microphone.

Mara looked behind her and was shocked she hadn't noticed that Drew moved his stool close enough to Mara's to rest his feet on her stool's spindles. His legs were long, so he was still a good twelve inches away, but the fact that she was almost sitting between them gave her a rush. When she turned her head to him to speak, he leaned towards her.

"She is really good. You have to really listen, though," she whispered.

Drew nodded his head and scooted even closer when Mara turned back around.

Red, blue, green, and white lights chased each other around the stage until a warm, amber light settled on Wisdom. She caressed the mic and spoke in a soft, deliberate tone.

"I can have my own vision
my own voice, my own decisions
I can walk into any space and command stares
from foot to face
it's not arrogance, you see
it took years to create this me
it took a father who was never there
who never told me that he ever cared
it took shame in the form of weight
like his face was on every doughnut I ate
it took me feeling like a burden
it took me assuming I wasn't worth it
it took gray days and it took pain
to know besides storms there are subtle rains
so now I can stand taller
I can see over mountains and skyscrapers
and the golden arches
I can write a new definition of me
of a self that longs to be cuddled and loved
appreciated and hugged
envied and desired, respected and admired
it's almost like I can feel the metamorphosis within me
from my replicating cells
to every pore in my skin
from the sad girl who sucked love from her thumb
to the stronger woman I am destined to become
because I know that nature is never wrong
that's why butterflies flutter by
after hiding their beauty for so long"

When Wisdom took a step back from the microphone, the audience showed love. She smiled and nodded her gratitude, holding up praying hands to each section of the small crowd.

"Thank you, sisters and brothers. Thank you so much. That one is called 'Self-ish'…"

Mara felt Drew moving behind her. She shifted slightly and he slid her drink to her. He rested his right hand on her arm as he did, and Mara hoped he didn't feel her tense up. She took a sip from her glass and tried to focus on the stage.

Wisdom introduced the next poet, and he received a relatively cool welcome. Wisdom signaled to the audience to increase their applause, and they did.

He began to recite a poem about the magic of being faded, and Mara's mind kept drifting to this gorgeous, strange brother a few inches behind her. And, damn, he smelled good. His leg began to bounce up and down beside her. She knew he was also checking her out. She could feel his gaze all over her back, all over her neck, and she was so glad she'd gotten that work out in earlier because—*and that's where I know him from*, she thought. The dude from Heaven's who got folded on the court. She envisioned Drew with some thick sports glasses and that mound of muscles was him, all right.

He started to drum his manicured fingers next to her on the bar. Fingers on the right, and a bouncing leg on the left. He was definitely bored with the people on stage, and he was waiting for a chance to talk to her again. Mara smiled and abruptly placed her hand on top of his fingers.

"That's rude," she whispered with a smile, and would have bet a paycheck that she saw a spark fly from their touch. She released his hand.

"Oh, sorry." He took a sip of his drink, not taking his eyes off her.

Mara turned fully back to face the bar and finished her martini.

"Look, do you want to go talk somewhere?"

Drew nodded. He took out some cash and put it beneath his glass.

"Where do you want to go?" he asked.

"Did you drive?"

He smiled. "Yes, I drove."

Mara stood and grabbed her purse.

"I want to tell my friends where I am – they're like my brothers and they will definitely start tripping if I don't."

Drew walked behind Mara, letting her lead him to a table where a man sat with a woman. He could have sworn she'd said "brothers", plural.

Jasmine was sitting next to Miles, and although they could not be heard, it was obvious they were in a heavy conversation. When Mara approached, they both looked Drew over.

Mara leaned down and whispered across Jasmine and spoke directly to Miles.

"We're going out to talk. Where's Si?"

Miles gave Drew a very serious once-over and looked back at Mara.

"Keep your phone on," he said loudly, ignoring her question.

"Boy, bye." Mara rolled her eyes.

She stood upright and walked out with Drew in tow.

Jasmine's eyes followed them out of the door, then turned to Miles. A hint of jealousy crept up and almost escaped her mouth, but she swallowed it back down.

"We'll have to talk later. I have tables to wait."

She started to stand, but Miles touched her arm.

"Fu—forget the tables right now, Jasmine."

She settled back into the chair and fidgeted with a table napkin, tracing the Black Café logo. Miles loved that about her. He used to love everything about her. Her curves. Her braids. Her sense of humor. Her passion.

"You just told me this shit and I have to make some kind of sense out of it. How could you not tell me you have a child? You know I would've...," he stopped himself and shook his head.

"No, you wouldn't have had to do anything. I just thought you should know. He was only four when I started seeing you and since he hasn't been staying with me, I had to kick in child support." She started to touch the book of matches near the centerpiece but pulled her hands back.

"So, you need extra money."

"Yeah. This job sucks, but it helps. I've been applying to different places."

"I can help you, too." Miles looked at her, searching for something, anything, in her face. Nothing. He reached under the table and his hand grazed her leg. She folded and unfolded the napkin between her fingers and Miles watched a small smile creep across her lips. She turned to look at him.

"Why are you such a nice guy?"

He shrugged. "Just one of my many traits you fell in love with two years ago."

Jasmine let out a quick laugh, then she exhaled.

"Well, you don't have to help, Miles. It's not your problem. It's mine." She patted his cheek then got up from the table, smoothing out her apron when she stood. Before she left, she squeezed one of Miles' shoulders, then walked to another table to take an order.

The audience rolled over in laughter and applause at someone's freestyle on stage. Miles watched Jasmine writing down orders from a group of people, and he hoped the two hundred dollars he'd slipped into her apron would help her out a little.

According to Drew's rear view mirror, it was around seventy-two degrees outside. Mara was loving the maple sugar interior of his massive SUV even more than she loved the metallic blue exterior. She checked out the smooth feel of the dashboard and admired the speakers over their heads and the shiny shield emblem in the center of his steering wheel.

"Do you know that this monster would crush my little car if it even bumped it?"

"Well, I'll make sure to never bump your car," he smiled back.

Mara ran her hand along her armrest and her eyes followed the interior lights around the perimeter of the floorboards.

"And, what's up with you men and these big ass trucks?" She thought of Sirue's huge truck and wondered again where he disappeared to before she left the lounge.

"Well...I can't speak for every man, but this definitely isn't an attempt to overcompensate for shortcomings." He smirked.

"I'll have to take your word for it, Mr. Collins," Mara gave him a quick glance and tapped the illuminated sound system. "Let's listen to something."

Drew looked through his phone, selected a song, and immediately a man's sultry voice backed by a smooth, slow track started filling the truck.

Mara closed her eyes and leaned her head back. She loved everything about this song, the lyrics reminding her that it's hard to hide if love is calling you. Then, she remembered she was in a stranger's vehicle and quickly opened her eyes.

"How are you going to put his sexy voice on when we're supposed to be learning more about each other?"

Drew let out a smile and turned slightly in his seat to look at her. He started to say something but shook his head and closed his mouth.

Mara sat upright and peered at him. "Just so you know, that annoys the hell out of me."

He laughed. "I apologize. It's just that you're...you're stunning. And, usually, I talk a mile a minute, but you have me tongue tied." He seductively bit on his bottom lip.

"Well, you need to untie that tongue of yours."

She licked her own lips and leaned closer to Drew. When she was an inch from his lips, she bypassed his mouth and reached over to turn down the music.

"Ahhhh," Drew threw his head back.

Mara laughed with him. "Thought you were getting lucky, huh?"

"That was cold, that was cold," he nodded.

"Are you still tongue-tied?"

"I'm not. But I could be."

His countenance turned serious, and he slid his right hand to her waist, pulling her closer to him. He smelled her fragrance, and the sensation only made his mouth hungrier. When his mouth touched hers, Mara felt the spark she'd seen earlier. His tongue was so strong. She felt hers succumb to its command to explore her mouth. He was kissing her so hard that he rocked her head and Mara put her hand on his face to slow him down. Her touched seemed to work, and Drew fell into a rhythm with her lips. A light moaning noise escaped his mouth. Mara loved inhaling his breath as he kissed her. She felt his hand gently squeezing her waist. After almost five minutes, Drew pulled back and rested his forehead on hers.

Their breathing was heavy and in sync.

"Come home with me."

Mara took another peck on those juicy lips.

"We're not going to your mama's basement, are we?"

He laughed and softly kissed her top lip, then her bottom.

"No, beautiful. To my house."

Mara smiled and raised an eyebrow. She pulled back a few inches from his face. "That's how women get abducted, sir."

"You're safe with me, I promise."

Mara stared at his moist lips. She licked her own and could still taste him. "Let's go, then."

In almost one movement, Drew threw on his seatbelt, put the truck into gear and maneuvered it out of its parking space and onto the road. Mara sat back in her seat, clicked on her own seatbelt and reached into her purse to grab her phone. She noticed a missed call from Miles and called him back.

"Why didn't you pick up?" he answered immediately.

"Hello to you, too, Miles," Mara replied, not really upset at all. She was already prepared for Miles' reaction.

"Where are you?"

Mara could hear the sounds of music and talking in the background. "I'm with Drew. I'm good," she tried to reassure him.

Drew glanced over and met Mara's eyes. They smiled at each other, and he looked back at the road. Mara's eyes followed the silhouette of his profile.

"So, you'll be back soon? We're still here." She could hear his concern.

"No. Look, don't wait for me, okay?"

"What? Mara, you just met him."

"I'll get a ride back to my car at Si's house."

"Tonight, or in the morning?"

Mara rolled her eyes. "Bye, Miles."

She ended the call and pulled down the visor to apply the lip gloss she also took from her purse. She checked her hair and was glad she decided to wear her braids down; they accentuated her almond-shaped eyes.

"You have protective friends," Drew commented.

"Told you," Mara smiled, and closed the visor.

"I better be on my best behavior, then, huh?" He glanced over at her again, and Mara could partially see his white teeth through his grin as he bit his lip, driving her wild.

Before she could answer, she felt her phone vibrate in her hand. She looked at the text from Sirue.

Miles just told me you left with a strangler. Be careful.

She laughed and wrote back.

I think you mean stranger, drunk ass

Seconds later, *shut up and be careful anyway*

Mara smiled and tucked her phone back into her purse. She turned up Drew's speakers and enjoyed the playful, flirty conversation they had as he drove. She even mentioned to him the plans she had with her best friend, Tea, tomorrow to look at houses together. And Drew shared with her his reason to go into the education field.

"I had one teacher who changed my life," he said when they were at a red light.

Mara liked how the glow from the traffic light settled on his facial features. She was liking so much about him.

"What grade did you have this teacher?" she asked.

"My whole life. It was my mother. She's retired now, but growing up, I saw how much she loved her career, and I also saw how much grief it gave her. I wanted to see if I could make it a little better. One change at a time." He looked over at her. "Corny, I know."

"Not at all," Mara said. She didn't know how much of what he said was true, but she wanted to hear more.

Chapter 6

It didn't take long to get to Drew's house in Maryland and even less time to make it upstairs to his sprawling bedroom suite. With their shoes deposited downstairs at the front door, Mara loved sliding her pantyhosed feet through his plush dark green carpet. She walked around, inspecting on the sly. She was on the lookout for anything too suspicious...pictures of ex-flames, handcuffs, serial killer biographies. Everything looked normal. One thing did stand out, though. An enormous framed black and white photograph. In the foreground stood two smiling white police officers while the scene behind them was total chaos. Women being dragged, cops spraying men and children with hoses. Mara was mesmerized and stood with her arms holding herself as she studied it. Drew walked up behind her, put his hands in his pockets and leaned down until his head was beside hers.

"You like it?" He broke the silence.

"McKenzy Moon, right?"

"Yeah. You know photography, too?"

"I know her work. She was amazing."

"I keep this above my bed, so I wake up and remember why I fight for my students and my mom every day."

Mara nodded and turned her head to give his cheek a soft kiss. She reached behind her to find his arms; he took the hint and wrapped them around the front of her. She closed her eyes and rested her hands on his arms and leaned back into him. She got lost in his embrace. His body felt so warm, and his tall frame seemed to conform behind her. They swayed slowly together, and Mara thought this felt too perfect. And suddenly, Aunt Esther's voice swam into her head.

"Baby," she used to say when Mara was little, "the Good Lord don't like to tease us. If something feels too good to be true, then it is, dammit." Aunt Esther always cussed when she gave her life lessons.

Mara let out a loud sigh to convince Drew that she wouldn't fall to fast. She shrugged out of his arms and moved to sit on the edge of his California king bed. Drew stood there looking a little confused and put his hands back in his pockets. She called him over with her finger, and he walked slowly towards her, bent down, and planted another kiss on her mouth. Mara tasted the sweet remnants of where they left off in the truck. He became more passionate with his tongue and Mara felt herself opening her blouse. He helped her and it was on the floor before she could catch her breath. She scooted back on the bed and Drew hungrily climbed on top of her. Mara tilted her head back and let him lick, tease, and nibble on her neck. As he did, he pulled down her slacks and stockings. Mara assisted, then helped him take off his shirt. She ran her hands over his toned torso and Drew did a faux muscle man pose that made her laugh.

"Come here," she said, meeting his mouth halfway. His body arched on top of hers and Mara wanted him so bad. Too bad. Drew's juicy wet lips moved down to her collar bone and over to her shoulder. With his tongue, he grabbed her bra strap and pulled it down. Mara's heart raced and she knew he could see it pulsing. He used his hand to remove her right breast from its cup and licked around her already aroused nipple.

Mara sucked her breath as she watched his tongue dance. He moved back up to her neck and buried his face as deeply as he could. She heard him moan into her skin. She felt the warmth of his mouth and instinctively spread her legs beneath him. She could feel the hardness through his pants and when she reached down to massage him, she quickly realized he wasn't exaggerating earlier. That truck was definitely not an overcompensation. He said something into her neck.

He began to suck the thin skin beneath her jawline and mumbled again. "I want you."

Mara moaned in response, then replied, "Drew."

He lifted his head enough to meet her gaze. His eyes were half-closed, strands of his dreadlocks fell from their ponytail and framed his face as he started to suck on her bottom lip.

"I don't...let's not do everything tonight."

Drew's eyes opened wider, but he was still momentarily in a daze. "Huh?"

"You heard me."

"Mara, I...I have condoms. I'll go put one on now."

"Not tonight. Not that, not yet." She kissed him and looked at his face for a reaction.

He let out a groan and mumbled an "okay." Mara smiled and ran her hands over his bare back, and he lowered his head to suck on her earlobe.

His back reminded her of her favorite-colored crayon when she was little. She loved coloring all the cartoon characters the warm shade of sepia. The muscles in his back relaxed under her touch. With his hands, he reached down and spread her legs even more, sliding his body downwards. His mouth roamed her thighs like they were on a treasure hunt and when he moved her silk panties to the side, his tongue found gold. Mara's back arched and two climaxes later, she pulled him up and told him to turn over. He happily obliged and softly stroked her braids as she kissed his chest, abdomen, and unfastened his pants. She took him into her mouth with no pretenses. Drew called out one expletive after another and invented some new ones. His eyes bulged when he could feel the back of Mara's throat. He came after only two minutes and Mara was silently glad they didn't have intercourse. She would have been highly perturbed at this two-minute man. But, when she kissed back up towards his throat and looked into his face, she wondered if she really would have cared. She liked him.

She kissed his neck again, then his mouth, and propped her elbow on his chest.

"I'm hungry."

He smoothed a stray braid from her face and put his hands behind his head. "I could tell."

Mara giggled. "For food."

"You want me to cook? Go to the store? Order something?"

"Hmm, got any rice?"

"Rice? Just plain rice?" he smiled, confused.

Mara nodded. "I like plain rice."

"So, I guess I'm going down to make plain rice."

"Thank you."

Drew pecked her lips, then started to sit up and Mara moved to her side. He stood, fixed his pants, and walked to his adjoining bathroom. He came out with a bathrobe in his hands.

"This is way too big for you, but…"

Mara stood, adjusted her bra and panties, and took the robe. "You mind if I take a shower?"

"Of course not. Here," he walked back inside the master bathroom and turned on the shower.

Mara leaned against the door jamb and watched him test the temperature of the water with his hands. She glanced around at the bathroom décor and fell in love with the African art adorning the walls. He even had kente-print wallpaper. Drew went to the sink to wash his hands and watched her in the reflection. When he caught her eye, he held her gaze and Mara felt her knees go limp. The steam from the shower started to float around them, and they both held their stares. Drew finally smiled and turned off the sink's faucet. He dried his hands on a hanging towel an pulled her to him.

"Mara No-Need-For-Last-Names, you are very beautiful. I can wash you if you want," he grinned.

She looked up at him. "It's Queden. And I can handle it, just go make my food. I'm starving."

"Okay, Ms. Mara Queden," he said softly. Mara loved how her name fell from his lips.

She reached up with her free hand and caressed the back of his neck, beneath his ponytail of dreads. She pulled him down to her mouth and kissed him passionately again. He pressed himself into her until she was fully against the wall beside the door. They breathed into each other's mouths and Mara wasn't sure if her skin was damp from the steam or from him. After another minute, she began to slowly kiss along his jaw, then pulled back to look at him.

They were both looking hungrily at each other's lips.

"I think I should go cook, or you'll never eat…," he ran his thumb along her mouth.

Mara nodded.

He kissed her forehead and walked out of the bathroom, slowly closing the door behind him. Mara looked into the mirror and wiped off the condensation that was forming.

"This is too sweet, Lord. Give me a sign. Something. Aunt Esther can't be right all the time." She exhaled sharply, then pulled her braids into a high ponytail, wrapping one single braid around to secure them.

Mara washed quickly, not really caring for his earthy-scented bar soap when she was used to her lavender and rose shower gels. She stepped out, dried off with a clean towel she found carefully folded on a small shelf, then wrapped up in the huge bathrobe. She opened the door to let the steam roll out. She loved the aesthetic of rolling steam. Drew's off-key voice could be heard from downstairs, singing horribly to the light music coming from the speakers that were apparently placed in every corner of his house. She smiled and shook her head.

She saw that he'd made the bed and placed her folded clothes at the end of it. Sitting atop her clothes was a small envelope. Her name was written neatly on the front and beneath it, a short message: "I owe you this."

She paused and thought for a second, then opened the flap. A small penny fell out and into her hand. She thought again for a second, then a broad smile spread across her face.

Chapter 7

Miles looked at the day's calendar on the desktop in his office. Besides the appointment he had today, it was otherwise empty. Just the way it was supposed to be, he thought as he propped his feet up on the corner of his large, oversized oak desk. The mounted sixty-inch television was the perfect distance away and allowed for ample walking room to his refrigerator and enough space for his miniature basketball hoop and dart board. He leaned back with his hands behind his head and didn't look up when his secretary knocked on his already open door.

"Mr. Puvi," she asked with an attitude. Old Mrs. Crawford always had an attitude. She hated working for such a young, lazy boss but sometimes, Miles' charm would win her over.

"Mr. Puvi," she repeated over her glasses.

"Wait a minute, Mrs. Cr---ooooooooh," he winced as he watched the sport network's replay of a seven-foot player's demonstrative dunk from last night's game.

Mrs. Crawford tapped her foot and pursed her lips, not believing she had two piles of work waiting for her and he had time to watch sports.

He picked up the remote and turned it down. "Yes, Mrs. C. How can I help you on this beautiful day?"

"Your ten o'clock appointment is here. She said she's here for an interview."

He took his feet down and opened a drawer beside his leg. He pulled out a slim manilla folder. "Yeah, I don't know her name. They sent her from FirstTemps, right? She's supposed to take Yvette's place for a few months while she has the baby."

"Yvonne, Mr. Puvi. Her name is Yvonne."

"Oh, tell Yvonne I'll be right out."

Mrs. Crawford adjusted her glasses. "No, the woman in accounting is Yvonne. Not Yvette."

Miles looked up at Mrs. Crawford. "You don't like me, do you?" he smiled.

"What do you want me to tell the ten o'clock?" Mrs. Crawford ignored his question but lightened her tone.

"I'll be right there. Is the...uh," he looked around his desk for a pen.

"The interview room is ready, yes." She walked towards him and handed him the black pen she was holding.

"What would I do without you?" he leaned back in his chair.

She headed for the door, stopped and turned around. "Remember to ask her for her identification and social security card so I can get copies started. And be firm with the start time. Eight o'clock sharp, no excuses. The last temp you hired wouldn't show up until noon."

Miles playfully rolled his eyes. "Yes, ma'am."

Mrs. Crawford turned to leave and closed his door behind her. Miles turned the volume back up and finished watching the last ten minutes of the sports recap before he stood up and grabbed the pen and folder.

He straightened his dark burgundy tie and cream starched shirt, then opened his office door. When he turned the corner, he had to blink twice. Sitting on the waiting couch in front of Mrs. Crawford's desk were two of the sexiest legs he'd ever seen. And the face gave them a run for their money.

"Mr. Puvi, this is Jasmine Coleman. She's here for the interview from FirstTemps."

Miles walked around Mrs. Crawford's desk and took Jasmine's outstretched hand as she stood. Her look of astonishment matched his.

"Wow," was all that escaped his lips.

"I didn't know you worked here," Jasmine said quietly.

"Yeah, I was transferred from the Rockville office. They needed a manager down here in Arlington and they offered me the position." Miles continued to shake her hand, then looked over at his secretary.

"Uh, we're going to um...we'll be in my office," he said, finally letting go of her hand.

Mrs. Crawford looked at him like he just said a curse word in church during a sermon. "I have the interview room all set up, Mr. Puvi."

"I know. But it's more comfortable in my office," he put his hand on Jasmine's back and led her towards his door. Mrs. Crawford grimaced and parted her lips to speak. The phone buzzed before she could give her two cents.

Miles closed the heavy door behind him and watched in amazement as Jasmine took a chair in front of his desk. The light rosewater fragrance she brought in with her was already permeating the large office and he tried to remain casual as he took his seat across from her.

"Wow, what a surprise," he said, trying to lean back in his chair and relax, but her sparkling eyes made it impossible. He rarely saw her with her natural hair pulled into a tight bun, but it was a very becoming look for her.

"Yeah." She nervously darted her eyes around the office. "I knew you worked for Cosmic Lumens but not down here, so when they sent me on the assignment I jumped at it, thinking maybe I would run into you."

"How long have you been with FirstTemps?" Miles asked for personal reasons, not for business. He wanted to know why she disappeared on him after they saw each other at the Black Café a month ago.

"About three weeks now," she looked down at the floor and pulled the strap to her purse over her shoulder. "Look, Miles, I can just ask for another placement. I don't want this to be awkward."

"No, it's cool. I'm fine with you being here. I can even get you here permanently when she comes back from maternity leave." He leaned forward on his desk, looking at her straight in the eyes.

Jasmine tried to hide her smile. "I don't want any special treatment. But I do need the assignment."

"You've got it. Welcome to Cosmic Lumens."

She exhaled what seemed like a long breath of relief. "I needed some good news today," she said as she toyed with her purse on her lap.

"Why? What's going on?" Miles leaned back in his chair again.

She shook her head. "Oh. Nothing. But…thank you for what you did. I never got a chance to say thank you."

Miles was confused, then suddenly remembered the two hundred dollars. "I hope it helped out some. How's…I don't know his name. How's your son?"

Jasmine tugged at her ear. "Fine. How's Tea?" she asked too quickly.

Miles smiled to himself. He remembered the jealousy Jasmine always felt towards both Mara and Tea, especially Tea. "She's fine, too, Jasmine."

"Well, since everybody's fine," Jasmine stood up and smoothed her red blouse and long black skirt. Miles walked from behind his desk and stood to walk her to the door. The rosewater was strong.

"I'll just give my information to the secretary," Jasmine said, looking up at Miles when they got to his door. He had his hands in his pockets and was staring at her, nodding his head.

"Miles, I'm sorry. I'm just not ready to talk about my son yet. With anybody. And the way we ended, with your friends getting in our business…it was just…ugly." Jasmine moved a little closer to Miles, who didn't budge.

"And now to see you twice in a month after so long…I can feel the old feelings again," she said as she adjusted her purse strap and ran her hand down Miles' face, playing with his left ear. He closed his eyes and recalled how she used to refer to that as *her* ear whenever they made out. He would claim her hands and she would claim his ear.

She pulled her hand down from the side of his face as abruptly as she'd lifted it. "See you on Monday?" she asked, taking a small step back.

Miles nodded and looked her in the eyes. She opened the door and softly shut it behind her, her scent lingering. Miles looked down at the floor and slowly blew out air. This was going to be a long three months.

Chapter 8

"So, you're officially a couple now?"

Tea was holding a framed picture of Mara's aunt and wrapping it in newspaper. She looked up at Mara who was on the sofa taking out her braids. A very cheesy smile formed on her face.

"Yeah. We talked about it last night. It's been a month, and girl he is so intense."

"Intense how?" Tea reached for another picture on Mara's living room wall.

"He came four times last night."

Tea almost dropped a seven-year-old pig-tailed Mara. "Whatever."

"In one hour," Mara clarified.

"Girl, what did you do to him?!"

Mara folded her legs up beneath her. She shrugged and pulled the loosened microbraid extension from a section of hair, then added it to the growing pile on the floor.

"I don't know if it was me, or if he was just horny, or what. He called me when I got home afterwards and, get this…he said he wanted to do it over the phone, too."

Tea grabbed more newspaper and wrapped the framed photo. "Have you done that before?"

She was always intrigued to hear about Mara's bedroom drama. And Mara was more than happy to oblige. Tea would gladly reciprocate the gesture, but she could almost guarantee that Mara wouldn't be interested in her all-too-frequent rendezvous with her battery-operated friend, Mr. Spanky.

"With Drew, no. But hell yeah, I've had phone sex. Remember Jackson from our sophomore year? He was in band? We did it all the time, don't act like you didn't ear hustle on us," Mara squinted at her and picked her fingers through another tiny braid.

"I did not!" Tea threw a balled-up newspaper page at her.

"It's some hot shit right there, though, if he knows what he's doing. Oooh, we should call one of those hotlines so you can get your freak on."

"Shut up, I'm not calling any hotline," Tea rolled her eyes and placed the wrapped photograph into a nearby box. "I mean, unless it's toll-free – no, no! I'm not calling a hotline!"

Mara laughed, but curiosity did get the best of her sometimes. She watched Tea as she continued to carefully pack up photos and other miscellaneous items. She pulled another extension out and tried to recall the last time her girl got some. Or the last time she told her about it. It was two years ago that she last had a serious boyfriend. Jonathan. The brother had it going on in the beginning. Got her a hook up with some real estate agents for Tea's salon. Would always want to be up under her, showered her with gifts. The whole nine. The only noticeable fault was that his six-five stature was too tall for Tea's small five-three self, in Mara's opinion. But she didn't want to burst her girl's bubble, so she kept her superficial opinion to herself. Tea was floating on clouds for seven months until the day Jonathan wanted to be the big man and his true colors came out. They'd gotten into an argument at his place over something stupid like turning the channel and he felt the need to go upside Tea's head. A few times. He followed that with some very rough sex. Tea claimed she was too stunned to say no, but Mara always questioned that logic. She was pretty sure he'd forced her against her will. Afterwards, Jonathan fell asleep, and Tea made a tearful phone call to Mara. Within an hour, Miles and Sirue had fractured his arm and knocked out three teeth. Mara keyed his punk ass white SUV and sliced his two back tires. Jonathan was never heard from again. Neither was any news of another love interest for Tea.

Mara looked at her best friend and the way she was buzzing around the apartment. Just as she was going to tell her to sit the hell down and take a breather, her cell rang.

"Tea, throw me my purse."

She tossed her the replica designer purse, a "Wendi" as she liked to call it, and smiled when she saw the name on her phone.

"Hey," she answered.

"Good afternoon, sexy."

Mara smiled again. "You just waking up?" She winced silently as she yanked a stubborn tangled braid from a back section of hair.

"No, I've been up for a while. Hit the gym."

"Oh, so you're gonna wait for a day when I can't make it because you don't want me to break your ankles on the court. I understand."

Drew laughed. "See, you're about to make me change my mind."

"About what, baby?" She sweetened her tone.

"Oh, now I'm your baby?"

"You're always my baby, baby," Mara said with a seductive moan. Tea shook her head and walked into the small kitchen.

"All right, since you sound so beautiful, I guess I can still do it."

"Do what, handsome?" Mara smiled.

"I remember you told me Tea was coming over to help you finish packing. I wanted to help and bring you some food. You hungry?"

"I could eat." Mara picked up the pace with her unbraiding.

"So, open the door."

Mara looked at her front door and ended the call. "Oh my God." She started scrambling to grab hair from around her on the sofa. "That negro is at my front door, girl! Look at my hair!"

Tea poked her head out of the kitchen's entryway. "Who, Drew?"

"Yes!" Mara grabbed more hair off the floor and sofa, then ran past Tea to the bedroom. "Let him in and tell him I'll be right out!"

Tea laughed to herself over how much Mara was tripping over something as petty as her hair. Drew had to have seen her in more embarrassing situations than this in the bedroom. She opened the front door and almost had to use the doorknob to keep her knees from giving out. Brother looked like a black Greek god. He was only grinning, yet she could see almost every perfect tooth in his head. And that smooth brown skin Mara told her about.

"You're Tea, right?" he smiled.

"Yep, come on in." She moved to the side but bent slightly forward to get a whiff of his cologne.

Damn, she said to herself. She quickly assessed his attire of dark denim jeans and a torso-hugging, very expensive white t-shirt.

"I wasn't sure if you liked shrimp or not, so I was safe and got plain chicken fried rice. That okay?" He stepped over boxes and newspapers and made his way to the small dining room table.

"Yeah. Please, if it's dead, I'll eat it." She locked the door and walked past him to wash her hands in the kitchen. She came back to help him take the food out of the bags. "Mara said she'll be out in a minute."

Drew glanced around and smiled that killer smile. "Don't tell me she ran to the back."

"Man, you know you don't run up on a sister taking her braids out."

He laughed and turned fully around to examine the apartment. Tea stole a long glance at his smooth appearance and perfect dreadlocks. She shifted her eyes before he spoke.

"I'm so glad she's moving and getting more space. It looks really cramped in here, she could do much better."

Tea nodded and hoped he didn't mean anything rude by that. "We both needed space. The new house is going to be amazing for us."

"That's good, that's good," he absently responded, rubbing his hands together and turning back around.

Tea started to remove two boxes marked "kitchen" from the table to make more room for the food. Drew immediately helped and took the boxes from her. Tea took the food cartons from the paper bags and set them out. She was about to say that she'd already packed all the plates when she heard the familiar ringtone of her phone. She looked around, trying to remember where she last left it.

"Damn," she mumbled. She told DeeDee at the salon to give her a call if she needed her for anything.

Drew looked around with her. "Um, what does it look like?"

"The house?" Tea asked, pausing to look at him.

He laughed. "No, what does your phone look like?"

"Oh, the new XR14, pink glitter case."

They both followed the ring into the living room near another group of boxes by the door.

"It sounds like it's over here. Hold these." Drew handed her the picture frames on the top box and started to dig through newspaper and empty boxes.

Tea had to laugh when he lost his balance and fell forward onto his knees, smashing one of his hands into an empty box.

"Ouch! Fuck!" Drew yelled when he saw the nearby stack of boxes starting to fall towards him.

Tea hurried to hold them up with her body, still laughing. Drew saw the phone on the floor where the stack of boxes once was.

"There it is!" He crawled towards Tea on all fours and just as he started to grab the phone, it stopped ringing.

"I knew that was going to happen," Tea said, trying to hold in her smile.

"Do you still want it?" he asked, trying to hold a rogue box at bay above his head while trying to keep from laughing at himself.

"No, I wanna keep it under the boxes," Tea laughed.

Drew also laughed and reached behind the boxes past Tea's ankles. She looked down and suddenly felt self-conscious with him so close. She eyed his brown leather belt and heard a throat clearing.

"Damn, I wanted y'all to like each other, but not like this."

Tea turned her head and Drew jumped when he heard Mara's voice.

He sat back, took the pictures from Tea and handed her the phone. When he started to stand up, Mara went over to help move empty boxes out of his way.

"Hi, baby," she said, taking his hand and leading him out of the mess. She started to pull him towards the dining room, but he turned her around and gave her a deep kiss.

Tea looked down at her phone. It was DeeDee's call she missed, just as suspected. She dialed her back, trying not to listen to the light moaning noises from Mara. She walked to sit on the sofa.

Drew pulled back and his eyes roamed over Mara's face. "You look beautiful."

Mara turned up her nose and tugged at the blue bandana on her head. "Whatever. I look like I'm about to hold up a bank."

He smiled and moved his hands up and down her waist, noticing she wasn't wearing a bra underneath her blue tank top. "Mmmmm," he said and pulled her to him.

Mara wrapped her arms around his neck but froze when she felt him lifting her shirt, exposing her bare breasts. His hands started to massage them until she leaned back and yanked her shirt down.

"Drew," she whispered, indicating with a tilt of her head that Tea wasn't sitting very far from where they were standing.

"What?" he said and inched forward to kiss on her neck.

"No, that's rude. She's on the phone," Mara whispered again. She took his hand and they walked to the small table. He sat down and helped her open the rice cartons. She angrily handed him his food.

Drew reached over and rubbed along her thigh. "What's wrong?"

Mara ignored him and moved his hand off her leg. She took the excess trash from the table and walked it to the kitchen. Drew stood up and followed her.

"Mara, what's wrong?" he repeated.

She dumped the trash and turned around fast. "That wasn't cool, Drew," she said in a harsh whisper.

His face showed his confusion.

"You don't go lifting my shirt and grabbing on me right next to my homegirl. I was half-ass naked and that's rude."

Drew rested both of his hands behind him on the counter.

"I'm sorry. I didn't mean to embarrass you, and I didn't mean to embarrass her," he said sincerely.

"And she doesn't have anybody right now, so I don't want to go showing off in her face." Mara stepped closer to him, her tone getting softer.

"She's cute. A lot of guys like that petite look, why doesn't she have anybody?" Drew whispered, kissing Mara's nose.

She shrugged and wrapped her arms around him, rubbing up and down his back.

"Do you like that petite look?" She kissed his chin. Mara felt her jealousy steadily rising and wondered if he'd been stealing glances at her friend's body. She had always been mystified by Tea's smaller form which somehow also supported pretty heavy breasts, while her own breasts were at least a cup and a half smaller.

His eyebrows wrinkled. "She's cute," he said slowly and smiled down at her.

"Mmmhmm. You said that already. Do you wish I was more petite?"

Drew looked towards the ceiling, feigning deep thought. Mara pulled her head back a few inches and looked hard at him. *This shit is starting to not be funny*, she thought.

Drew laughed. "Baby, she's cute. But you're fine. You're sexy. I love all this ass and all these thighs," he gently squeezed her body.

"So...," Mara couldn't believe she was about to ask him this, but she was suddenly curious. "...if you saw both of us walking down the street, you'd try to talk to me and not her?"

"Hell, yeah."

"Why? 'Cause I'm taller? You know what they say about tall women," she said as she toyed with a few strands of his dreads.

"Because I like my women to have cushion." He pecked her mouth.

"So, now I'm fat?" She peered at him in mock anger.

Drew looked into her eyes. "You're not fat. You're perfectly created."

Mara playfully turned around and rubbed her rear end against him. She backed into him and started to grind more, giving her spandex a workout. Drew let out a small laugh, but his mood quickly changed when he started to get excited. He rested both hands on her hips as she got into a groove. He squeezed her hips and Mara slowed down, getting into a deep rhythm. She circled to the left, pushed back even farther, and circled to the right. One of Drew's hands slid beneath the front of her shirt. They both heard a box fall in the living room and they broke out of their freaky trance when they heard Tea swear.

"Uh," Mara cleared her throat. "You all right, girl?" she called out.

"Yeah," Tea appeared in the entryway. "DeeDee told me that one of my regulars dropped in looking for me, but she said she'll come back later on tonight."

"Oh, okay," Mara said absently, opening the refrigerator for no reason.

Drew clapped his hands once. "I'm starving! Let's eat, ladies."

They made their way to the table where they all sat and went to town on the food. Tea knew Mara was embarrassed from earlier and loved how her friend tried to lighten the mood by talking about the new house.

She just wished Mara knew how thin those kitchen walls really were.

Chapter 9

At the end of the meeting with the homeowner, Mara and Tea could not believe they had the keys to their rental town house in their hands. It was going to be their new home. With both of their salaries, they knew they'd be able to swing the rent plus utilities for the three-bedroom, two and a half-bathroom dwelling. Mara was excited to get out of her tiny apartment, and Tea was thrilled to finally move out of her father's house. Now, a few days after the meeting, Mara's small red car was in the driveway and Tea pulled up in her own four-door compact to the curb in front of their shared home on Summer Hill Drive in Mitchellville. It was so beautiful. Charcoal gray shutters on the top floor. A large ornately decorated front door, with a huge brass knocker that Tea absolutely adored. She especially loved how the huge bay windows in the living room protruded out over the garden. She was having fantasies about the flower bed the owner said she could put there when Mara swung the front door open.

"Come on, Tea! Everybody'll be here in less than an hour!" she called down then disappeared back into the house.

Tea turned her car off and retrieved the box of food Anna made for them. She was shocked when she stopped home from the salon earlier that day to finish packing and smelled the sweet potato pie and greens in the kitchen. Anna told her that she had to tutor that evening, but she'd stop by with her dad later on in the week. Tea knew Anna couldn't wait to have her out of the house so she and her dad could fight without being scolded. She lifted the box, slammed the back door with her hip, and smiled in relief when she saw Drew walking towards her. He took the box out of her arms, and she tugged at the back of his tan shirt.

"Aw, shucks. Loving the linen suit, Drew."

"Thank you, Tea, I'm glad somebody does. Please tell your girl that because she hates this color on me. Told me that if it wasn't so close to chow time, she'd make me go home and change. Said I look like a custodian."

Tea laughed and ran to hold the front door open for him. "Drew, don't pay her any mind, you look great. She's just stressed out about today."

Drew bumped against the door jamb as he entered. "You're telling me."

"Whoa, don't spill the greens, bruh, don't spill the greens."

They walked inside and she saw Mara on her cell, straightening the fluffy brown couch pillows. She looked more tense than usual. Tea loved what she did with her hair: it was still in its natural state because Tea hadn't had time to re-braid it for her yet. It was pulled up into a huge twist-out afro puff, accentuated by medium-sized silver hoop earrings. *Two thumbs up*, Tea thought. But what was plaguing her? She chalked it up to pre-hostess jitters.

"Hold on, talk to Tea." Mara rolled her eyes and tossed Tea her phone. She mumbled something about not having time for drama and marched back towards the kitchen.

Tea glanced at the caller's name on the phone and instantly put it up to her ear. "Si?"

"Yeah," he answered. "Look, I was trying to ask Mara if it's cool that I'm bringing Teresa."

"Teresa?! Since when are y'all back together?"

"We're not really. Not officially, anyway. She just called me again, telling me she's lonely. I told her that if I bring her, it won't mean anything. I'm just being nice."

Tea knew Sirue like the back of her hand. His deep voice wavered a little and it gave his true intentions away. "Sure, Si. Just make sure double-oh seven brings something from our list."

Sirue laughed and agreed. They both hung up and Tea commenced to cleaning. At Mara's request, she vacuumed the rooms again and checked the downstairs guest bathroom for the fourth time. Everything was in its place, the food was warming, and the house smelled like potpourri. Tea went upstairs to take a shower and Mara followed, telling Drew she had to freshen up.

Tea grabbed her robe from the back of her bedroom door and almost bumped into Mara when she turned around.

"Girl!" she said, clutching her heart.

"Tea, come here." Mara pulled her into the bedroom and closed the door. She sat on Tea's bed and looked up at her with pleading eyes.

"Tell me I'm trippin'."

"Huh? Mara, what's up?"

"Just please tell me I'm trippin'." She started to bounce her leg while wringing her hands.

"Honey, what's wrong?" Tea asked with concern, and quickly went to sit next to her friend.

Mara licked her lips, the dark ruby lipstick staying in place. "He…before you got here…Drew…" Both legs started to bounce now.

"What? What did he do?" Tea asked softly, rubbing her back.

Mara swallowed and memories from an hour ago came flooding in.

Mara quickly became more and more annoyed with Drew. He seemed to be in her space whichever way she turned. The housewarming was starting at two and it was already half past noon. Tea was nowhere to be found. And Drew was following her around like a puppy, interrupting her frantic cleaning and cooking.

When Drew followed her out of the kitchen, and she suddenly realized she left her gloves on the counter, she turned abruptly. The bottle of bleach cleaner fell out of her hands when she bumped into his chest.

"Drew!" she yelled.

He was startled.

"Baby," she said more softly. "Okay, see, I'm trying to finish everything and you're…" Mara's voice trailed off.

Drew bent down to pick up the bottle. He handed it back to her. "I'm just trying to help."

"I know, I know…," Mara sighed, and Drew held her arms.

"Relax. Everything will be fine. I'll…I'll do whatever you need me to do, even if that's sitting my ass down." He smiled the smile she loved.

Mara looked up and nodded. "Thank you."

He leaned forward and gave her a sweet kiss on the forehead. "I love you and you'll be fine. Tell me how I can help."

Mara remembered blinking but wasn't sure if she'd even moved.

Drew lowered his head a little to get level with her eyes. "Mara..."

Now she blinked hard. "Um. No. I mean, yeah. What did you just say?"

"How can I help? What do you need me to –"

"No. You said you love me?"

He shrugged with a smile. "I thought you could tell."

"Say it again." Mara stared him down.

"I love you, Mara."

"Say it again," she repeated with a smirk beginning to spread across her lips.

"I love you, Mara Queden." Drew leaned forward and touched his mouth to hers.

"He told me he loves me." Mara said, a single tear rolling down her face. She bit her bottom lip, remembering the taste of Drew's gentle kiss earlier.

Tea smiled. "That's all? Girl, I was about to go down there and kick his big ass in the kneecaps," she said quietly, realizing her best friend was still upset. "So, what's wrong?"

"He's the first one to tell me that." Mara's legs stopped moving and she wiped her tear away.

"Well, that's hard sometimes for guys to do," Tea comforted, hiding her surprise. Mara's told her about her experiences for the last seven years and through all the wild sex and situations, it rang true that Mara was never really in a committed relationship with any of them.

"No." Mara interrupted Tea's thoughts and looked at her. "The first one...ever."

Tea stopped rubbing her back and made a confused face. "Mara, you know how we feel about you. And Auntie Esther loves you like she gave birth to you. You know that."

"Nobody's ever *said* it to me, Tea." Mara sounded deflated. "There's a difference."

Tea pouted and held Mara's hand, resting her head on her shoulder. "I'm sorry. I don't know why I've never said it to you. I love you, poopie. You're my sister." Tea's eyes welled up.

Mara wiped fresh tears with her free hand. "Aw. Thanks, girl. I 'm so mad I'm sitting here crying like this. It must be PMS."

Tea laughed and wiped the remaining tears from Mara's cheek. "So did you tell him you love him, too?"

Mara nodded. "And then I told him he needed to change out of that tired tan suit."

They laughed and the doorbell downstairs sounded.

"Oh crap, I still need to get ready," Tea said, throwing her robe over her shoulder. She stood up and helped Mara stand.

"You good?" she asked.

"I'm straight. I look all right?" Mara turned to the side and showed off her outfit. It was definitely a new one. A light blue pair of denim jeans that closely hugged all of her curves and a deep red tube top that perfectly matched her lipstick. She topped it off with a pale pink short-sleeved shrug sweater. She looked phenomenal, and she knew Mara wanted her to say so.

"You look amazing, girl. Now, hurry up downstairs before Drew tells a corny ass joke to our first guest."

Mara smiled and headed down to make her grand entrance.

Chapter 10

Fifteen minutes later, Sirue, Teresa, Drew, and Mara were sitting in the front room having drinks and talking about the heightened security around Georgetown University. Since all of the chaos downtown lately, Homeland Security made sure that the area's prestigious campuses were adequately protected.

"What I don't understand," Teresa started, putting down her white wine and locking her arm inside of Sirue's, "is how they can have all this money to protect these PWIs, yet the public schools with small children get those raggedy ass security officers."

Sirue nodded and took a long swig of his drink.

"Point taken," Drew said. "At my school –"

"Where do you teach?" Teresa interrupted.

"I'm a vice principal at Marshall," he corrected. "So, at my school, we got a lot of –"

"Oh," Teresa interrupted again. She looked around at the decorations in the living room. "These colors are so nice together. Love all the tans and grays. Did y'all hire somebody?"

Mara cut her eyes quickly to Teresa. She held her wine glass in mid-air.

Drew put his hand on her lap. He continued. "So, at my school we received a lot of push back when I discussed our specific needs with my direct supervisor. I've requested five times to have someone from the police department come and speak to my kids about the severity of our safety. Has anyone showed up? No. Has anyone even called me back? No."

Mara looked back at Drew. "That's a shame. And those kids are right in the middle of –"

Teresa interrupted with a long sigh. "Sirue, can you get me some water? This wine is too much before I eat," she said loudly.

Mara poked her tongue inside of her cheek and gave her a *no, this heffa didn't cut me off* look. Sirue turned his head to Teresa and whispered something inaudible.

"If I'm thirsty, I'm thirsty." Teresa was still loud and Sirue whispered for her to be quiet.

"Why?! Why?" She raised her volume and Drew took another sip of his wine.

"Because you're being fuckin' rude in somebody else's damn house, that's why!" Mara snapped.

Everyone got silent. Sirue ran his hand over his face, groaned, and shook his head. Drew stood up and held Mara's arm as he did.

"We're going out back, to…uh…look at the back yard," he said, and they started to walk. Mara snatched her arm free and led the way, mumbling "yellow ass bitch" loud enough for everyone to hear.

"Are you happy now?" Sirue glared at Teresa, who was cowering next to him.

"I'm sorry. I forgot how sensitive she is," Teresa whined and put her hand on his knee.

"Two things." Sirue cleared his throat. "First, take your hand off my leg."

She did.

"Second, if you even look like you're going to come out the mouth wrong to her for the rest of the day, I'm taking you home," he said evenly. "That's a promise."

He stood and took her glass with him towards the kitchen.

Teresa folded her arms and crossed one leg over the other. "Always defending her," she said with attitude.

Sirue stopped walking and turned around. "What?"

"Nothing."

After a few minutes of sitting alone, Teresa noticed that no one had come back into the living room. She made her way through the kitchen to the open back door where she heard laughter and voices. She saw Sirue, Mara, and Drew sipping drinks and sitting in deck chairs overlooking the fenced-in yard. She stepped out and caught Mara's hard stare as it followed her to the empty chair beside Sirue.

"It's such a beautiful afternoon," Drew said, looking at the few scant clouds in the otherwise clear blue sky.

"Right, and not humid for once," Sirue added.

Before Teresa could comment on the weather being too hot for her tastes, the back door opened. Tea emerged, wearing a cute pair of sandals, a pair of black wide-legged yoga pants and a close-fitting white t-shirt. She smiled when she saw Sirue and hurried over to him.

"Si!" She leaned down to hug him. "I didn't know you were here already."

"Hey, Big Head," he said endearingly, and hugged her back. "Yeah, we haven't been here long."

Drew suddenly stood. "Here, Tea, take my seat." Then to Mara, "You want another drink, beautiful?"

Tea sat, then glanced at Mara, smiling. There was love all over her friend's face, and it looked damn good on her.

Mara nodded, handed him her glass and watched him walk back into the house. She crossed one leg over the other and swung her leg, looking down at her fingernails, smiling and in her own world.

Tea asked Sirue about work and they began a quiet conversation. Teresa looked over at them and studied how Sirue looked at Tea. She often wondered if they ever had a fling, but she remembered once that Sirue told her he wasn't really attracted to very short women. She instinctively sat up taller in her chair, trying to display all of her five feet and seven inches.

Drew partially opened the back door again and called to Mara. "Baby, your aunt is here."

Mara was surprised. She grabbed her phone from the small deck table near her. "She is? I thought she was gonna text me when she and her new beau Matthew were on their way. Oh...she did."

"You never check your phone, I don't know why you even have one," Sirue commented.

"Shut up, jerk," she laughed. Mara followed Drew back into the house.

"She really never looks at her phone," Tea agreed.

"It's just an accessory at this point," Sirue said.

Tea laughed. "So, what did your department chair say about it?" she asked, getting back to their conversation.

He shook his head and took a sip of the cola in his hand. "Just gave me the same bs about there not being another open position right now, blah blah blah. I could really teach that class."

Teresa leaned even closer to Sirue. "What class?"

"Advanced Parasitology," Sirue answered, then added to Tea, "I mean, given my proven track record, do you think there's any legal justification for not allowing me to teach it? Other than it being at their discretion."

Tea shook her head. "Talk to the dean. You need to go over everyone's head since no one is giving you the answer you deserve to know, Si. They seem hell-bent on overlooking you for every higher-level biology course."

He nodded his head in agreement and took another sip just as Aunt Esther called to them from inside the kitchen.

"Sirue Oseon, if you don't bring your giant self in here to say hi to your Auntie, I'm gonna chop you in your throat! Tea! You, too!"

They laughed and headed back inside, with Teresa trailing behind them. They walked into the kitchen, which seemed to miraculously fit seven adults comfortably. Aunt Esther hugged Tea, who walked in first.

"Sugar, are they feeding you?!" She squeezed Tea's back, then held her at arms' length.

"Yes, ma'am."

"Matthew, look at this child! Skin and bones," she tsked her teeth and looked up at Sirue. "Whew, handsome. Come give me a hug!"

"Hi, Auntie, how are you?" Sirue said, giving her a strong bear hug.

"I'm fine now," she let out a deep laugh and patted his back. She glanced over and noticed Teresa scowling her face at their hug. "You all right, young lady?"

Teresa jumped and forced a smile. She nodded and moved closer to Sirue.

Aunt Esther's glance lingered, then she cleared her throat and gave Sirue a quizzical look. He made a face and stuffed his hands into his pockets.

"Well, we do have to get goin' though. Just wanted to stop through with my food and gifts. Got a cabaret downtown I don't wanna be late for." She laughed again and danced a jig.

Everyone laughed with her, and Mara went to hug her again. "Auntie, thank you for everything."

"You're welcome, my sweet girl," she said, hugging her warmly.

Mara wouldn't let go. Instead, she leaned into her aunt even more. It quickly became oddly quiet when everyone noticed Mara burying her face into her aunt's neck and mass of hair. Tea motioned for them all to leave, and they started to pile out. She lightly rubbed Mara's back on her way out of the kitchen and left them alone.

Aunt Esther softly pushed Mara back. "Baby? Tell me what's the matter." She held and rubbed Mara's arms.

Mara's eyes were tearing up and she tried to wipe them before tears fell and ruined her mascara. She shook her head. "I don't know. I'm just…everything is…"

"You're growing up, sweetie." Aunt Esther fought back her own tears. "You remind me so much of my baby sister. So feisty. So strong. Such a big, loyal heart. I see you pushing yourself to be better with your education and she always did the same thing. All the way to the end," Aunt Esther placed her hand over her mouth to keep from sobbing.

Mara wiped her face again using both hands. She rarely heard Aunt Esther talk about her mother. When she did, it was both comforting and difficult to listen to her speak about a woman she didn't remember. Her cry became a steady stream of tears that seemed to be waiting to fall.

"Don't be getting in over your head, now," Aunt Esther said, taking a few deep breaths. She motioned at the air. "All of this is nice as hell, love, but so is a one bedroom and a den. You hear me?"

Mara nodded. "Yes, ma'am."

"I'll be over next weekend, let me see…" she checked her phone. "Yeah, I can come on Friday night to help you decorate some more like I promised. Damn, who am I talking to? I mean to help Tea decorate. You ain't gonna do shit, are you?" she laughed.

Mara shook her head, finally smiling.

"I know you won't. Come here, sweet girl." She grabbed Mara and held her, softly rocking her. "Baby, I'm a phone call away. Bills get too high, you let me know. Not every damn month, though. Hell, I'm on the VIP list for three nightclubs and I gotta have enough to tithe every Sunday!"

Mara laughed and managed to pull away from their embrace.

"I like your new friend. Matthew seems really nice."

"Yeah, he's solid. Ten years my junior and rocking my world, you hear me?" She let out another hearty laugh. "Now, go tend to your party, baby girl."

"Yes, ma'am." Mara wiped her face one last time and put her hands on her hips. "I look okay?"

"You look great. Just keep your eye on Light Bright out there. Something about that child just ain't right."

Chapter 11

After Aunt Esther and Matthew left, Sirue and Drew drifted into another heavy conversation about the country's lack of educational priorities. They were agreeing and disagreeing with the same concerns and Mara thought it was great how well they seemed to get along. They headed back to the deck while Mara and Tea tended to the food in the kitchen. Teresa tried to hang around the stove but felt out of place. When she stood near the refrigerator, she was in somebody's way. When she moved next to the counter, Mara let out a hard sigh as she tried to reach around her to grab a serving spoon. Teresa finally took the hint and walked out back to the deck and sat in a chair.

Tea opened the oven and licked her lips. The two dishes of mac and cheese and pans of turkey wings and ribs were smelling like something from heaven. "Ooooh, good Lord. Can Auntie please come cook for us every week?"

Mara laughed. She looked around and found the potholders. "Girl, right? Miles is about to be so short 'cause I'm ready to eat."

"Yeah, where is he, anyway?" She looked at the wall clock. He was already forty-five minutes late.

At that moment, there was a loud knock at the front door. Tea made her way to the living room and opened the door in Miles' mid-knock. He dropped his hand from the air and tried to read Tea's face.

"How late am I?" he said as apologetically as he could.

Her gaze dropped to the huge shopping bag at his side.

"All I know is there'd better be some kitchen appliances in there."

Miles held the bag in front of him and pulled apart the handles, exposing a new electric can opener, a tabletop grill, and a hand mixer. Tea frowned up her face and grunted.

"Well, I guess you can come in." She pulled him inside and he gave her a hug with his free arm.

"You look nice," he said, admiring her attire. His attention turned to the surroundings. "Daaaaaamn, I'm loving it."

He put the bag down and walked around the living room, taking off his light leather jacket as he checked out the pictures on the walls and the faux fireplace. "Still don't know why y'all didn't get me and Si to help move you in."

Tea shrugged. "We had enough to hire movers. Plus, we wanted to surprise y'all. But, forget all that." She checked out Miles' threads. "I see why you were so late, friend. Where you comin' from? Smelling all Sachi'd out."

She was loving his coordination. She wasn't surprised, though; he always made sure he was decked out. This time he was wearing a cream silk shirt and perfectly creased cream slacks. His jewelry was blinging, and she could have sworn those shoes were spit-shined. His whole ensemble went so well with his neatly trimmed curly 'fro.

Miles let out a slick smile and she could read his mind.

"So, where'd you take her? And who is she? Do we know her?" Tea interrogated.

Miles looked flustered. He definitely didn't want to relive any old animosity between Jasmine and Tea right now.

"Well," he started slowly. But, before he could finish, Mara appeared from the kitchen.

"Ohhh, shit! Lookin' like you just shot a music video!" She gave him a quick once over.

"Shut up," he said and walked over to give her a big hug. "Okay, you owe me one for being so late, so I'mma let that one slide."

"Yeah, you gonna be slidin' for real in them shoes, bruh." She reached down and shook his pants leg. He playfully pushed her away.

"Wait," he sniffed. "I know y'all ain't eat yet," he said, hoping Tea would forget her questions about his whereabouts.

"Naw. But ooooh, come on, let me show you around!" Mara said with the enthusiasm of a kid. She took his hand and led him out to the back deck first to say hi to everyone else. They all exchanged greetings and Mara told everyone to get ready to eat while she showed him the rest of the house.

The table was set with Tea's favorite new dinnerware and while everyone washed up, Tea filled serving bowls full of collard greens, macaroni and cheese, stuffing, potato salad, and flaky buttered rolls. She positioned the platters of sliced glazed ham, fried turkey wings, and ribs on either end of the oblong table. Next, she filled the glasses with ice cold water and placed wine glasses at each setting. By the time she sat down, everyone was making their way to their seats. It took less than ten minutes for the men to start on their second helpings. Tea and Mara kept making faces to each other about how fast they were devouring the food.

"Si, y'all don't eat at home?" Mara asked, looking at Miles stuffing his fork with food while still chewing.

Teresa laughed and looked up from her plate. "I know, that's what I was going to—"

"ANYway, y'all like my potato salad?" Mara interrupted, rolling her eyes at Teresa.

Miles almost choked and had to look down at his plate to stop from laughing. Tea, Drew, and Sirue also tried to stifle laughs.

Drew put his hand on Mara's leg beneath the table. "It's delicious, baby," he said and leaned over to kiss her on the cheek. When his mouth was near her ear, he whispered," You know that was wrong."

She looked at him and shrugged. He squeezed her knee and couldn't help but smile as he continued eating.

Once everyone was thoroughly stuffed, a few of them retreated to the living room to play games. Only Drew, Sirue, and Tea wanted to play the tiled word board game, so Miles and Mara decided to stay at the table, play cards, and talk about Teresa. She was quickly becoming Sirue's shadow as she sat as closely to him as possible on the sofa while she watched him play. Miles and Mara both got bored after a few hands and started to purposely walk by their board game and knock tiles out of place. That only warranted a few evil stares from Drew and Sirue and a couch pillow thrown by Tea.

They ended up moving the game to the dining room table while Miles helped Mara set up the picture drawing game. They used a dry erase board and not the small sketch pads included in the box, so they took a few pictures down and hung it up on the nails above the mantle. Mara turned on her portable speaker and found a soul compilation playlist on her phone. She sat with her leg drawn under her, facing Miles on the sofa. It felt good to sit and talk to him, and for some reason, it seemed like they had a lot to catch up on.

"I like you and Drew."

"Yeah. I'm really feelin' him," Mara said honestly.

"I can tell." Miles looked into her eyes and could see happiness.

"So." She hit his chest. "What about you? Who were you creeping with today?"

He shook his head and tried to hide his smile.

"Why all the mystery?" she asked inquisitively but knew the answer before she finished the question. Her eyes widened. "No. You're seeing Jasmine, aren't you?"

Miles wasn't really shocked that she'd guessed so soon. He put his arm over the back of the sofa.

"I mean, not really seeing her. She's working for me now." Miles told her what happened in his office a few days ago.

"Are y'all going anywhere with this? Or y'all just messing around?"

He rubbed the back of his neck. "It's…complicated."

Another thought entered Mara's mind. "Tea doesn't know, does she?" She mentally recalled the intense argument Tea had with Jasmine when she found out she dumped Miles so coldly eight months ago, even after Miles had taken her cheating ass back. "That didn't end too well."

He shook his head. "I think I'll make it a need-to-know kinda thing."

"Yeah, that's best. It's funny how Tea's little self is so protective of us."

Chapter 12

After Sirue narrowly beat Tea in the board game by making the word 'quartzy', they all joined them in the living room and Miles went to take a bathroom break. Drew looked at the set-up and couldn't believe how serious they were about this next game. The game board was spread out on the coffee table with the pieces already in their starting places. The powdered timer was in the center. There were pillows set on the floor and a package of unopened dry erase markers in various colors beside the board.

A mellow old school song about having a crazy love played softly in the background.

Drew walked up behind Mara who was sitting on the sofa. He leaned down to her and wrapped his arms around her chest. He whispered something in her ear, and she smiled, then whispered something back. Teresa took Sirue's hand and led him over to the corner, standing with her back to the wall. He stood in front of her and lowered his head, placing his hands on her hips. She ran her hands across the back of his fade and they both swayed to the music.

Tea walked into the room from the kitchen after putting the last of the food away. She instantly felt out of place. There was a lovefest going on and she had no partner. The sweet music didn't help at all. She grabbed the pack of markers and plopped down into the huge armchair, lifting one knee up to her chest. She sighed and watched as Drew's and Mara's love whispers started to grow into smooth kisses. Mara dropped her head and Drew began softly kissing the nape of her neck.

"Juuuuuuust great," Tea said to herself and glanced at Teresa's hands sliding up and down Sirue's shoulder blades. She wanted so badly to have that feeling again. She watched them moving together and jumped when she felt someone's hands resting on top of her shoulders.

"Whoa. Relax, it's just me," Miles whispered in her ear. He continued to knead her neck and shoulders. "You're so tense."

Tea let her head drop and the long bangs of her short pageboy fell into her face. She matched the rhythm of his hands, which matched the slow rhythm of the song. She rolled her head, which suddenly felt twice as heavy, from left to right and back again. He used his thumbs to massage her neck. He seemed to apply all the right pressure in all the right places. She moaned.

"Feels nice, doesn't it?" he smiled.

Her eyes lazily closed. "Yes."

Miles knew she had a lot going on and must have been stressing out over getting the house. His thoughts made him unconsciously move his hands down the sides of her arms. She moved slightly in the chair.

Tea felt awkward when she felt one of his hands move up to smooth the back of her tapered hair. She turned her head a little and Miles took his hands off her. He sat on the arm of the huge chair and loudly cleared his throat.

"Uh, there *are* rooms upstairs," he said grabbing the markers from Tea and tossing them at Mara.

The song ended and everyone started to break out of their cuddles. Drew suggested they do women versus men, but after Mara shot him a look, he changed his mind.

"I'll be on Sirue's team," Teresa said, sitting on a floor pillow beside his leg as he sat on the couch.

"So damn pressed," Mara said, shaking her head.

Teresa laughed. "Yep," she agreed, putting an arm around his leg.

Sirue rubbed his face, then said, "Okay, me, Teresa and Miles against y'all."

"No! We want Miles, that is so not fair!" Mara looked seriously angry, and Drew wondered what the big deal was. She explained to him that Miles was by far the best artist of them all and every team he was on for this game seemed to win.

"Baby, don't even sweat it. I told you about the comic strip contract I almost had when I was young, right?" Drew stretched his fingers and tightened the elastic on his dreadlock ponytail.

Mara looked at him unbelievably.

"Oh, Lord," Tea mumbled.

"No, I'm serious. Trust me ladies, we will beat these amateurs!"

Halfway through the game, Miles' team was sixteen spaces ahead. Drew was at the board, his sleeves rolled up, scribbling something indecipherable. Mara sucked her teeth when she watched the last of the white powder fall from the timer. She looked at Tea and couldn't believe the crap Drew was sketching in front of them.

"Drew...what the HELL is that?" she asked through clenched teeth.

He slowly put the cap back on the black marker with emphasis and set it down angrily on the mantle.

"If y'all would *look*, you would see the horse back there in the stable." He jabbed at his work on the board. "And *obviously*, these are somebody's shoes, because *obviously* this is a closet!"

Tea bit the corner of her mouth. "Um. Drew. Hold up. Your word was horseshoe? You had to draw a horseshoe?!"

He nodded. "Duh! Yes!" He jabbed at the board again. "Horse and shoe!"

Mara threw her hands up and stared at the ceiling while Miles and Sirue bust out laughing. Sirue stood up and grabbed his card from the box. He shooed Drew away from the dry erase board. Drew went to sit next to Mara on the couch, but she put her legs up and blocked him. He rolled his eyes and sat on the floor in front of her mumbling to himself, "If y'all blind asses knew how to look at pictures."

Sirue rolled the dice, then read his card and gave his team a smirk. Tea reached over to flip the timer. When she did, a noise sounded.

Drew looked down at his phone. "That's me – y'all go ahead, I'll be right back."

Mara lightly kicked him on his leg as he walked past her, and he paused to give her a quick kiss on her cheek before heading to the kitchen.

Sirue deliberately cleared his throat to get his team's attention and began sketching a fluffy animal.

"What the hell?" Miles squinted.

"Puppy!" Teresa shouted.

Sirue kept drawing furiously.

"Move, man, so I can see...oh, um...dog! Canine!" Miles tried.

"Poodle!" Teresa screamed.

Sirue threw his marker down and pointed at her. "Yes! Yes! That's what I'M talking about right here. Move me, please! That's four more, thank you," he shouted.

"Oh, shut up and sit down." Mara threw a pillow at him. "My go."

She intentionally walked the long way around the coffee table to disrupt the jovial high fives they were giving each other. She picked up the dice and heard another phone chime.

Everyone looked around. Miles pulled out his phone.

"Hey, Jazz," he answered, then suddenly regretted it.

Mara's eyes bugged wide open, and she looked at Tea, wondering if she'd heard. And by the look of her face, she did.

"Jasmine? What the hell is she doing calling Miles?" she asked Mara, pointing towards Miles.

Miles stood up and walked towards the dining room.

Sirue picked up Teresa's drink and finished it off.

Mara shrugged then walked to sit back down. "Girl, who knows?"

Tea looked at Sirue from the armchair. "Si, you knew about this? Since when have they been back in touch?"

He held out his free hand and shrugged. "Uh, Teresa, I'll fill this back up for you."

Teresa responded by leaning back against the couch, pulling her feet beneath her. She liked the drama about to unfold.

Miles ended the call and headed back to the front room to see Tea glaring at him. He sat beside Mara on the couch and slid his phone onto the coffee table. Mara braced her face for whatever was about to go down.

"Tea, that was almost a year ago," Miles said, almost apologetically.

"Yeah, well once a freak always a hoe."

"Tea!" Mara's eyes widened. She wondered where the hell that came from.

Miles let out a small laugh. "I don't believe you just said that."

"And I don't believe you'd go back to her. You know that I literally walked in on her and Kelvin, right? They were in mid-sex, Miles. On your living room floor, or don't you remember how mad you were?" Tea could feel her face heating up.

Miles stared ahead and clenched his jaws, resting back on the couch. He rubbed his left temple, then shot a look over at her. He didn't want this to happen this way. His voice was level when he spoke.

"People can change, Tea. She changed."

"Okay, whatever, Miles. Mara, it's your go."

Mara bit her lip and started to stand up.

"No, you know what, it's not whatever, Tea," Miles said, his voice getting louder.

Mara sat back down.

"Miles, I don't feel like it right now. Mara, it's your –"

"You called her a hoe and now you don't feel like it? Nah, come on…you have so much to say, let me hear it." He leaned forward and rested his elbows on his knees, exaggerating with his hands. "Why the hell are you still pissed about that shit and I'm not?"

"Miles, chill," Mara said.

Tea looked at him. "You really want to know?"

"That's what I said."

Tea scooted up to the edge of the armchair and counted on her fingers. "One: she's a liar. Two: she's rude as hell, and three: Kelvin's not the only man she fucked while she was with you."

Mara and Teresa both made "oh" shapes with their mouths. Miles lifted his head a little higher.

"How do you know that?"

"Well, just like people can change, people can talk, too. I heard two different women at the shop on two different occasions talking about her. But, if that hoe life is what you want, do you. Don't say I didn't warn you. Again. Let's finish this damn game." Tea waved him off with her hand.

"I hate it when you do that shit," he shook his head and stared at her full on.

"Miles, that's enough," Mara warned again.

"Do what shit?" Tea asked, staring back at him.

"When you act all opinionated one minute then want to end a conversation when you don't feel like bein' bothered. That shit."

"Don't be mad at me, I'm not the one who slept with Kelvin...and Jermaine...and Lionel," Tea ticked her fingers off as she recited the names, then rolled her eyes.

Miles seethed in his skin. He clenched his jaws again and, from the floor, Teresa shifted slightly farther away from him.

"Well, I don't think you've been sleeping with *anyone* since Jonathan, so maybe that's the real problem. How many names can you count now?" Miles knew the moment it slipped from his mouth he'd gone too far.

Mara and Teresa looked over at Tea, who put her hand on her stomach.

"Fuck you," she said quietly and stood up.

"Tea." Mara called her name gently, but she'd already started jogging up the stairs.

Miles watched her leave and then stared absently at the game on the table.

"Damn, Miles." Mara understood his anger, but knew she'd never go as far as throwing Jonathan's abusive ass in Tea's face. She threw the dice back on the table and picked up her drink, sinking back into the couch.

Teresa unfolded her legs and stood up from the floor. "I'll go talk to her."

Mara shot her an evil look. "No, the hell you won't."

"I'm saying...she's crying," Teresa said, almost in a whisper as she sat down in the armchair Tea just vacated.

"And I'm saying leave her alone. You don't know her." Mara sipped on her drink again. "Why the hell are you even still here?"

Teresa pouted but started smiling when she saw Sirue walking back in with her glass.

He had a strange look on his face and didn't know quite what to make of what he'd just overheard in the kitchen. When he left to refill Teresa's wine, he saw Drew leaning back on the kitchen counter, smiling a very wide-toothed grin. He acknowledged Sirue with a nod, then proceeded out the door to the deck and lounged in a chair.

Sirue took the wine bottle from the bucket of ice in the sink and opened it then walked toward the window when he heard Drew's voice.

"Yeah...no, no, I'll come past later," Drew laughed. "I know...don't worry about it...can't wait to see you, either...yeah..."

Sirue went back to pouring the wine and didn't glance up when Drew walked back in, showing more teeth.

"Hey, man, I was thinking. Would you mind coming to my school for career day? It's next week and the science department would be more than glad to have you." Drew walked to the refrigerator and took out the French onion dip they'd put back earlier.

"Yeah, sure. Just give me a call."

Drew continued to talk about his school and some of the lame career days they'd had the past few years. Sirue feigned interest, all the while wanting to knock those damn teeth out of his mouth for possibly playing Mara. He didn't want to jump to false conclusions, though, and he was relieved when Drew excused himself to the bathroom. Sirue headed back into the living room and instantly felt the tension.

He handed Teresa her drink and, by the silence, he knew things didn't go too well.

"Where's Tea?" he asked.

"Upstairs," Teresa answered, reaching up to hold his hand.

Mara rolled her eyes. "What a fucked up evening."

"I'm sorry," Miles said, almost inaudibly.

"It's not just you. Her, too. Both of y'all with this old, tired shit. Damn." She leaned forward and started putting the game away.

Sirue picked up the pillows from the floor and Miles stood to dislodge the dry erase board from the wall. Drew walked into the living room clapping his hands and rubbing them together.

"All right, all right, what's the score?" He was all smiles.

No one answered him. He stood with his hands out.

"So, what did I miss?"

Chapter 13

Beep, beep.

Tea clicked on her car alarm and adjusted the duffel bag over her shoulder. She was at the mall an hour before the stores opened and couldn't wait for the solitude of her quiet shop. It was almost like she ran out of the house that morning. She wasn't sure if Mara was even home. She faked a deep slumber when Mara knocked on her bedroom door after everyone left last night. Maybe she was going to tell her that she planned to spend the night at Drew's. There was just no point in talking to her because she didn't even know what to say to herself other than Miles was right. Why had she been so angry? The whole marrying Sandra on a whim thing didn't get her as worked up as him getting back with Jasmine.

"Whatever," Tea mumbled to herself as she opened the huge glass door and entered the mall.

On the way to her shop, she stopped at her favorite kiosk, Common In-Sense, because she knew Kadari had beaten her again. And there she was, always earlier than Tea, no matter how early she thought she arrived.

Tea made an obvious gesture of looking at her watch.

"Daaaaamn, K," she said with mock annoyance. "What do you do, sleep in your car to beat me here?"

Kadari smiled and squatted to unlock the heavy black tarp at the bottom of the stand.

"Wah gwaan, Tea, girl," she said in her light Kingston accent, "you know I must get here earlier than you to grab your customers." She laughed and unhooked the tarp from the metal lock. "So how is your new place? Did you enjoy your days off?"

Tea described her new house to Kadari and told her about the housewarming, minus the details about the argument.

"Ohhh, it sounds so nice. You know, my brother came by to work my stand for two days, but I think he really wanted to be here to see you. He was so upset he missed you, though," Kadari said with a match-making smirk. She stood and put one hand on her curvy hip and the other through her blonde-tipped twists.

"If you don't stop trying to hook us up, K." Tea walked over to smell the new lavender incense sticks that she hadn't seen before. "When did you get these?"

Kadari sucked her teeth and finished pulling the covering from across the rest of the stand.

"Listen, I just think you two would be cute together –"

"Kadari!" Tea rolled her eyes.

"No really. Hear me out, sistren. He's a good man, has a good career, and since I haven't seen you with a gentleman caller lately..."

Tea tuned her out, an all she started to hear was white noise laced with a patois accent. Why was everybody so concerned about her not having a man? Wasn't owning her shop at twenty-four years old good enough? Wasn't finishing college a year early good enough? She was surprised her father hadn't started up with her yet, but she knew he was too wrapped up in fussing with Anna to be worrying about her not dating. *Damn, how Freudian was that?* She felt a poke in her arm.

"Tea," Kadari called her name again.

"Oh, my bad."

"Where did you just go?"

Tea shook her head. "Girl, don't mind me, I'm still waking up," she lied.

"Mmmmhmm." Kadari looked at her and sucked her teeth. "You look awake to me. So anyway, if he comes by today, I'll tell him you're interested in a conversation?"

Tea shrugged. "Yeah, sure." She knew she had zero intentions of meeting, let alone talking, to her brother. She ran her hand over the tapered part of the back of her head. "Well, let me get to my shop. I'll stop by later on to get some of that lavender."

"Okay, girl. See ya, walk good."

Tea didn't offer any more greetings to her fellow early birds at the mall, and instead made a beeline for her shop. She unlocked the gate, lifted it, and walked through, then lowered it halfway. The moment she stepped inside she felt her spirts lift a little. This was definitely her sanctuary. Even after two years of running it, it still felt new each time she crossed the threshold. She dropped her duffel bag on the floor and sat at the front reception desk, thumbing through the appointment book. DeeDee took great care of the shop for the last three days, but she was glad to be back. She ran her finger down today's clients and almost jumped out of her skin when the store's phone rang.

"Hair by Tea," she answered.

"Do I know you well or what?"

She knew the baritone voice instantly.

"Si, why are you calling me here?"

"Because, woman, if I called your cell, you wouldn't pick it up, just like last night when I called for thousand times."

"Oh." Tea smiled and realized she hadn't even bothered to turn her cell phone on yet this morning. What was the point?

"So, are you feeling better this morning? Mara filled me in on what I missed."

"Not really. I'm a little bummed out." She played with the container of pens in front of her.

"You know Miles was just talking out of frustration. He feels bad as hell if that's any consolation."

"But it's not just him. He's right, and he was only saying what I know all of y'all are thinking anyway. I haven't dated anyone since Jonathan, and I'm just bitter, frigid, uptight and need to get laid. I know how y'all think." Tea sighed.

"Are you finished?"

Tea was quiet.

"Tea, listen. Nobody thinks that. Just you."

"Sure. Okay." She rolled her eyes.

"Is this what you were telling yourself over and over last night when you were holed up in your room for hours? Tea, I haven't been in a serious relationship in a while. Before Drew, Mara was proud to be single and mingle, and Miles steps in and out of relationships like shoes. C'mon, none of us can judge you."

She let loose a half-smile. "God, but I felt so out of place last night. You and Teresa were booed up. Mara and Drew were all kissy face. Miles had just come from seeing Jasmine's cheating ass...," she shook her head.

"Speaking of Drew," Sirue hoped to get off of her date-less subject. "Tell me what you think of him."

"They're cool together. They seem to get along well, and it doesn't hurt that he's fine as hell. Why?"

Sirue told her what he'd overheard in the kitchen.

"That could be anybody, Si. His mother maybe."

He groaned. "I don't know. Didn't sound like he was saying goodbye to his mama. Just keep an eye on it. Let me know if Miles and I need to hurt him."

She laughed. "Always choosing violence."

"All right, I better get to work. I'm making an appointment with the Dean today."

"Tell me how it goes."

"I will. What time do you get off tonight?"

"I'm not sure. I'm closing, but looking at the appointment book, my last client might talk me to death." She made a face and pushed the book forward.

"Just tell her you have a headache and she'll get the point."

"Nah, that won't work. It's Mara."

He laughed. "Yeah, plan on being there for a while."

"Bye, Si."

"Bye, Big Head."

Chapter 14

After hanging up with Tea, Sirue changed his mind about calling Teresa back. She raised hell when he dropped her off at her place last night instead of letting her spend the night. She retaliated the only way she knew how: by blowing up his cell. He looked at his phone again as he waited at the traffic light. Twenty-two missed calls. She was quickly getting back to her stalker ways. He decided against calling her and dropped his phone into the passenger seat and smiled. Then he wondered why he was smiling.

His SUV made its way down Canal Road and easily found a convenient parking spot near his office in the Saldisch Science Building. He loved arriving before eight a.m. when he could still manage to get so close to the science complex. The less walking, the better. Sirue had been meaning to meet up with Miles and Mara at the gym on Saturday mornings. Just to tone up. That's what he kept telling himself. Teresa pointed out to him last night that he'd picked up some weight. And Mara did seem to pat his stomach more when she walked by him. Sirue shrugged and balanced his large soda, briefcase, and box of donut holes as he made his way through the doors, up the elevator and into his office.

Before he could get situated, there was a knock at the partially open door.

"Hey, man. There's definitely going to be a revolution. Did you read the paper yet?" Sedrick strolled into the office, ignoring Sirue's disinterest. He tossed the folded campus newspaper on top of his desk and took his usual seat across from him. Sirue shoved a confection into his mouth and glanced up to scan the article in view. He wiped some glazed icing crumbs away and re-focused his eyes. Another university was in the media again for refusing prestigious teaching positions to yet another African American professor. He read the quarter-page article, swallowed half the box of sweets and finished his drink.

Sedrick watched him eat. "You know diabetes is a thing, right?"

"Shut up," Sirue wiped his mouth. "So, are you going to have my back when they write an article about me?"

Sedrick gave a short laugh. "Brother, how can I not have your back? That opening is perfect for you. Right up your alley, too. Not this weak intro to biology shit they got you slaving away at now." He shook his head.

Sirue yanked his briefcase onto his desk and popped it open. He removed the papers bound together by a clip and dropped them in front of him. As he opened a drawer to look for his record book he'd mistakenly left there over the weekend, Sedrick leaned forward and grabbed the papers.

"You graded their symbiosis reports already?" He thumbed through them, noticing Sirue not only marked them but gave feedback on each one. "Duly impressed, man."

"Yeah, why?" Sirue opened the record book and powered on his desktop. "Don't tell me you're still behind on your students' papers. C'mon, Sed, they took that exam three weeks ago."

Sedrick tossed the papers back to him and shrugged. "They'll get 'em back before the semester's over."

Sirue hated his friend's blasé attitude towards his job. Sedrick was a damn brilliant research scientist, but never quite seemed dedicated to being a professor. Sirue began to record the grades both into his record book and his online grading portal while Sedrick picked the newspaper back up. He wondered if they remained acquaintances only due to circumstances. There weren't many professors who spent their duty-free time socializing with Sedrick. It was usually the other way around. Sedrick was the only colleague he knew who consistently used his time hopping from one office to the next, looking for gossip or otherwise wasting his energy. If he wasn't in Sirue's office, then he was across campus in Samantha Hedgley's office in the history department, or downstairs in the chemistry offices bugging Taylor Hughes.

"All right, man, I'm heading to the café. Want something?" Sedrick stood and stretched. "Preferably something with actual nutrients?"

Sirue laughed. "No, thanks. Got class in an hour and need to get these entered."

"The consummate professional. Be easy, man. Peace."

He tapped his newspaper against his hand as he walked out.

"Remember to bring your sketchbooks to the laboratory tomorrow. You'll be viewing and sketching three types of bacteria directly following your exam. If you're running late, don't bother coming. I won't distribute any late copies. All right, I'll see you then."

Sirue looked down and gathered his materials from the large black lab table at the bottom of the small auditorium. The students in his early class were all freshmen majoring in a non-scientific discipline. They all complained ad nauseum to deaf ears that he gave them too much work and too many assignments for an intro class. He piled his notebooks into his briefcase and turned to wipe the wall-sized white board when he heard someone tapping on the lab table behind him, obviously trying to get his attention.

"Yes?" he answered, but his voice trailed off when he turned and saw her standing there, her hands resting on the table between them.

Teresa had an expressionless look on her otherwise perfectly made-up face. She was wearing a zipped pink athletic jacket and a short pink skirt the same shade as her manicured nails, which she started tapping again.

"You had me worried about you all night." No smile. No contempt.

"What are you doing here?" Sirue glanced behind her at a few straggling students talking at the top of the steps.

"Well, I wouldn't have to come all the way out here if you would just call me back." She smoothed a few big curls behind her ear, and now Sirue could sense the attitude creeping in.

"Teresa, don't start this shit." Sirue leaned forward and spoke in a harsh whisper. "You don't come to my job and show out."

She rolled her eyes and forced out a laugh loud enough for the students at the door to look down at them.

"Show out? Ohhhhh, okay. Now I'm showing out." She smoothed her hair behind both of her ears and attempted to calm herself down. "Look,

I'll wait here for you to finish so we can talk. You fuckin' danced with me last night, grabbed on my ass, but couldn't even call me back after you dropped me off."

Sirue glared at her and wondered how fast he could strangle her without leaving any evidence. He looked up at the students who hurriedly tried to avert their attention back to their conversation. He turned back around and wiped the board spotless, all the while fuming. When he was satisfied, he grabbed his briefcase and stormed out of the metal door adjacent to the podium. Teresa ran to catch it before it closed.

"Sirue!" She called, jogging to keep up with his stride.

He continued his brisk pace through the tiled hallways, nodding greetings to his colleagues. He knew they were silently questioning the presence of the pretty woman struggling to catch up to him. *Great*, he thought. A public strike against him. Just what he needed right now.

He rushed into the closing elevator, but the doors were held open because another professor was behind him and saw Teresa waving her hand at him. When Sirue got off, he sped to his office and before he could get in and lock it, she maneuvered her way inside. He looked down at her in disgust, then closed his door shut. He walked to a file cabinet, located the papers he wanted, and sat at his desk, abruptly picking up his desk phone and dialing.

"Hi, this is Dr. Sirue Oseon from the biology department...yes...well, I'd like an appointment with Dean Simon...yes, as early as possible." Sirue let out a severely fake laugh. "I can imagine...yes...both personal and professional." He scribbled something on a sticky note. That is perfect...yes, I will, thank you...you, too."

He replaced the receiver and fingered through the papers he'd retrieved, fully aware that Teresa had made herself comfortable in the empty chair across from him. He opened his briefcase and fumbled through it until he found his record book.

"So, you're going to ignore me?" She crossed her legs and shook her foot furiously.

Sirue looked up at her and slammed his case shut. He looked back down at his papers, at his computer, then ran his hand over his head. He exhaled, then grabbed a red ink pen and began marking the assignments.

Teresa unzipped her jacket, removed it, and laid it on her lap.

"Why do you hate me?" she asked quietly.

"What?" He looked up.

"You heard me."

Sirue sighed and rolled his head back, then rubbed the back of his neck. It was too early for this shit.

"When I called you a few weeks ago, it felt so good to hear your voice again. And you keep throwing me these mixed signals. One minute I'm good enough for you to feel up on, the next minute you hate me again."

That was true. He didn't know what had gotten into him at the housewarming. *Oh*, he remembered. It was the wine. Plus, she did look and smell damn good yesterday.

"I don't hate you. I … we just can't date again, Teresa. We're dysfunctional together. I don't even know if we can be friends when you pull shit like you did just now."

She looked down at her hands. "I won't do this again." She looked up, her tone softening. "I hate feeling like I'm losing you. You're the only man who ever had sex with me and still wanted to take me out the next day. I loved us being a couple. I miss you."

Sirue looked at her full pink lips as she spoke and tried to tell himself that soon she'd switch up and start flipping out again. His eyes slid down to her full breasts that rose as she breathed, and he could see headlights through her thin shirt. The twitch in his pants made him focus back on her face.

Teresa noticed his roaming eyes and licked her lips.

"If we can't be a couple, what if we just… hang out?" She uncrossed her legs and slowly lifted her snug skirt, revealing her black lace panties. "Nobody has to know. Just you and me."

Sirue's eyes hungrily stared between her legs, remembering the warmth they held. His gaze moved all over her body as she stood and slowly sauntered towards him. She came around the desk and nudged his legs open with her knees, then stood directly between them. She moved closer to him, pressing her chest against his face. He lifted her top enough to unfasten the clasp of her bra. Sirue held her breasts with his hands, rubbing them over his face. Teresa moaned and smiled as she lowered her body enough to unzip his slacks. He grunted as she ran her hands all over him, then put him into her mouth.

"Shit," Sirue whispered as she slid her lips down to the base of his penis. Just like that. He always loved how she never needed any prep time. He could feel the warm, wet walls of her throat and he wanted more. He slid his hands through her hair and guided her along. Teresa took his hands from her hair and held them down on the arms of his chair. He leaned back and let her work her spell over him. In about five minutes, Sirue knew he was going to erupt. And he knew she'd let him do it in her mouth. After she swallowed, she wiped the corners of her mouth and pulled her bra and t-shirt back down while he fixed his pants. She walked behind him and rubbed his shoulders.

"Do you think I'm beautiful?" she asked.

Damn, Sirue thought. He closed his eyes.

"Yeah, you are."

Teresa kissed his head and smoothed the collar on his shirt. "Well, I have to get to work early today. I'm training new people and I told them to get there by eleven."

Sirue just nodded, uneasy with her standing behind him, her hands massaging his shoulder blades. She was getting very comfortable again, and he knew where it was going. He knew where the whole thing was going, but he didn't want to take advantage of her. He ran his hands over his face as if he was wiping his own exasperation off.

She leaned down and whispered into his ear. "So...can I come by tonight to cook for you and Miles?" She sucked on his ear lobe.

He nodded. "Yeah. That's...sure, okay," he stammered.

She stood and walked back around to retrieve her jacket from her chair. With her hand on the knob, she turned and blew a kiss to him.

Sirue picked up a hand and gave her a weak wave. When the door closed slowly, he knew it wasn't just Teresa who left. His common sense went right behind her.

Chapter 15

After two consecutive days of trying to contact Tea, Miles decided it was a lost cause. It was too juvenile to chase somebody to apologize when they didn't want to be chased. There were even worse squabbles they'd had, though, that they managed to make it through. This time seemed different.

Miles was in the large upstairs spare room which he declared as the game room, yet Sirue called the study. Two of the walls were covered with six-foot bookshelves which flanked a very comfortable reading chair and lamp. Across the room, there was a small ping pong table, two mini-fridges, a mounted seventy-inch plasma screen TV, a cabinet with three different gaming consoles, two oversized leather recliners, and a beverage station. Miles sat in his favorite recliner and grabbed his tablet that was charging in the side pocket. He sat in his sweats and a loose gray muscle shirt and scrolled through different tabs, not really focusing on the screens he conjured up. It was late Wednesday night and since he'd just come from Heaven's with Mara, he already had his shower and heated up leftovers Teresa made earlier for dinner. Miles glanced at the time. It was nearly half past eleven. Too late to try Tea again. Miles scratched his goatee, then ran his hand over his face. He laughed because he reminded himself of Sirue.

He couldn't figure out why he felt so bad about saying what he said to her three days ago. It needed to be said. Maybe not in front of so many people. And definitely not in the manner in which he said it. Miles still believed it to be true. Tea needed some hot sex. Everybody does. He recalled the last sex partner he had before getting back in contact with Jasmine. Her name was Monica, and she was his old supervisor from the Cosmic Lumens offices in Rockville. She called him about a month ago wanting to hook up. Miles obliged, and after a delicious meal at a local cheesecake restaurant, they drove back to his house and had incredible sex, amplified by the innuendos and flirtations they shared over dinner. Miles absently scratched his temple, trying to remember how Monica had her hair styled that evening. He could envision everything else about her curvy body, but for the life of him, he couldn't see her hair. A smile spread across his face as he remembered Tea once said that she always made it a point to focus on people's hair. But Monica definitely confirmed his notion that casual sex is as good a stress-reliever as a forty. Not better, just the same.

Then, his thoughts flew to Jasmine. The sex they had recently was so familiar. Her beautiful hands on his body, her loud orgasms, the way she enjoyed sucking on every surface of his skin. And then he remembered the random phone interruptions during their encounters, seeing her flirt with almost every man in the office, and the confirmation from Mrs. C. that Jasmine was indeed dating at least two of his co-workers.

He shook his head clear and he saw the back of Tea's dainty neck in his mind. She really needed something to relieve her stress. He wished he'd said it in a gentler way instead of saying she hadn't been laid since that asshole Jonathan. He should have been more considerate, already sensing that she was tense when he massaged her shoulders before they played the game. He could feel it all throughout her muscles.

Miles went back to the home screen of his tablet and opened his favorite sports app. He recalled how her shoulders felt beneath his hands. She was so petite and smelled so good, and he loved that about her. But what did her neck and shoulders and scent have to do with anything? This was Tea. Big Head.

Didn't she relax under my touch, though? he thought as he scrolled to the recent basketball scores. She even started to get uncomfortable. Or nervous. But why –

A notification on the screen alerted him that he just received an email from *shopgirl*. He frowned his face, wondering why she'd be emailing him when she could just text.

He fished his phone from between the cushion where it fell. He sent her a text.
Hey
Tea wrote back fast. *Yes, that email is from me.*
I didn't read it yet. Wanted to catch you before you fell asleep
Oh. Go read the email first.
Ok hold on
Miles tapped his email app and quickly tapped the inbox, opened the email and read at double speed.

Miles, what you said really hurt me, but I know I went too far. I am sorry for the mean words I spoke about Jasmine. I called myself looking out for you when all I did was piss you off. It's just that sometimes I see you make these impulsive decisions. I think you can do much better than her. That's all. And I know this could have just been a text, but I felt less nervous this way. Love, Tea.

A wide grin spread across Miles' face, and he went back to his phone.
I'm sorry, too
That only took you like 2 seconds. Did you actually read it?
Yeah I always got As in English
Not in college you didn't
Oh yeah
LOL
You never let a brother use your notes though
Because I did MY work while y'all were out playin
No, that was called pledging
That was called dumb
You sound like mara. she's rubbing off on you. she's a bad influence.
LOL mara is snoring like she's got emphysema
What impulsive decisions do I make?
Huh?? Tea sent a question-faced emoji.
From the email
Ohhhhh miles, um...the wedding for one. And that dirt bike last year.
Which I still plan to give to your brothers when they're older

Miles saw that she was in the process of writing something back, then deleting it, then writing again. He tapped the side of his phone, wondering what was taking so long to type.
So...are you and jasmine a couple now?

Miles froze at the question. Is this what she was typing and re-typing for the past minute? What took her so long to write that? His mind raced, thinking of something funny to say. Anything to say. He looked blankly at the screen, wondering how much to tell her about Jasmine. He was no longer giving her money, splurging for lunch, nor paying for her parking at the job. He admitted that he wanted something more from her, but after experiencing her roaming eyes for himself, he quickly remembered why they didn't work out. Not to mention the son she kept hidden from him. It all still stung.

Hello??
Oh sorry, Miles typed.
Was my question too hard?
No
What were you thinking about? Or did you go take a leak?
I'm not with jasmine
Thanks for telling me because you didn't have to
I know. I wanted to.
Well she's lucky to have you as a friend
I thought you said I can do better than her 😊
You can but she can't get a better friend than you
I hope you're not trying to borrow any money
Shut up
Hey what's up for Friday night? Your turn with granny again?
Nope. I wanna get out of here though. mara is cooking for drew. All that lovey dovey crap will make me sick

Miles smiled to himself. *Come with me to a cabaret my line brother is throwing*
You're not taking jazz??
I asked you. Miles tapped his thumb against his phone again. He waited at least thirty seconds for Tea to reply.
Okay I'll go
Cool
See if Sirue wants to tag along
Ok
Well I need to get to bed. Tea sent the yawning emoji.
Goodnight

Bye. don't be a stranger. you should call people sometimes.
Funny. Bye.

Miles noticed that he was wearing a very big grin. He silently scrolled back through their conversation and re-read it. He looked at the timestamps and knew he wasn't imagining that it took her long to respond when he asked her out. Why was he so upset that she suddenly wanted Sirue to come? He kind of wanted her to himself. Miles shook his head. He wasn't thinking straight. He ran his hand through his hair and wondered when he could persuade her to touch it up. He smiled at the thought of her fingers in his hair, and quickly concluded that it was time to get his tired ass to bed, too.

Chapter 16

"I know you wish you could make him staaaaay…"

Mara sang along with the track playing through her speakers as she looked in her full-length mirror. She dried off from her forty-minute shower, inhaling the fruity aroma of her body wash. In a half an hour, Drew would come sauntering through her front door, smelling delicious and looking like an African king. She could imagine his broad shoulder blades busting through his shirt as he hugged her. Mmmm. And she would drown in his scent. She opened her eyes, not realizing they'd been closed, nor that a new song was on. She started to hug herself and move to the rhythm, using her towel as her dancing partner. She smiled at her own silliness. It was almost scary how much she loved him. No one ever spoiled her so much. No one ever made her dance in a mirror, and no one ever made her so horny. When they went clubbing last weekend, he couldn't keep his hands off her. And he made her so hot in his truck that she gave him head while he was driving. Tea scolded her for that one when she told her, but Mara didn't care. They were both caught up in the heat of the moment. Damn the highway.

Tea was always so damn prissy about sex, anyway. They had a very deep sister talk late on Monday while Tea twisted her hair, and although it felt good to share with her girl, she knew her limits. She almost let it slip that she and Drew don't always use condoms. And Tea would have had a conniption if she knew how much Drew was into spanking during sex. It shocked the hell out of Mara the first time, too. They were in his favorite doggy-style position, and out of nowhere, the light smacking turned into something else. She almost did a rear kick on his ass, but he adjusted his tempo enough that it started to turn her on, too. Mara knew not to let him get carried away with the shit, though. She also knew that Tea would take it to the next level of paranoia, so it was best to keep that information to herself.

Mara shook her shoulder-length natural twists free from their ponytail and admired how fresh they still looked. She lotioned up, put on her red lace lingerie and spritzed on the citrus cologne she loved. Her red cocktail dress was laying on her bed, so she slid into it, grabbed her makeup pouch and sat at her vanity.

"Mara, I'm gone...," Tea called through Mara's bedroom door.

"Wait, come in." Mara turned down her music a few notches.

Tea opened the door and Mara glanced back from the mirror.

"You look beautiful, Tea," Mara smiled.

Tea looked down at her tie-front blue chambray sleeveless top and snug white jeans. She tugged at the tie of her shirt, pulling it down an inch to cover her almost bare midriff.

"It looks okay? I hope I don't sweat it out. Or my hair," she said, sweeping her long bangs to the side and smoothing down her tapered shave in the back.

"Just sit down when you feel yourself getting overheated. Make Miles get you a cold drink. That's what he's there for." Mara turned back around, crossed her legs beneath her vanity, and applied the liquid eyeliner.

"Yeah, or Sirue."

"Si's going?"

"Yeah. I'm surprised his shadow won't be there."

"Right. She'll probably be hiding in the parking lot, you know her ass," Mara laughed. "And I'm glad you and Miles are cool now. Damn, y'all were stressing me out."

Tea smiled.

"All right, girl, I'm out. What are you cooking? It smells good as he—"

"Shiiiiiiit!" Mara zoomed past Tea, almost knocking her over, and doubled down the steps. She ran to the kitchen, yanked the oven door open, grabbed a potholder and removed the quiche just in time.

"If you didn't take seventeen-hour showers you wouldn't be burning your food," Tea teased as she bounced down the steps.

"And if you don't get your four-inch-tall ass out of this house!" Mara called from the kitchen.

Tea laughed on her way out the door.

Despite having to drive the thirty minutes to the hotel, Tea was in a great mood. She called DeeDee at the shop to remind her to confirm their water delivery for tomorrow, then called to check on her brothers. Anna said, in a very annoyed tone, that they were at a sleepover, but even she couldn't ruin Tea's spirits.

She let down her back windows to enjoy the warm early October breeze. She cranked up the radio because they were playing some old school go-go, and she seat-danced to the infectious beats. Her body was itching to get on the dance floor tonight.

In the parking lot, she saw Sirue's truck and managed to park her car a few spaces down from it. Fortunately, the lot didn't look overly crowded yet. She grabbed her clutch and as she walked, she felt her phone vibrate.

You here yet? Sirue texted.

Yes, Tea replied

Ok meet us at the door

She didn't have to look very hard to find them. Sirue stood a few inches above everyone else there, and his head served as a beacon to guide her towards him. She smiled to herself at the analogy and walked through a few small groups of people until she caught up with her boys. She hugged them both. They were looking mighty sharp. Sirue was decked out in an all-black ensemble, his silver jewelry popping. Tea noticed he kept his silk shirt untucked, probably because of his tummy. He still looked smooth, though. Miles wore a black short-sleeved mock turtleneck and dark blue denim jeans that were the perfect fit. He looked hip, especially with his fresh tapered mini afro, lined up goatee, and wire-rimmed personality glasses that he sported every now and then.

"Y'all look really good," Tea commented, then turned to Miles. "And you look all collegiate," she added to him.

"Thank you, thank you. I'm trying to attract some educated honeys tonight." He stroked his goatee and looked around at the plethora of women standing outside seemingly at his disposal.

Tea rolled her eyes.

Sirue looked at him. "Brother, first you need to get us in here. You got our cover, right?" Sirue asked, getting impatient.

"I invited y'all *and* I have to pay?"

"Yep!" Tea and Sirue said in unison.

"Cheap ass friends. Don't y'all work?" Miles shook his head and took out his wallet.

When they entered the rented dance hall inside the posh Region Hotel, the space was large and had a receiving entry area connected to a wider expanse of open dance space. Tea instantly fell in love with the decorations. There was a Mother Earth motif everywhere. The tables around the walls donned muted brown tablecloths with small beige floating candles as their centerpieces. The walls themselves had climbing ivy interspersed with clear lights going around the hall. In this immediate area, there were four beige hanging chandeliers and framed posters depicting various black art pieces; but Tea's absolute favorite touches were the oversized twin punch bowls. They were black ceramic sculptures of a nude male and female with drinks spurting from different bodily orifices.

"There's gotta be almost two hundred people in here," Sirue said, looking around.

"Yeah. My LB Travis said he invited like two-fifty, but you know how we go. It's gonna get packed in here because we always bring like ten cats with us." Miles craned his neck as he glanced at the people trickling inside.

"Oh, Lord, Tea. He said 'cats'."

"I heard," Tea winced. "If he says 'groovy,' I'll race you out of here."

Miles ignored them as they all made their way to the nude statues. He flashed his teeth at two women standing to the side of the table. One was medium height, on the heavier side, and sported intricately pinned up locs. The other was almost Miles' height with her heels on and had the body of an athlete. And both looked interested in him.

"Ladies," he greeted, giving them inquiring eyes.

They both waved. Tea noticed that Miss Kinky Locs couldn't stop smiling at Miles. He filled his cup and moved a few feet to sweet talk the women.

Sirue poured Tea's cup, then his own, and they both turned to survey the growing crowd.

"You look really nice, Tea," Sirue stood back and checked her threads out. "I meant to tell you that when we were outside."

Tea almost blushed at his sincerity.

"Thanks. And I'm feeling the blackness, Matrix," she tugged at his sleeve then looked at the people beginning to migrate towards the open dance floor. "Damn, I hope it doesn't get too hot in here."

"Yeah. Wonder what kind of ventilation system they have," Sirue commented. He glanced up at the ceiling.

"Like if it'll start pumping the AC once it reaches a certain ambient temperature."

Sirue nodded hard. "Right. They can have them pre-set to do that."

Tea looked up at Sirue. "Oh my God, we are such geeks."

He smiled and started to speak but noticed Miles motioning him over.

Sirue leaned down closer to Tea. "I'm gonna go see what he wants. You cool?"

"You better get over there, player," she smiled.

Sirue obliged and Tea deposited her drink on the side of the table. A waitress quickly emerged and removed the used cups.

Tea strolled around the perimeter of the anteroom, pausing to admire some of the artwork. She immediately recognized Annie Lee's "Blue Monday." She had the same print across from the chair dryers at the shop. She gazed at the next poster that caught her attention. She had to squint to see the artist's name. John Holyfield. It had such rich colors. The title was "Family Fellowship." She thought it would go great near the front of her waiting area.

"Shcooooz me?"

Someone tapped her shoulder. Her voice caught in her throat when she turned and saw a very short incisor-less man grinning at her. He had to be about an inch shorter than she was and had a gap for days. Strikes one and two.

"Heeeeeeeey, baby. Shweet thang you. Damn, mama." He could barely hold his drink steady from all his pelvic gyrations. "I know you tired 'cause I been dancin' in your mind all night, girl."

Screwing up an already tired line. Strike three. He's out.

Tea gave a short fake laugh and excused herself like she had somewhere to go. She wondered who the hell's plus-one he was and how the hell he got so drunk already.

"Oh. It's like that, jack? Okay, okay, pretty mama."

She heard him call after her until the sounds of music and conversation muted him out. She wondered if he was drunk enough to follow her. Tea walked around deeper into the dance area for a few minutes just in case. The floor was filling in and she soon became aware of the very fine men. All sizes. All builds. Some were dancing. A few were being wallflowers. She wished one of the tall, lanky ones would come and approach her. Mara wouldn't have a problem going up to any of them. Tea sighed. She looked around for Sirue and Miles but didn't see either of them. She sighed again and wondered how fast she could get to her car.

Chapter 17

As Tea started to head out, a member of the live five-piece band spoke into a microphone in an accent heavier than Kadari's. He said their next set would get everybody out on the dance floor. Even though he was way on the other side of the hall, the speakers along the walls made Tea feel like he was talking just to her. The percussion started up first, kicking up the volume a few decibels. They started their own remixed version of a popular reggae song, and the beat was infectious. She hated being so lame and not enjoying herself just because no one took her hand and led her to dance. Screw them. She had a lot on her mind lately and felt her confidence growing. Shaking her body was the remedy, at least for tonight.

She started to loosen up and move to the rhythm, clapping above her head and winding by herself. The band played an extended reggae mix for the next twenty minutes and the bass was pumping through her bones. She half-closed her eyes and felt her hips swiveling as she moved deeper into the crowd of dancers. Some women smiled, some women gave her dirty looks, and most of the men couldn't take their eyes off her as she put her hands on her knees then back to her hips then up above her head. Her backbone felt as pliable as a snake.

Suddenly, she felt heat behind her. She rhythmically turned around and began grooving with the stranger in front of her. He kept his eyes on her body as she circled around him. He matched her groove and Tea thought he felt so natural. His chin as a few inches above her head, and his hands seemed permanently attached to her hips. Tea looked up intensely, not missing a beat, and noticed his loose shoulder-length black dreads were almost covering his face. *Yum*, she thought and danced even closer. He lowered his body and wedged his thigh between her legs and she grinded on it for the next five minutes until he turned her around and virtually made love to her backside.

Tea alternated between reaching behind her to run her hands through his dreads and through her own hair. This felt damn good. How long had it been since she felt freedom like this? She could feel the sweat dripping down the nape of her neck, and strands of her long bangs were plastered to her face. Situations like this made her thankful for her short hairstyle. She wished she had a towel, though. But what she really needed was for this fine brother to stop getting so hard it felt like he was penetrating something. Tea wiggled back around to face him and slowed down as, thank God, the song started to end. Mr. Rock Hard wiped his face with both hands, and Tea peeped his finger for a wedding ring. Nada. He leaned into her, touching her cheek with his. She thought she was going to melt. How the hell can he still smell so good after dancing for half an hour?

She felt his mouth brush her earlobe.

"Can you come talk to me?" he whispered.

Tea nodded and took his hand, leading him towards a wall. Any wall. The closest wall.

They actually lucked out and found an empty table that looked like its occupants just left. He pulled out her chair and as she sat, she wondered where Sirue and Miles were. She tried to peek through gaps in the crowds on the dance floor, then along the walls near their seats.

"Looking for someone?" he asked, scooting into his chair. His voice was liquid velvet and even deeper than Sirue's.

"Yeah, the friends I came with." Tea turned her attention back to him. He never took his eyes off her. "So, what's your name?"

"Terrance. And what's yours?" He wiped perspiration from his face again.

"I'm Tea. Like the drink." She fanned herself. "Speaking of drinks..."

"Yeah, I'm thirsty, too." Terrance looked around. "What would you like?"

Tea smiled. *You naked in a bed*, she thought.

"Um. Punch is fine."

"I'll be right back." He got up and Tea watched him walk away. He looked amazing. She wanted to yank her phone from her pocket and call Mara, but she didn't want to be premature about it. He could have tried to talk to every female in here. Hell, he might not even come back to the table.

Tea nodded her head in time with the smooth mix of one of her favorite reggae songs about winding and going down "deh" the band was now playing. Part of her wanted to get back up and start dancing again, but the part that didn't kept sitting right in the chair.

She looked out at the couples getting their dirty dances on. One looked familiar. Miles was wrapped up in some woman that wasn't either of the ones he was talking to earlier. This one had long, flowy bright auburn hair that Tea quickly surmised was a lace front. She was thick all over, wearing a red stretchy capri pants suit with red pumps, complete with climbing straps up her calves. Tea made a face as she also checked out how her arms were flung over Miles' shoulders and how his hands were squeezing her ample hips. She also realized he'd removed his glasses when he saw their foreheads and other body parts were touching. They might as well have just made out right there on the damn floor. Tea rolled her eyes but couldn't break her stare.

Before she knew it, Terrance was strolling back towards her carrying two drinks and a hefty plate of food. They shared curry chicken, yellow rice, and bean salad while sipping their drinks and having light conversation. Between glances at Miles and Red Capri on the dance floor, she learned that Terrance, who was thirty, owned a musical instrument shop with his older brother and he professionally played six instruments himself. He was a friend of the keyboardist who invited him to the cabaret. She also found out that he had twin baby girls. Tea tried not to look taken aback.

He quickly added that the girls' mother had an affair, re-married (*re-married?* Tea thought) and took her new family to Atlanta, where she felt more comfortable as a stay-at-home mother. She sent him pictures of the girls every week and he video called them every other day.

"What are their names?" Tea asked, suddenly thinking of her brothers.

"Amelia and Jessica." Terrance said slowly.

"Beautiful names." Tea wondered why their marriage didn't work out. But that was enough personal information for right now.

"You're a great dancer," she smiled at him, dabbing her mouth with her napkin and trying to read his face. He seemed lost in thought momentarily but refocused and let his eyes fall on her.

Applause interrupted him before he could respond, signifying the end of the band's recent set. Terrance checked his watch, then looked apologetically at Tea.

"When I was getting our food, I promised Phil that I'd relieve him of the keyboard for a while since he has an emergency. Um...will you be around for the rest of the night?"

"Oh." Tea was disappointed but tried to play it off. Damn. She wished she was smoother about showing her emotions on her face. She wanted to talk to him all night. She wanted to kiss him. "Uh, I'm not sure. I can give you my number in case we don't see each other again before we leave."

Ughh. That was too forward, Tea thought.

"I was just about to ask for it," Terrance smiled.

Tea held out her hand and asked for his phone. She dialed her number.

"Now you don't have to ask." She smiled back and stood up.

He stood also and walked around the small table to stand in front of her. They smiled at each other, and he leaned in to give her a tight hug, then whispered in her ear.

"I think I'm lucky, because I'm sure a lot of other guys wanted to dance with you tonight." He kissed her on the cheek and walked away, quickly disappearing into the mass of dancers.

Tea stood motionless, trying to calm the fire between her thighs. She knew that he intentionally touched her earlobes again with his lips. She needed a real drink now.

"Hey. Tea!" She heard Miles' voice as she started to walk.

He eased beside her and put his arm heavily around her shoulders.

"Damn, you're harder to catch up with than Si. You seen his big ass?" He was leaning a tad too much on her, and Tea could tell he'd already had a couple of spirited beverages.

"Probably all holed up in a corner somewhere, you know him." Tea lifted his arm from around her.

"Yeah. Always hookin' up. Whenever we go out, always hookin' up with the fine ass women."

Tea rolled her eyes. She was getting tired of this conversation already. Even with his smart glasses back on, he was starting to sound dumb and slightly inebriated.

"Well, I'm going to the bathroom. If you see Si, tell him I'm probably leaving soon," Tea said, deciding she could skip the alcohol.

"Leaving?" Miles continued to walk closely behind her, keeping pace through the sweaty dancers.

Tea nodded. As they reached a small clearing, she glanced toward the band and saw Terrance talking to the other band members. He looked down from the partially elevated stage and caught her glance. He smiled and waved. Tea did the same.

She continued walking and felt Miles beside her.

"Leaving?" he repeated. "We just got here."

"Hi, Miles," Red Capri said out of the blue, grinning hard as she walked past them. "Don't forget you owe me another dance, handsome." She ran her hand over his chest and tugged at the sleeve of his shirt. Miles nodded faint recognition as she moved away. He turned to Tea and saw her glaring at the woman.

"Yep. Leaving. It's late. I'm tired." Tea stepped aside to let a few people pass between them. They were standing inside the oversized arched entrance to the dance hall, with the doors propped open.

"Tired from dancing with Savion over there?"

She heard his voice drop about an octave. He didn't sound so inebriated now.

Tea was tongue-tied for a split second. "Uh. Who? Terrance?" She pointed absently behind her in the vicinity of the band.

Miles was looking directly at her now, leaning against the wide-open double-door jamb, with his hands shoved into his jeans pockets.

He shrugged. "If that's his name."

His eyes remained fixed on hers.

Okay. Miles is being weird, Tea thought.

"Yep, that's why I'm tired. He's a good dancer," she added, unsure why, and folded her arms. She leaned against the opposite side of the opening. Even from this distance, she could see Miles clenching his jaws.

"You're a good dancer, too. I never saw you dance like that."

This has to be the liquor talking, Tea thought as she squinted at Miles. She wondered how long he was staring at her and Terrance together.

"You saw me dancing?" She crossed her feet and tried to figure out their exchange.

Miles nodded. Tea wanted him to smile, crack a joke, something. He was being too intense.

"Well, I need to go pee," she blurted out.

"I'll be here when you get out," he said quickly, his eyes still locked on hers.

Tea was confused and she knew her face showed it. She didn't realize she was shaking until she pulled her pants back up in the stall. What in the world was going on with Miles? Why was he being so protective and so strange? Then Tea figured it out. He probably saw Terrance checking out other women and didn't want her to get played. Always the damn big brother like she couldn't handle it herself. Wasn't he the one who said she needed to get laid, anyway? Plus, he was tipsy and was never good at holding his alcohol. She washed her hands, grabbed a mint from the dish, splashed her face with cold water, patted it dry and pulled her lip gloss and eye liner from her tiny clutch. After another three minutes, she saw that he'd kept his word. Miles was still standing in the same position as she walked out towards him.

Tea walked right up to him, stood on her tiptoes and held his face as she kissed his cheek.

"I love you for caring about me, but I'll be fine. I can handle Terrance," she smiled.

Miles didn't speak. She looked up at him and he still wouldn't break a smile. She patted his chest.

"So, tell me about all the numbers you got tonight. I know Miss 'You Owe Me a Dance, Handsome' is one of them."

"I didn't get any hook ups."

Tea made a face, then cupped her ear. "Huh? What was that?" she asked loudly.

Miles gave a faint smile and repeated, "I didn't get any hook ups. I didn't get any numbers. Nobody got my number. I already have the numbers I want."

"Oh, just making sure I heard you right, bruh." Tea laughed and turned when she heard the band start playing again. She peeked through gaps and around people to catch a glimpse of Terrance playing. He was getting into his groove, his dreads freely swinging. She wondered how many people in the place knew he had twin baby girls in Hot-lanta missing their daddy.

Tea noticed more people starting to dance again and move towards the middle of the floor. Some of them seemed to come out of the woodwork. The music was getting louder and people on the floor were getting hornier. Herself included. Something about the rhythm of reggae music made her want to move. It pulled her farther into the crowd and farther away from the exit she'd planned to make a few minutes ago.

She felt a familiar heat behind her. Hands were on her shoulders, then slid down the sides of her folded arms. She knew it was Miles. He squeezed them, then let go. She felt him shove his hands back into his pockets because he was standing so close behind her that their bodies were touching.

What's wrong with this negro? Tea thought.

She stepped up a few inches, playing like she was swaying with the music. He stepped up right behind her. Tea could feel her breathing get a little faster and she moved around again, dancing. Miles fell in step with her, moving his body in time with hers. His hands lightly rested on her hips, as if he was afraid she'd walk farther away. She didn't.

Miles gently squeezed, then massaged her hips and waist in small circles. Tea dropped her hands and gave into the pulse of the music, leaning her body back against his. They moved together; Miles' cheek pressed against Tea's hair. By the time she looked up, she saw they were back under the entry way.

His hands were higher up her waist now, sliding down and back up. Tea's throat got instantly dry. Is this why he was tripping? It had to be something he was drinking. It had to be. She chewed and swallowed the rest of the mint in her mouth but was too stunned to turn around. The music pounded louder in her ears, and she pressed her cheek against the cool archway entrance. Miles pressed himself into her body and barely left any space between her and the wall. His motions became more deliberate, and she could feel his breath on her hair.

Tea started to slow her moving and didn't budge when she felt his hands beneath her blouse on her bare stomach. He drew figure eights with his fingertips and Tea's breaths came faster. No one was paying them any mind. Everyone was wrapped up in their own pleasure. There was a throbbing between her legs when his fingers played under her waistband. She swallowed hard and closed her eyes.

"Teeeea," Miles dragged out her name in a long whisper. He dropped his head and leaned his forehead against the wall, his mouth against her ear, his arms now snugly around her waist.

Her breathing accelerated even more. *This was so weird. This was Miles.*

"Did you...," he said softly, his warm breath in her ear sending tingles down her spine. He paused. "Did you let Savion touch you like this?"

Tea snapped her eyes open and put her hands on his arms, pushing them down and off her body. She turned and saw a mixture of sex and smugness on Miles' face.

"You asshole," she said, shaking her head and deliberately shoving him hard as she stormed into the hallway and out of the hotel doors.

Miles caught his balance and looked regrettably down at the floor.

"Fuck," he said, hitting his forehead.

Chapter 18

Mara called his cell phone again.

Two hours and still no sign of Drew. What could he be doing? He said he called an emergency faculty meeting after work to discuss budget cuts. But a meeting that ran until after nine o'clock? On a Friday? That just didn't fly.

She got his voice mail. Again.

"Damn."

Mara threw her phone on the dining room floor and walked back into the kitchen. She looked at the casserole dish and bread keeping warm on the stove. She piled two huge slabs of quiche onto a plate then took out one of the glasses of ice she put in the freezer. She opened the icebox and took out the wine. She changed her mind, put it back, then took out a six-pack of beer instead.

She grabbed a bag of chocolate chip cookies and a box of graham crackers from the pantry on her way back to the dining room table. For the next twenty minutes, she called Drew every motherfucker she could think of while she stuffed her mouth. Afterwards, she was thoroughly upset at herself. Not because she'd eaten everything so fast, but because she forgot the butter pecan ice cream in the freezer.

Emotional eating only forced her to work out twice as hard the next morning, but she didn't care right now. This bastard stood her up. He knew how excited she was to cook for him. It was their two-month anniversary. Not a big deal to him, but Mara could count on both her pinky fingers the number of times she could boast about being exclusively with someone for that long.

Leaving the crumbs and dishes on the table, she grabbed her phone and dragged her bloated stomach up the steps and to her bedroom. She started to take off the dress when her phone rang. It sounded like a symphony of ringtones because the alcohol was starting to play tricks on her, and she hated to feel the buzz by herself.

She picked up her phone and saw the call was from "My DrewBae" and threw it back down on her bed.

Fuck you, she thought and let it ring.

She pulled off the dress, watching it fall to the floor. Her twists went back into their ponytail, and she caught her reflection as she walked past her closet door mirror. She jumped when she saw herself. In her mind, she looked fifty pounds heavier. She patted her stomach, then wished she hadn't. Her gas was no joke. Stupid graham crackers.

Her phone chimed again.

Mara slammed her bedroom door shut and climbed into bed. The comforter was cool and warm at the same time. She wanted to hurl but didn't feel like getting a bag, though she sure as hell wasn't going to mess up her sheets. She steadied her breath to keep her nausea at bay. A fleeting thought almost made her pull out her Global Marketing Strategies textbook to get some studying done. The thought didn't last long. Sleeping off her heavy stomach sounded more inviting.

The sound of her phone next to her pillow interrupted her dream of walking through ice cream clouds. She yanked it to her ear.

"What the hell do you want?" she said evenly.

"Why haven't you been answering your phone?" Drew asked, almost yelling.

The background noise let her know he was in his car. She wished he was under it.

"Me? Where the hell were you tonight?"

"At work. I told you it was going to be a long night. We –"

"No, Drew. Don't." Mara rolled onto her back and stared into darkness.

"Don't what?"

"Don't lie to me," she said quietly.

Drew made a sound somewhere between a laugh and impatience.

"Mara. The faculty meeting ran over and from there I went straight to my cousin's ceremony," he explained slowly and deliberately.

"That's tomorrow night, Drew," Mara said flatly. "Not tonight. Get your damn story together then call me back."

"Wait! Mara, it was tonight. I swear. I got the dates wrong. He called me to remind me today. I'm sorry, I should've called you after the meeting, but I was rushing and already late." He paused to take a breath. "I should've called earlier in the day."

Mara let out a heavy sigh. She mumbled something into her phone and a tear fell back towards her ear.

"Huh? What was that, baby?"

She sighed again. "I said, you should have tried harder."

"Let me make it up to you."

"Fine." Mara wiped her single tear away.

"I'm coming from Columbia but I'm on my way."

In thirty-five minutes, Mara opened the front door in her red bra and panties.

"Mmmm," Drew moaned his approval and bent down to hold her.

She turned away before he could embrace her and without speaking, she walked back upstairs. In her room, she made her way through the darkness to her bed and used the faint glow from the hallway light to watch Drew undress. He secured his dreads into a ponytail, removed his boxer briefs and rubbed his stomach.

"I'm starving, baby. Got any food left?"

"Fuck the food. You should've been here," Mara said angrily.

"Damn. You still mad?" Drew crawled onto the bed, slowly kissing her thighs, then pulled down her red panties with one finger. He resumed kissing her stomach, collar bone, then lips. She turned her head slightly to the side.

"Just hurry up and get inside of me," she said quietly.

He sat up on his knees and with his hands on her hips, turned her over on her stomach. Mara tiredly got on all fours and felt one of his hands groping under her bra. His other hand guided himself inside and she felt her walls respond immediately. It was soothing to have him fill her up, especially when she was feeling so empty. As empty as his damn story for his whereabouts. Why was he so hungry if he just came from a dinner engagement?

"That's it," he grunted. "Bend down some."

She lowered her torso and flattened her hands against the headboard. The last thing she wanted was to become one of those ditzy ass females who knows her man is cheating but tries to ignore it. That just wasn't her. But why now? Everything else was so good between them. Maybe she was overreacting after all. She squeezed her eyes and shouted a few expletives as Drew dug his fingers into her round flesh and pounded deeper and harder. The sound of his body slamming into hers matched the squeaking of the headboard.

After almost ten minutes, Drew finally collapsed next to her.

"Fuck." He wiped the sweat from his face.

Mara laid flat against the mattress and was also panting, although she didn't get to climax. But she had other things on her mind. She flipped her head over to look at him.

"Are you cheating on me?" she asked softly.

"What?" He turned and rubbed her moist back. "Is that what you think I was doing tonight?" he whispered, moving closer to her face.

Mara nodded.

"Aw," he moved a few twists behind her ear. "Mara. Baby. I'm in love with you. I am not sleeping with anybody else. I have my cousin's number if you want to call him." He smiled at her.

"I don't want to call anybody," Mara lied. She kissed his lips and wanted to get lost in them again like when they first met. She thought again of his cheesy excuse for tonight and decided she'd take his word for it this time. She'd keep her senses alert just in case.

But for now, having him here was what she needed.

Chapter 19

Miles knew he had gone too far this time. He went outside and found Tea sitting on a bench. He slowly approached and let out a long breath. She saw him and rolled her eyes. This was going to be harder than he thought.

She started to stand to walk away but stopped when he held out his hand.

"Wait. Look, you stay here. I'll sit way over here and leave you alone. I just don't want you out here by yourself."

Once he saw that she conceded, he sat down at the other end of the bench and let out a sigh of relaxation as he rested his tired back.

They silently watched a hotel shuttle bus pull up and drop off passengers. A few people walked past, some strolling, some rushing. In front of them, at the curb, a girl and a boy, both toddlers, were at a minivan with their mother. The girl dropped her soft soccer ball and it rolled towards Tea. The little girl came running and tripped forehead first on her own shoestring. There was a stunned look on her face and her mother called to her while she installed the car seats.

Tea and Miles both ran over to the girl. Miles gingerly picked her up and Tea grabbed the ball. They both asked her if she was okay, which is when she started to cry.

"I told you to put that ball down, girl!" The mother called to her over her shoulder and put the boy in the van. "I knew we should have left earlier today!"

She walked towards Miles to retrieve the sobbing toddler. "Thank you. Come on, sweet pea."

"No problem," Miles handed her over.

Tea smiled at the girl. "Here's your ball, honey."

The woman thanked them both again and rubbed her daughter's head, giving it a kiss. Miles and Tea walked slowly back to the bench and noticed the girl was waving to them as she rode away.

"Awww," Tea gushed and waved back. She turned to smile at Miles and wanted to comment on the girl's adorable dimples, but remembered she was still mad at him. Her smile faded.

"I meant to call him Terrance. Not Savion."

His voice jarred her.

"No, you didn't," she tsked her teeth.

Miles crossed his heart and held his hand up.

She sucked her teeth again and cut her eyes away.

The wind was picking up. Tea crossed her legs and folded her arms. Too much nonsense was running through her mind. Too many questions. But only one that really need to be answered.

"Is mine the number you already have?" Tea turned to look at him.

He thrust his hands into his pockets and grinned at her choice of words. He tongued his cheek and looked down at the sidewalk. This is insane. This is Tea. *Tea.*

His bashful reaction made her heart jump.

Ohmygodohmygodohmygodohmygod. Her breath seemed to get caught in her lungs because she couldn't exhale and tried to play it off like she wasn't half-choking.

He gave a single nod and turned his head to her. The way he looked at her from follicle to toenail polish and back up again gave her goose bumps.

"You're beautiful, Tea." His voice was steady although his heart was beating triple speed. "You're beautiful to everyone around you. You make everybody feel good. You make me feel like I'm fourteen," he smirked.

Damn that sexy ass goatee, Tea thought as she bit her lip. She nodded slightly because she didn't know another appropriate response. She watched him intently as he continued.

"I've...I've been feeling this for a while now, and I...," he blew out a long breath. "I'm very attracted to you." He looked directly at her.

Tea's eyes widened momentarily, but she caught herself.

"Whoa," she said aloud, but to herself. "Miles, I'm...wow." She put her hand on her chest.

"I just sprung that on you. You don't have to –"

"No!" She cleared her throat. "I mean, no, I know. Can we go walk? I need some fresh air."

"We're outside," he said softly, trying to hide his smile.

"Shut up. Come on," Tea stood up and held her hand out. He looked at her as though he was seeing her beauty for the first time. He clenched his jaws, took her hand, and they strolled down the sidewalk.

They walked in silence for a few minutes, making their way around to the side of the hotel. Tea didn't know what to say. She could feel his hand squeezing hers and she could feel his eyes on her every few steps. Either he was tongue-tied, too, or he was waiting for her to speak.

Across the street to their left was a rather large business park containing three semi-tall office buildings. A few random cars and vans were in the otherwise deserted parking lot, and Tea wondered what kind of people would work this late on a Friday night. Of course, it was probably the cleaning crew, although she couldn't help but think that inside there were husbands who'd called home to their wives, claiming they had to work late. There were probably wives in there doing the same thing. How many marriages were being tested in those offices right now? Which lights were trying to fool the world? Tea thought about other people fooling themselves, too.

There was another bench alongside the hotel where considerably less pedestrian traffic walked by and Tea led him towards it. Miles sat much closer to her this time, and when he released her hand, he slid it behind her, loosely resting it on her right hip. Tea blinked slowly when she felt his hand but kept her gaze on the unfaithful couples across the street.

"So..." There was no other way for Tea to ask it. "What about Jasmine?"

Miles glanced at her, but Tea kept looking at the buildings. A light on the top floor turned off.

"There's nothing to tell. I mean, she worked for me. You knew that, right?" he asked softly.

Tea shook her head.

"Yeah, started a few weeks ago. I'll be honest and say that we...went out a few times that first week –"

Tea lifted her head and turned to look at him.

"—but I had to end it. She was flirting with everyone at work, right in my face. I told her it wouldn't work out with her there. She's getting moved to our Clinton office. I was helping her out financially, but...," his voice trailed. "That's a wrap, too."

Miles remembered how tough that conversation was with Jasmine that had quickly turned into an argument. He didn't want to bring up the fact that it was the reason he was late to their housewarming party. Or the fact that they continued to see each other for another week. That is, until he walked down to the mailroom after a hint from Mrs. Crawford and saw Jasmine and Ronnie entangled on the sorting table. But he knew that this wasn't the time for the full explanation. Not right now.

Tea looked back across the street. "What kind of hold does she have on you?"

He let out a small laugh. "Why do you think she has a hold on me?"

"Because she does. There's something about her...about what y'all had."

"I think I must have wanted something that was never there."

Tea nodded to herself. Another light turned off across the street.

Miles squeezed Tea's side then let go. "Hey," he said softly.

Tea looked over at him. He looked into her eyes and Tea could see him clenching his jaws. He never looked so handsome. He looked so damn kissable. She examined the lines in his face, noticed the curly hairs in his goatee. The shape of the goatee itself was perfect. Tea hoped she wasn't drooling.

"I want to...um," he whispered.

"Kiss me?" Tea whispered back and inched closer.

He looked momentarily confused. "Oh. Yeah, but I was going to say that I wanted to tell you something."

Tea made a face. "Ohhhhkay. That's embarrassing."

Miles laughed a little. "Don't be embarrassed."

"What do you want to tell me?" she asked, leaning back to a more comfortable distance from him.

Miles immediately got serious again. Tea knew this had something to do with Jasmine.

"What's up?" she urged.

"It's...well, I never told y'all, but when we were together, me and Jazz...she was pregnant."

Tea's eyes widened. "Pregnant?"

He nodded. "From what I knew, it was mine. She had an abortion even though I begged her not to..." His voice trailed off.

"Is that when y'all started having problems?"

Miles nodded. "We kind of tried to work it out for the next few months, then I started hearing more and more stories from everyone about how she was sleeping around."

Tea slowly looked away. He knew good and well people were telling him about Jasmine way before that, but he was too sprung to listen. She squinted. A man and a woman were leaving one of the office buildings together, laughing and talking. Who's to say they were creeping? Maybe they were strangers who just happened to bump into each other on the elevator. They stopped in the middle of the parking lot and continued talking. What could they still be talking about after hours of hot and heavy adulterous sex? They had to have just met a few minutes ago.

"...and then I saw her in my office, felt sorry for her, and wanted to give her the job. I guess I still felt guilty...," Miles continued as Tea's attention was elsewhere.

The conversation across the street was getting more intense. Her hand was on his arm now. Tea wished she had binoculars to see what kind of wedding ring her husband gave to her. She could be screwing up an otherwise wonderful marriage. And him, what if his wife was having suspicions? What if they had children? She watched as they gave each other a lingering hug then walked to their respective cars. Tea shook her head and noticed that Miles had stopped talking. She turned her head towards him and wondered if he'd stopped because she had tuned him out.

He was glancing towards the mysterious couple, too, but looked down at Tea as she looked up.

"Did I tell you how pretty you look tonight?" he asked.

"No."

"You look very pretty, Tea Racker." Miles moved his face forward a few inches and lightly pecked her soft lips. He slid his hand up her back past her neck and rested it on the back of her head. He tilted it slightly and kissed her again.

Tea closed her eyes and at first didn't know what to think. She quickly became lost in his passion, especially after she felt his soft tongue slip into her mouth. Everything about his mouth was juicy and she hoped she wasn't sucking too hard or being too eager or anything that would make him pull back and laugh. She tried to relax and let his strong jaws take over, but he was becoming more intense. Tea put her hand on his chest. He misread her gesture and covered it with his free hand and started to kiss her even faster. She lightly pushed his chest again, and Miles squeezed her hand, softly moaning. Tea's eyes popped open, and she saw Jonathan kissing her. She felt her throat close up. She pushed his chest hard enough to send him back against the bench.

"Tea!" He wiped his mouth.

She turned completely around towards him and felt her hands shaking as she ran her hands over her face. Her heart was racing, and she covered her mouth.

"You didn't want me to kiss you?" Miles was confused but managed to move closer and put his hand on her lower back.

"No, that's not...I mean, yeah, I did. I do...sorry." She smoothed her hands against her white jeans and felt incredibly humiliated.

"No, that was my fault. I finally get to kiss you and I can't control myself."

Tea let out a fake chuckle, knowing he probably thought she was a psycho.

"Si's probably looking for us, we should go." She stood up and folded her arms across her chest. Her heart was still thudding, but it was beginning to slow down.

"Um." A disappointed look spread over Miles' face as he stood. "Do you want to talk about this some more? About...this?" He pointed at himself and then at her.

"Miles, let's just...we're better as friends, you know?" It felt like a lie before it even came out of her mouth, but Tea knew it was the right decision.

Miles looked deflated. He jammed his hands into his pockets and just nodded his head to himself. She knew she probably hurt his feelings, but she started walking away. There was too much on her mind. All of this was too much. He kept pace with her, and they remained silent as they turned the corner. When they reached the spot where the little girl had been, Tea stopped walking. Miles continued, then noticed she wasn't next to him. He turned and saw her staring at him.

He walked back towards her, furrowing his brows, wondering what was wrong.

"You okay?" he asked.

"Are you being real with me, Miles?" Tea bit her bottom lip.

He nodded sincerely, still confused.

"I'll find Si and tell him I'm taking you home. You go get a room for us." She tip-toed, flipped her bangs out of her eyes, kissed his cheek, and walked double speed to the hotel and through the doors.

Miles stood motionless, trying to register what just happened. A broad smile crossed his lips and he exhaled, placing his hand over his heart.

Chapter 20

The doors of the fabric-lined elevator opened with a chime and Tea stepped off alone. The walls on the seventh floor were decorated with the same gold-embossed upholstery as the interior of the lobby. She listened to complete silence until the doors closed behind her. According to the plaque in front of her, room 7003 was immediately to her right. She let out a long breath and walked a few feet to the door. She stared at it and before she could succumb to the hundred and one reasons why she shouldn't, she lightly tapped near the peephole.

In a few seconds, the lock clicked, and the door quietly opened.

"Hey," Miles grinned.

"Hi."

Tea walked into the room and Miles softly touched her hand, then let it go as he closed the door.

"There are some drinks in the fridge," he pointed. "You want?"

Tea shook her head and gently hopped up onto the edge of the bed. She noticed his eyeglasses next to the TV as he pulled the chair from the desk and sat down across from her. He watched her carefully. A million thoughts were running through her head now. She wondered if he was still a little tipsy from earlier. She wondered if he was going to change his mind about the whole thing. She wondered what the "whole thing" really meant.

"Why don't you tell me what's on your mind and maybe it won't be so bad," Miles interrupted her thoughts.

Tea brought his face back to focus. She squinted at him.

"How do you know I have something on my mind to tell?"

Miles smirked. He leaned forward with his elbows on his knees, clasping his hands.

"Let's see…you're wondering if you're making a mistake, but you don't know what that mistake actually is. You want to know if I'm being for real."

"Are you?" Tea studied his face.

He nodded, his eyes never leaving hers. "It feels right. You and me."

Tea scooted back on the bed and crossed her legs. Her cheeks inflated as she blew out a long puff of air. She rubbed her eyes and ran her hands over her cropped hair, resting them on the back of her neck. She looked up at Miles who was still staring at her.

"You okay?" he asked. He knew she needed some time to think. She reminded him of Sirue in that affect. Always needing to mull things over. He clenched his jaws, wishing she would just go with her gut and let him make her happy.

She didn't answer. Instead, she rested her elbows on her legs and looked down as she twiddled her thumbs.

Miles sat back in his chair and gave her some space. He wanted to get up and hold her in his arms. She looked so adorable, yet so fragile. He couldn't believe he'd ever said those hateful words to her a few weeks ago. He suddenly felt the need to protect her against everything.

Her head had been down for the last four minutes by his calculations. He got up, then kneeled on the floor in front of the bed with his hands rubbing the outsides of her thighs.

"Hey," he whispered.

Tea looked at him with watery eyes. "You can't screw me over, Miles," she said quietly.

"I won't."

"I can't take that again."

"I know." It stung a little that she could compare him to Jonathan, but he understood.

She bent forward a few inches and gave him a light kiss on his lips. She kept her face close to his. "This is too weird," she said and pecked him again.

"No, it's not," Miles replied, then initiated another soft kiss.

Tea sat upright and stretched.

"You know what?" she asked.

"What?" Miles stood and found it hard to contain his smiles now.

"You haven't officially asked me to be your girl."

"Wait a minute. Yes, I did."

Tea shook her head. "You didn't." She folded her arms.

"Okay." He cleared his throat and leaned down onto the bed, his hands on either side of her. "Will you be my lady, Tea Racker?"

His lips looked so kissable, three inches from her own. Tea answered by giving him a quick kiss.

"Or," Miles kissed her again. "I can go old school on you." Another kiss. "Tea, can I have a chance? Check yes or no."

Tea laughed and flung her arms around his neck. He held her as if to pick her up and she jumped.

"I forgot how ticklish you are," he grinned.

"Nooooo," she attempted to scoot back on the bed even more, but he grabbed her legs and started to mercilessly tickle anywhere he could reach. After almost a minute, Tea ended up underneath his torso, almost in a complete fetal ball.

He stopped once he was on all fours and panting just as heavily as she was. He kissed her earlobe, then her neck, and Tea felt the room suddenly get warm. She turned onto her back and couldn't believe this was Miles on top of her. The same guy who told her she needed to get fucked.

She lightly pushed him on the chest. He moved aside so she could sit up against the headboard. "I need to catch my breath," she lied.

Miles smiled. "You want a coke or something?"

He went across the room to the small refrigerator.

"No, I'm good." She watched him open a can and down its contents in less than sixty seconds.

"You need to stay over there and burp because you are not coming over here with all that gas." She covered her nose.

Miles pounded his chest and let out a very long belch then another. He smiled at Tea's look of disgust and excused himself to the bathroom.

Tea exhaled when he closed the door. "What the hell am I doing?"

She figured she could make a run for the door and down to her car in five minutes. Three if she didn't wait for the elevator. Then she could

Impulsive

just blow this off like it never happened. Miles would be pissed, but he'd get over it.

Tea stood and slid back into her shoes. She looked around for her clutch and grabbed it from the floor. She figured it fell during the tickle session. She smiled to herself at how much they'd both laughed, then shook her head. *No, this won't work. There's nothing wrong with things staying the way they were.*

As she moved closer to the room's door, she heard Miles' horrible rendition of a rap song by one of his favorite Canadian-born rappers. She smiled again because he always tried so hard to sound like him knowing good and hell well that was determined to be a lie. She shook off her smile again and started to leave.

The view from the window gave her pause. Oddly enough, she could see the same business park she'd seen earlier. This time, her vantage point gave her another perspective. The lights across the street were still on in one of the windows. She bit her lip. Who was to say it wasn't just a cleaning crew?

She heard the bathroom door open but didn't turn around. There were soft footsteps on the carpet. Miles leaned down and rested his chin on her shoulder, and they were cheek to cheek.

"I can go get myself a separate room for tonight," he said quietly.

She lightly shook her head. "I want to stay up and talk."

"Until the sun comes up?" He pressed his cheek against hers.

"Until the sun goes back down."

Chapter 21

Sirue could barely make sense of Tea's story about taking Miles home. He was leaning against a wall talking to the cute, thick, kinky loc'd sister Miles introduced him to earlier that evening. He found out they didn't have much in common. She was a pediatric nurse who despised cooking and loved traveling. But he did enjoy her company. She laughed at his corny jokes and looked interested when he went off on tangents. He was deep into his conspiracy theory about the lunar eclipse and the space program when Tea rushed up to them.

"Si! There you are!" Tea looked flushed. "Oh, sorry. Hi, I'm Tea," she said to the woman.

She smiled warmly at Tea and sipped her drink. "Hi."

"Tea, this is Renee. Renee, Tea." He looked at Tea, wishing she would hurry up with whatever she needed.

"Hi, Renee. Si, I'm not feeling all that great. I'm gonna leave. I think Miles is riding with me, so I'll drop him home."

Sirue gave Tea a quick once over. "Everything okay?"

She nodded. "Yeah, sorry to interrupt. I'll talk to you later." She gave Sirue a quick hug and waved a quick goodbye to Renee.

Sirue watched her weave her way through the dancers on the floor, then turned his attention back to Renee, who was watching him intently.

"She's cute," Renee commented.

Sirue smiled. "She's like a sister."

Renee raised an eyebrow and sipped her drink again. "Well, tell me more about this lunar eclipse."

After an hour of talking, laughing, and walking around the perimeter of the dance floor, Sirue and Renee exchanged phone numbers. He wondered if they would connect on a romantic level, especially since he really did enjoy her conversation. She left soon after and Sirue quickly found himself with another woman who'd introduced herself to him.

When he finally made his way to his truck to leave, Sirue rolled his eyes and decided to call Teresa back. He had deliberately missed six of her calls that night and ignored all of her texts. He needed the space.

"It's about time!" She screamed into his ear.

"Teresa. No. I can't do this right now." Sirue started the ignition and pulled the hand sanitizer from his center console.

"Can't do what? Talk to me?"

He sighed. "I'm tired, Teresa. I'm about to drive home."

"I was calling you all night to tell you that I got off earlier than I thought. I wanted to come hangout with you," she said, sounding hurt.

"I didn't even check my phone until I got into my truck," he lied and tossed the small bottle back into the console.

"Too busy dancing with the sluts, huh?"

Sirue didn't answer.

"Well...can I come over at least?"

"Teresa, I'm really –"

"Tired. I heard you," Teresa interrupted. He could hear her tapping something.

Sirue shifted the truck into drive and carefully navigated his way out of the busy parking lot. He slid his phone into the mount on his dashboard.

No one spoke for the next minute.

"I won't bother you. I just want to lay next to you," she said quietly.

Against his better judgement, Sirue told her he'd be home in the next forty-five minutes. He didn't know why it was so hard to say no to her sometimes.

The hotel room's bathroom was beautiful. Tea admired the coordinating mauve and pale pink colors of the tiles and wallpaper. She washed her hands and the remaining makeup off her face, then looked at her reflection in the large mirror. Her hands were shaking, so she steadied them on the cool sink. It was still so surreal to her. Crazy, goofy, irresponsible Miles? She stared directly into her own eyes. But he was also gentle, protective, and extremely affectionate. Being handsome and sexy as hell were also major pluses. Tea smiled and held herself. She decided she was going to take him at his word that he wouldn't break her heart.

When Tea opened the door, Miles was sitting on the edge of the bed wearing his white undershirt and holding the remote. She glanced at his black mock turtleneck draped over the nearby chair.

He looked over at her and smiled. "Hope you don't mind if I catch the end of this game."

Tea shrugged and stood beside the bed. "I know you love watching basketball, even though your team is sorry."

"It's...the...coach," he replied with an eye roll that made her laugh and turned his attention back to the television.

She walked to the telephone on the desk, then studied the room service menu beside it.

"Want me to order something?" he asked, looking at her then back at the screen.

"Uh...," she made a face at the selection. "Only if you want something."

"Okay," he said. "Damn! Get the damn rebound, why the hell are you even on the floor?!"

Tea walked to stand next to him and tried to catch the rhythm of the game, but she wasn't interested in the least. Miles reached over and hugged her hips while Tea played mindlessly in his hair.

"You really do love watching this game, huh?"

He looked up at her. "I love watching you more."

Tea bit her lips and tried to fight a smile.

"Too cheesy?" Miles asked with a nod.

Tea responded with her own nod. "I mean, it was cute, though."

Miles laughed and gave her hips a squeeze, then resumed fussing at the millionaire athletes.

Tea retrieved a bottled water from the fridge and drank half of it before putting it on the nightstand. She wanted to crawl into the bed, but she didn't want to do it in her snug white jeans. She also didn't want to take them off and give him the wrong idea. Her comfort won the battle and she quickly pulled them off and hopped beneath the thick blankets. She propped herself up with a few of the plush pillows against the headboard.

After a few minutes of the game, Miles turned down the volume, stood and stretched. Tea watched him pull off his shirt, and even in the low light, she could see his beautiful form. Those arms, that chest...all toned in the right places.

"Mind if I get in?" he asked sincerely.

"I'm not gonna make you sleep on the floor," Tea smiled. She lifted the blankets and Miles slowly slid into the bed next to her.

She scooted over enough so that he could share her mound of pillows. They were facing each other, and Miles propped himself up on his arm. Tea laid with her arm folded beneath her head. They smiled at each other.

Miles gently moved her bangs from one side to the other and traced the contour of her face with his finger. Tea felt her cheeks blush from the intense way his eyes followed his traces. She reached up and took his hand, then kissed each finger. Miles smiled.

"What do you want to talk about?" he asked softly.

The dim light from the lamp behind her danced in his eyes and she felt her throat go dry.

"Everything," she managed to say.

He briefly looked to the ceiling then back to her. "Hmm. I was born on a stormy Sunday night..."

Tea sucked her teeth. "I'm serious."

"Me, too. Birth stories are important," he smiled and moved his fingers back to her mouth and lightly touched them across her lips.

Tea reached out and put her hand on his bare chest. His heart was pounding, and she smoothed her hand up to his shoulder and back down to his chest. His skin was so warm, and his muscles were so perfect. Not too big on his frame and so incredibly toned. It was still strange that this was Miles beside her.

"I can really get used to you touching me," Miles whispered.

Tea continued to watch her own hand move across his brown skin. She got lost in its warmth. She could feel his breathing getting shallow and she slid her hand up to his neck and to his soft, curly hair. Without any pretense, she pulled him towards her and passionately kissed his lips. She moaned lightly as he wrapped his arm beneath her. Tea felt his body pressing against hers and she slowed their kiss down.

They both pulled away and tried to temper their fast breathing.

"We're supposed to be talking," Tea said, wiping his mouth.

"Okay, you're right. Talking." Miles exhaled and adjusted the pillows behind them both again.

Over the next hour, they laughed and talked. At half past one a.m., Miles ordered a sub from the menu and Tea shared his fries. They fell asleep not long after, Tea snuggled inside of Miles' arms.

The early Sunday morning sunlight woke Tea up out of her comfortable sleep. She was momentarily confused when she sat up in the empty bed, not sure where she was. Her glance fell on Miles' clothes in the chair, and she heard the water running in the bathroom.

Memories flooded back and she remembered their post-midnight conversations about their childhoods, most embarrassing moments, favorite teachers, least favorite college courses, and what they found attractive about each other. The last thing Tea remembered before drifting to sleep was hearing Miles' compliments.

When Miles emerged from the steamy bathroom, Tea was waiting at the door doing her pee dance.

"You take longer than Mara," she complained and pushed him out of the way to get in. "You're just gonna put the same clothes on, anyway!"

Miles held up his hands and laughed. "I'm sorry," he yelled through the closed door.

In less than fifteen minutes, Tea came out and saw Miles standing at the large window wearing just his boxer briefs. His back looked so sexy. Tea crawled back onto the bed, sitting back against the headboard. When he turned, he looked at her.

"You think we should tell them about us tonight?" he asked.

Tea drew her legs up, and slightly open. She fingered for Miles to come closer, and he walked over and slid towards her. He positioned himself between her legs, laying back against her chest. Tea ran one hand through his hair, then over the front of his shoulder, then down his torso. His bare skin felt so smooth. She could touch him all day. Her hand moved in deep circles from one pectoral muscle to the other.

"You feel so comfortable to me," she whispered into his ear.

Miles closed his eyes.

"If you want to tell them, then let's tell them," she continued. She was very unsure last night, but after thinking about it, she knew it would be futile to keep their new relationship from Sirue and Mara.

Miles cocked his head over enough to look at her sideways. "You sure?"

She nodded. "Mmmhmm."

"Okay," he held both of her hands beside them. "We can all go out to eat or something. Sirue ain't turnin' no food down."

Tea smiled. "I hope Mara can come alone. I don't want Drew tagging along for this."

"We'll work it out. And if it doesn't feel right, we can just plan it for another day. I want it to be the way you want it to be."

"Miles…"

"Yeah?" He leaned his head back again.

Tea wanted to tell him how good he made her feel. There had to be a way to let him know how easily she was going to fall for him without making herself look like a simp. His mere proximity made her feel safe. Not to mention how moist her kitten was getting just from his body heat against her. And it wasn't like a typical relationship because she didn't have to put up with the phony phase when meeting someone new. It was like they'd stepped over that part and headed straight for the courting and romance. But it was just too soon to express all of this. She feared he would jump out of the bed so fast she'd think it was all a dream.

She sighed. "I guess we need to get moving soon. It's almost check-out time."

He leaned closer and kissed her mouth. "Okay," he whispered.

Chapter 22

Sirue looked at his cell phone with confusion intended for Tea.

"You want to meet tonight? Two nights in a row? That's a lot for you."

"It will be later, after I get back from the shop. I've just been wanting to get out more."

"Could it be because of the new guy you hooked up with last night?" Sirue asked, not really teasing, but genuinely curious.

He heard Tea's voice catch. "N-noooo. Well...no, not really. Just don't tell Mara that I hooked up with anyone, okay? Not yet anyway."

Sirue was even more confused when they hung up. What kind of secrets was she keeping from Mara of all people? He shrugged and resumed slicing the boiled potatoes on his cutting board. *These were going to taste good as hell*, he thought to himself. Teresa was probably just getting out of the shower, and he knew he wouldn't have to share much with her since she typically ate like a bird around him. He started to envision the double helpings he was going to put on his plate.

The onions were quickly becoming translucent in the skillet, and he turned the fire down. He liked a little crunch with his; nothing worse than slimy onion slices. The paprika was within arm's reach in front of him in the cupboard. He took it down while it was on his mind and finished cutting the last half of the last potato. The contents were wiped into sizzling oil and Sirue shook enough paprika to give them the desired color. Salt, pepper, and more paprika were added, the lid was placed on the skillet, and Sirue set the timer on the back of the stove. When he started to put the knife and cutting board in the sink, his vision went completely black.

Cold fingers were pressed against his face, covering his eyes. "Guess who?"

"Somebody who really shouldn't be doing this while I have sharp objects in my hand, that's who."

Sirue shook his head free, and the fingers fell. He went back to soaping the water.

"Damn, excuse the hell out of me." Teresa closed her pink satin robe and leaned against the opposite counter. She was glaring at Sirue's back. "Why do you always do that?"

He rolled his eyes, dried his hands on a paper towel and turned around.

"Do what, Teresa?"

"That. You get so mad at me. You snap at me."

"No, I don't, Te—"

"Whatever! I don't even want to fuckin' hear it! Why do I keep getting pulled back in?"

She snatched her robe closed even tighter and folded her arms.

Sirue let out a sharp laugh. "What? You've got to be kidding me. Aren't you the one who called *me* last night and practically begged to come over?"

"Yeah, throw that in my face." Teresa's tone quickly turned into a whine. "But wasn't I good last night? I almost had you in tears."

"What's *wrong* with you?" Sirue said through clenched teeth, his hands on the side of his face. He thought she sincerely needed medication. He would go drive to a pharmacy and pick some up if he had to. Hell, he'd find somebody on campus to write a prescription for her. Her moods jumped from one second to the next.

He looked at her like she had three heads.

"Nothing's wrong with me. You just make me go a little crazy." Now her tone was back to semi-normal.

Sirue squinted at her for a few seconds, then blinked. "I have breakfast to cook, you should probably get dressed."

"Whatever you say, sweetie." She stepped closer to give him a quick kiss, then noticed his phone on the counter and stood back to look at him. "I heard the phone ring earlier, who was that?"

He sighed. "It was Tea."

"Oh. Tea I can deal with. Mara I can't stand." Teresa tried to make her voice syrupy when she saw Sirue's expression harden. "Heeeey." She gently rubbed the side of his arm. "Can you finish this later? I want you to help me get dressed."

She took his arm and put it inside of her robe, resting it around her bare waist.

Before Sirue could answer, his cell rang again. Teresa reached to the side and grabbed it.

"Good morning!" she said cheerfully, before looking at the caller's name.

"Who is this?" the voice asked.

Teresa rolled her eyes when she saw her name. "Ugh. Of course, it's you. Speak of the devil and she will appear."

"Well, keep my name out your mouth, Lucifer, and you won't have that problem."

"Uh. You're the one who called –"

"Just give Sirue his damn phone," Mara snapped.

Teresa rolled her eyes at the screen and shoved it in Sirue's face. "I told you I can't stand her," she said loud enough for the neighbors to hear.

Sirue glared at Teresa as she stomped out of the kitchen.

"Hey, Mara, what's up?" He attempted to sound more upbeat than he felt. "Sorry about her."

"Don't apologize for that, Si. She's the ignorant ass. But then again, you keep dealing with her so I'm starting to worry about you, too."

"Mara, it's early. I'm cooking. What do you need?" It wasn't quite the time to get into that nonsense. He knew he was so grumpy that he might say something he'd regret.

"Okay, my bad. Have you seen Miles? I'm on my way to the gym and he's not picking up his phone, which is odd."

Sirue opened the refrigerator and took out the eggs and the package of bacon. "No, he's not here."

"Damn. Oh well. Did you see who Tea was boo'd up with at the cabaret last night? I called her just now and she's being all hush-hush about it, won't tell me anything. I was hoping to get the scoop from Miles this morning."

"Nope, I was kind of into my own thing last night. Met some nice ladies, got a few new friends," Sirue said, starting to put his phone on speaker, then deciding against it. He grabbed a mixing bowl from the cabinet.

"Mmhmm, well, what about the lady-thing you have right there? I don't blame you for creeping out on her, though."

"I'm not creeping. We're not exclusive. Yet." He didn't mean to let that slip.

"Yet?"

He sighed while he cracked the eggs.

"I need to make sure it's what I want. That's all."

"And you really don't care if none of us likes her? That doesn't faze you at all, does it?"

"Nope." The eggshells went down the disposal.

"I can respect that. I don't understand that shit, but I can respect it. Well, look, after you eat you should come down to the gym and work off that stomach, brother. Getting a little soft around the middle," Mara laughed.

"Shut up. Goodbye."

Teresa made it back downstairs as Sirue was placing their plates on the table. During their breakfast of scrambled eggs, fried potatoes, bacon, and biscuits, Sirue's attention was on his phone. Teresa made several attempts to pull his phone away from him, but he just moved it to the other side of his plate.

"You don't even talk to me while we eat," she complained, stabbing at potatoes with her fork.

Sirue sighed hard and turned his phone over. "So, let's talk."

Teresa stared at him, then rolled her eyes. She took a sip of her juice, then lifted up her own phone and started scrolling.

He looked from her phone and back to her face. "Teresa. You have my attention. Let's talk," he repeated.

"Nope," she replied, picking up a strip of bacon and taking a small nibble. Her eyes never left her phone's colorful screen.

"Why would y...," Sirue stopped himself and rubbed his forehead. "Fine. Okay." He shook his head. He didn't have the energy to engage with her this morning. He turned his phone back over to check his email.

When he finished eating, Sirue stood to clear his dishes. Teresa watched him intently as he grabbed his plate and cup and walked to the kitchen. She followed him and stood behind him as he washed his dishes.

"I can wash up for you," she said quietly, sliding her hands under the back of his t-shirt.

"I've got it, Teresa," he answered coldly.

She continued to massage his back until he placed the plate and cup in the dish drainer and turned around. Her hands slid around to the front of his torso. He lowered his head and watched her. Teresa looked up and grinned.

"We can't keep ignoring our problems and using sex to fix everything," Sirue said, his eyes contradicting his words.

"It's so good, though," Teresa moaned. She took her hands from beneath his shirt and moved them to the back of his neck. She pulled his head down and kissed him hard on the mouth.

"Tere--," Sirue started. He grunted and began to kiss her back. With her mouth on his, she took one of his hands and guided it between her thighs. When he felt the moisture, he grunted again and lifted her body up as she wrapped her legs around him.

They continued to kiss passionately and loudly as Sirue carried her upstairs an into his bedroom. Throwing off their clothes, they climbed onto the bed and Teresa quickly mounted him in reverse.

She dug her nails deep into Sirue's knees. She leaned forward and remembered why she hated this position so much. He was so far inside of her, and it seemed to hurt more than it felt good. But she opened her eyes and saw his toes flexing and crossing each other. She knew it was worth it. She bounced faster.

Sirue threw his head back deeper into his pillows. *This was some leave-your-wife shit right here*, he thought. He managed to lift his head up enough to see the sweat rolling down her back. With his finger, he wiped some off and licked it. He grunted more and grew inside of her wetness as he grabbed her hips and helped her move up and down.

Teresa moaned along with him. She knew he was about to erupt.

"Come on, baby...come on...," she pleaded.

Sirue let out a very long expletive and Teresa stopped moving enough to reach down and bring herself to climax a few moments after he did. She pulled off slowly and fell next to his heaving chest. She ran her fingers through his curly chest hairs and gave him small kisses on his shoulder.

"That was good, huh?" she whispered, still panting.

Sirue nodded, his eyes closed.

"You like how tight I am, don't you?" she said in the same sweet voice.

He nodded again, not sure where she was going with this nor why she was so damn talkative right now.

"I started doing special exercises for it. I'm reading this book all about vaginal muscle control." She got up on one elbow and an excited gleam came over her face. "One exercise has me squeezing my muscles while I hold small objects —"

"Teresa, stop."

"I'm serious—"

"Me, too," Sirue shook his head. The post-orgasmic elation was fading fast.

Teresa sighed and leaned back onto the bed. "Fine. Do you mind if I take another shower? I need to get to work soon."

"Sure, go ahead."

Teresa got up slowly, grabbed the towel she used earlier and headed to Sirue's master bathroom. She turned around and smiled at Sirue while she stood in the doorway. He felt her eyes on him and lifted his head to meet her glance. Teresa's smile quickly disappeared, and she slammed the door hard enough to make a few framed pictures on his dresser shake.

Sirue didn't know whether to laugh or call the men in white. She was officially losing it. Maybe he was, too.

Chapter 23

"I knew we'd be the only ones here."

Miles had just walked up to Mara's coupe, which was parked a few cars ahead of his on the busy downtown street. He waited and tried not to laugh when she stepped out and had to lock the door several times before it finally caught. She hit the window with the palm of her hand. "Stupid ass car."

"But, man, you know Tea's gonna be late to her own burial. And Si's only late if Teresa's still picking out his outfit. He does dress fly as hell, though."

"Wait, so what do I look like? A gym teacher?" Miles slowed his pace to touch the lines on his freshly shaped goatee.

Mara looked him over.

"Nah. More like a black Muslim straight out of prison with those damn glasses on again, bruh."

"These are different glasses," he said, taking off the black-rimmed designer personality spectacles and showing them to her.

She waved them away from her face. "Whatever, the temple's that way, Brother Miles."

Miles laughed. "See, I was thinking about paying your way tonight."

"All right, I take it back."

"Nope."

"Jerk."

They reached the front door and Miles pulled out enough money to cover them both.

There was a faint smell of herbal tea mixed with deep incense. A variety of colognes and perfumes permeated their nostrils as they stepped down into the venue. The Black Café had its usual array of Saturday night customers. The younger twenty-somethings. The sugar daddies. Singles. Couples.

Instinctively, they both headed to the bar.

"It's kinda packed tonight, huh?" Mara asked the unfamiliar bartender. "Wisdom must be on the mic."

"Yep, she always turns this place out." The bartender's eyes wandered then landed directly on her chest, and he smiled a toothy grin at her. "What's your pleasure?"

"A toasted dentist."

"Excuse me?"

"I mean, a toasted almond," she said quickly.

Miles fought back a smile. "Make that two, please."

The bartender looked Mara up and down and made a show of rolling his eyes before he walked off.

Miles shook his head. "That was cold, what did that man do to you?"

"I'm saying…his teeth were all in my face. And what if you were my man? He didn't know." She tilted some peanuts into her hand and caught a glimpse of herself in the wall mirror. With her twists still looking nice, she'd decided to pin some up and keep a few out in the front. She pressed her lips together to ensure her berry crème lip stain was holding in place. While she chewed, she found herself wishing she had a full-length mirror to check out her flowing khaki pantsuit. She spread open the oversized overshirt as if to air it out and patted her stomach through her white tank top.

"Miles, am I getting fat?"

"Yeah." He turned in his stool to survey the patrons.

Her eyes widened. "What? Where? My stomach, right?"

Miles tossed some more nuts into his mouth. He gave her a quick once-over. "No. More in your ass. I wanted to say something about it when we walked in, but I knew you'd be all sensitive and shit."

"Miles, stop playing." She pouted to herself and stood up, trying to gauge the size of her rear end.

He started laughing. "Damn, Mara. Your man got you trippin' or something? Girl, sit the hell down." He took her arm, but she snatched it away.

"You play too much," she said, giving him a shove that almost sent him to the floor.

The bartender brought their drinks and Mara sipped on hers immediately. She twirled her straw with an attitude. Miles looked up at one of the two televisions above the bar. He nudged her.

"Look. The game's on."

Mara didn't answer. Instead, she finished her drink and pushed it forward, motioning for a refill. She tapped the bar and looked around while she waited for it to arrive.

"Damn! Play some D!" Miles yelled. He got a few shared sentiments from the other people watching the game.

He half-turned to Mara. "See, told you they need to get rid of his ass. Too many – OHHHH!" A player from Boston just cut through three defenders to increase their team's lead to sixteen. The home team's coach called a much-needed timeout.

Miles looked over at Mara, who was sipping away at her second drink. He nudged her elbow and she simply slid it over a few inches away from him.

"You mad for real?" he asked. "You know I was just messing with you."

"Shut up."

"Love you."

"Shut up," Mara repeated.

He laughed and just then, the lights dimmed. There was a mild applause as Wisdom stepped to the mic. All eyes were on her, and she swayed behind the microphone, continually thanking the crowd for their love.

"You're a beautiful audience, thank you," her soulful and raspy voice spoke again and again.

From their vantage point, Miles and Mara could look straight ahead and catch a full view of the stage. When Wisdom concluded her set of new material, Mara realized how much the words applied to her. Why was she so heavily into Drew when she had so many other things going on in her life right now? She had a new home to take care of, classes that were kicking her ass, and a job she was overqualified for. But ever since her freshman year in high school, she'd had a boyfriend. Sometimes two or three. And usually, she just wanted them there to take up space. She thought about needing Drew next to her last night just to take up the empty space. She chewed on her lip and got lost in everyone's applause.

"Thank y'all for feeling me. Thank you." Wisdom bowed her head in appreciation to the audience a few times. She turned to thank the musicians behind her and got back to the microphone.

"All right, first up tonight is…"

Miles spotted Sirue walking through the doors.

"Finally. C'mon, let's get a table," he whispered to Mara.

He got up but Mara didn't. Her stare was fixed on the stage. A single tear appeared at the corner of her eye and began to roll.

Miles stepped closer as it fell to the edge of her mouth.

"Hey," he put his hand on her back. "What's wrong?"

Mara wiped the tear and cleared her throat.

"I'm good."

Miles' countenance tightened and his voice hardened.

"I was bullshittin' before, Mar, but did Drew really say something to you?"

Mara's gaze fell on her protective friend. "No."

He put his hand on his chest. "Is it because of what I said?"

"No." She smiled and stood up. "I'm good. Her words just touched me. Must be PMS, come on."

They started walking and Miles continued to study her. She was very emotionally wired tonight. He wondered how she was going to take his news.

Mara waved Sirue over to a table that was still being wiped down. The three sat and they noticed how relaxed he seemed.

"Damn, man, you are almost an hour late and you come in all gums," Miles said across the table as Sirue eyed the menu.

"I know why he's so happy," Mara cut in. She squinted at him. "It's Teresa. He's in looooooooove," she teased.

"Wait – what?" Miles inquired.

"You need to get the facts straight before you go stating random opinions," Sirue said, eyeing the tasty shrimp platter entrée pictured at the bottom. "That looks good."

"Whatever, just come with it – are you and Teresa together again?" Mara snatched the menu from his hands.

He looked from her to Miles and frowned at their nosy stares.

"Since you two are obviously desperate for gossip—"

Mara and Miles nodded in agreement.

"—we're not exclusive. I'll leave it at that. Besides, *you're* the one who invited us here for the news tonight," he looked at Miles. "Where is she?"

"Yeah, where is this mysterious lady you've been seeing?" Mara asked, glancing at her phone and silently wondering what Drew was doing.

Miles shrugged. *Where was Tea?* "Uh...she'll be here."

They collectively looked for a waitress but couldn't locate one to save their lives. The third poet's set was almost over, and Miles was about to pull out his phone to call Tea. Before his hand reached his pocket, he looked up and saw her paying the cover at the door. It was all he could do to keep from jumping out of his chair.

Mara tapped Miles on the arm.

"There she is," she waved until she got Tea's attention.

Miles suddenly felt acutely aware of his mannerisms. He quickly took in her form-fitting long-sleeved olive top, accentuating her beautifully full breasts, her tight black jeans and black boots. As she walked over and maneuvered between tables, he remembered why he'd been missing her all day. She brightened the entire night club.

He stood and Sirue pulled her chair out.

"Sorry, y'all. I got caught up with my brothers."

"Oh, where'd you take them?" Mara wondered.

Tea hesitated. "Um. To get some dinner and to the park. I'm starving. Did you order something yet?" She grabbed the one-page menu from the center of the table.

Mara looked over at Sirue. He seemed to read her mind and tried not to show it on his face. Sirue gave his attention to the next artist on the microphone while Mara noticed Miles was drumming his fingers on the table and stealing glances at Tea.

Tea frowned then put the menu back.

"I love this place, but the food sucks."

"Miles, what time did you tell her to meet us here? It's getting late." Mara looked down at her phone again. She wasn't in the mood for all of this, especially since Drew had yet to reply to texts she sent to him hours ago.

"Um." Miles looked to his left at Tea, attempting to read her eyes. "Well," he sat forward with his elbows on the table. "She –"

"You brothers and sisters ready to order yet?" A head-wrapped waitress materialized out of nowhere. She flashed them a forty-something plastic smile.

"Yes!" Tea nodded.

Miles sighed and wished the waitress would have come past a few minutes later. They all ordered their selections and she left as fast as she'd appeared. The poet finished his two rather humorous pieces and the audience erupted with laughter and snaps.

Too much noise, Miles thought. Too many distractions. He wanted to call off the announcement but saw Tea glaring at him and urging him to speak. Mara was getting bored fast. Sirue was probably the only one paying any mind to the performers while thinking about the food he just ordered. Miles let out another breath.

"Well, I wanted everybody here because y'all are my family, and I wanted you to find out together."

"I'm surprised you didn't invite us out to Pennie's," Mara quipped.

"Right, like last time," Sirue added, slow on the uptake.

"Duh, Einstein. That's what I meant," Mara responded, completely aggravated now.

"I know that's what you meant, why else would I say 'Right'? What's your problem?" Sirue didn't like her attitude nor her tone.

"I don't have a problem." Mara waved him off. She motioned at Miles to get on with it.

Tea's eyes darted from Mara to Sirue. There was no time for a bitch session right now. *What was going on with Mara?*

"Is she here?" Sirue looked towards the front door. Mara did the same.

"Yeah." Miles smiled.

Three women had just paid and stepped down into the lounge area. They were gazing at the tables near the stage area.

"Which one? The tall one?" Sirue asked, craning his neck.

"No," Tea answered, her eyes on Miles. "She's not tall."

Miles smiled at Tea. Mara looked between them and suddenly realized why she couldn't get in touch with either one of them earlier that morning.

"Which one?" Sirue asked again. "They're all attractive."

"It's --," Miles started.

"It's me," Tea blurted out. "It's us. Miles and I are going out."

Sirue's jaw dropped. Mara forced a surprised expression.

"Wow," she replied quietly.

Tea bit her lips, looking across the table and bracing herself for more of Mara's response. She knew more was coming.

"Well, damn!" Sirue stood up and went to hug Tea hard. "Big Head and Miles? Damn," he laughed.

Miles chuckled and gave Sirue daps. Sirue stood again and hugged Miles.

"I'm happy for you man," Sirue scooted his chair closer and wanted to hear everything.

"Thanks. I feel so lucky," he smiled and was glad he didn't have to contain it anymore. He reached for Tea's hand on the table and held it. He wanted to go grab the microphone and let the whole place know.

Sirue fired question after question and while they talked, Tea wanted to have some girl-talk time with Mara. She moved closer to Mara and followed her eyes towards the people at the next table.

"Wow," Mara repeated.

"Can you say something else? I know you hate me for not telling you first," Tea stated the obvious.

Ding, ding, ding, Mara thought. "No, it's...wow. I'm shocked, that's all." Mara's flat voice screamed of irritation.

"Mara."

"Tea," she lowered her voice. "I'm happy for you. I am."

Tea twisted her lips in disbelief.

"Girl," Mara walked over to give Tea a small hug.

Tea hugged her back, but before she could say anything else, the waitress appeared with their drinks and Mara went back to her seat.

As the waitress turned to leave, Sirue touched her arm.

"Excuse me, I want to order another round of drinks for the table."

She smiled a real smile at his excitement. "Sure. What's the occasion?"

"My two best friends just came to their senses!"

Chapter 24

Tea rolled the vacuum cleaner back into the hall closet and peeked around the corner at the clock on the kitchen wall. It was almost noon and Mara was still asleep on a Sunday morning. That struck her as odd, then again, she remembered how late Mara talked on the phone the night before. When Tea got back from the Black Café, she found Mara already home and on her phone. She'd decided not to bother her but could hear her fussing with Drew until late into the night. Tea figured she would still be asleep, too, had Miles not called and asked her to a movie that afternoon.

After a small breakfast of cereal and juice, Tea finished loading the dishwasher and headed upstairs to take a shower. She passed Mara's room twice, then stopped the third time when she thought she heard voices. *No*, she thought. *It couldn't be.* Was that Drew's voice she heard? Tea leaned closer, so that her ear was nearly pressed on the door. She tried to make out the muted conversation but couldn't.

Tea debated for a full minute whether she should knock on the door. The hushed voices sounded like a quiet argument, so she decided to leave it alone.

Twenty minutes later, she walked back to her bedroom from the bathroom, turned on her speaker and decided she felt like some smooth nineties R&B. She danced to herself while she picked out an outfit.

Tea sang along to the hook about moths being attracted to flames as she pulled on a sheer-sleeved salmon-colored peasant blouse from her closet and held it against her body. She figured it would look nice with her light blue denim jeans and salmon pumps.

She applied copious amounts of lotions and fragrances then got dressed between dance moves and imaginary singing competitions. She didn't realize how loud she was becoming until there was a knock on her door.

"Hold on!" she called and turned her speaker down. She opened the door, fully dressed, except for the silk scarf on her head and bare feet.

Mara stood in front of her with bloodshot eyes and twists all over her head.

"Is my music too – girl, are you okay?" Tea opened her door wider to get a full view of her friend. Her red satin robe was pulled closed, and her arms were folded across her chest.

Mara gave her a tired nod. "Yeah, I'm fine," her voice answered in a throaty monotone. "Nikki's been calling my phone."

"Oh, damn, thanks," Tea said, looking her friend over again as Mara turned and walked back to her bedroom, quietly closing the door behind her.

Tea exhaled, then grabbed her phone. There were so many missed calls. She dialed the shop.

"Hair by Tea," a very stressed-out voice greeted.

"Nikki? Hey, it's me. Is everything all right there?"

There was a loud sigh on the other end of the phone. "Oh my God, I've been trying to get ahold of you, Ms. Tea. I left about eight messages and I sent text after text, but you never –"

"Nikki. Take a breath. It's okay, I was just in the shower. Now, what's going on?"

Nikki proceeded to tell her that DeeDee's daughter had to be picked up early from swim practice, so she wouldn't be able to cover the salon that afternoon. Tea sucked her teeth. She hated to change plans at the last minute. She thanked Nikki, reassured her again that she did a great job of trying to contact her, and arranged to get there before four o'clock. She'd just have to haul ass from the movie theater.

Tea removed the silk scarf from her head and fingered out her wrapped hair. It fell into place perfectly, her bangs swooping to the side. She then looked in her mirror as she quickly refreshed her eyebrows. Within ten minutes, her pumps were in her hand, and she headed downstairs. The smell of bacon didn't surprise her as much as Drew's presence in front of the stove did. He looked over and flashed her a quick smile and wave. Tea nodded her greeting, then made a quick right into the den, out of his eyesight. She sat down and read through the texts Nikki left earlier and shook her head, envisioning her panic when Tea never responded. She started to call Miles when a figure appeared at the den's doorway.

"Knock, knock...," Drew said as he tapped the already open door. He stood in a very muscle-revealing t-shirt, black sweatpants, his dreads in a ponytail, and a spatula in his hand.

Tea looked up. She instantly noticed his eyes weren't as red as Mara's had been. In fact, his whole demeanor said he'd slept like a baby.

"Hey, I'm just throwing together some food for us, you want some?"

"Nah, no thanks. I ate." Tea turned her attention back to her phone.

"I heard you grooving up there when you got out of the shower." Drew's voice dropped to a lower decibel.

Tea didn't like him thinking about her bathing herself. And she definitely didn't like the way his eyes were studying her chest.

She nodded her head in response, not sure what to say. He tapped the spatula against his free hand a few times before he spoke again.

"I can give you something else to nibble on if you don't want breakfast."

Tea suddenly felt the hairs standing up on the back of her neck. "What did you just say?"

"I said I can cook something else for you since I'm already in there," he broke out in a grin. "If you're not hungry, that's okay, too."

"I told you I already ate," she said firmly.

He held his hand and the spatula up in surrender. "I was just asking."

"And I was just calling Miles."

Drew smiled and slowly walked back to the kitchen. Tea tried to make sense of what just happened as she slipped on her salmon pumps. She couldn't wrap her mind around it fast enough. Was she tripping? She dialed Miles and told him to hurry up. She stayed downstairs in the den while she waited. Within five minutes, the aroma of fried meat met her nose, and she patted her growling stomach.

"Mara!" She heard Drew calling upstairs. "Come down! It's ready, baby!"

Tea listened as she heard Mara's door open upstairs.

"Damn, what would be so hard about bringing it up to me?"

"Because I already set the table! Now, come on down so I can make your plate!"

Mara said something Tea couldn't decipher, then heard her stomp down the steps.

"See, that wasn't too hard, was it?" she heard Drew ask Mara once she reached the kitchen.

There were loud kissing sounds and moans from Drew, and Tea's stomach turned. He was such a pig. Why was he making her best friend so miserable? She stood at the door of the den and listened.

"Get off of me, I'm hungry."

"Mmmm. Me, too. Come here, sexy."

"I know you're not standing here all horny after last night."

"I told you I wasn't finished. Just come here."

"Drew..."

The next sound Tea heard was something smashing to the floor. She was motionless, not sure if she should run in there or not.

"Look what you did," Mara fussed. "I'm really not in the mood for this, Drew."

"Baby, it's just a plate. I can buy you another one."

"Well, shit, clean it up."

"I will if you turn around," Drew's voice started to get lower, and Tea had to strain to hear what he was saying.

She couldn't hear Mara's response.

"Baby, come on, I'm all worked up now," he moaned. She could hear Drew's horny ass but didn't want to charge in and embarrass Mara. She wasn't sure if Mara was whispering or if she wasn't answering him at all.

"Lift that up." Drew started to make sounds like he was breathing through clenched teeth. "Bend over, baby."

"Drew, stop," Mara whispered in a tired voice.

Tea let out a horribly fake sneeze and yawned loudly before she walked out of the den. She stretched with added noise when she reached the kitchen just in time to catch Mara squatting down to pick up the pieces of shattered glass with her hands. Drew was sitting askew in a dining room chair that he obviously just ran to sit in because he was out of breath. Tea looked around nonchalantly and peeked in the skillet on the stove.

Mara stood and tossed a few of the bigger pieces of the broken plate into the trash and pulled her robe closed again, looking exhausted.

"Here, watch out," Tea said kindly and opened the broom closet to get the broom and dustpan. She swept up what remained of the plate while Mara watched blankly.

"Thanks," she finally mumbled and walked sadly to the dining room and fell into the chair next to Drew. Tea wanted to throw up when she noticed him rubbing her leg under the table.

Mara piled the sausage and bacon onto her plate followed by a large helping of eggs. She started to eat before she saw Tea standing in the kitchen staring at her.

"What's up, Tea?" Mara asked, her fork in midair.

Tea reluctantly shook her head and got something to drink.

"You look nice. You and Miles going somewhere?" Mara asked quietly, biting a forkful of eggs.

Her question seemed more rhetorical than inquisitive.

"Yeah. Movies." Tea drank a glass of apple juice and put the empty glass in the sink. Her phone buzzed in her pocket, and she read the text from Miles saying he was almost there. Tea glared at Drew and started to worry about leaving Mara alone with him.

"Do you...do you want to come with us?" She directed her invitation at Mara.

Mara gave her a weak smile and shook her head.

Tea sighed. "Okay. Well." She looked at her friend. "Call me if you change your mind."

Mara nodded. Drew reached over and held her hand while he continued to stuff his face.

Tea rolled her eyes and headed to the front door. On her way, she stopped at Mara and bent down to give her a hug.

"I'll text you," she whispered to her sad friend, then left the house.

Mara watched her walk out. She knew Tea was worried about her. She just wished she could tell her everything.

Chapter 25

Miles wondered why they were so late. He checked his smart watch for the third time in two minutes. The clock above his office door tauntingly clicked to the next minute. Twelve past one. *What the hell was taking them so damn long?*

"Shit," he muttered to himself. He angrily flipped to the next page in the file on his desk. He carelessly scanned the data while tapping his pen. Another minute passed. He knew it was the wrong decision when he called forty minutes ago. He should have gone with his first instinct and dialed the other number. This was getting ridiculous.

Miles threw his pen across the room. He pushed back from his desk and walked to his small office window, folding his arms. *Out of all the options, I had to pick this one,* he thought. He wished he could take back the last hour of his life.

Mondays were always rough, but this was reaching the point of insanity. He punched his fist into his palm.

Suddenly his desk phone buzzed, and he walked back to sit down, pushing the speaker button. Mrs. Crawford's raspy voice talked to him.

"Mr. Puvi, your carry-out order is here."

"It's about damn time!"

"Mr. Puvi, there's no need to shout. Your food has been late before."

Miles laughed. "Mrs. C, just remind me to never call this restaurant again."

After a lunch of greasy, but tasty fried wings, a large fried rice, four egg rolls and a large soda, Miles was ready to work. He turned down the volume on the sports network and stretched loudly.

He wondered what Tea was doing. He missed her smell. At the movies yesterday, he noticed she was a little tense. She definitely had something on her mind, and he loved the way she snuggled against him in their seats. There was something about her he wanted to protect. She seemed so vulnerable sometimes, yet so strong and invincible. He couldn't believe how much he thought about her now. She consumed most of his thoughts during the day and all of them at night. He had to get it under control, though. There was nothing that could turn off a woman more than a man being overly interested. At least, that had been his experience. There was no reason to call her every few hours. He'd talked to her already this morning when she got to the shop. What purpose would another call serve, anyway?

He picked up his desk phone and dialed.

"Hi, Miles," she answered.

"Hi, baby. How's it going?"

"Just wiping down the dryers. It's not that busy today."

"Yeah, same here. I had a scary moment earlier when my lunch was late."

Tea laughed. "Okay, do you actually have work to do?"

"Yes. For instance, I have a meeting in a few minutes. It's not all gravy, you know."

"Mmhmm. Really? I think your frat brother hooked you up with that job just so you could chill all day. Tell the truth," she teased.

Miles smiled, but feigned seriousness. "Oh, because I got a hand up from another black brother, I don't know the value of hard work?"

"I didn't even say all that –"

"And just because I got some ends, y'all want to assume I don't deserve the job?"

"See, now you're just –"

"I mean, what? You want me to come home with dirty fingernails and greasy hands?"

Tea paused. "Are you done?"

"Yeah." Miles could almost hear her smiling through the phone.

"Good. I'll call you tonight. I wanted you to come by the house. We can order out and watch some TV or something," Tea said sweetly.

"Sounds like heaven to me. Talk to you later."
"Bye. Have a good meeting."
"Thanks, baby."

Miles tried to get rid of his cheesy grin before his meeting. He did the only thing that could possibly work. He turned up the volume and watched the highlights from last night's hometown team. Nothing could put a frown on his face faster.

Mara loved having the house to herself. Not that Tea was ever in her way when she was home, it was more Drew who was crowding her. She stood with her hands on her hips and looked out of the wide bay window in the living room. The drapes were pulled back, and sunlight was dancing its way all around her. She rolled her neck and absorbed the radiant heat. It felt great.

She picked up the window cleaner and resumed spraying it. The clean smell of it alone was enough to intoxicate her back to normalcy. Cleaning was never a chore she enjoyed, but she needed the mental distraction. There was so much she had to wash out of her head, too. She was tired of snapping at Drew whenever he made a comment. She was sick of her unsettled feeling that started to come over her whenever he was near. There was an untrustworthiness he carried around lately. Mara couldn't put her finger on what it was. He even wanted the sex to be when and how he wanted it, which was increasingly more and more. It was still good, and he knew how to make her climax better than anyone ever had, but she did notice how demanding he was becoming. He seemed to never be fully satisfied anymore.

Mara wiped the blue liquid off the glass and stood back to admire her handiwork. Streak-free and spotless, just like the bottle claimed. Now for the upstairs bathrooms.

She lifted the bucket and rags, but before she made it to the steps, her cell rang.

Mara was surprised that her ringer volume was even on. She grunted, freed her hands, and went to pick up her phone from the coffee table. She held the phone face down and said a quick prayer that it wasn't her supervisor asking why she called out of work today.

She peeked at the caller's ID and it read *unavailable number*.

"Hello?"

There was static on the line.

"Hello," Mara repeated louder.

"Who am I speaking to?" a woman's soft voice asked.

"You should know, *you* called *me*. Who is this?"

The woman hung up. Mara looked at her screen and rolled her eyes.

"Who the hell…whatever," she said and shoved her phone in her bra strap, grabbed her cleaning supplies and went upstairs.

The bathtub in the main bathroom wasn't in as much need of a scrub as the sink. She turned on the hot water and looked for a fresh sponge underneath the basin. She almost hit her head when her phone rang again.

"I swear," she muttered to herself and accidentally kicked the bucket as she tried to regain her balance. "Shit!"

She hobbled around and sat on the edge of the bathtub as she looked at the caller's name and answered her phone.

"Hey, girl, OUCH!" Mara said, rubbing her toe.

"Um…you okay?" Tea asked, laughing nervously.

"Yes, bumped my damn toe. That's what I get for cleaning. What's up?"

"I just wanted to see how you're doing. I noticed you were still asleep when I left this morning, and I didn't see you when I came back from the movies yesterday."

Mara thought for a second. She remembered how crazy she must have seemed yesterday. "Oh, yeah, I'm good. I just really needed today off."

Tea let a pause linger.

"Is…um…are you and Drew okay?" She rushed her words out.

Mara was thrown off. "Yeah. He just gets on my nerves sometimes. I know I didn't look like myself yesterday and I knew you would be all worried, girl. A lot of studying and shit on my plate, that's all."

"Well, all right," Tea paused again. "Since you're cleaning, make sure you scrub the scum off my soap dish in my bathroom. Oh, and the towels need to be washed."

"So, you must be putting me on payroll or something."

Tea laughed. "I invited Miles to come by tonight."

"Ohhhh, okay. So, you want some fresh linen for you and bae?" Mara smiled. "Ugh, it still doesn't sound right. You and *Miles*. I'm gonna throw up."

"Shut up. We're taking professional pictures tomorrow night, too. I made an appointment." Tea sounded so proud.

"Oh, Lord. Not those ghetto poses in matching outfits, please. I would never let y'all live that down."

"Whatever. Bye, Mara. You don't have to cook dinner after you clean the kitchen, we're going to order out tonight."

"You must really think I'm hired help. Bye, girl."

Mara hung up and found herself in good spirits, despite her aching toe. Tea's giddiness was certainly contagious. New love did that to you. She could remember the first night in Drew's truck. The first night he showed her his house and described the paintings in his bedroom. Bedroom. Everything always came back to sex with him. She sighed and tried to keep her good mood going while she went back to cleaning.

Chapter 26

"All right, Mrs. C. I'm off early today." Miles stopped at her desk and swung his keys in his hand. He was leaving the Cosmic Lumens building the same way he'd arrived that morning: empty-handed. No briefcase, no attaché case, no crossover bag. No files to take home and look over. Just how he liked it.

Mrs. Crawford made a show of looking at her watch. "Thirty minutes until quitting time, Mr. Puvi."

"Yeah, but I had a long day. You know, the late lunch, the meeting..."

"The meeting was cancelled," she reminded him, peering over her glasses. Her grim expression didn't faze him one bit.

"But I still had to prepare for it," he winked and headed to the glass double-doors. "Oh," he turned around. "Anyone calls for me, just –"

"Forward them to your cell phone. I'm well aware of the protocols, Mr. Puvi, since I came up with them."

He flashed her another quick smile and blew her a kiss. She dodged the invisible smooch, and he laughed all the way to the elevators.

It was a beautiful Monday. He jumped into his black sedan and was glad he was going to beat at least some of the traffic from Virginia to the District. His commute was crazy, and with the soaring gas prices, it was starting to make a dent in his extra change fund. He turned on his music and blasted his favorite hardcore rapper from his speakers. Tea wasn't fond of his music, but Miles loved his lyrical masterpieces. He pounded his steering wheel with the rhythm as he crawled his way up 495.

An hour later, he was parking his car in his driveway.

Inside, he decided to return a text to his Aunt Carrie that he missed on the way home. He thanked her for the care package she sent him last week. It was full of goodies and homemade desserts. She said she'll continue to send them until he finds a good woman to take care of her baby nephew. Miles smiled as he typed that he already found one.

A call came through as he hit send. He answered and placed it on speaker, not sure of the number.

"Hey, Miles," the voice said.

"Yeah, who's this?"

"Hey man, it's Drew. How's it going?"

"All right, can't complain."

"Uh, look. I heard about you and Tea. I wanted to congratulate you."

"Oh, thanks, man. I appreciate that."

"I guess we both lucked out and found some smart, beautiful women, huh?"

"Yeah, we did." Miles wondered where he was going with this, and why he was wasting his time.

"Speaking of which, I uh...had to talk to you about something. Mano y mano. I can't really talk too candidly here at work," Drew's voice dragged on.

Miles looked at the time. "Aren't the students gone by now?"

"Yeah, for the most part. I guess I could close my office door. Hold on."

After a few seconds, Miles heard muted conversations in the background.

"Look, Miles, there's a parent here. I'll have to talk to you later."

"Sure, man. Anytime."

With that, Miles' phone fell silent, and he was completely puzzled. He shrugged it off and went to take a quick shower. Thoughts of Tea made his shower slightly longer than he'd planned. As he got dressed in jeans and a simple athletic brand t-shirt, he found himself trying to keep her smell out of his memory. Any recollection about her small waist, ample bosom, fresh aroma, or delicate fingers could make blood flow to all parts of his body. He knew he had to get a handle on it and fast. He wasn't lying when he told her she made him feel like a teenager. Maybe it was the anticipation that made her so incredibly sexy. *No*, he thought. *It was her scent.*

On his way to Mitchellville, Miles stopped to pick up a few boxes of chocolate covered peanuts, a couple buckets of popcorn, and a six-pack of soda. It was almost seven-thirty when he reached the house. The smell of pine and lemon met his nose as Tea opened the door.

He looked down at her with a wide grin. He pecked her lips and inhaled her sweet, fruity scent.

"You smell so good," he said, stepping inside.

"Thank you...ooooooh," she said, grabbing the bag from him when she saw the candy. "These are my favorite." She turned around and left him standing in the entryway.

"Damn, can't even get a wardrobe compliment, a hug, nothing..."

Tea laughed as she plopped on the living room sofa. She shook the box of candy and began to rip the plastic covering off. Miles stood there, staring at her incredulously.

"So, that's how it is, huh?" he asked.

Tea tore the box open and started to shake a round piece of confection into her hand, ignoring both his question and his glare.

"Nah, you gonna give me my hug." Miles ran over to her, and Tea playfully screamed. She tried to kick at him, but he grabbed her legs and gave her a huge bear hug while spitting wet raspberries into her neck.

"Ewwwww! Okay! Okay!" she laughed, but the words wouldn't come out. He began tickling her, completely unfazed by her pleas and whining.

Miles finally stopped harassing her long enough for Tea to catch her breath. She held the candy close to her chest, hugging it tightly with both arms. She kicked at him again.

"Meanie," she pouted.

He leaned over her, his arms on the back of the sofa. He was also slightly out of breath and couldn't resist kissing her soft cheek.

"Don't kiss me," she whispered, turning her head to the side.

"I sowwy," Miles said and kissed her cheek again.

She turned her head the other way. "You messed up my hair."

"You're still the prettiest girl I ever did see."

Tea squinted at him. "You can get off me now," she said, fighting a smile.

Miles looked down and wanted nothing more than to make love to her right then. He was sure his feelings could be read on his face, so he slowly stood up and held out a hand to help her from her curled up position. She smoothed her hair down and he assisted by sliding her bangs to the side.

"Good as new," he whispered and landed another kiss on her cheek.

Tea smiled and took his hand as she lifted the bag and led him to the kitchen.

Mara jaunted down the stairs.

"I thought I heard you down here. What's up, M?" Mara gave him a side hug.

"Nothing, M," he said as he hugged her back. "You seem chipper."

"Yeah, brushing your teeth will do that to you, you ought to try it."

Tea let out a loud laugh, then caught herself. Miles looked at her, then back at Mara. "Oh, you got jokes?"

"I'm playin', maaaaan. Try the mouthwash first." Mara pinched one of his cheeks and he swatted her hand away.

Tea noticed Mara's spandex shorts and fitted tee. "You about to go work out?"

"Yeah," Mara grabbed the bag of snacks from the counter, looked inside and frowned. "Ooooh, chocolate. But I feel bloated as hell. What movie are y'all watching?"

"Faster Driver IX. Can't believe Tea hasn't seen it yet," Miles said excitedly.

Tea made a face. "Who wants to see the same actor ride in a car for like the twentieth movie in a row?"

Mara looked at her and raised her hand. "Ummm. I do! Especially if he's doing it without a shirt on, ya feel me?"

Tea slowly nodded and gave her a high five. "You right, you right."

Miles rolled his eyes and put the sodas in the fridge.

"All right, y'all. I should be back in a couple of hours so don't let me walk in on something freaky."

Tea blushed. "Whatever."

Chapter 27

The movie began as loudly as expected. Tea had positioned herself between Miles and the back of the big couch in the den. It felt so right laying on him. He was completely into the scenes of the movie, though. She looked up and studied his goatee. She picked at it, loving how the hairs felt between her fingers. She traced the perfect lines around his chin and beneath his nose. He didn't budge once. His attention was completely on the flat screen. *What was so interesting about the movie, anyway?* Tea wondered if he knew the real reason why she invited him over. She'd been thinking about him touching her all day. Now, here they were. Just the two of them on an oversized couch. Laying down. And he was paying her no mind.

She'd take care of that.

Tea looked back up at his face. She touched his lips, rolling her finger around their curves. She parted his lips with her index finger and slowly inserted it inside. Without taking his eyes off the screen, Miles circled her finger with his tongue. Tea played with it, making it chase her finger around his mouth. His tongue was so soft and warm, she could feel her body getting the same way. Her breathing picked up. She slowly slid her finger out, then back in, and repeated it a few times. She moved it down to his Adam's apple and with her entire hand, she caressed his neck then the underside of his jawbone.

Tea felt his arm reaching up and her body was primed, ready for his touch. To her dismay, he grabbed for the remote and turned the volume up a notch. Tea looked up at him and could see a faint smile. He was playing with her now. Well, she could play, too.

She slid down on the couch so that her face was at the level of his navel. She got from behind him and put her body between his legs, making one leg fall to the floor. Miles looked down at her momentarily, but when he caught her gaze, he quickly turned his attention back to the movie. Tea knew his body would betray him, just like hers was doing right now. She lifted his shirt up enough so that her mouth could rest on his stomach. Her tongue licked wherever there was flesh to meet it. She felt his breaths become shallower. He even flinched once. This was definitely working.

Tea licked the line of hair beneath his navel. He smelled so good. She partially held herself up by the elbows so she could unfasten his belt. She fumbled with the button a little bit when she felt how hard he just got beneath the denim. The zipper opened slowly, and she heard him exhale. She cupped her hand around his erection through his boxer briefs. Her eyes enlarged when she felt how thick it was. She managed to pull it through the opening of the fabric and the sensation of her skin on his made him grow even more. She squeezed it softly, then moved her hand from tip to base. She let it rest on her cheek. Miles was holding on to the back and arm of the couch.

Tea slowly pulled his boxers back together and zipped his jeans partly. She slid her body upwards and laid her head beneath his chin. She felt his hand on her back, rubbing hard, small circles.

"You're teasing me," he managed to say once he got control of his vocal cords again.

"Turn the TV off," Tea said, looking at the screen.

Miles reached for the remote and clicked the power off. Tea inched up a little more and touched her lips to his. She kissed him passionately and could feel her body succumbing to his strong hands. He lifted her slightly so he could sit up and allow her to straddle him on the couch. She ran her hands through his hair and let her mouth make love to his. A vice couldn't remove her from his lips. She felt her toes curling as he moved his hands across her butt and along her legs. She wanted to take off her pants and his jeans so she could feel his skin. Finally, Tea lifted her head from his and caught her breath.

"You...taste so good," she said, panting as she kissed him again.

"Let's go upstairs," Miles whispered into her mouth.

Miles softly closed the bedroom door behind him. He watched Tea as she walked to her speaker and cued a playlist from her phone. This amused him, but he kept his smile to himself. He'd never made love to music. But with Tea, everything felt new. She probably wanted this to be perfect and had already envisioned how the scene would play out. He wanted everything to be just right for her.

He removed his shirt and let it fall to the floor. His jeans followed as she turned shyly away from him to lift her top over her head. He watched as she unfastened and removed her bra. The sight of her nude breasts when she turned around made his boxers grow even more. On her frame, her full-sized D cups looked humongous. She removed her pants and looked at the floor. He licked his lips, admiring the way her lavender panties looked against her skin and hugged her hips. She climbed onto her bed as the neo-soul ballad came through the speaker.

Miles placed his condom on the nightstand, turned on the bedside lamp and turned off the overhead light. There was a definite ambiance being set and it made him even hornier. He wanted to express so much to her. He gently laid her back onto the pillows, his mouth finding her neck. Tea lifted her chin so he could navigate. Miles wanted to taste every inch of her. His hands found her round flesh and his face was lost between her breasts. Tea watched as he licked and sucked her hard nipples. She moaned in pleasure, grabbing handfuls of his hair, and getting lost in the sounds that filled the room.

After a few minutes of his mouth sucking every surface of her breasts, Miles started to move back up to the side of her neck. Tea let out a sound.

"No, don't stop," she requested softly, nudging him back down and offering her nipples to him again. He eagerly obliged and quickly covered them with his dripping mouth. Her whimpers made him hungrier, and his mouth pleasured her for the next ten minutes.

Finally, he made his way back to her neck. He sniffed her skin.

"Damn, baby, your smell turns me on," he whispered, then sucked on her earlobe.

Tea moaned again and rubbed his back. His skin felt like warm butter beneath her hands. She massaged his shoulder blades, feeling his muscles relax. Her hands slid down both sides of his spine and back up to his blades. His body weight on top of her made her back arch and her legs instinctively spread beneath him. She enjoyed the warmth of his breath against her skin and the heat between her legs from his body.

Miles grunted as his mouth moved to her throat, then to her other earlobe. He pressed his lower body onto hers and had to pause his movements when he felt Tea's wetness through their clothes.

"Shit," he whispered, and sucked air through his teeth. With his right hand, he reached down and rubbed her moist panties. Tea's fingers climbed his neck and landed in his hair.

"Yessss," she moaned.

Miles slid the fabric aside and slowly pushed a finger inside. He felt Tea's body arch beneath him again, and his mouth moved to hers. Tea hungrily kissed him back and moaned louder as he slid in another finger. They moved in a strong rhythm, his fingers dancing slowly and deeper.

When he started to pull his fingers out, Tea moaned. "No," she whispered into his mouth and reached down to put them back in.

Miles smiled against her lips and followed orders. He felt her excitement all over his fingers. A few minutes passed and when he slid them out again, he pulled away from their kiss. He put his wet fingers into his mouth, sucking each one dry as he looked into her eyes. Tea bit her lips, watching him and gently caressing the side of his face.

He smiled again, then moved his body down hers. His mouth ended at the top of her panties. Tea pulled at the sheets, not sure what was coming next.

Miles saw her hands grabbing the bed. "Just relax, baby. Trust me, okay?" Miles said over the soft music.

Tea nodded but didn't feel her body relax at all. She hated that she felt like such a virgin and a prude.

He used his fingers to pull her soaked panties down to her ankles, then off her feet. He maneuvered his own briefs off, then reached across to the nightstand. Tea watched as he sat back on his heels and slid the condom on. She gulped when he placed her leg over his shoulder.

Miles loved how her body made his feel so big. He kissed her calf, her heel, then back down her calf and massaged it as his mouth sucked on her soft skin. He glanced down and noticed her eyes were closed and she had the comforter in a death grip. He lowered her leg and crawled back on top of her.

"Baby," he said twice until she pried her eyes open.

"Sorry," she said quietly.

"Do you want to stop?"

Tea shook her head.

"When you want to stop, will you tell me?" Miles asked, his eyes focused on hers.

She nodded. "I will."

"Okay," he said, gently kissing her lips, then her chin.

Miles spread her legs slowly with his. Just feeling the softness of her inner thighs made him delirious. He raised her hips and Tea's legs fell open wider. He teased around her entrance, then began to push inside.

Tea moaned at how incredible it felt. She knew she was already overflowing like the Mississippi, and she didn't care. When he pushed a little harder, though, she tensed up.

"I'm halfway in, baby. You're so damn tight," he mumbled into her hair.

He gritted his teeth. It was taking all he had not to pound away and have her muscles squeeze him to ecstasy. He pushed harder. Tea's nails were deep into his back, and he could feel her teeth on his shoulder. She was groaning above the sounds of the music.

Her fragrance was mixing with his and Miles couldn't stand it anymore. He pushed as hard as he could, then froze. He wanted to give her time to adjust. Tea let out a loud shriek that he hoped was more pleasure than pain.

"It's okay, it's okay," he heard himself say into her ear. He pulled out slowly while her muscles and flesh stretched with every centimeter.

Tea grabbed onto his lower back to keep him inside of her. Miles pushed back deeper, and he held on to her shoulders to keep her from scooting back to the headboard. He kept a slow rhythm to pace himself. He didn't think he'd be so close to climaxing already, but Tea was the most amazing woman he'd ever made love to. He lifted his head to look at her beautiful face. She was biting the hell out of her bottom lip and wincing each time he moved deeper.

She managed a half-smile at him and affectionately rubbed the back of his sweaty neck to let him know she was okay. Miles knew he was in love. He didn't dare say it in this moment, since he knew that could be easily dismissed as lust. There was a strong sensation in his groin, and he was going to have an orgasm any second. He tried to hold it a little longer by burying his face into her neck.

"Oh my God, Miiiiiiiles," Tea screamed, and she spread her legs open as far as they could go. He pumped faster as he held onto the bed next to her. He would have bet money that he was hitting her lungs, he was so far inside of her. There was no mistaking she was about to come. Her muscles twitched all along his shaft now. Tea's hands found her own breasts and she grabbed at them until she felt herself shaking beneath him. She moaned through clenched teeth and let the tremors move through her body. Miles grunted and sucked on her neck as he felt his own climax take over. They were both panting as he pulled out and removed the full condom. He let out a long, drawn-out groan.

"Damn." He leaned back down to kiss her tired, open mouth. "You okay?"

She nodded. "Yeah."

He fell to her side and wrapped a leg around her as he pulled her body to his. "That was beautiful. *You* are beautiful." He kissed her forehead and wiped her sweat-drenched bangs from her eyes, then kissed her eyebrows.

Tea held onto him tightly.

A 90's boy band song started to play from the speaker.

"No." Miles pulled back and looked at her.

"What?" Tea smiled.

"No, we are not listening to this after we just made love."

"But I love them," Tea gushed, hugging him closely again.

Miles laughed and ran his hands through her hair.

When the song went off and a slow jam ballad came on, Tea excused herself and went to the bathroom to take a shower. She was a little sore and told him not to look while she walked, but she knew he would. When she closed the bathroom door and turned on the shower head, she sat on the edge of the tub. Her hands were shaking, and she used them both to cover her mouth. She couldn't believe what they'd just done. They made love. And she didn't crumble and fall apart.

Miles was definitely the one.

Chapter 28

Mara sang along to her playlist. Her calf muscles were pounding away on the elliptical. She gripped the bars, sweat dripping from her neck and face onto her shirt. She checked the digital numbers again. Forty-seven minutes. She knew she could hang for sixty, no problem. The queasiness she'd felt on and off all day was starting to surface again. She pounded harder against the pedals. Now she was panting harder and singing louder along with the catchy song in her ears. She noticed the woman on the machine next to her was staring at her in the mirror. Mara changed the next line in the song to "What the hell are you looking at?" loud enough for the woman to get the point.

Fifty-nine. Sixty. Mara turned the machine off and as the pedals slowly stopped moving, she jumped off, grabbed her towel, and wiped her face. She tapped the earpiece and stopped the music from blasting in her ears. The gym had become much busier in the last half hour and a few people had begun to line up for the stationary bikes. Mara muttered expletives to herself. She wasn't in the mood to wait in line. She felt incredibly too fat and too amped up to be standing around waiting.

The weight room was packed, too, and Mara wondered if everybody in the county worked out on Monday nights. There weren't too many people on the indoor track, so Mara rolled her eyes and decided to jog a couple of miles. When she finished, there was a free quad machine, so she dashed to it. After fifteen minutes of leg extensions, she threw her towel over her shoulder. It was time to call it a night.

On her way to the front door, she noticed one of her sneakers had come untied. She squatted to tie it and didn't notice the man who'd spotted her first. His back was turned as he feigned interest in a brochure stand.

Mara stood and scanned her card at the reader on the counter. At least Pierre wasn't here to gawk at her tonight. The way she was feeling, she would really have lost her temper and said something meaner than usual.

When Mara left the gym, Drew turned back around in time to watch her walk to her car and drive away. He was glad she didn't notice his truck parked a few rows down.

Mara didn't bother checking the clock on her dashboard. It still needed to be fixed. She picked up her phone from the passenger seat and decided she could make it to the drugstore before they closed at ten. As she drove, she figured a bag of chips would burn off pretty fast after a workout like the one she just had.

"Mmm, and so would a honey bun," she said to herself as she parked. "And a bottle of soda would practically metabolize before it even reached my stomach."

Convincing herself that the extra calories weren't too counterproductive, and knowing her own arguments were weak as hell, she dragged her suddenly sore legs out of her car. She picked up the snacks she wanted plus the other items she needed. On her way home, she was lost in deep thought.

Miles dried off and put on the same clothes he'd taken off forty minutes ago. He tossed the towel into Tea's hamper and made her bed. When she came out of the shower earlier, she almost broke her neck trying to get dressed and back downstairs. He tried to slow her down and talk to her, but all she did was throw him a clean towel and said, "The shower's all yours."

He walked down the steps and the sound of the blender puzzled him. He peeked into the kitchen and saw Tea standing in front of the counter, absently watching the pale pink liquid swish around the container. She turned when she heard the floor creak beneath his feet.

"Hey," she smiled faintly, then turned back around.

"Hey."

Miles walked behind her and massaged her shoulders. The citrus scent of her body wash was just as intoxicating as it was earlier. He could feel her tense muscles even through her thick, terrycloth robe.

"What'cha making, baby?"

"Um. Strawberry smoothies. You want one?" She maneuvered from his grasp and removed two glasses from the cupboard.

"Okay, sure." Miles took the hint and moved back a couple of steps.

Tea turned off the blender and poured the cold refreshments into the glasses. She turned and handed him one.

"Thank you," Miles said, his eyes on her.

Tea smiled another quick smile and they both took a few sips. Miles followed her into the dining room. He watched Tea as she watched him. He scooted his chair closer and held her hand.

"How do you feel?" he asked, focusing on her eyes again. Her eyes never lied.

"I feel...good." She looked down at her drink. He would've missed her shrug if he wasn't looking for it.

"You hesitated."

"Well, I'm still kind of letting it sink in. There's a lot I'm thinking about."

"Like what?" Miles slowly let go of her hand to give her some space. "Talk to me."

Tea sipped some more and played with the edge of the placemat. The only light around them came from the kitchen and Miles' face looked painfully serious as half of it was drenched in shadows. Tea swallowed.

"It was –"

Keys jingled and Mara walked in, startled to see them sitting in the dining room.

"Hey, y'all," Mara said quietly. "Don't mind me, I'm going straight upstairs."

She tossed her keys on a small table near the door.

"Hey," Miles absently responded to her as she went up the stairs. His attention was still on Tea. He watched her eyes follow Mara and he knew she wanted to go talk to her about their first sexual encounter.

When they heard a door close at the top of the stairs, Tea pulled a foot underneath her body and tugged her thick robe tighter.

"It was what?" Miles urged her to finish her thought.

Tea looked him over. "It was different than it was with Jonathan."

Miles blinked and checked his reaction. He was quickly getting tired of being compared to that piece of shit.

"And that's a good thing...?" he asked.

She nodded. "A very good thing."

Miles reached up and held her face with one hand. He leaned in slowly and passionately kissed her. He pulled back and looked into her eyes, debating if now was the time to tell her he's fallen in love with her. *Not yet*, he told himself. She could still take it the wrong way.

Tea's loud yawn broke the silence.

"So, my kisses are already boring you?" he joked.

"I'm just tired. I need to go to bed, sweetie."

Sweetie. He loved how that sounded on her lips.

"Okay." He stood and she held his hand as they walked to the door.

Tea gave him a small kiss. "Call me when you get home."

He nodded and waved good-bye. She watched him until he drove away, then couldn't get upstairs fast enough.

She knocked on Mara's door, then heard the shower come on in the bathroom, so she ran to that door instead and knocked harder.

"Mara!"

The water stopped running. Tea heard some sounds, then banged on the door again.

"Okay, girl, dang." Mara yanked the door partially open.

"Dang, nothing, you can take your shower later." She pulled on Mara's arm, but Mara didn't move.

"No, I am funky as hell. I won't be long, I promise."

Tea crossed her arms and stomped her foot. "You can't come talk to me for a minute?" She glanced behind Mara at the sink, but Mara moved to block her view. She pushed the door closed a little more.

"What was that noise I heard?"

Mara made a face. "Nothing, Nosey! Goodness, girl." She closed the door, then talked through it. "I'll be out after my shower!"

Tea rolled her eyes and went back downstairs to wash her smoothie dishes. When she finished, she went to the den to straighten it up, and ended up watching the last part of a re-run playing on the television. She headed back upstairs and noticed Mara had come out of the bathroom. She knocked on her bedroom door.

"Hey, Mara, I'll just talk to you tomorrow. I'm going to bed."

There was a pause, then Mara answered through the door. "Okay, thanks, I mean okay."

Tea looked at the closed door, sighed, then went to climb into her own bed. Her phone rang as soon as she got comfortable.

"Hi, Miles," she answered sleepily.

"Hi, beautiful."

"You're just getting home?" Tea yawned.

"Yeah, picked up a number three on my way here. You know I gotta eat."

"We never got a chance to order any food, did we?" Tea pulled her comforter around her neck.

"Nah, but I wasn't hungry for that, anyway."

"Whatever...if you had to choose between a quarter pound burger or me tonight, which would you choose?" she asked.

There was a long pause.

"Miles!"

He laughed. "That's tough, though. Does it have cheese?"

"I'm hanging up."

He laughed again. "Oh, Si's having a cookout here next Saturday for his birthday. Plus, he said he has some news for everybody."

"All right, I'll tell Mara. I wonder what he has to tell us."

For the next ten minutes, they brainstormed the possibilities. He was marrying Teresa. He was officially breaking up with Teresa. He was trading in his truck. He got the new faculty position. He and Teresa were moving into their own place. Miles even speculated that Sirue wanted to call everybody together to let them know he was growing his hair out to loc it.

"Yeah, that is something he would do," Tea agreed. "Well, I'm gonna get some sleep. Early shop day tomorrow."

"Okay, I'll talk to you in the morning. Sweet dreams."

"You, too." She wanted to say she loved him, loved his company, loved his hugs, and loved his voice.

"Bye. I miss you."

Tea smiled. "You just saw me."

"And I miss you."

"You're so cute," Tea mused. "Bye, sweetie."

"Goodnight."

Tea ended the call and couldn't stop smiling until she fell asleep.

Chapter 29

Sirue hated Wednesdays. It was the day he taught two introductory biology classes. It was also his turn to re-stock all the biology labs. His lab assistants did the grunt work, but he resented that he had to be "available" in case they had questions. Not to mention the fact that the clean labs wouldn't directly benefit him, since all his lab days were on Tuesdays.

After two extra hours in his office, the walls were closing in. When the last assistant poked her head in the door and said goodnight, he was not far behind her. He dragged his energy-deficient body to the parking lot and found his truck. Almost too exhausted to push the ignition button, Sirue noticed two first-year professors walking to their cars. One he instantly recognized. Taylor Hughes, a chemistry professor and one of Sedrick's gossip partners, pointed him out a couple weeks ago as the newly hired biochemistry professor.

The morning she told him, he was in her office.

"No, Taylor, you're not serious." Sirue sat down across from her while she typed away on her laptop.

"Yes, I'm telling you, man. I even mentioned to Dr. Parsons that you were interested." Taylor stopped typing long enough to glance at him. "I think he went to Penn with his son."

Sirue rolled his eyes. "Assholes."

"You know Jesse from HR? Well, she told me they're looking to hire Dr. Parson's niece next semester, too."

"Let me guess...," Sirue looked blankly at her.

"Yep. Evolutionary Genetics."

"So, he's just trying to overrun the whole Natural Sciences wing of the university. I worked too hard for this shit. I busted my ass getting my doctorate so I could teach what I want to teach."

"Tell me about it. I have one more year 'til tenure, and I don't know if I can make it."

Sirue empathized for a few more minutes but got bored with Taylor's personal problems. He had his own professional ones. After hearing that news, then meeting with the Dean, he'd made his decision. Now, getting through these last few weeks of the semester was torture.

The two young professors in the parking lot noticed Sirue and waved. He returned a death glare and they hurried to their cars. Professor or not, he was still a big dangerous black thug to them all. He gritted his teeth and couldn't get his truck to Brooks Bar fast enough.

Three hours later, Sirue was staring at his dashboard. His truck was parked in what looked like a semi-deserted mega mart parking lot. He picked up his phone and dialed.

"Hey," Mara answered.

"Hey."

"It's ten thirty, bruh. What's up?"

"I'm drunk and don't know where the fuck I am." Sirue's dry voice was hardly audible.

Mara sighed. "Damn, Si. Hold on."

Sirue stared at the lamp post directly next to his window. He stared until the white light turned about four different colors then amalgamated back to one again. He watched as the moths danced circles around the lights and disrupted his line of vision. He wondered what moths tasted like. *Were all insects crunchy?* He could remember eating them as a little kid until his mother found out. She found him outside in her flower garden, picking ladybugs off the stems and putting them in his mouth like candy. She yelled, washed his mouth out with diluted floor cleaner, and smacked him so hard that he lost a tooth. Luckily, it wasn't a permanent one. Sirue tongued the spot in his mouth and could remember the copper taste of the salty blood.

"Hellooooo!" Mara shouted.

"Oh. Didn't um…I didn't really hear the bugs."

"Boy. You are tore *up*."

"I know. My life is tore up." Sirue's bass coupled with his low volume made his voice sound like a gravelly whisper.

"No, it's not," Mara said. "So, what happened today?"

There was silence.

"Si?"

"You remember when I used to call you…all the time from my dorm when I was fucked up? Nobody else…would know what to say. I think I got fucked up a lot. Fucked *uuuup*, fucked up."

"Hell, yeah, I remember. And stop trying to cuss just because your ass is drunk."

Sirue let out a sharp laugh. "Today. You asked about today."

"Yeah."

"Today I'll tell you about on Saturday. Happy fuckin' birthday to me."

"Tea told me about Saturday. Me and Drew will be there. I've been pressed for some of your potato salad. Make sure you have a separate bowl just for me."

"Where did you go?" Sirue asked quietly.

"Huh? When?"

"When you telled me…when you told me to hold on just now." Sirue's words were starting to slur, but he tried to maintain his grasp of the language. He was absently touching different buttons and knobs on his dashboard displays.

"I told Drew I'd call him back. See how I got off the phone with my man to talk to you?"

"Your man, your man. You need to watch your man."

There was a short pause. "Si, you're wasted."

"Nooo, no, hear me out, hear me out, hear me out. He's shady as fuuuuck. Probably has four other women right now –"

"Sirue."

"—that he's fucking." He looked back up at the lamp post.

"Sirue, shut up."

"Huh?" He scratched the back of his neck, totally confused.

"I'm about to hang up on your sorry ass. Do you need me to come get you or what?"

Sirue didn't answer. He stared straight ahead and chewed on the inside of his cheek.

Mara spoke slowly. "Do you need me to come and fucking get you?"

"It's the alcohol, Mara. I shouldn't have said that shit. I'm sorry." He closed his eyes, shaking his head.

"It's cool, Si."

"No, it's not. I'm sorry, Mara. I can't do shit right today. Fuck." He hit himself hard on the forehead twice.

"Si. I'm good, okay?"

He didn't answer.

"Where are you?" Mara asked.

"WorldMart."

Mara let out a quiet laugh. "Only your ass would drive drunk to a WorldMart."

"Mara, I really am sorry. Next time you see me, punch me in the jaw."

"Shut up."

"I'm serious. I won't even ask why. Punch me in the jaw then in the stomach."

"My fist would get lost in your jelly belly," she teased.

Sirue laughed. "Damn the fat jokes. It's muscle. And Teresa isn't complaining."

Mara made a vomiting sound. "She gonna be at the cookout? Can't you just tell her it's on Sunday?"

Sirue laughed again. "Okay, why is this wrinkled old lady pointing me out to the security guard? And now he's flashing his light on me."

"You're probably parked all crooked and shit with your hazards on. You better get out of there."

"Yeah." Sirue pushed the ignition. "I think I can get home from here...wait, where the hell is the exit?"

"All right, I did my AA counseling for the night. Be safe. Don't hit any black people."

Sirue chuckled.

"Now get off the phone so you can focus, okay?" Mara said, worry creeping into her tone.

"Oka—FUCK! Well move the hell out of my way, asshole!" Sirue honked out his frustration with the oncoming car.

"Sirue, go park. I'm coming to get you."

"I'm good. I promise."

Mara was quiet. "Call me when you get home or if you pull over, okay?"

"Will do."

"And stop drinking so damn much!"

Mara ended the call and Sirue tossed his phone on the passenger seat. As he drove onto the Beltway, he wondered how much vodka he had left in the wet bar at home.

Early Friday morning, Mara found herself unable to stay asleep. She reached over to look at her phone. It was too early to start getting ready for work, but too late to try to sleep again. Part of her wanted to catch Tea before she left for the salon because it was killing her to keep the news to herself. Another part of her was terrified. She sat up in bed, put her hand on her belly, and said a quick prayer before heading to the bathroom.

After brushing her teeth and washing her face, Mara opened the bathroom door. She could hear Tea moving around downstairs, so she took a breath and walked slowly down the steps, pulling her robe closed.

"You're up early," Tea said cheerfully when Mara turned the corner and headed towards the dining room. She was placing a plate of toast and a boiled egg on the table along with a mug of coffee. "You hungry?"

Mara shook her head. "Nah, just couldn't really sleep." She sat down across from her.

"Do you feel okay?" Tea asked, shaking pepper on to her egg.

Mara nodded. She watched her friend take a bite of her food and a sip of her coffee. Tea frowned at her.

"What's wrong?" she asked.

Mara blew out a breath and looked down at the table. *Now, never, or whatever.*

"I took three tests a few days ago. I'm pregnant, Tea."

Tea dropped the piece of toast she just lifted. Her eyes widened, then she covered her mouth. "How...like, oh my God, how do you feel?" Tea stammered.

Mara shrugged. "I'm okay, I guess. I don't know."

Tea looked her friend over. She pushed her chair back and went around the table to give her a hug. "Oh my God, Mara." She sat in the chair closest to her. "What did Drew say?"

"I finally told him last night. He had mixed feelings."

Tea tried to keep from making a face. "Mixed feelings?"

Mara noticed and shrugged again. "Yeah. He's probably just nervous. I am, too." She looked down at her hands. Tea reached over and rubbed her arm.

"What did he say?"

"Ummm...just that he'll be okay with whatever I want to do, but he doesn't really want a child right now." Mara glanced up at Tea.

Tea nodded slowly and bit her lips to keep from saying what she was thinking. Mara sighed.

"I know, I know...," she rolled her eyes upward. "We weren't careful, so that falls on both of us. I'm twenty-five, he's thirty. We should've known better. But I can't be upset with him for how he feels." She shook her head.

"Well, what do *you* want to do?"

"I want to keep my baby." She looked directly at Tea and her own eyes widened at her declaration. "*My baby?* Wow."

Tea smiled and hugged her best friend again.

Chapter 30

Sirue dropped the two heavy bags of charcoal next to the grill. He silently cursed Miles for being AWOL when he knew he needed him to straighten up the inside of the house. In his absence, Teresa was scrubbing away, preparing for the guests to arrive in a few hours.

He didn't mind having her here, really. Over the last week, her craziness subsided a little, and he didn't feel quite as upset as he normally did with her. Sirue inspected the inside of the grill and then glanced up at his bedroom window. He shielded his eyes from the sun and squinted to make sure his vision wasn't playing tricks. Teresa was standing in the window staring down at him. *How long had she been up there watching?* He slowly waved to her, and she waved back. She blew him a kiss and disappeared behind the window frame.

"What the hell?" Sirue asked himself and shook his head. He hoped he didn't think too soon about her moods improving.

Looking around the yard, he decided it needed much more work than he thought. He checked his watch and decided he could spend a maximum of one hour in the backyard if he wanted to stay on schedule. He got to work.

With ten minutes of his estimated time remaining, Sirue locked the leaf blower back into the shed. He managed to fill two large paper lawn bags and stood them up along his back fence out of the way. Giving the backyard a final onceover, he was pleased with its appearance. Chairs were placed in various locations, the long picnic table was covered, and his favorite yard accent piece – a red cedar lawn bench framed in wrought iron – was placed near the large oak tree. Sirue's glance lingered near the grill and remembered what was missing. He'd get Miles to grab the extra table from upstairs when he arrived...whenever that happened.

Sirue went up the deck steps and into the house and was taken aback by its cozy setting. There was easy jazz coming from all the speakers on the first floor. The sofas were rearranged to open up the space even more. There were scented candles lit everywhere, letting off a soothing cinnamon fragrance. Festive streamers were hung throughout the living room area, Teresa even had white helium-filled balloons around the space, suspended by weights.

An instrumental version of a soulful song played from the speakers and Sirue followed the sound of Teresa's voice singing along. She was in the kitchen preparing what looked like a fruit bowl. Sirue stood in the entryway and stared at her. She was wearing a short black shawl over black jeans and had her hair pinned into a tight bun. He looked back down at her ass and felt the blood rushing south as he walked towards her and sniffed the back of her neck.

"You're gonna get me all dirty," she said, reaching behind her and resting her hand on the side of his face.

He took a long whiff of her skin and lightly sucked her neck. "Mmmmmm," he moaned.

She smiled and resumed singing as she rinsed the strawberries.

Sirue knew he was smelly and didn't want to get his sweat on her. He leaned back against the counter and checked out the food she'd prepared on the stove.

"You went all out for this huh?" He lifted the foil from one of the glass dishes and saw the thick baked beans.

"Well, this is a big deal." She turned to face him. "It's your birthday. Plus, you're about to tell the people you love the biggest news you've had to tell them. I'm happy for you and for us."

Sirue took a step forward and kissed her. "Me, too. I guess I need to get ready."

"Yeah, it's late, they'll start coming soon. And I still want to put some decorations out back." She nudged him out of the kitchen.

"I'm going, I'm going...," he grabbed two strawberries on his way out and she lightly slapped his arm.

"Go!"

Sirue chuckled and took off his shirt as he made a right and headed upstairs.

"Oh, honey, I have your outfit on the bed. I decided on the dark blue sweater instead of the cream shirt since you'll be on the grill," she called up to him.

"Okay," he replied back down and thought he could really get used to this. Maybe it wasn't such a bad idea after all.

About an hour later, Teresa saw the blue four-door sporty sedan trying to squeeze into the driveway behind her car.

"Honey! Sedrick's here," she called to Sirue who was putting on his apron and heading to the backyard with his grill utensils.

"Here, I'll take these out back and you can get the door," she said.

Sirue thanked her and headed out the front door. He heard Sedrick's wife, Rita, before he saw her get out of the passenger's side.

"See, that's what I'm talking about – why couldn't you just park on the street?" She emerged, holding a large plastic container and noticed Sirue on the porch laughing at his henpecked friend.

"You got energy to laugh, you got energy to come and get this food from me," she said to Sirue as she closed her door.

"I was going to carry it, sweetcakes," Sedrick said with frustration. He grabbed two twelve-packs and two six-bottle cases of beer from the backseat.

"Yeah, but you didn't." She handed the food over to Sirue. "Hey, Sirue. How have you been?"

They greeted each other with kisses on the cheeks.

"I'm good, Rita, what about you? How's the internship in Baltimore?"

They headed back towards the house with Rita leading the way.

"Oh, it's finally over. I was actually hired at a dental practice in Bethesda."

"Wow, Sed, you never told me that."

Sedrick shrugged and closed the front door behind them as they all stepped into the house.

"Why am I not surprised?" Rita asked condescendingly, looking at her husband.

"Not now, sweetcakes, not now."

Rita rolled her eyes and put down her hobo crème designer handbag. She nodded at the bowl in Sirue's hand. "Those are the ribs I told you I would bring. They're marinated and ready to go on the fire."

"Mmm. Nothing like Rita's ribs." Sirue licked his lips. "Sed, I made room in the freezer for some of those drinks. There's a cooler on the deck for the rest. And you know anything leftover stays with the host."

Sedrick laughed and headed to the kitchen.

"Come on, Rita, I don't think you ever met Teresa."

They walked onto the small back patio and down the steps. Teresa looked up from poking the charcoal. She put the stick down and smoothed her hands on her jeans as they approached.

"Hi, I'm Rita. You must be Teresa. Nice to meet you."

She firmly shook Teresa's hand and Teresa was immediately on guard. She quickly assessed Rita's appearance. Her frosted flipped curls were very hip and professional, and they showed off the dangling diamond earrings. Her body was voluptuous, and her pink cashmere short-sleeved sweater hugged everything in place. She was wearing matching pale pink slacks with open toed slip-ons. Teresa's insecure gaze was nothing but obvious when she frowned at the coordinating finger and toenail polish.

Yeah, Sirue definitely had sex with her, Teresa thought. If not, then he wanted to.

"Nice to meet you, too," she lied. She'd have to stick like glue to Sirue. No question.

Sirue put the container of ribs next to the grill and adjusted his apron. Teresa's eyes were on him. She knew he was probably trying to hide an erection.

"Baby, can you go ask Sedrick to bring me the tray of sauces I have on the counter? Plus, I'm not sure when Miles will get here, so Sed can grab the card table in the hall closet upstairs."

Teresa was clearly torn between leaving them alone and going inside for what might be a few minutes. She nervously rubbed her hands together.

"Sure," she hesitated and stepped closer to his side. "But not without a big kiss from you first."

Rita rolled her eyes and sat down in a nearby plastic chair.

Sirue put a hand on the small of her back. He sensed what she was feeling.

In a whisper he warned, "Teresa…"

"I just want a kiss," she desperately hissed back at him. "What? You can't kiss me in front of your friend?"

"Baby, don't do this right now."

"Don't do what –"

"We had a perfect day so far, don't ruin it with your jealousy. Again." He looked hard into her eyes.

Teresa's face tightened and Sirue had never seen her that angry. The veins in her forehead were prominent and her lips were pursed. He couldn't believe this was happening.

"That's the meanest thing you ever said to me," she strained to whisper. "I ask you for a kiss and you call me jealous? Jealous of what? Is there something I should be jealous about?"

"No, there's not." He shook his head in disbelief and removed his hand from her back.

Teresa folded her arms and stared at the glowing charcoal. Sirue ran his hand over his face then turned to look at her again. He spoke slowly and deliberately, trying to maintain his composure.

"Will you please go ask Sedrick to get the sauces and the table?"

"I'm not doing shit," she said without looking at him. She went to sit a few chairs down from Rita.

"Fine," Sirue snapped and flipped a pair of tongs from the grill, and they were airborne until they clanked to the ground. He stormed the few feet to the steps and into the house. The sliding door slammed closed behind him, causing both women to jump.

Rita caught Teresa's gaze long enough to give her a disapproving look and went back to scrolling on her phone.

Chapter 31

Inside, Sirue took a bottle of beer from Sedrick's hand as he put the last of the bottles strategically into the freezer. He popped it open and fell into the armchair in the living room. Sedrick followed him and watched him down the entire beverage without stopping for air.

Sirue wiped his mouth and rested his elbows on his knees, dangling the empty bottle with one hand.

"What's up, man?"

Sirue shook his head. He didn't want to get into it. All he wanted was for the taste of the alcohol to soothe his unrest. To bring him some calm. To remind him why he even continues to deal with her. He closed his eyes as if in meditation and slowly tapped his foot.

"Well, by the way you punished that beer, I'd say it was Teresa-related, so I'll leave you to your thoughts, brother." He stopped in the kitchen, grabbed a couple of sodas for the ladies and headed outside.

Sirue was still in deep thought five minutes later when Tea and Miles walked through the front door laughing.

"Whatever," Tea was saying, "you did not say that to Old Mrs. Crawford!"

"I mean, c'mon, how can she not try to push up on this?" Miles retorted. They stopped cold when they saw Sirue leaning over in the chair.

"Hey, Si," Tea said warily as she walked over to him.

He opened his eyes and slowly gave her a weak smile. Tea put her hand on his head and bent down to give him a kiss on the cheek, then felt his forehead.

"Do you feel okay? You got a headache or something?"

He nodded. "Yeah, and she's out back."

Tea hit his shoulder and sucked her teeth. She saw the empty bottle in his hand and took it into the kitchen for him. Miles put the huge, wrapped present that he carried in next to the sofa, out of the way.

"Come on, man. Cheer up!" Miles clapped his hands. "You got food to make and news to tell us."

Sirue smiled weakly again.

"Yeah, I'm dying to know," Tea added, walking back into the living room.

"Come on," Miles repeated. He moved over to Sirue and gave him a few encouraging pats on the back. "Stop moping. Tell me what you need me to do around here."

Sirue looked up at him and made a face. "Well, if your ass was here on time, I wouldn't have had so much shit to do."

Miles laughed. "There we go. Sirue's back!" He held out a hand to help him up.

Sirue shoved his hand away and stood on his own. He looked at Miles who thought for a second that he might really be upset. Then, Sirue broke into a smirk, and they gave each other pounds and half-hugs.

"Hey, I do need you to get that card table from upstairs, though."

"No prob." Miles jogged upstairs singing. "Guess who's back? Back again? Moody's back! Tell a friend…"

"That's your boy," Sirue said to Tea.

"And I'm gonna stick beside him," she chuckled and followed him into the kitchen. "So, give me a heads up on the news. Good news or bad?" She opened the refrigerator and retrieved a can of orange soda.

"Definitely good news." He thought for a second. "Maybe a little of both, though. But there's a bowl of fruit in there, I'll carry that. Can you handle the platter of chips and dip?"

She nodded. He grabbed the tray of sauces as well as the fruit bowl and they went outside. They walked to the bench on the side of the yard and put everything down. Tea noticed familiar faces.

"Hey, Teresa. Hi, Sedrick –"

Rita stood when she looked up from her phone and heard Tea's voice.

"Tea!" she smiled.

"Rita! Hey, girl!"

Rita carefully made her way through the grass over to the picnic table and gave Tea a big hug.

"I haven't seen you in months, Miss Lady! How's the shop?"

"Oh, it's fine. Great, really. I have a student working there part time to help me and DeeDee out. I'm still waiting to see your face in my booth. Your hair looks great, by the way," Tea said, admiring Rita's big bouncy curls.

"Thank you, but I know you would've made me look extra fierce," Rita smiled.

They sat at the bench and caught up with each other's lives. This was only their fifth time meeting, but when Sirue introduced them all two years ago, Rita instantly hit it off with Tea and Mara. She was professional, down to earth, and always spoke her mind with tact. Miles came out with the table and set it up for Sirue near the grill, then said his hellos to everyone. He walked over to the bench, hugged Rita hello, then moved to Tea and whispered something in her ear that made her smile, then kissed her on the cheek and headed back to the grill area.

Rita couldn't help grinning. "Well, well, well. I heard you two were an item, but I had no idea you were still in the cute lovey stages."

Tea blushed but tried to hide her embarrassment by picking some fruit from the bowl and onto a plate. "You heard about us, too?"

"Girl, if Miles could have posted it on the announcement board in Ben's Chili Bowl, I'm sure he would have according to Sirue." Rita took a grape from Tea's plate. "But that's okay, it just means he's proud of what you two have. I think it's sweet."

"Yeah," Tea agreed. She glanced over at her man, who already had everyone in stitches and was quickly becoming the life of the party. "It doesn't hurt that's he's fine as hell, either."

"Girl, you ain't lyin'! Right here," Rita held up her hand and Tea gave her a high five.

After about twenty minutes, the aroma from the barbeque started to drift its way over to the picnic bench and everyone could feel their stomachs growling. Miles, Sedrick, Rita, and Tea began a serious game of spades –

couple versus couple – while Teresa continued to sulk in a chair next to the grill. Her legs and arms were crossed, and she swung her foot furiously, staring at the grass.

Sirue was humming to the music coming from the speaker on the patio. He turned over the half smokes and lifted the ribs to see how they were coming along.

"Psst, psst," he called to Teresa. She didn't respond.

Sirue sighed and closed the lid over the grate. He wiped his hands on his apron and stood in front of her chair. He leaned down towards her, placing his hands on the armrests.

His face was so close to hers that their noses were touching.

"I'm sorry I called you jealous."

Teresa still didn't budge.

"You can't stay mad all day," he said softly and pecked her lips twice.

She unfolded her arms and put her hands on both sides of his face. She opened her mouth, parting his lips with her tongue. Sirue felt her intensity and matched it with his own.

"So, this is why nobody can open the front door – y'all are out here playing cards and kissy face!" Mara yelled over the music and the chatter. She and Drew emerged from around the side of the house.

"Hey Mara! Hey Drew!" Everyone from the spades table greeted them.

Sirue finished his kiss and stood up, turning around.

"It's about damn time," he called over to them, and Drew walked over to give him daps.

"What's up, chef?" Drew asked, peeking under the lid of the grill.

"Same ole, same ole. You met Teresa, right?"

Drew nodded and said hello, shaking her hand.

"Let me introduce you to my colleague and his wife," Sirue said, leading him to the bench where Mara was already headed.

Teresa felt completely left out as she watched them all joke around together. She folded her arms again, and intensely scrutinized Sirue's interactions with Mara and Rita. She couldn't wait until he told them the news. Then they'd see who was laughing.

Sirue walked closer to Mara and bent down to give her a hug. When he pulled away, she held his hand in an arm wrestle grip.

"Hey, I owe you a punch in the jaw, remember?" she whispered.

Sirue lifted his head to expose his jaw. He tapped it with his free hand, encouraging her to hit him. She playfully pushed him away and he squeezed her hand before letting it go.

"You just better have my potato salad, sir."

"I got you. Your rice is in there, too. But what took y'all so long to get here?" he asked, directing his question to Mara.

"We're not even that late, stop trippin'." Mara looked over at Drew who was sitting next to her. "Babe, can you go get my jacket from the car? I told you it was gonna be cold."

"It's not that cold out here, you'll be all right," Drew said dismissively, watching the cards being played. He reached for some chips.

Mara sucked her teeth. Miles held a long glance at Drew and Tea caught his glare.

"Go, Miles. Your turn," she said, trying to get his attention. Miles looked back down at his cards.

Sirue also heard the exchange and clapped his hands together. "Well, back to the food."

"How much longer? I'm starving," Rita asked.

"Patience, patience, can't rush the chef," Sirue called back over his shoulder.

"Yeah, whatever, just *rush* back over there and finish cooking," Mara quipped.

Everyone laughed and he gave them all the middle finger.

Chapter 32

"You are looking so healthy," Rita commented to Mara when the game was over and the women, minus Teresa, went inside.

Mara and Rita were on the sofa, and Tea had her legs drawn under her in the cushioned oversized armchair.

"In other words, I'm fat," Mara pouted.

"No! You know I didn't mean that," she playfully hit her arm. "You are nowhere near fat. Look at me in my size eighteen."

"Shut up, you are not an eighteen. You don't look it at all," Tea said.

Rita nodded. "Yep, when I met Sedrick, I was a loose ten, now both of us have gained weight. Don't worry, it'll happen to you, too."

Tea rubbed her stomach, realizing that she and Miles would be in the same boat, eventually. He loved to eat, and she loved to cook. Deep down, she really didn't care, though. Some extra happy weight wouldn't be a bad thing.

Mara debated whether to share her pregnancy news with Rita. She decided against it. Miles and Si should be told next before anyone outside of their circle.

"Well, you are working your eighteen. It looks good on you," Mara said.

"Thank you, sis," Rita smiled. "Hell, Sedrick doesn't complain, why should I? He likes holding on to all this padding." She patted her rear end.

"Yeah, Drew says that about the junk in my trunk, too," Mara half-smiled. "Guys like having something to grab."

Tea suddenly remembered overhearing them in the kitchen back in Mara's old apartment. She recalled the way Mara commented on Tea's smaller frame and the way they seemed to laugh at her expense.

She shook the memory away when Teresa opened the back screen door, saw them sitting there, then changed her mind and headed back outside in a hurry.

"What is up with that one?" Rita asked.

Mara shrugged. "I don't know. I've been asking Si that forever."

Rita recounted the events that occurred before everyone arrived. She explained how Teresa became instantly jealous at the sight of her.

"Girl, she's like that with everybody. Thinks all women are out to steal her man," Mara said. "Well, except for Tea. She likes Tea for some reason."

"Well, damn, thanks." Tea rolled her eyes.

"You know what I meant, boo."

Tea nodded. "I think it's because Si told her once that he's not attracted to smaller women. Isn't that crazy?"

"She is crazy personified," Rita agreed. "Definitely something wrong with her. I just might have to tell her about herself today. You know, in a sisterly way."

"Good luck with that," Tea said.

Mara shrugged her shoulders in apathy. She couldn't care less if Teresa ever got the stick out of her ass.

Rita stood and stretched. She walked over to a shelf of photos that stood by the door.

"Aw, Tea, this one of you and Miles is so adorable," she gushed, holding the silver-framed photograph.

"Thank you," Tea smiled.

"And, um...y'all notice how Teresa is in all of these photos with Sirue?"

Mara said, "Yeah. I think Si likes for his women to be obsessed with him. Definitely a complex his mother gave him."

Tea shot a glance at her and thought for a second. She recalled the stories Sirue told them one night when he'd had too much to drink about a year ago. The subject of mothers came up and he just lost it. He disclosed the physical abuse he endured and her mental illness that caused her to ignore him for days at a time. When he was ten, she even picked him up from school early wearing a nightgown just to make him go back home and clean the kitchen that *she* dirtied up that morning, then spanked him before taking him back to school. By the end of that evening, after they all heard about his trauma, there wasn't a dry eye left.

"You know what – I think you're probably right. Mothers can do some serious harm to their sons' sense of worth," Tea commented vaguely, not wanting to divulge Sirue's secrets to Rita.

Mara looked at her knowingly and nodded.

Rita glanced over the photos again. "So, when his women are making him the center of their worlds, he sees it as comforting."

"Facts," Mara added. "And can't nobody be more pressed for him than high yellow out there."

Tea nodded, feeling emotional. "I guess all of us have some kind of complex."

Rita put her hands on her hips and shook her head. "Damn shame."

She walked around the living room, admiring the décor. She passed by the back sliding door and her jaw dropped.

"Ladies, if we plan on eating, we'd better haul ass. They started without us!"

Mara and Tea followed Rita down the steps. Miles, Sedrick, Sirue, Drew, and Teresa were all at the tables, their faces buried in ribs and hamburgers.

Rita stood behind Sedrick and hit him on the back of his head. She took the hamburger from his hands before he could take a bite of it.

"You know I'm hungry. You couldn't come get us?" she scolded him as she sat beside him at the bench.

"We sent Teresa to get you," Miles said through a mouthful of beans.

Tea looked down at him in disgust, while Mara went and sat across from Drew at the other end of the table, helping herself to potato salad and rice.

Miles swallowed, then took Tea's hand. He gently pulled her down next to him.

"Here, sit down. I'll get your plate."

She rolled her eyes and squeezed onto the end of the bench. He got up and fixed her a healthy plate of ribs, a hamburger, baked beans and a few deviled eggs. He put it in front of her and sat back down, sliding his arm around her waist.

"I'm sorry," he whispered into her ear.

"No, you're not. Breath smelling like pork," she smiled back at him.

"I am," Miles grinned and pulled her a little closer to him. He leaned to her as if about to whisper a secret in her ear, but instead he kissed the skin right beneath her earlobe. He pecked there again when he felt her jump.

Tea could feel his goatee and although it tickled, it started to turn her on. She pulled her head teasingly away as her hand found his thigh under the table.

Mara was witnessing their exchange from the other end of the bench. Her heart felt like it jumped a beat as jealousy crept its way in. She wanted to kick Drew for not showing her half the affection Miles showed Tea. She glared across the table at him as he shoved a spoonful of beans and potato salad into his mouth. And here she was, fixing her own plate, pregnant, and all the other couples couldn't get enough of each other. Next to her, Rita was quietly telling Sedrick something about their plans for later on that evening and Sedrick was hanging on her every syllable. As much as they argued, there was so much love between them. And next to them, Sirue and Teresa were giggling across the table at each other. Even Crazy had someone showing her attention. Drew hadn't said one word to her since she sat down. He was focused on his plate and his phone.

Mara could feel her eyes starting to sting with tears and she tried to hide her face with her hand as she chewed. She knew she never cried this easily and wondered how bad her hormones would get in a few months.

"It's good, huh?" Drew finally asked her as he put his phone face down and heaved more potato salad onto his plate.

Mara nodded. She played around with the rest of the food in front of her. He used to be so attuned to her every mood. Why was it so fucking hard for him to read her emotions now? He could see good and well that she was fighting back tears. A child could see it.

Mara cleared her throat. "I'll be back."

She stood and walked back inside the house. Tea was eating, but turned her head when Mara walked past her. Her eyes lingered after she disappeared inside because she couldn't decide if Mara was upset or not. Miles followed Tea's glance, then looked back at her.

"She okay?" he asked.

Tea shrugged and thought to herself that if she didn't come back out soon, she'd go check on her. When she turned back around, Miles was helping himself to a deviled egg from her plate.

She sucked her teeth. "You have the whole tray full of them over there, why would you take mine?"

"'Cause those are waaaay over there. Yours are right here." He deliberately ate it in her face, and she hit him with the side of her arm.

After a few minutes, everyone started to talk more and eat less. Mara came back outside, and Tea grabbed her hand as she walked by. She gave her a questioning look.

Mara bent down to hug her. "I'm cool."

She walked back to her seat at the end of the bench and kicked Drew in the shin. "Are you still eating?"

He nodded and took a long sip from his can of beer. "See, if I had somebody cooking for me like this all the time, I wouldn't be so hungry."

Mara's jaw dropped.

Sedrick and Teresa laughed. Rita looked at Drew like he lost his mind. "You do. Your mother."

Mara co-signed. "Yeah, as much as she calls you, why don't you just ask her to bring you meals, too?"

Drew held up his hand. "Whoa, whoa, didn't mean to call out the firing squad."

"Right, can't a man complain about food without his woman catching feelings?" Sedrick asked.

"I know you didn't just ask that," Rita said, cutting her eyes to him.

"Mmmhmm, trying to jump all in the conversation while everybody was laughin'," Tea added. "You ain't slick, Sed."

"Do you have any complaints about my food, Sirue?" Teresa asked.

She knew he loved her cooking, in the kitchen and the bedroom. But she wanted to make it known.

Sirue was finishing a bite. "No," he said quietly with a full mouth.

"Uh, what was that, man? We couldn't hear you," Miles teased.

"I said NO," then to Teresa. "No, baby, I don't. No complaints."

Mara rolled her eyes.

"Damn, I'm still hungry," Miles said rubbing his stomach. "Si, hand me some of those WHIPPED eggs over there."

Everyone started laughing and then a 70s television show theme song chimed from Drew's phone.

"Oooh, that was my show," Rita said, and started talking about her favorite episodes.

Drew looked at his phone, then put it back in his pocket. Mara didn't say a word, but she wondered if it was his "mother" again.

Chapter 33

Thirty minutes of talking and some silliness went by, and Teresa, Sirue, Rita, Sedrick and Drew moved the chairs closer to the grill so they could catch what was left of the sunlight. Tea was laying her head on Miles' arm as they sat across from Mara on the picnic bench.

"So were y'all able to pick up a present for Si?" Tea asked.

"Yeah, just some gift cards to the bookstore and the appliance store. Nothing as big as that box I saw in the living room from y'all. Damn showoffs." Mara picked at the remaining fruit in the bowl.

"Girl, it's that robotics kit and VR headset he wanted," Tea shrugged.

"He literally sent me the link to buy them," Miles explained, drinking an iced tea. "But he'll love your gift cards, too."

Mara smiled. "Yeah, when were out today, Drew was trying to figure out why we were buying appliance gift cards for a man." She shook her head. "He actually asked me if Si used to be gay."

"*Used* to be gay?" Tea asked. "Because of appliances? That doesn't make any sense."

"How can someone formerly be gay?" Miles said, his disgust with Drew compounding even more. "He really asked you that?"

Mara nodded. "I checked him, don't worry. Drew's just a real macho man and always ignorant about shit like that."

"Yeah, well it's usually the 'macho men' who are the first to be on the DL," Miles said angrily.

Tea lifted her head and looked up at him. "Miles, calm down."

Impulsive

"Yeah, I told you I checked him, damn." Mara wasn't in the mood, but she still wanted to pry. "You don't like him, do you?"

Miles shrugged. "I don't like some things he does. I'll leave it at that."

Tea sat up and sighed. "Y'all, c'mon, talk about it another time."

Mara held up her hand to Tea. "No, I'm not mad or anything," then to Miles, "it's just that I respect your opinion. I really want to know what you think."

"About what?"

"About him, about us."

Miles eyed her and started to talk, then suddenly stopped and picked up his drink. "Nope, you ain't setting me up."

Mara picked up a slice of an orange and threw it at him and he threw it back. Drew headed towards them, stretching and yawning.

"Babe, I'm so tired," he said, standing behind Mara and rubbing her shoulders. "You think you'll be ready to leave soon?"

Mara turned her head to look up at him. "No, we came to celebrate his birthday, we didn't even cut the cake yet."

Drew stopped rubbing her shoulders and dug his hands into his jeans pockets. He sat next to her on the bench with his back to Tea and Miles as he leaned against the table. He spoke in a very low whisper.

"Mara, I'm tired. It's getting late," he complained.

"We haven't even been here that long," Mara said softly. She knew Tea and Miles were pretending they didn't hear a thing but were listening to every syllable. She hoped Drew didn't cause a scene.

He rolled his neck back and forth. He looked at Mara with an indescribable gaze. She couldn't read his emotions, nor could she find the softness in his face that she used to love. He looked tired, all right. And bored. And unhappy with her. Or maybe she was reading too much into it. He did have a long week at work.

She leaned towards him slowly to peck his full lips. His kisses had a way of igniting dormant sparks in them both, and maybe this time it would work again.

Drew withdrew his head slightly when she was within an inch of him.

Mara was hurt and embarrassed. "I can't get a kiss?" she tried to whisper.

"I said I'm ready to go."

"All of a sudden, right?" Mara knew it had something to do with the phone call from earlier.

He snapped his head in her direction again. "What?!"

"You heard me," Mara said, her tone tense.

Drew leaned back against the table again. "That shit right there is gonna stop." He shot her a sharp look, then glanced back towards the grill.

Tea and Miles both looked at Drew then back at each other. Tea put her hand on top of Miles' hand to try to temper his anger.

"Shut up, Drew," Mara said quietly.

"Yeah, I'll shut up, but your ass is gonna be figuring out how to get home in a few minutes," he responded with another hard look at her.

Mara rubbed her temples and just looked down at the table. She mumbled to herself.

Drew rolled his eyes. "We're leaving after I get a drink," he said and left to go back into the house.

Mara bit both her lips and felt the sting of tears again. She could feel Miles glaring at her, probably wondering why she accepted such behavior from Drew. She could also feel Tea's eyes and knew she was wondering if she was okay. It was hard trying to live for everyone's emotions when she couldn't even understand her own.

"You all right, girl?" Tea asked.

Mara looked up and shrugged. "I'm gonna be all right. He's just being a big ass baby right now."

Miles drummed his fingers and stared off towards the house.

Tea knew it was more than him being a baby. It was more like a narcissistic power trip with him. "What's wrong? He didn't get his way?"

Mara sighed. "Pouting 'cause he's ready to go. Whatever." She pulled a few grapes from the bowl and played with them in her hands.

"You haven't even been here long," Tea mused.

Mara gave her a look of agreement and shrugged.

A few minutes of silence went by and each of them had deep thoughts running through their heads while they mindlessly observed the nature around them. Miles suddenly checked his watch and patted his stomach. He stood up.

"I'm gonna hit the bathroom, baby," he said and leaned down to kiss Tea on top of her head.

Tea watched him as he walked up the stairs and into the house. She knew he was upset and hoped he could control his impulses.

She stood up and walked around the table to sit next to Mara. She looped her arm inside of hers.

"I don't like how he talks to you," she said carefully.

Mara sighed and looked to the side, tears threatening to fall again.

"Feel like talking about it?" Tea asked her friend.

"No," she answered quietly.

Tea leaned her head on Mara's shoulder, and Mara leaned her head on top of hers. She knew Tea was probably going to force her to talk sooner rather than later.

Chapter 34

Miles could hear Drew before he saw him. He stood next to the entrance of the kitchen, trying to catch the conversation.

"Well, I could have told you that...," Drew laughed. "Are you going to be there, too? Yeah, of course she's here...yeah, she's trippin'...so maybe I should give you your own ringtone...okay, midnight, but you better be ready this time...," he laughed again.

Miles stepped into the kitchen and stood almost motionless. Drew was caught by surprise, but instantly tried to mask his shock.

"All right," he continued, his tone much different. "Okay. Yep...okay. Bye." He ended the call and met Miles' stare.

Miles cut his eyes and moved to the refrigerator and pulled a soda from the top shelf. He opened the can, took a long sip, and wiped his mouth. So much anger was boiling inside of him, it was hard to swallow.

Drew turned to head out. Miles' eyes followed him.

"A little too old to be playing games, don't you think?"

Drew stopped in his tracks. He whipped around. "What?"

Miles took another sip. "You heard me. I didn't stutter."

"Look, brother –"

"I'm not your brother." Miles calmly put the soda beside him on the counter.

"Well," Drew scratched his dreads. "What I *heard* was somebody minding business that isn't his."

Drew's body squared with his. There was still a four-foot gap that Miles wanted to close. He took a step forward.

"Mara *is* my business," Miles said.

"Wait, I thought Tea was your business."

Miles tensed up and his eyes narrowed. He took another step forward. Drew matched it.

He looked at Miles with a smug grin. "As a matter of fact, you might want to mind that business a little closer. If you were, maybe she wouldn't be sniffin' around me like a little dog."

Before Drew could blink, Miles' hand was around his throat, and he was leaning back against the counter. The dish drainer, along with some plates and glasses, crashed onto the floor and into the sink. His attempts to dislodge his hand were futile and he continued to struggle beneath him.

"Let...go...of...me, man," Drew tried to say, pulling at Miles' hand.

Miles' grip tightened with each word he spoke. "You need to keep her name out of your motherfuckin' mouth."

Drew managed one more bout of strength and with both of his hands, he was able to twist Miles' arm enough to loosen his hold. He shoved Miles hard against the other counter, causing him to lose his balance. In his attempt to keep from falling, Miles knocked a blender and the toaster to the floor yet moved in time to dodge Drew's punch.

Miles threw two of his own body shots to Drew's abdomen, then felt the sting of a hit to his jaw. He saw another one coming, ducked it, and made hard contact with the side of Drew's face.

Neither of them saw Tea standing in the entryway.

"What the hell?!" she screamed. She couldn't believe her eyes. "Miles! Drew!"

They were exchanging blows and she did not want to get between them. She ran back outside. By the time she returned with Sirue and Sedrick, the fight had migrated to the living room. Miles was on top of Drew, then Drew shoved him onto the coffee table. Miles retaliated by yanking him down by his shirt to the floor. They both landed punches as they scuffled around the floor. Miles started to pound his fists into Drew's face.

"Shit," Sirue said as he walked in on the scene. He was able to put his arms around Miles' torso and pull him back. Sedrick raced towards them and pushed Drew back away from Miles.

"Cool off, man," he warned Drew.

Drew held his hands up. "I'm good, man, I'm good."

Sirue turned Miles around and forcefully pushed him into the kitchen.

Just then, Mara, Teresa and Rita entered from outside. The men were pulled apart, but it was obvious what had gone down.

"Oh my God," Rita exclaimed.

Teresa's hand flew to her mouth.

Mara looked from Tea to Drew and then to Sirue and Miles in the kitchen.

"What the hell happened?" Mara asked to everyone around her.

Drew was straightening his clothes, still catching his breath. He wiped his bleeding mouth.

Sedrick, Teresa, and Rita started picking up pillows and magazines from the floor.

"Somebody fuckin' answer me! What happened?" Mara screamed.

"Mara, you have to calm down," Tea said, not wanting her to get more worked up than she was. She held her arm.

Mara yanked it free. "No, Tea." She walked over to Drew. "Were you *fighting*? Huh? Were you fighting? I don't believe this shit, I really don't." She shook her head and ran her fingers through her braids.

"Maybe you should be talking to your boy over there," he said loud enough for everyone to hear.

Miles fumed in the kitchen, but Sirue kept him from leaving. "And maybe your punk ass should learn how to treat your woman," he called back.

Drew let out a sardonic laugh and shook his head. He looked near the front door and found his keys. He picked them up, patted his jeans to make sure he had his wallet, and looked at Mara who was staring at him in disbelief.

"I'm gone. You can have this ghetto shit." He turned to leave.

"Drew," Mara called.

He held up the hand with his jingling keys as if to say "See ya" and walked out of the front door, rubbing his sore cheek.

Tears streamed down Mara's face and when she turned around, she saw everyone's eyes on her.

"I'm sorry, y'all. Sorry, Si," she said and before anyone could respond, she was already out the front door.

Chapter 35

Mara's senses were in overload. This craziness could not be happening. Not right now. It was astounding how juvenile and selfish Drew had been acting lately. And the more she thought about it as she stood on the front porch, the more she realized that it didn't happen overnight. He'd been distant since even before he found out about the pregnancy. Everything she did or said pissed him off. He flew off the handle when he didn't get his way. He made her feel like everything she did was wrong.

She jogged across the front yard to Drew's truck. He was already climbing in and as he pulled the door closed, he noticed her on his heels.

"What the hell is your damn problem?" she yelled at him through the window he'd just rolled down.

"Hold on, Mara. Let's get it straight. You're not going to stand out here in the street like some ghetto baby mama who didn't get her check," Drew's voice was slow and steady like he was addressing his high school students at an assembly.

"I'm a ghetto baby mama because I want to know why you were in there fighting? So what does that make you? My baby daddy?"

Drew looked at her with empty, disapproving eyes. "Your boy in there went for my throat first but you're out here causing a scene with me? That's who you need to be talking to."

"Well, I'm not. I'm talking to you, Drew. You're my man, even though *that's* been a little shady, too." Mara didn't try to hide the frustration in her voice.

Drew let out a hard laugh. "What the fuck does that mean?"

"Dammit!" Mara hit the door of his truck with the side of her fist. "Stop talking to me like I'm a fuckin' idiot. You heard what I said, Drew!"

Angry tears rolled down her cheeks and she stared at him, trying to read his expressionless face. He looked at her, and his eyes roamed her facial features. After a few seconds, he held his hand out to her.

Her muscles were tense. She lightly shook her head, looking at his open hand.

"No," she said softly.

"Babe —"

She shook her head again and wiped tears.

"Babe, come on. Come sit with me for a minute. We can talk in here." Drew softened his tone.

Mara finally recognized the face in front of her. It was the kind face she first met. The one that made her laugh, that made her feel beautiful. But there was still a hardness in his eyes. She knew it was just a matter of time before she did something to upset him again.

"I need to get back to Sirue's party." Another tear fell. "What's left of it."

With that, Drew pulled his hand back and started his truck. She folded her arms across her chest and watched him make the most detrimental decision about their relationship, about their family. He looked at her, shook his head, and tongued his bruised lip.

"Guess you made your choice," Drew said. He put his truck into gear and drove away.

When she watched him turn the corner, Mara exhaled. She hoped he would turn around and apologize because she wanted to forgive him. But instead, she stood there in a silent vigil wiping the last of her tears.

Mara turned around in time to see the living room curtain move back into place. She knew her nosy friends saw everything that just went down. She didn't care, though. She knew they meant well.

With her arms still folded, she slowly made her way back across the yard and inside. Tea was standing in the doorway almost blocking Mara's entrance. She reached out to hug Mara before she could get the door closed behind her. Mara laid her head on her friend's shoulder, holding back tears.

"You okay?" Tea asked her quietly.

Mara didn't respond. She saw Miles sitting on the sofa, staring at the coffee table. Still fuming. Sirue and Teresa were in the kitchen, and they both glanced her way.

"I'm all right, girl." She gave her a weak smile and walked past Miles into the kitchen.

She stopped in the entryway and Sirue leaned the broom he was holding against the counter. He looked at her, tilting his head.

"Si," she started, but the rest got caught in her throat.

"Hey," he walked over to hug her.

Teresa rolled her eyes and turned around to grab the broom and finish sweeping.

Mara pitched in to help straighten up. When everything was back in its place and conversations resumed to a more normal level, Teresa turned the music up. Miles continued to sit speechless while Tea sat beside him on the couch, rubbing his back every few minutes.

Rita persuaded Sedrick to tell some of the jokes he'd been working on to liven the mood. He did a dead-on impression of a comedian, down to his crooked fingers, that cracked everybody but Miles up.

"That's who you look like!" Teresa yelled and pointed at him. "The actor with the Asian guy! 'Do you understand the words I'm saying'?!"

Rita patted her back. "Honey," she said, taking the half-empty beer from her hand and putting it on the coffee table. "Let's just put this over here."

Everyone laughed and Teresa looked confused.

Sirue leaned into her and whispered the name of the comedian Sedrick was mimicking.

"Ohhhhhh," she nodded.

"Bless her heart," Rita said to Tea and Mara, slightly shaking her head.

Chapter 36

After he cut the cake and opened his presents, Sirue felt himself getting a bit nervous. It was showtime. Teresa whispered in his ear, and then turned down the music.

"Okay, okay," Sirue tried to get everyone's attention and cleared his throat.

"Maybe you should stand up," Teresa eagerly suggested.

He rolled his eyes but stood anyway.

"Hey, lovebirds, I need your attention," he said to Miles and Tea, who were talking quietly to each other at the end of the long sofa. They paused at his request.

Mara was sitting at the other end, chatting with Rita. She was half-listening and half-wishing the damn party would hurry up and end so she could go home. She'd definitely have to tell them her own news at another time. She suddenly wasn't feeling like having the extra attention.

Sirue cleared his throat again.

"I don't even know how to start this," Sirue said, running a hand over his head. He looked at his friends and took a deep breath.

"I'm...we're," he gestured at Teresa, "moving to Nashville. I got a position teaching both Neuroanatomy and Human Anatomy at Skiff University."

Teresa was all gums watching their reactions, her eyes bouncing from face to face.

Tea's eyes widened and she put her hand over her heart. "Wow. Si, for real?"

"Yeah." He smiled at her, then looked over at his best friend. "Miles, I'll be leaving in two weeks, man. A little sooner than expected so I can prepare for the next semester. You know I'm good for the rent the next couple of months."

"Whoa," Miles said, taken aback. "I'm...whoa. Congratulations, brother. I mean it." He stood and walked to Sirue, giving him a firm hug and a few pats on the back. "Kept this shit quiet for a minute, didn't you?"

"Had to make sure I got the job first." They shared another brotherly handshake and pulled each other into another quick embrace. Miles grimaced from being in pain.

Sirue released him. "Oooh, sorry, man."

"You know I'm so happy for you!" Tea stood and moved Miles out of the way so she could hug Sirue.

Miles grimaced again and held his side as he leaned on the wall near the group, still managing to smile for his friend.

Sedrick and Rita came over to him with more hugs. They all stood around, talking about Tennessee and Sirue's new position.

Mara could feel Teresa's eyes on her. She glanced at her friends, huddling together, talking happily about Sirue's news. This was what he was waiting to tell them for almost a week? Why didn't he just send a group text? Hell, why even tell them at all? Why not just pack up and roll out in two weeks then call them from Nashville? Two damn weeks. He was leaving in only two damn weeks. Why was everything changing so fast?

She stood and glared at Teresa, whose smug grin she wanted to slap off her face. She pushed past her and walked out the sliding back door, ignoring calls of her name.

The sun was setting, and the sky seemed to hold on to its purplish hue. Mara sat on the back porch steps and stared up at the endless horizon. It was so beautiful. She rested her hands on her abdomen and closed her eyes. *I'm never going to leave you, my angel*, she mouthed to herself. *I'm going to pour so much love into you.*

The sliding door opened, and she didn't turn to see who opened it. She wiped the tears that streamed down her cheeks and rested her arms on her knees, opting instead to look down at the cement steps.

Sirue grunted as he sat down next to her on the steps, his leg resting against hers. He took her hand, and she laid her head on his arm, the tears starting to fall again. After a few silent minutes, she sat up and wiped her face again.

"I'm always making a scene."

"Because you are the drama queen," Sirue finished.

She smiled and knew he was telling the truth. "I don't want you to go."

"I know you don't."

She could have sworn she heard his deep voice catch a little bit.

"But you have to go." She briefly looked over at him.

He nodded. "It's not that far. I'll be calling you all the time."

Mara thought for a few seconds. "Si, I'm pregnant."

She could feel him take a huge breath as he turned his head to face her. "What?"

"Yeah, I was going to tell y'all tonight, then all this shit went down. Only Tea knows. And Drew, of course...," her voice drifted off.

He reached around and gave her a warm side hug. "How far are you? How do you feel about it?"

"Um, I'm eight weeks." She shrugged. "I don't know how I feel. I do know that every damn thing is making me cry, though."

Sirue played with her braids and squeezed her shoulders again.

"Mara is a mommy."

"I know. Blows my mind, too." She sniffed.

"No, you'll be a great mother. You know what it takes."

Mara felt a lump in her throat again. She tried to swallow it back down before she spoke.

"Hey," she wiped a tear. "You better call me from down there when you get to drinking again, okay? You know if she's gonna be with you, you'll be hitting that bottle hard as shit."

Sirue laughed and they sat quietly for a few minutes, looking at the sky.

Teresa stood to the side of the closed glass doors, arms folded, staring at their backs, and wondering why he was sitting so close to Mara.

Rita and Sedrick said goodnight to everyone and thanked Sirue for letting them be there for the big news. They promised to come visit his new place in the summer, and Sirue gave Sedrick the green light to join the gossip train at work on Monday. He could almost see Sedrick's mood improve at the prospect of being the juicy news-bearer.

They offered to give Mara a ride home, and she gratefully agreed. She said goodbye to Sirue, telling him she'd give him a call the next day. She hugged Tea and whispered that she'd told Sirue already. Tea asked her if she wanted to get Miles so she could tell him also, but Mara declined. She said she'd probably just wait to tell him after he cooled off.

"He's really sorry about what happened tonight, Mara," Tea tried to explain.

"No, he's not because I know that's Miles. He'd do it again in a heartbeat, but I'm just not feeling him right now."

Tea nodded sadly and said she'd see her later at home.

Miles was in the kitchen, hearing all the goodbyes and fixing a plate of ribs and beans. He watched it heat up in the microwave, took it out, and leaned against the counter to eat it. He knew he had to simmer down, because even an hour after the incident, he still wanted to finish the fight. What did Drew mean that Tea had been sniffing around him? He recalled a moment outside when Drew walked up the steps beside her with his hand briefly on her back. But he also noticed that Tea spoke a few harsh words to Drew earlier that day, so he didn't think twice about it. Drew was just yanking his chain and trying to get under his skin. He knew the game. There was no way Tea wanted that asshole.

Chapter 37

"You have a scar on your cheek."

It was a few minutes past midnight and Tea was cuddled next to Miles upstairs in his bed. She was examining his face while he absently watched the moving images on the television screen. The three-inch scratch was already starting to heal.

"I do?"

"Mmmhmm," she kissed it lightly.

Miles rubbed her back, his eyes still blankly glued to the re-run playing before him.

Tea kissed his neck, then his shoulder and draped her leg across his body. She rubbed his chest through his undershirt.

"You're still quiet," she said and turned his head to face hers.

He grinned and inhaled sharply as he pulled her on top of him. Tea straddled him and began massaging his torso in small outward circles. She heard him wince a little when she touched his left side. She rubbed it gently and then slid her hands up his chest and rested them beside his head on the pillows. She placed her lips on his and felt Miles' hands rubbing all over her back. She thought he had the juiciest, most edible lips she'd ever tasted. It was still breathtaking that she could be so free with him. In some ways, their familiarity felt like an old couple, yet the newness of being together was still fresh.

Miles reached down and smoothed his hands over her round cheeks. He wished she didn't have any panties on, but he wished even more that he wasn't still wearing jeans. He was about to burst through his zipper seam. It didn't help that he could feel Tea's bare breasts against him. He didn't even see her remove her bra.

"Take these off," he whispered into her mouth, tugging at her panties. Tea smiled against his lips. "Take 'em off for me."

Miles pulled his head back a few inches and raised his eyebrow. She didn't have to tell him twice. In a swift motion, he pulled her panties down and from around her ankles, while Tea carefully helped him remove his jeans and boxers. He watched her as she climbed back up his body and he reached for a condom beside his bed. Tea helped him put it on and Miles almost lost control watching her pretty hands and fingers touching him. He held his hardness down as Tea straddled him again, resting against his length. Her warmth made Miles throw his head back against his pillows.

Tea licked the hollow spot on his throat and dragged her tongue around his neck, driving him crazy. She gasped when she felt his long fingers behind her, poking and probing in her wet spots.

"Relax, baby," Miles whispered and continued to slowly move his digits around.

Tea moaned slightly and buried her face under his jaw. Her body kept the slow rhythm with his fingers, and she knew he would need to dry his hands when they were done. He was turning her on so much and so fast that she ignored her ringing phone on a chair across the room.

Sounds from her mouth were muffled against his own when she found his lips again. Tea wasn't sure if it was his warm breath meeting hers, or if it was the sensation of his tongue roaming aimlessly in her mouth, or even if it was the increasing speed of his fingers inside of her, but she could feel her body about to climax.

Her phone rang again.

It was just background noise to them both. Tea spread her legs more on top of him and the wet sounds of his fingers inside of her made her delirious. She began to suck the skin on his jawline and Miles bit his bottom lip, pushing his fingers deeper and faster into her moistness. He could feel her body about to release.

"Come on my hand," he whispered hoarsely. He matched her moans and felt her body tense, then begin to shake uncontrollably. His fingers remained in motion until her spasms quieted and he rested his hands on her hips.

Tea wiped her sweat-drenched bangs and planted a soft kiss on his lips.

"Mmmm," she smiled at him. "Damn."

"Your orgasms are so beautiful."

Tea smiled, a little embarrassed. She pressed her mouth against his again and got lost in his tender kiss. She felt his hands squeezing her hips and rubbing the outside of her thighs. She wanted more of him. Her body moved farther up his body until she felt his hard shaft behind her. Miles helped her raise her body and ease her slowly back down.

Tea softly moaned as one hand gripped his shoulder and the other held the back of his head. She looked into his eyes as she felt him enter. She paused just after his tip filled her up.

"Oh my God," she sucked in a breath and leaned forward to push her mouth onto his.

Miles jumped as he felt her thighs squeezing his sides. He was still sore from the fight but didn't want her to stop. Her hands through his hair, her moans, her whimpers, her moist heat drenching him the more passionately they kissed...Miles didn't want any of it to stop. Instead, he held her hips and moved his mouth in a hard rhythm with hers.

He guided her lower down and Tea allowed it as much as she could. With most of his length inside of her, she rocked her hips slowly back and forth. Miles sharply inhaled, feeling the sensation of her snug, warm walls.

"Shit, baby...yessss." His hands moved her faster.

Tea's mouth opened on top of his and she could barely talk, let alone breathe. He felt so good inside of her. She brought her mouth to his shoulder and started to suck on his skin.

"My beautiful baby," Miles whispered, slightly turning his head until his lips grazed her ear. "You're so beautiful. You feel so good. Don't stop."

Tea's mouth left his shoulder and began sucking on the side of his neck. "I'm gonna come agaaaain...," she moaned into his skin.

"You feel so damn good." Miles grunted as he felt her breasts against his chest.

"Come with me, Miles," Tea managed to say through her staggered breaths. Her fingers grabbed at his curly bush and her mouth slid to his. She kissed him hard, and her orgasm exploded while she sucked his bottom lip.

Miles couldn't stop his own release when he felt her muscles squeezing and contracting. He wrapped both arms around Tea's torso and held her close until he finished. Tea's breathing slowed and she gently rubbed her hand through Miles' head, looking directly into his eyes.

He smiled at her smile. Their foreheads touched and Miles gave her nose a quick kiss.

"I'm gonna lift you off, okay?"

Tea nodded, though she wanted him to stay inside a little longer. She let him raise her body and she helped pull him out, then sat back once he quickly removed his condom. Tea kissed along his jawline while Miles softly massaged her back.

"You get very wet, huh?" he quietly asked, smiling.

Tea pulled back a few inches and looked at him. She bit her lip and nodded, wondering if he didn't like that.

Miles' eyes roamed her face and smoothed her bangs away, tenderly lifting her chin. He leaned forward and softly touched his lips to hers.

"You need me to get you a towel?" Miles asked, sensing her uneasiness.

"I should be asking *you* that, I guess," she said. "Sorry."

"No, no, don't be sorry. That wasn't what I meant. I love how you get so turned on."

Miles carefully moved her from on top of him and went to the bathroom, quickly coming back with a small towel. Tea was bashfully covered with his comforter. He kneeled one knee onto the bed and tugged at the bedding. With it pulled back, he licked his lips.

"I can uh...lick it off for you instead," he said hungrily, his eyes moving up to hers.

Tea giggled nervously. "I'll just take the towel, please." She held out her hand.

Miles handed it to her. "Next time, then?"

"I'll think about it," she smiled.

"Okay," Miles whispered and slowly climbed back into the bed beside her, assisting her with the towel. He pulled her close and enjoyed the feeling of her warm skin on his.

"My beautiful Tea," he said into her hair.

They laid quietly for a few minutes until Tea's phone rang again from across the room.

"Damn," she muttered, and looked behind her towards the chair near his television.

"I got it, baby." Miles got up and retrieved the phone. He glanced at it, then handed it to her and gave her a quick kiss. "I'm gonna jump in the shower."

Tea pouted. "You sure?"

He nodded, and kissed her mouth again, then went back to his adjoining bathroom.

Tea looked at the caller's name.

"Hey, what's up?" she asked.

Mara's voice was hardly audible. "Tea, I'm sorry I kept calling. You got a minute?"

"Yeah. Are you okay?" Tea positioned herself against the headboard and pulled up the blankets.

"No," Mara sniffed. "I just broke up with Drew. It's over." She started to cry into the phone.

Tea listened and tried to console her friend. After a few minutes, she was able to calm Mara down and convince her not to drive past Drew's house. And after a few more minutes, when she knew her friend wouldn't end up in a holding cell overnight, Tea told her they'd make plans to go out tomorrow, just the two of them.

Chapter 38

Tea flipped through the channels, then stopped on an old episode of a rerun she loved. She laughed as the smart-mouthed snarky waitress made a remark about another waitress' bra seeing no action.

The shower water stopped running and Tea replayed the night's events over in her head again. Miles had been unusually quiet since the party. Even while they made love, she could sense something was bothering him. He was still gentle with her, and his sweet words always made her smile. But he didn't seem like himself.

He emerged from the bathroom wearing a towel around his waist. She admired his damp body and how sexy it looked in that towel. She felt a sensation between her legs and craved him again.

Miles took a bottle of cocoa butter-infused lotion from his dresser and rubbed it on his skin, while absently watching the show on television. Tea suddenly understood one of her favorite soul singer's fascination with brown skin. It glistened and his ab muscles flexed as his hands worked over his torso and stomach.

Tea held out her hand. "Come here, I can help you," she said.

He walked around to her side of the bed and sat in front of her, handing her the lotion. He grabbed the remote and turned to the sports channel.

"Um, no, I wasn't watching that," Tea said with mock irritation.

"I'm sorry, want me to turn back?" he asked sincerely.

"No, it's okay."

She slowly applied the aromatic lotion to his shoulder blades. His taut muscles felt so good under her hands. And he smelled so damn tasty.

"So, how's Mara?" he asked.

"She's better now. Said they just officially broke up."

"Good. So today was the last time he should show his ass around here."

If you only knew, Tea thought. Drew would probably be in the picture for at least the next eighteen years.

"It's a two-way thing, though," Tea started. "It's easy for us on the outside to say something should be over. When you're deep in it, then it's a whole different perspective. It's not that easy."

Her hands moisturized the length of his spine.

He nodded. "Yeah. True. But he's an asshole, so..."

Tea rolled her eyes behind him. "You can be so close-minded."

He cocked his head half-way around. "No. He's an asshole," he repeated over his shoulder. "He told me today that you've been sniffin' around him."

"What?!" Tea dropped her hands.

"Yeah. Why do you think I wanted to kill his sorry ass today?"

"Sniffin' around him? Like I wanted to get with him?" Tea had to make sure she heard him right.

Miles nodded, his attention slightly back to the scores running across the bottom of the television screen.

"That's funny, because *he's* the one who's been trying to push up on *me*." Tea regretted it the second it left her lips.

Miles turned his head abruptly and met her eyes.

"What did you say?"

Tea swallowed. "He's...he tried to come on to me," she explained quietly.

"When?"

"Like, I don't know." She shrugged. "A few times, I guess."

"Hold up." Miles' body was turned completely around now, facing her on the bed. "Did he touch you?"

Tea rolled her eyes. He couldn't be serious.

"Did he put his hands on you?" Miles restated.

"No, Miles."

He held her gaze for a few moments. "When were you going to tell me this?"

Tea didn't like his tone.

"You need to calm down."

He looked at her for a few seconds, then cut his eyes and turned back around. When Tea tried to resume the lotion massage, he stood up and she watched him walk to the other side of the bed.

"Oh my God. What the hell is wrong with you?" She looked at him in shock.

"There's definitely something wrong when my woman can't tell me another man is hitting on her." Miles kept his eyes on the television.

"It wasn't a big deal, Miles. Damn," Tea shook her head. She felt oddly out of place now without a bra on, so she searched for it under the blankets.

"If it wasn't a big deal, why didn't you tell me?" He turned to look at her.

Tea didn't like his accusatory tone.

"Well, why didn't you tell me?" he repeated.

She found her bra and caught his inflection. "Wait," she paused. "What are you trying to say? That I encouraged him? Is that what you're saying?"

Miles exhaled and shrugged. "I don't know. Maybe you are attracted to him. I saw his hand on your back today."

He watched as she hooked her bra together.

Tea let out a short laugh. "You have to be kidding me right now."

"And you didn't care it was there."

"When did he have his hand on my back, Miles?" Tea asked, not believing they were having this conversation.

"On the steps." Miles' stare didn't leave Tea's face. His jaw clenched.

"Miles. He was helping me up the stairs if that's what you're talking about."

"Oh, so now you can't walk up five steps?" He finally cut his eyes away and looked back at the television screen.

Tea frowned her face and felt her pulse quicken. She did not like this hyper-jealous side of his at all. It had remnants of Jonathan written all over it. She knew Miles was fiercely protective, but this was on another level. Is this why he was so quiet tonight?

She spoke with as much evenness in her voice as her frustration would allow, despite the thump in her heart. "Do you want me to tell you whenever anyone anywhere tries to flirt with me, Miles? Huh? I could keep it recorded in my phone for you anytime it happens."

He gave her a sideways glance that said he was fed up with the games. "No, but I do want you to tell me how he came on to you."

"Whatever. I said it was no big deal. I don't want to talk about this anymore." She waved him off and scooted back against the headboard.

Miles shook his head. "Here we go again. *You* don't want to talk about something, so we don't, right?"

Tea blew out a long breath, her eyes on the television.

"So, what did he do? Did he try to kiss you?" Miles continued.

She looked over at him, caught his glare, then rolled her eyes.

"Wait, *did* you kiss him? Or you just want to keep that a secret between you two?"

"Fuck you. Don't talk to me right now, Miles."

"Just a minute ago, it wasn't a big deal, but now you're getting all defensive over that asshole?" His tone rose again. "Damn, *were* you sniffin' around him?"

Tea picked up the big bottle of lotion and threw it at him. It landed with a hard thud near his temple and bounced back to the bed. His hand flew to the point of contact.

"Ow, fuuuuuuuck," he said, inhaling sharply.

Tea stood and found her pants on the floor. She yanked them on and sat on the loveseat to put on her shoes. Miles rubbed his head and watched her. Tea stood and calmly looked at him with her hands on her hips.

"Take me home."

"Tea," Miles said quietly.

She saw her shirt laying against the back of the loveseat and picked it up. She slipped it on and saw that he hadn't budged.

"Fine, I'll call a ride." Tea grabbed her phone and started to walk out of the bedroom.

"Give me a minute," Miles said tiredly.

Tea shrugged. "No, I'll get a ride." She started tapping an app on her phone screen.

"Tea," Miles said firmly. "Give me a minute. I'll take you."

She stood in the doorway for almost two minutes while he threw on clothes and groaned about his head. As they walked down the hall, they could hear Sirue and Teresa making very passionate love through Sirue's bedroom door. Tea became even more angry, and she stomped down the stairs and out of the house.

Chapter 39

Neither spoke for the first few minutes of the ride. Tea drew her leg up in the passenger seat and stared out of her window. Was she upset because he was accusing her or because he was right? Drew was definitely fine, but she'd never made a move on him. She would never do that to Mara nor to Miles. There was a loud exhale and groan from the driver's side that interrupted Tea's thoughts. She didn't turn her head, but she knew Miles was probably rubbing the newly formed bump on his temple. She felt kind of bad about throwing that huge bottle full force at him. But a part of her was glad that her aim was so good. He had no right to say what he said. No big deal means no big deal. It was over, but he wanted to keep going. They would probably still be in his room arguing if he had his way. Tea slid her bangs behind her ear and watched the scenery flying by in the darkness. The Jonathan flashbacks were bad enough, and now this. She leaned her head back against the seat, memories and emotions playing back in her mind.

The night she and Jonathan fought about the television channel turned into a fight about all the men he'd seen staring at her earlier that day when they were out together. He described each one precisely, down to his shoes. He also fabricated Tea's alleged responses to each guy. With one, she supposedly smiled back. With another, she supposedly whispered something provocative. He became more and more enraged until he grabbed her arms, slapped her into the wall a few times, and eventually threw her onto his bed and forced himself inside of her.

Tea shuddered at the memory and wrapped her arms around herself in the passenger seat.

When they got onto Route 50, Miles felt the throbbing pain in his temple increasing, but he knew he deserved it. He glanced over at Tea and couldn't believe he was stupid enough to give her a reason to say, "Take me home." He'd never had a woman tell him that, and he especially didn't want to start with her. He wanted to be back home with her right now. Making her bite her lips again, scratch his back again.

Miles glanced over at her. She hadn't turned to look at him since she got into the car and slammed the door. She was sexy when she was angry, but he knew better than to tell her that right now. He had to tell her something, though. He couldn't let his baby go home so upset, even if she did put a throbbing knot on his head.

"Tea," he said softly, reaching over to put his hand slowly on her left thigh.

She moved it off.

Damn, he thought.

"I want to apologize, Tea," he said sincerely.

Tea continued to look out of the window.

"I took it too far. I should have let it go and I'm sorry."

Tea sighed and reached over to lift his right hand. She kissed his palm and put it back on her leg. He squeezed it.

"I forgive you, but...we have to talk." Tea finally turned her head in his direction.

"Okay," Miles nodded, looking at her and back at the road. "Feel like going back to my place?" he asked.

Tea shook her head. "No."

He looked at her again, then towards the rear lights of the cars ahead of them. "Okay," he said quietly.

"I just need to be alone."

This time, his glance at her lasted a few seconds longer before looking in front of him. He clenched his jaw and lightly rubbed her leg. "You mean...alone? For just tonight, or...? What do you mean?"

Tea smiled a half-smile. He looked so worried.

"Just for tonight."

He nodded and gave her another quick glance. "Okay."

Miles pulled up to the curb in front of Tea's house. He put his car into park and rubbed his left temple. He had a killer headache starting to radiate from the lump. But, more than the headache, he worried about their relationship. Worried how much he screwed it up. Tea had been quiet again for the last few minutes of the ride, and now that they were in front of her house, she still sat and stared into the darkness of the night.

"I'm sorry, baby," Miles apologized again.

Tea exhaled, then turned in her seat to face Miles, folding one leg beneath her. Her eyes widened when she saw the growth on the side of his head.

"Oh my God, you need some ice on that," she gently turned his head so she could get a closer look.

He winced when she lightly touched it. "I'm okay."

"C'mon inside," she said, her tone a mixture of guilt and concern.

In the kitchen, Tea grabbed an ice pack from the freezer and wrapped it in a paper towel, then placed it inside a plastic sandwich baggie. Miles was standing against the counter, watching her move around the kitchen. She walked over to him and slowly placed the cold pack against the side of his head. Next, she took a water bottle from the refrigerator and pulled a bottle of medicine from the cabinet. She handed him the water and two pain relievers, and he swallowed them immediately.

Tea gently took his free hand and started to pull him to the dining room, but Miles didn't move. She turned and looked up at him, almost melting from the intense look in his eyes. She placed a hand on his cheek and smoothed his skin with her thumb. His eyes closed and he allowed his head to rest in her hand. After a few moments of stroking his cheek with her thumb, Tea tried again.

"We need to talk," she said softly and took his hand. They walked to the dining room and after he sat, Tea moved her chair closer to his.

They looked at each other, and Tea thought carefully about what she wanted to say. She noticed he looked defeated and a little nervous, slouched back in his chair. It was hard not to reach over and hug him, but she knew if she did, she wouldn't get through this. She took a deep breath.

"So...this," Tea motioned between him and herself, "...what happened tonight, we can't do this."

Miles dropped his eyes momentarily, then looked back at her and nodded.

"I need you to trust me when I tell you things. I wouldn't lie to you, especially about somebody like Drew."

Clenching his jaw at the sound of his name, Miles slightly rolled his eyes and gave her a quick nod.

Tea leaned her head to the side. "See? You're still upset."

"He's an asshole, Tea," Miles said quietly, adjusting the pack on his temple.

Tea sighed. "Okay, but do you believe me?"

"I believe you," he said without hesitation. "He just really got under my skin, and I'm sorry about what I said to you...but not for defending you and Mara."

Tea nodded and looked down, slowly tapping on the table. After a minute in deep thought, she finally looked up and saw Miles' eyes were directly on hers.

"Miles, I just can't...," she rubbed the back of her neck and shook her head, trying to find words.

Miles narrowed his eyes, searched her face, and studied her body language. He lowered the ice pack and patiently waited for her to finish.

"You know how my father and Anna are," Tea started. "You know how abusive Jonathan was, and I can't..." She chewed on her lip and looked hard at Miles, who was breathing faster and starting to shake his head.

Miles looked into her eyes, his jaws tightening. There was his name again. He was being compared to a punk who put his hands on her and raped her. Miles felt like he was going to come out of his skin. *She's about to break up with me*, he thought. *I fucked this up.*

"I can't do dysfunction again, okay? I want something healthy and fun and safe," Tea said, crossing her arms and holding herself. "And I want it with you."

Miles let out a breath and put a hand over his chest. "Then, that's what I'll give you. I promise."

A smile started to form on Tea's lips, but she remembered something else she thought about during the car ride home. "Ummm. One more thing." She made a face.

"Anything," Miles said seriously.

"I...think we should abstain for a while."

Miles raised his eyebrows, then squinted at her. "Ab-*what*?"

"Ab*stain*," Tea repeated.

"Okay, I was just making sure...as in, um...from sex?"

Tea nodded.

"Why? Did I do something you didn't like tonight?" he asked, truly confused. "Just tell me, I can fix it –"

"No, nothing like that," she interrupted. "You made me feel really good tonight."

"So...okay, I don't understand, then, baby." Miles shook his head, his eyes directly on hers.

"I just want us to have a closer bond."

Miles opened his mouth, then stopped himself, then opened his mouth again. "We've...known each other for seven years. That's a seven-year bond."

Tea smiled. "That's a friendship bond, I want a relationship bond."

"My headache is coming back," Miles groaned and put the ice pack on his head again.

"Your bump is on the other side" Tea smirked, pointing to his head.

Miles cut a sharp look at her and moved the ice pack over.

Tea giggled. "It won't be that bad."

He made a face and exhaled with puffed out cheeks. "You're talking maybe for a week or so?"

Tea shook her head. His eyes widened.

"Tea, okay, wait, wait," Miles started.

She failed to fight a smile. "We can do it. I think it will make us stronger."

He looked to the side at the dark living room, talking to no one and gesturing with his hand. "I'm already pretty strong. I mean, I workout...could probably do a hundred push-ups right now, for real..."

"Miles," Tea laughed and stood in front of him, rubbing his head.

He groaned and leaned his head forward onto her stomach. "Okay, baby. If that's what you want, we'll do it." He groaned again.

She laughed and kissed the top of his head.

Chapter 40

Mara's senses were too stimulated to continue her fitful sleep. The strong aroma of cinnamon, the sound of clanking dishes in the sink downstairs, and the sunlight coming through her window shades were all enough to awaken her completely from her slumber. She swung her legs over the bed, then rubbed her belly. She said a silent good morning to her baby and smiled. Her clock read 7:42 and, if it wasn't for her growling stomach, that would have been reason enough to lay back down. It was Sunday for crying out loud.

So, she stretched, then stood and stretched again. On her way to the bathroom, she stubbed her toe on two of her textbooks that were lying on the floor. She strung three or four curse words together at how clumsy she'd been lately, then hobbled to go wash up.

Fifteen minutes later, she was following the scent of food.

"Good morning, sunshine," Tea cheerfully greeted her when she reached the bottom of the steps.

Mara couldn't keep her eyes off the spread on the dining room table. French toast, bacon, a pitcher of orange juice, applesauce, scrambled eggs, and biscuits. She couldn't sit down fast enough.

"Tea, girl, I could get used to this. That's two days in a row."

She took a long sip of her juice and they both started fixing their plates.

"So, I'm like definitely at the top of your friends list now?" Tea joked while spooning heaps of applesauce.

Mara shot her a quick glance then continued to pick up slices of bacon. "Please. You know you're my sister. Nobody else would put up with my ass."

Tea shrugged a 'that's true' response.

They finished piling food and began to eat in relative silence, save for the sounds of forks scraping against glass.

"Hey," Mara said between bites. "What are you doing up so damn early, anyway?"

Tea buttered a biscuit. "Miles didn't leave here until about six this morning. I couldn't get to sleep, so I tried to read but that didn't work either."

"Six?" Mara's eyebrow went up.

"We were *talking*."

"Ain't that much to talk about. Did y'all have a fight or something?" Mara stuffed a forkful of French toast in her mouth.

Tea shrugged and took a bite of her biscuit. "Not really. Kind of. A small one."

Mara noticed her uneasiness. Maybe the fight was about her? "About what?"

"Stupid shit." Tea shrugged again and avoided her eyes.

Yeah, it was about me, Mara thought. So, they stayed up all night talking about her. Miles probably said something dumb about her and Tea came to her defense. Miles hated to just leave shit alone. He always picked at something until it was raw. Mara took another swig of her juice. She wondered if Tea ended up telling him about the baby.

"...so do you want to come with?" Tea was talking.

Mara was confused. "Huh?"

"I said I was probably gonna get to the shop early today. Do you want to come?"

"Oh," Mara shook her head. "Sitting around those hot ass dryers all day would make me pass out. Plus, Si's taking me out to lunch today. Look at me, already planning my next meal."

"That's nice."

"Yeah, when I got off the phone with you last night, he called to check up on me. Said something told him he should call me. Girl, why was Teresa's ass all in the background trying to suck his peen off?"

Tea looked at her. "Are you serious?" Tea remembered hearing sounds coming from Sirue's bedroom as she stormed out last night.

Mara nodded. "I heard it." She made a fake vomit action. "Told him I'd talk to him later and he said he'll take me to lunch."
Tea was quiet and poked her food around her plate. "Ewwww. You heard Si and –"
"I don't want to talk about it."
They laughed and tried to finish their breakfast.

Sirue didn't know he'd accumulated so much art. Paintings, prints, and a few originals from local artists all crowded box after box in the living room and hallways. He stood in front of his favorite – a medium sized canvas he'd bought at an art fair a few years ago. Sirue scratched his head and smiled. Mara had actually been the one who'd persuaded him to purchase it. They'd stared at the young girl and boy, both with big, round brown eyes. In the background, a woman who was obviously their mother sat at a small, messy kitchen table, doubled over with her head in her hands, crying. The boy and the girl held hands in the foreground, staring out at the viewer with a defeated gaze in their eyes. Sirue wasn't sure if it was the pale browns and grays the artist used or if it was the title of the piece, "Waiting," or even if was the barely visible pot of food burning over the woman's shoulder, but he would always get lost in this painting.

"Hey."

Sirue hadn't heard Miles come downstairs and his voice startled him.

"Damn." He shook his head back to the present.

"Panting sucked you in again, huh?" Miles glanced at it. He still couldn't see the fascination.

"Always. Here, give me a hand," Sirue said, starting to hoist the heavy framed piece from the wall. Miles pitched in and they bubble-wrapped it then placed it in a nearby box. There were a few smaller prints to be packed away and Miles let Sirue handle them while he went into the kitchen to fetch cereal, bowls, and milk.

They ate, looking around at the bare walls and sealed boxes.

"You know what? You might have to get Tea to pick out some new artwork. You can't leave the walls like this."

Miles nodded and slurped his spoon. "That or just paint 'em."

Sirue made a disapproving face, then poured his second bowl. "Still feels unreal. One more week, man."

"Oh yeah, I was able to get that whole week off to help you out. I meant to tell you."

Sirue looked at Miles. "Every week is a week off at that fake ass job of yours," he quipped.

"Y'all gonna chill with that job shit." Miles poured another bowl.

"Yeah, yeah, yeah. How are you getting down there? Flying with us?"

"Nah, I'll fly the company pl—"

"Don't even tell me. The job's going to pay for it." Sirue held his spoon in mid-air.

Miles shrugged. "Fringe benefits, brother."

Sirue shook his head. "So, Tea and Mara will come down later?"

"Yeah, like two weeks later. I might be able to take off again and come with them. And before you say it, shut the hell up."

Sirue laughed and looked at his friend. "Damn, I'm going to miss you."

Miles nodded. "As will I. But look, don't let me come down there and find you dressing all country."

"Don't worry about me. You just need to make sure you clean this house more than once a month."

"I know how to clean a damn house," Miles retorted, slurping his spoon again.

Sirue put his down dramatically. "Where do I keep the extra vacuum bags?"

"Huh?"

"How do I sanitize the kitchen?"

"How the hell am I –"

"And where's the mop?" Sirue stared at him.

"I'll just buy new shit, damn!" Miles stabbed at the cereal in his bowl.

Sirue laughed and stood up, grabbing the cereal and milk. "Just like I said. Worry about keeping this house clean and I'll worry about my clothes."

Miles talked with his mouth full of sugary squares. "Nah, you mean Teresa will worry about your clothes," he called to him as he walked past.

"Good point," Sirue nodded.

"She lays your clothes out like you're a damn invalid."

Sirue laughed again. "Don't be mad because Tea doesn't pick out your shit."

"Yeah, 'cause she knows I'm a whole grown ass man over here," Miles replied louder than he had to. "Big ass overgrown Webster."

Chapter 41

"Dinner was delicious."

Tea was standing behind Miles in his kitchen, rubbing small circles in between his shoulder blades. He was rinsing off plates from the pesto chicken and veggies meal they just finished and loading the dishwasher.

"Thank you," he smiled and turned slightly to kiss her.

"I still feel bad leaving Mara by herself tonight. She had a pretty rough week."

Miles lifted the door shut and turned the appliance on. He dried his hands, leaned back, and pulled Tea to him. She stood between his legs and was expressionless as he moved her bangs from her face and tucked them behind her ear.

"She knew she could come over," Miles said softly, looking down at her. "But I think she still hates me."

Tea wrapped her arms around his torso and rested her head on his chest. She could hear the strong rhythm of his heartbeat and it soothed her.

"She doesn't hate you," she whispered.

Miles rubbed her lower back and slipped his hand beneath her pink t-shirt. Tea loved his big hands, and she especially loved the massages they gave. She was glad Sirue was out with Teresa. She wanted some private time with Miles. Her shop seemed to be overbooked the last few days and although the money was terrific, she was getting home close to midnight. All day at the shop today, she couldn't stop thinking about having Miles all to herself. She knew they weren't going to have sex, but she couldn't wait just to be near him.

She lifted her head, and he lowered his to meet her lips. They quickly found a strong groove and moved their heads in sync with one another. Miles explored her mouth and finally settled on circling her soft tongue with his own. He moaned sounds of hunger as he pulled her even closer into his body. Tea slowly pulled away from the kiss.

The look of lust in his eyes and the way his mouth hung open as he licked his moist lips made Tea drop her forehead onto his chest.

"Shit," she muttered to herself.

Miles managed to chuckle, and he kissed the top of her head. "This isn't easy, is it?"

Tea shook her head. It had been a week since their declaration of celibacy. It wasn't too bad of a transition during the week since they were both at work, although his naughty texts didn't help. She stood up straight and took a few steps away from Miles, shaking her bangs from her face and smoothing the back of her shaved hair. She blew out a hard breath towards the floor.

Miles smiled at her attempt at self-control.

"You want to find a movie to watch?" he asked, looking her over. His eyes landed on her chest, and he felt a twitch in his briefs. He loved the full cleavage visible from the top of her low-cut shirt. Damn the movie, he really wanted to bury his face in her flesh.

Tea nodded, but neither of them moved. Miles wiped his mouth with his hand and stroked his goatee as his eyes roamed over her body again. He licked his top lip. Tea bit both of hers.

"I'm still hungry," he said quietly, his half-open eyes staring at her mouth.

Tea motioned towards the refrigerator. "We just put the food away," she smiled.

Miles slowly shook his head. "Not for that."

"Oh," Tea's eyes widened, and her legs felt like jelly.

"I just…I wanted to taste you all week," he said, his face intense.

"Uhhh," Tea blew out air again and rubbed her forehead. "Miles…"

"Okay," his face softened, though he let out a small groan. "Okay."

"Okay," she repeated. "Let's go find a movie?"

Miles took her hand, and they bypassed the living room which was full of moving boxes. Upstairs in the game room, Miles pushed the oversized recliners together and they settled on the newest comic superhero release. Tea grabbed two sodas and chocolate from one of the mini fridges, then made a bag of microwaved popcorn. Tea broke up the chocolate candy into the popcorn, saw a bag of gummy worms and added those, too. Miles made a face when she handed the bag to him.

"I'm not eating that," he said, pushing it back to her.

Tea laughed. "Try it, I'm serious, you'll love it."

He looked inside the bag at the colorful melted chocolate concoction. He wasn't a huge fan of popcorn anyway, so none of it looked appetizing. He shook his head again.

Tea squinted her eyes at him. "If you try it, we can make out."

Miles grabbed the bag from her hand and started dumping it directly into his mouth. Tea cracked up laughing and took the bag back.

"I knew that would work!"

He chewed and swallowed the mouthful of popcorn in his mouth and leaned over for a kiss. Tea wiped his lips and brushed crumbs off his goatee, then planted her mouth on his. Miles moaned and reached his hand over to her chair to pull her body towards his. He slid his free hand beneath her pink top until it rested on her breast. He gently massaged it through her thin bra. Tea slightly moved her head back and smiled, their lips barely touching. Miles got the hint, pecked her lips one last time, then shook his head in frustration. He wanted her so bad. Instead, he reached for the remote in the side pocket of the chair and started the movie.

They held hands, talked, and laughed during the film. Tea enjoyed all the gentle kisses he placed on her hand, and Miles loved the way she'd look over at him and smile each time he did. When the movie was over, he walked her outside to her car.

"Thank you for coming over tonight, baby," he said, hugging her once they reached the driver's door.

"I couldn't wait to see you," Tea said, looking up at him.

Miles smiled and took both of her hands into his own. He brought them to his lips and kissed each hand.

"Still on for bowling tomorrow when you're done at the shop, right?" He was excited for the double date with Sirue and Teresa.

Tea nodded with a slight pout. Miles looked at her face.

"What's wrong?" he asked.

"Nothing…just a little sad Mara doesn't want to come with us."

Miles nodded. "She can still change her mind."

"Yeah," Tea gave a half-smile. She reached up and wrapped her arms around his neck. "I love you."

Miles froze and pulled back to look at her.

"Baby," he started. He put his hand on his chest. Even though he sensed she did, he never heard her say the words within the confines of their relationship. As friends, they would say it often. This felt different. "I love you, too."

Tea stood back fully on her feet and couldn't stop smiling. "And I'm *in* love with you."

He stared at her, and his eyes searched her face. "I'm in love with you, too, Tea."

They both smiled full grins and Miles suddenly reached down to lift her up. He gently swung her around and they laughed until her lips met his again.

Chapter 42

"Whatever, shit don't just happen like that," Mara spoke into her cell phone.

"What do you mean?" Sirue asked.

It was Tuesday morning and Mara was at her desk, eating her second snack in thirty minutes. There was nothing she hated more than being stuck in a cubicle at a company that devalued her. She peeled the candy bar wrapper back so she could get a better bite.

"I mean," she bit off a chunk, "that I'm surprised you let that shit slide."

"I didn't let anything slide."

"Uh-huh. So, what do you call it when Teresa just happens to be looking through your phone when you walk in, and you don't confront her? She knows what she's doing, Si."

Sirue evened out the bass in his tone. "Well, obviously you didn't hear what I said. I said she was *holding* it, not looking *through* it."

Mara let out a sharp laugh. "Yeah, okay. Think what you wanna think. But you brought it up, so it must have seemed fishy to you. Am I right?"

She flashed a phony smile at a coworker who nosily walked by her cubicle.

Sirue was quiet for a few seconds. "Anyway. That's not the reason I called. I wanted to check up on you."

Mara quickly considered letting him know that she wanted him to be the baby's godfather, but decided she'd hold off on that until he was in a better mood. She tossed the candy bar wrapper in the wastebasket.

"I'm good. Auntie came by last night and we hung out. She went crazy at BabyTowne and brought me so many things. Almost bought up the whole store."

"Aw, damn. I missed Aunt Esther? How is she? I need to make sure I see her before I leave."

"She's wild as ever. You know she's engaged to two men now. Doesn't know which one to keep, if any. Hold on." Mara spoke a few words to another coworker who paused at her desk. "Hey, Si. I need to go. There's some meeting I had no idea about. I'll talk to you later."

"Okay."

"And go handle your business with your CIA boo thang."

"Bye, Mara," Sirue said with a smile.

When Mara pulled in front of the house that evening, she rolled her eyes at the sight of Miles' car.

"Damn," she said to herself. She knew Tea took off from the shop today, but she didn't think he'd be here, too. Didn't he ever work?

Mara cut off the engine and sat for a minute. She considered going through somebody's drive-thru since she was starving, but she also had to use the bathroom. She'd gone right before she left work, but now it felt like her bladder was being squeezed.

"Oh, well, hopefully Tea will keep him out of my face," she muttered and walked to the front door. Before she could throw her keys down, she heard feet running through the house.

James rounded a corner, his padded feet making thud noises on the carpet. He was holding a game controller and running from his big brother Damien, who was a few steps behind him.

"Give it here!"

"No! Teeeeeeeeea!" James yelled then saw Mara and ran to hide behind her. "Aunt Mara, help!"

"Give it to me!" Damien reached for his brother's arm, but Mara held him back.

"Damien, chill," she yelled.

He continued to grab around Mara's body. "No! Tell him to give it here! He's always taking my stuff! Give it to me, you brat!"

James started to laugh once he realized he was protected. "You shoulda' let me play then," he teased. "That's why I got this." He dangled the controller.

Damien managed to land a punch on James' head, causing him to scream and Mara grabbed both of them by the arms.

"I said chill out! Both of y'all, stop!"

Just then, Tea came flying down the stairs and saw Mara taking them both to the sofa.

"Oh, hi, Mara." She noticed the annoyed look on Mara's face. "I'm sorry, girl. Y'all, what happened?"

Both of the boys started to give their own version of events simultaneously. Tea held up a hand to James. "Damien, go."

"He's always taking my stuff! Me and Miles were playin' then he got mad —"

"No, I didn't! He punched me!" James pushed his big brother and hit him with the controller.

"James! Give it," Tea said sharply, snatching it out of his hand and he kicked Damien in the leg.

Damien tightened his face and balled his fists, glaring at his little brother.

"Yo, Day!" Miles' voice called from the den. "Day! I figured it out, man, come on!"

Damien rolled his eyes and started to stand up, still fuming. Tea nudged him back down.

"I want to talk to you. Wait." She turned to James. "You. You don't like your brother hitting you, so don't hit him. Apologize for taking this."

James looked down at his feet and stuffed his fingers in his mouth.

"Apologize," Tea repeated.

"Sorry, Day. But you don't never let me play nothin'," he mumbled.

Damien rolled his eyes again and folded his arms.

"James, you can't always play with him. He's bigger than you."

Normally, Mara would have had enough of this Child Rearing 101, but she sat on the arm of the sofa and watched Tea handle her brothers like a pro. It was like she knew exactly what to say. She wondered if she'd know what to say to her little crumb snatcher and her hand instinctively went to her abdomen.

"Go ahead back to the den. Just watch them play for now, and maybe you can try it later. Walk!" Tea added when he started to run.

She sat down beside Damien whose eyes were still blazing beneath his curly, dark lashes. She bumped his arm, but his lips remained pursed as he stared at the floor.

"Hey," she said.

Damien turned his head to her, and she could see his watery eyes.

"You can't get so mad at him, Day."

"Nobody takes my side. Not Daddy, not you."

"I know how you feel. I was the same way when you came along. Everybody loved some Damien. I would get fussed at if I even looked at you wrong."

"For real?" he asked, looking up at his sister.

"Yep. And I was almost grown myself, but Daddy wouldn't let me get near you. You know you're his number one boy. You just need to look out for James, that's all."

Damien nodded and dug his heels into the carpet.

"Day!" Miles called again and he came from around the corner. His gait slowed when he saw them all on the sofa. "Hey, Mara," he said.

She raised her eyebrow in response, then grabbed her purse and walked past him.

"Everything okay?" he asked Tea and stood in front of them. "You get in trouble, man?"

"James got me in trouble!" Damien said, his anger building again.

Miles squatted to his level. "Well, I tell you what. Let's go back and finish the game until it's time to eat. Then we'll find something for all of us to do."

Damien got up and stomped his way back to the den. Miles stood, then leaned down to kiss Tea quickly on the mouth.

"I'm sorry, baby. I didn't know they started fighting."

"How could you not hear them yelling at each other?"

Miles smiled. "I was fixing the game. I'm sorry. I'll keep them out of your way. You know Miles loves the kids."

He slipped his hand around her waist when she got up. "Miles loves his baby, too."

Tea playfully rolled her eyes and pushed him away. "I need to go cook something. I know they'll be hungry again soon." She also wanted to see what was wrong with her girl. She didn't look too good. Tea started to turn away but felt him pulling gently on her arm.

"Hey, you," Miles said softly.

Tea looked up at him but gave no response.

"I know you had a headache and were trying to lay down. I'm sorry, baby."

She shrugged. "No, I know." She folded her arms. "I'm just tired."

"How 'bout this? I'll take them to the court, then I'll take them home. Don't worry about dinner, we'll pick up something on the way."

Warming up to the idea, Tea started to smile and looked relieved. "You will?"

He nodded and pulled her closer. He planted a soft kiss on her forehead, then down the bridge of her nose, and finally on her lips. "Why don't you lay back down?"

"Yeah, I need to." Tea didn't tell him that her headache had been long gone, but what he didn't know wouldn't kill him. She missed her brothers, but they were starting to wear her patience thin. They'd been rowdy since she picked them up from their dual dental appointments. Anna wasn't able to stay for the duration and was overjoyed to find out Tea was off work and available. Tea really didn't mind since it had been weeks since she'd last seen them.

Miles headed back to the den and Tea glanced in the direction of the bathroom, but the door was wide open. She peeked in the kitchen and on the deck. Mara was nowhere around. She walked upstairs and lightly tapped on her door. She opened it at Mara's request.

"…yes, okay and make sure you add extra black olives," she was saying into her phone. She waved to Tea, who waved back. "Yes. Wait, no, not green peppers, nothing I said sounded anything like green peppers." Mara rolled her eyes. "Look, nevermind. I'm just gonna use the damn app like I should've in the first place." She ended the call.

Tea sat at Mara's vanity and finger-fluffed her pageboy. "You know they're going to spit in your pizza sauce," she laughed, glancing at her friend behind her in the mirror's reflection.

Mara laughed and tapped out her order on her phone. When she finished, she stood and walked to Tea.

"Hi, lovely," she smiled and hugged Tea from behind. They smiled at each other in the mirror, and she played in Tea's hair.

"Hi, girl. I guess that's a solo pizza you ordered?"

"Sorry. I thought you already ate. I smelled something in the kitchen."

"Oh. Miles made some pepperoni pockets for the boys earlier." Mara nodded like she couldn't care less.

Tea looked at her. She knew when to pick her moments with Mara.

"He's really sorry, Mara. He keeps apologizing to me like somehow it'll make you forgive him."

For a few seconds, she wasn't sure Mara heard her because her face was blank. Then, Mara blinked hard and rested her hands on Tea's shoulders.

"I don't know...it's starting to become this thing now. Everybody's tiptoeing and shit. Si keeps telling me Miles is sorry, you keep telling me he's sorry. I know you and Si are talking behind my back." When Tea started to object, Mara gave her a look, and Tea made a face of agreement.

Mara sighed and sat down on the side of her bed.

"I'm not even mad at him anymore. He was just defending me, I guess." She intended to say it to herself but was loud enough for Tea to hear because she nodded hard. Mara stared at her friend. Words weren't necessary. They weren't in college or high school anymore. *Get the hell over it.* Tea's message was silent and clear.

Mara rubbed her belly for about a minute, and then stood and looked at her friend. On her way to the door, she patted Tea's shoulder a few times. Downstairs and in the den, her stomach growled because she smelled nacho-flavored chips, then wanted to vomit when she realized it was just the boys' sneakers by the wall. She stepped across their legs to open a window.

"Aunt Maaaaaaara!" Damien whined when she partially blocked his view of the television screen.

"Yeah, yeah, yeah." She shoved the window up and could instantly feel a breeze.

Miles was on the sofa behind the boys, who were sprawled out on the floor. He glanced at her fanning herself and noticed she was packing some extra pounds in her waist and hips.

Mara turned back around too quickly for him to avert his gaze. She definitely saw him looking at her, and being the paranoid self-image conscious person she is, Miles knew she'd say something to him. Or want to know if she looked fat. *Just great*, he thought when she stepped back over the boys and stood in the doorway. She's going to cuss me out for looking at her ass.

"Hello?" she said as he tilted his controller and got back into the game.

Miles turned his head to look at her.

"I need to talk to you," she said.

"Right now?"

"Um, no. In the Year of the Tiger." Mara stared at him for two seconds, then rolled her eyes and walked out.

Miles laughed. "Hold up, lil' soldiers. I'll be right back."

In the dining room, Mara was lowering herself into a chair as he approached. He pulled a chair from the head of the table and placed it a few feet from her.

"What's up?" His eyes studied her face.

She cocked her head and peered at him. "I don't like what happened between us," she started. "I don't know. I don't want to be upset anymore."

He nodded. "Okay. I accept your weak ass apology."

"What? See, I knew –"

"Mara. Mara," he held his palms up. "Kidding. I was joking."

"Oh." She sucked her teeth.

"No, really, I feel you. I know how hard it was for you to come to me," he said seriously.

"And I'm really angry with *him*, not you. It's just that he's not here for me to be angry with. You are. I'm sorry, though. I should've just...," Mara shrugged.

"I'm good," he waved off any further apologies. "We're good."

Miles leaned over to give her a quick hug and sat back down.

Mara bit her bottom lip and looked down at the burgundy place mats. She blinked and a small stream of tears fell from each eye. Miles scooted his chair closer and put a hand on her back.

"Mara…"

She knew he was not accustomed to seeing her emotions all over the place, and neither was she. Everything made her cry lately. And now, here he was, one of her best friends in the entire world, who defended her honor and her name, who was there for her no matter what, and she'd ignored him for two weeks. He didn't even know she was expecting a child. What if something happened to her or to him? Mara couldn't process the thoughts fast enough.

"Miles," she decided it was now, never, or whatever, as Aunt Esther would say. Her words came tumbling out so fast she couldn't control them. "I'm pregnant. I'm almost ten weeks now. I'm sorry I never told you. I told Si and Tea not to say anything because I wanted to tell you. I was just so mad I couldn't think straight. Now, with Drew gone, I know I'll have to lean on y'all, and I don't know what to do sometimes. Like with Tea and the boys when I came home. She is so good with them. I wanted to jack them up for running all in my house, but she was so calm. Y'all are so cute together, Miles. I can't believe I'm just now telling you. I need you to help me out. Si and Tea can get psycho, you know how they are. I can't do it by myself. I can't do this by myself," she stopped and took a short gasp of air. "My baby's not gonna have a daddy, Miles. I didn't have a daddy. I never wanted a child without a father. Oh my God." Mara's tears began to fall as freely as her words, and she sobbed into her hands with the revelation that she would be a single parent.

Miles was caught off guard by everything she said and now he rubbed her back to console her.

"Shhh, it's fine, it'll be all right." He hated the look of fear that was in her eyes. "Come here."

He pulled her to him. Her entire body shook and all he wanted to do was protect his friend.

Chapter 43

Sirue looked out the window. The clouds were floating above and below the wing of the plane. With all the beefed-up security at Dulles, he was surprised they'd even made the flight. Especially since Teresa insisted on re-packing every suitcase at the last minute. He wished Miles was on the same flight, then at least he wouldn't have to listen to her complain. Sirue slipped on his earpieces. The movie showing as some lame romantic comedy that he wasn't in the mood for, but it beat the alternative since he forgot to take out his tablet. He felt her shifting in her seat and looked over at her.

"What are you doing?" he asked, removing an earpiece.

"This damn seat is uncomfortable. Excuse me! Excuse me, stewardess!" Teresa waved her hand in the air and the uniformed woman walked briskly down the aisle.

"I'm a flight attendant, ma'am," she corrected with a taut smile, then narrowed her blue eyes. "How may I help you?"

"Well, Miss Flight Stewardess. I need a pillow."

Sirue shook his head and went back to watching the movie.

"If you look right there," the woman pointed, "you'll see we have provided extra pillows."

A few other passengers were becoming agitated at the interruption.

"I can see that, I'm not blind. I need *another* pillow. Now, please." Teresa flashed a fake smile and rolled her eyes.

The woman pursed her lips and hurried back down the aisle. Teresa folded her arms across her chest and sighed loudly.

"Sick of this already," she mumbled.

"What's wrong with you?" Sirue leaned into her, his voice a harsh whisper.

"Everything, Sirue. You yelled at me –"

"Keep your voice down, please, Teresa."

She lowered her volume and glared at him. "You fuckin' yelled at me at the house and I heard you call Mara's fat ass before we left."

Sirue was incensed and couldn't spit his words out fast enough. "I already apologized to you for yelling, Teresa, but you didn't have to pack those damn suitcases three times. And Mara is not fat, so you need to chill with the name-calling shit."

"Oh, what the hell ever. Take up for her like you always do." She waved a hand at him. "What were y'all talking about?"

He shook his head. "I'm not doing this with you right now."

"Oh, you better believe we're gonna finish this shit later, then."

Teresa snatched the pillow from the flight attendant as she approached. She looked across the aisle at an elderly woman who was grinning while she watched the movie overhead. She started a conversation with her, then asked if she would switch seats with her because her boyfriend was getting on her nerves. The woman smiled and said she went through the same thing with her ex-husband.

As the old woman sat down next to Sirue, he glared over at Teresa.

Teresa gave him the finger and stuffed the pillow behind her back.

Sirue jammed the earpiece back into his ear and wondered if she honestly needed an intervention. Did he have to deal with her mood swings in Nashville on top of adjusting to a new job in a new city? What was he getting himself into?

The green LCD on his watch read 11:48pm. Sirue unlocked the door to their garden apartment and said a silent prayer that Teresa would be asleep. During their first week in Nashville, he was meticulous enough in his planning that he arrived home just in time to hear her mumble "goodnight" as she turned over in bed. He hoped his new colleagues attributed his late hours to an overzealous work ethic, especially since he was literally the last professor to leave the Natural Sciences compound every night. Dr. Sinclair, the biology department head, found it remarkable that Sirue's office and labs were already prepared for students, although it would be another week before his new classes actually began.

He stepped in slowly, then saw the slit of light beneath the bathroom door straight ahead.

"Shit," he said to himself.

Not caring how much noise he made now, he loudly locked the front door and lowered his briefcase. He started to remove his tie and shoes as he entered the master bedroom on his right. The lamp on her nightstand cast a soft amber glow across the room and the sheets were ruffled. It was evident that she'd just gotten out of the bed. He sat down on the other side and continued to undress.

Teresa walked into the bedroom and stood in the doorway. Sirue could barely make out her form in his peripheral vision, but he didn't turn to greet her, either. He knew from her silence that this would be a long night.

"Damn, hello to you, too." Her voice didn't have the raspy tone of someone just waking out of sleep, rather the accusatory tone of someone ready for combat.

"Hello, Teresa." Sirue pulled the tails of his blue dress shirt from around his waist and lay it next to him.

She sucked her teeth and folded her arms across her chest, still glaring at him from the door.

Sirue did his best to ignore her and removed his slacks, then socks, and gathered his clothes to deposit them in the hamper near the closet. He stopped at the wide mirror on their dresser and rolled his neck as he removed his class ring and watch. He examined his reflection for an uncomfortably long time and finally turned to walk out of the room, fully aware that Teresa had yet to budge. She held her ground as he approached.

He stood silently in front of her, waiting for her to move.

"Excuse me, please," he finally requested. He put a reluctant hand on her waist.

She shoved his hand down and resumed her stance. Sirue sighed and rolled his eyes upward, then back down to her.

"You're not leaving this room until you talk to me. You haven't talked to me in five days."

"Tere—"

"FIVE days!" She held up her fingers for emphasis. "You're gone all fucking day and night, leaving me alone in this fucking apartment watching fucking TV—"

"Teresa," he steadied her with his hands on her arms.

She violently shook herself loose from his grip and pushed him away with enough force that he stumbled. She screamed. "GET OFF OF ME! Get off of me!!!"

Sirue held his hands up. "Okay, okay, Teresa. Shhh." He just knew the neighbors would be banging on the door any minute now.

"No! Don't shush me, Sirue. Don't you dare fucking shush me. Did you turn your phone off? Huh? Is that why you haven't answered my texts? I texted you thirteen times today!" She was shouting every word at him now.

Sirue's instinct was to exude calm or else he knew the situation would escalate. He wanted nothing more than to shake the hell out of her, but he fought the temptation and merely spoke through clenched teeth.

"Teresa, stop yelling," he repeated over and over as he took a few precautionary steps backward.

His composure seemed to fuel her fire and she charged toward him, pounding his chest between incoherent words. Although each punch she landed was intended to hurt him, the only discomfort Sirue felt was the realization that his own apathy about their relationship caused this outburst. He managed to hold her wrists at bay while she struggled to pull them free.

"Get off of me," she grunted in a low timbre he'd only associated with someone possessed. She was stronger than he'd thought, and she managed to pull an arm free. Teresa started to attack his face, shoulder, and torso with as many hits as she could land before he forcefully grabbed her arm and restrained both behind her back. He squeezed them tightly and pressed her body against his. Sirue held her firmly in place for a full minute until her breathing regulated and her forehead fell against his heaving chest. The loose bun of curls she'd had in her head was now messy and falling to the side.

"Let me go," she uttered quietly with exhaustion.

"You going to keep your hands to yourself?" he asked evenly.

She nodded. Sirue released his grasp and she pulled completely from him, rubbing her soon-to-be bruised forearms. Without speaking, she quietly walked to her side of the bed, gingerly touching her sore wrists.

Sirue couldn't believe this scene had just occurred. This was insane. It had never gone this far before. Her outburst was ludicrous. Still, he felt enormous guilt over leaving marks on her arms. His own body and face were still giving off heat in the wake of her punches and slaps, but there was no excuse to put his hands on her. He should have kept trying to walk away.

Torn between conflicting emotions, Sirue rubbed his head with both hands and hit the doorjamb twice on his way out of the room, causing Teresa to jump. In the bathroom down the hall, he splashed cold water on his face and neck, then stared absently into the mirror. Before he allowed himself the solace of contemplation, he abruptly turned the lights off and walked to the living room. There were still a few unpacked boxes, but as he sat on the sofa, he noticed that Teresa had already made their home cozy. Some paintings, including his favorite, were strategically hung on the walls. Knickknacks and photographs were on their mantle above the faux fireplace. The drapes were hung. There was a latent candle fragrance in the air. The place was starting to take a life of its own while he was hiding at work, and he never once said a word of appreciation. He went out of his way to avoid her because of her psychotic episodes, but he started to wonder if he aggravated her psychoses in any way.

Instantly, thoughts of his mother flooded his memory. She often blamed young Sirue for her manic episodes. On more than one occasion, he would get yelled at for needing help with normal children things – getting dressed, brushing his teeth, homework. But there were other times when he would be expected to parent himself with chores like cleaning the house, reminding her when certain bills were due, or setting alarms to get them both up in the mornings. Any deviation from these duties would lead to a barrage of blame from her. He was the reason she missed a bill payment; he was the reason she couldn't keep the house clean. Or, most often, he was the reason she either screamed or locked herself in her bedroom for days.

Sirue shook his head, trying to gain some clarity, and leaned forward with his elbows on his knees and hands rubbing his eyes. He heard Teresa moving around, then the bedroom went dark. After a few more minutes to himself, he slowly walked back to bed and climbed in. Teresa was motionless, her back to him. Sirue laid on his back, unsure if he should speak. He wanted to apologize, but he didn't want her to think it was okay to physically attack him at her pleasure. He also wanted to discuss their relationship, because there were a lot of things that needed to be said.

"Teresa," he whispered.

"What?"

"I'm sorry for putting my hands on you the way I did."

She mumbled something in a low whisper.

"Huh?" Sirue leaned into her back and strained to hear.

"I said it's not the first time somebody hurt me."

Although her words weren't spoken with enough sadness to warrant it, Sirue slid his arm around her and clasped his hand in hers. He half-expected her to shove him away, but her body went limp as he pressed against her. He was painfully aware that he didn't know much about her past but was sure she had plenty of demons in her head. A casual onlooker could see that. In their relationship, he'd actually revealed more about his own history than she'd ever divulged to him. But, then again, he never pushed her for answers.

He smoothed his thumb along the soft skin of her palm. He wanted more of her vulnerability. It made her seem more human and less erratic. Sirue nuzzled his nose into the crook of her neck and inhaled. He suddenly wanted to push.

"Who hurt you?" he whispered just below her earlobe.

He could feel her breathing getting shallow. He attempted to soothe her into speaking by kissing the back of her head through her mass of wavy curls. Instead, she led his hand to her right breast, which freed itself from her small cotton nightshirt. Sirue willingly played along and massaged it. Her aroused nipple hardened even more between his fingers. It turned him on as he continued to fondle it, but he wanted to maintain his train of thought and moved his hand down to her stomach.

"Talk to me. Who hurt you?" he asked softly.

Teresa shrugged away from his closeness. "I'm tired," she said, despite sniffing tears away.

"You can trust me," Sirue said, sliding his hand to her hip and giving it a gentle squeeze.

Suddenly, she whisked around, partially knocking Sirue onto his back, and flung the bedsheets off them both. In one swift motion, she mounted him and reached down for his semi-swollen manhood inside his boxer briefs. When she had it exposed, she shifted enough to move her panties to one side and started to insert him.

"What are you doing?!" Sirue asked, wide-eyed at the speed with which she was moving.

"You want to fuck me, don't you?"

He couldn't see the features on her face, but her silhouette of frayed hair and disheveled clothes was more than enough to know she wasn't completely lucid.

"Teresa," he started to object again, but she'd already put him inside of her and he felt himself growing despite his intentions.

She leaned forward and gyrated her hips, her arms on the bed beside his body. Sirue placed his hands on her waist and spread his bent legs beneath her.

"Uh huh," she moaned. "That's what I thought. God, you feel so good." She surprised them both with a bounce so severe that her skin smacked his on every downward motion. She grimaced with the pain of taking him in so quickly.

Sirue let out a long sound and turned her over. As she lay beneath him, he entered her more steadily and deeply, leaning back and grabbing onto her thighs. He pulled her body to his.

"Shiiiiiiiiiiiit," Teresa yelled and Sirue leaned down to her. He grunted with a passion he hadn't let surface in weeks. He looked at her breasts bouncing through her thin shirt.

"It's yours, Siruuuuue…oh my God, fuck me harder," she repeated in breathless spurts.

Sirue groaned his response, and his thrusts became deeper. He didn't know why he was pounding her so roughly, although she sounded like she was enjoying it. His fuzzy brain could barely make sense of the words she spat out. He loved the familiarity of her warmth and the sensation of their juices blending. Without losing his rhythm, he leaned back again and pulled her even closer by her thighs. She let out a yelp as he did. It was too dark to see, but he knew he was probably grabbing her legs too hard. He didn't want to stop. He felt her insides tighten around him and he released his death grip long enough to feel the friction inside of her. His senses were beyond overload.

Teresa contracted her muscles and Sirue exploded his frustration and confusion deep inside of her. He caught his breath then lifted himself off of her writhing body. She turned away from him and he immediately felt like he'd been manipulated.

A part of Sirue still wanted to push for more answers, but now he was too exhausted. They'd never had sex that intense before and his body was still resonating. He knew she didn't climax and normally he would make sure she did. Tonight, though, he wanted to exert some sense of control, so he just let her stay as physically frustrated as he felt mentally. He drifted off to sleep while the scenes of the last hour replayed in his mind.

"Sirue?" Teresa turned to face him and lifted his resting eyelid.

He shook his head free, upset at the sudden irritation of being jolted awake. He grunted, not sure how long he'd been asleep. The room was still dark.

"Sirue?" she asked again.

"Hm?" he answered groggily.

"Do you think I'm crazy?" She traced the profile of his face with a finger.

He opened his eyes. "Huh?"

"I want to know…do you think I'm crazy?" She kissed his cheek, then went back to touching the lines of his face.

"What? Teresa—"

"Because, if I was *really* crazy, I would go to the police station right now and say you raped me. I'm bruised up pretty bad."

Siure looked at her, not sure he heard her right. The concentrated look in her eyes told him he did. He sat up with a quickness that defied his lethargy.

"What the hell did you just say?"

"You heard me." Teresa shrugged and turned back around. "Goodnight."

How could she say something like that so casually?

"No, no, uh uhnn, get up, that shit is not a joke, Teresa."

"I didn't say it was. Goodnight."

"Goodnight my ass! What kind of shit is that to say to me?"

"I'm tired, Sirue. You're overreacting, damn. Good. Night." Teresa pounded a few times on her pillow, then plopped her head back down.

"Yeah…well, we have some serious shit to talk about in the morning," he dug his finger into the mattress for emphasis, "because that right there ain't funny."

"Whatever. Now you have so much to say, huh? Just keep ignoring me like you were doing all week."

Sirue glared at the back of her head. He wondered if his leg could reach up and kick it. No, the base of the lamp would do a much better job, but that's too much blood splatter.

"Psycho," he muttered and wildly turned over on his side, yanking the covers.

"You ain't seen psycho yet, gimme the damn blankets," she said and yanked them back.

Chapter 44

"Are you serious?"

Mara was in the den, rubbing the small swell of her belly. She had been about to call Tea at the shop when her phone rang and Sirue was on the other line sounding distressed.

"Do you think I would lie about this?" he replied.

She chuckled and used the remote to turn the volume of the television down.

"Can I say it, Si?"

"Don't say it."

"Can I please say it?"

"Mara."

"I TOLD YOU SO! I knew she needed intense therapy, but did y'all listen to me? Noooooo. I just ended up looking like the crazy evil bitch. That heifer is loony!"

"Are you finished?" Sirue said.

"It's whatever, man. I just got my justification. So, whatcha gonna do now? How fast are you kicking her out? And can you put me on speaker phone when you do?"

Sirue let out a short laugh. "Well, we didn't get that far yet. We're going to have a talk this morning before Miles gets here. Did I tell you yet that I'm glad you forgave him? It's about damn time."

Mara rolled her eyes. "Yes, you told me." She looked down and stretched the elastic waistband of her sweatpants. "I'm getting so big, Si."

"Well, my nephew or niece needs nourishment. What did you eat today?"

Mara couldn't help but smile. "It's not even eight o'clock, young."

"Mara –"

She sighed. "I got some food in the fridge. I'll eat in a minute, but I haven't been that hungry. I threw up twice at work yesterday and I'm feeling nauseous right now."

"What did your doctor say?"

"My appointment's on Monday. Auntie's driving up to be with me."

Her phone beeped and signaled another call coming through.

"Si, hold on, the other line –"

"Hey, just hit me back later. Like after you eat."

"Okay, okay. Bye." She accepted the incoming call. "Hey, you."

"I knew you'd be up!" Miles' voice came through her phone.

"You in Nashville yet?" She stood and felt a small cramp in her side. "Ouch!"

"Ouch what?"

"Nothing, it's my side," she rubbed it as she walked slowly to the kitchen. "Where are you?"

"In my small ass rental car now."

Mara reached the refrigerator and peeked inside. Nothing looked appealing.

"You heard from Si? He's not picking up his cell. I need the address again. I'm not trying to end up at a nigger check point down here in Redneckville." He glanced around at the unfamiliar signs pointing every which way.

"Yeah, I just got off the phone with him. His ringer must be off. Hold on, I have his address." She clicked through her contacts and read it off to him. "Oh, and you are definitely going to walk into some drama at his place, though."

Mara grabbed a small carton of blueberry yogurt. She gave him a brief synopsis of Sirue's story as she fished for a spoon.

"Damn. Don't know whether to laugh or feel sorry for him," he concluded. "That's some toxic shit."

"Right. Well go ahead and put in the address before you really get lost. I'll talk to you later."

"Peace."

Mara put her phone down on the counter. The yogurt was good enough on the first spoonful, but then she started to get a bad taste in her mouth.

Then, there was a stabbing pain in her abdomen. She held the edge of the sink. The spoon and yogurt went falling to the floor. Mara screamed as the throbbing intensified, then doubled over before dropping to her knees.

Tea was pacing back and forth in the waiting room when she finally saw a woman in scrubs approach. Tea hurried toward her.

"Were you working on Mara Queden?" Her speech was choppy, as she could hardly form the words.

The doctor nodded grimly.

"I'm...sorry. There was significant scarring. Her body couldn't support the embryo."

Tea's hand flew to her mouth as she tried desperately to keep her composure.

"So...is she okay? Can I see her?"

A nurse emerged from around a corner and practically bombarded the doctor, shoving a clipboard in her face. The doctor scribbled her signature and returned her pen to her pocket as the nurse sped away.

"Yes, well, she'll be moved to her room in a few minutes. I'd wait about an hour, give the medication some time to kick in," she nodded her sincerest sympathy and touched Tea's arm as she walked away.

Tea tried to keep it together. She knew she had a propensity for falling apart in stressful situations, so she told herself to think and furiously dialed numbers on her cell. Within the hour, she'd received at least ten phone calls from Miles and Sirue.

Aunt Esther arrived minutes before they were allowed to see Mara. They walked in together and saw Mara laying on the bed with tubes in her arms. Aunt Esther rushed to her side and hugged her as best she could.

"My baby..." was all Mara could get out before she sobbed into her aunt's shoulder.

"It's all right, sugar, it's all right. We don't always know God's plans." She hugged Mara even tighter, and Tea walked around to the other side of the bed. She rubbed Mara's back and wished there was so much more she could do for her.

Chapter 45

Mara reached over and answered her ringing phone.

"Hey," she answered with a sleepy attitude.

"Hello, beautiful," Sirue's chipper voice sounded.

"Beautiful these."

He laughed. "Well, you told me to call you and tell you how my first few days of classes went, but first I want to know how you're feeling today."

Mara rolled her eyes and sighed. She was already over being constantly asked how she's feeling. She'd had her miscarriage almost two weeks ago and if it wasn't a text from Sirue, it was a video call from Miles, or Nurse Tea giving her hourly check-ups.

"I'm okay," she lied.

Sirue paused. "Would you tell me if you weren't?"

"Yes…no…maybe," Mara shrugged. "But are you sure I told you to tell me about your classes?"

"Don't start with the bull."

She let out a weak chuckle. "See, I was half-drugged last week so that didn't really count."

Sirue ignored her comment and went on to tell her about his first week of teaching at Skiff. It was definitely what he'd expected. He missed the camaraderie that Sedrick provided, but he was adapting to the other like-minded professors in his department. He had about the same course load, so he wasn't overwhelmed at all. The facilities were also similar, but the actual material he covered was more challenging. The anatomy and physiology courses seemed to invigorate him, but the genetics course was his favorite. It was a totally different beast instructing actual biology majors and not students who just needed the science credit.

"I even started jogging this week," he added proudly.

Mara coughed and laughed at the same time. "What the hell...Si, stop playing."

"No, I'm serious. And Teresa jogs with me. It's kind of our planned time together."

"So, how's that working out?" Mara couldn't care less, and it was evident in her tone.

"It's working. She's...doing a lot better. Some things have changed for the good."

"Well, I'll be glad when you send Miles back home so Tea can stop fussing over me," she commented, changing the subject.

"It's that bad, huh?"

"You know how she is. I sneezed yesterday and she called her doctor, my doctor, and Aunt Esther because she thought I got an infection."

"Damn," Sirue said with a knowing smile.

"And my class is going okay, thanks for asking."

"Hey, I was going to –"

She laughed. "Whatever. But my professor's giving me an extra week to turn in my semester project. I'll get it done if Miss Red Cross would give me a minute to breathe."

As if she heard her cue, there was a light knock on the door, and it creaked open. "Mara? I heard your voice, I wanted to make sure you weren't talking to yourself."

Mara rolled her eyes. "I'm talking to Si, Tea. It's all right, I haven't gone crazy on you yet."

She sat up taller in her bed and tried to arrange her pillows behind her back. Tea rushed over and adjusted them for her.

"I can do it," Mara tried to say, but Tea refused to let her.

"Tell BigHead I said hi," Sirue said.

"I would, but she's too busy treating me like I'm disabled," Mara snapped, and Tea stopped cold.

"No, I'm treating you like someone who's been through hell, Mara," she commented patiently, then resumed fluffing the pillows.

"What did she say?" Sirue asked.

Mara ignored his question and could feel her irritation with Tea growing. She let out an aggravated sigh and Tea moved to pick up the dishes on the nightstand. Been through hell? How did she know what hell was like? How did she know how it felt to wake up from a nightmare and have an emptiness so deep you wanted to die yourself?

"Hellooo?" Sirue called into the phone.

"Oh. My bad. Um, what was I talking about before I was so rudely interrupted? Oh, about how Miles needs to hurry his ass home so somebody won't have as much free time on her hands and will leave me the hell alone?" After it left her mouth, she knew she was wrong.

Tea stood with the dishes in her hands and gave Mara a sharp look. She shook her head and left the room without a word, closing the door behind her.

"Shit," Mara whispered.

"Damn, Mara," Sirue said.

"Me and my big trifling ass mouth. Shit," she repeated. "I'll call you later."

"All right."

Mara hung up and continued to sling expletives at herself as she slowly swung her legs around and stood next to her bed. Her abdomen felt sore, but much better than it did the days before. It didn't feel like her uterus was being tugged by a rope anymore. She slid her feet into her slippers, threw her robe on and slowly made her way downstairs.

Tea was rinsing a plate and putting it into the dishwasher. Mara stood at the entryway of the kitchen and leaned on the wall, watching her close the dishwasher and turn it on.

"Tea," she started.

"You should be in bed," Tea interrupted. She dried her hands off on a dishtowel and walked past Mara to jog up the steps. Mara flinched when she heard Tea's bedroom door slam shut.

Miles drummed his fingers as the city of Baltimore came into view. He hadn't originally planned to stay the extra week in Nashville, but he took advantage of his job's flexibility. He checked his watch again. Tea would definitely be at the shop by now. He figured it was fate when he reached the Nashville International Airport two hours ahead of schedule and was able to catch an earlier flight back home after a seat became available. He wanted to surprise his lady. She was expecting him later that evening, not around lunch time.

After retrieving his luggage and his car, he started the forty-five-minute trek south on the BW Parkway. There wasn't too much traffic, so he was able to enjoy his favorite trap music playlist and get some thinking done. It was time to ask her. Definitely time to ask her. Hopefully, she wouldn't think he was just jumping into another adventure or acting without thinking. Tea was perfect for him, and he knew it. He'd talked Sirue's head off all week, going on and on about her. He loved her feisty nature when the situation called for it. He loved her nurturing spirit. He enjoyed her playful side, her business side. Her eyes, her smile, her soft skin. Her body.

Damn, Miles thought. He could see her long bangs partially covering her big, brown eyes. The way she'd shake her bangs away from her face or pull them behind her ears was so sexy to him. The way she licked her lips. The way her shirts held her breasts just right. He silently thanked all the Racker female chromosomes in her ancestry and smiled to himself. And it wasn't just the way she looked. She made him feel complete, like she was the piece that had been missing all along. Why did it take him so long to realize it?

Thoughts of Tea kept him company until he was just outside of Largo, Maryland. He made a quick detour before heading to the mall. When he arrived, he could smell her salon before he even reached it. He nodded a hello to Kadari at her kiosk and turned to see a lot of women in Tea's shop.

Nikki greeted him with an energetic smile.

"Hey, Mr. Miles," she said, then picked up the ringing phone next to her. "Hair by Tea, how may I help you?"

Miles excused himself and grooved to the infectious sounds of the smooth R&B coming through the overhead speakers. He walked past a few women in the reception area. Every seat was full.

"For me? You shouldn't have," DeeDee said, commenting on the contents in his hands.

"Hey, Dee," Miles gave her a quick hug and glanced around. "Y'all are busy busy, huh?"

"Yeah." DeeDee quickly resumed working on her customer's wet set. "Usually is on Sundays, though. Your lady is in the back mixing colors." She winked at him.

Miles strolled past a few more women under dryers; some were reading books and the rest were on their phones or tablets. When he saw her, he felt his chest jump a beat. Her back was facing him, but he could see her clear gloved hands meticulously pouring liquid from one bottle to another. He watched for almost a full minute, then cleared his throat.

Tea whipped around, startled.

"Miles!" She hurriedly removed her plastic gloves and went to hug him.

"Hi, baby, I missed you." He hugged her as best he could with his hands full.

"Oooh, what's all this?" she smiled.

He handed her the bouquet of assorted flowers and gently smoothed her bangs from her forehead. She buried her face in the colorful foliage and inhaled deeply.

"This is exactly what I needed today," she said quietly. She looked up at him, and with her free hand, pressed it hard against the back of his neck and lowered his face to hers. She kissed him intensely, pulling aggressively on his bottom lip as she pulled away.

Miles looked at her again, then remembered he had something else to give her.

"And there's food." He held up the greasy bags displaying the signature blue and green logo of Hungry Boy's Soul Food.

Tea's eyes widened.

"I'm soooo hungry," she whined.

"Me, too." Miles licked his juicy lips and his eyes bore into her like she was on the menu.

"Don't start back here," she playfully warned through clenched teeth.

He chuckled and gently took her elbow, leading her to the back office.

"Hold on," she told him and headed to DeeDee's station. Before she even spoke, DeeDee held up a hand.

"Girl, go handle your business. I got this 'til you get back," she said discreetly.

Tea was a little embarrassed. "No, he just brought me lunch. We're just going to eat, Dee."

"Mmmhmm, okay. And I look like Meg the Stallion."

Tea rolled her eyes and couldn't get back to Miles fast enough.

The food was in clear containers, and it was all still warm. Fried chicken, mac & cheese, mashed potatoes with Hungry Boy's famous gravy, and cornbread. Plus, two bottles of iced tea, paper plates and plastic utensils. They spread the food out and as they fixed their plates, Miles explained to her how he was able to catch the earlier flight.

"I'm glad you did," she said from across the small desk that separated them.

He handed her the potatoes and picked up on her tone. "How's Mara?"

Tea scooped out the creamy spuds and lightly shrugged. "She's all right, but she won't let me help her get better." She recounted the scene from earlier that day.

Miles fed himself forkfuls of food as he listened. When she finished, he washed it down with half of his beverage before he spoke.

"She probably just needs some space, some time to herself to get her head straight." As he said it, he realized how perfect it all was now. It was in the stars for him to ask her at this moment.

Tea opened her mouth to speak, but Miles cut her off.

"Wait, baby, I need to talk to you."

Tea closed her mouth. "Okay."

"How would you…," he tapped his fork for a few beats, then looked directly into her eyes. "How would you feel about moving in with me?"

Chapter 46

Sirue lifted the vented lid off the pot of steaming vegetables to examine the contents. He moved the mixture of carrots, broccoli, and cauliflower around. Perfectly tender. He turned off the burner and set the pot aside. The rice was nearing completion and the seasoned chicken thighs in the oven smelled divine. He reached above and grabbed two plates from the cabinet. As he did, the front door opened.

"Hey, honey," Teresa called out. She hung her keys on the wall and deposited her purse on the sofa as she walked to the kitchen.

"Hi, you," Sirue said when he turned around. He gave her a quick kiss which led to a longer one.

"It smells so good in here," she smiled. "I'm so hungry."

"I'll plate us up, then you can tell me about your day," he returned a smile.

Teresa went to wash up and change clothes. Sirue removed the pan of chicken from the oven and inhaled slowly as he placed it on top of the stove. As he plated, he thought about how different their relationship had been in the last two weeks.

The morning after the crazy and confusing night of sex, Sirue insisted they talk before he left for work. He convinced her to see a therapist that very morning, and she hesitantly agreed, as long as he did the same. Since then, they have had civil exchanges and he could see an immediate change in her demeanor. He had yet to divulge to her that he never scheduled his own appointment, and he also realized she never really asked about it.

The small, four-seat dining room table was adjacent to the open kitchen. Sirue set their dinner down and retrieved two wine glasses and a bottle of Chardonnay.

Teresa walked in with her bouncy curls freshly set free form the tight ponytail she'd sported earlier. She also changed into a comfy gray and pink lounge set; her face washed clean of makeup.

"This looks so good," she said as she sat across from Sirue, admiring the food.

"So do you," he replied, taking a sip of wine. "How was your day?"

"My session was great today," she said as she reached for his hands. "Let's pray."

Sirue obliged and they said grace over their meal. He grabbed his fork and started eating after she took a few bites of her rice and veggies.

"I told her the pills seem to be working, even though I know it's kind of early to tell," she offered.

Sirue shrugged and looked at her. "If you're feeling a difference, it's good that you let her know."

She nodded. "So...what about you? How was today? Any cute underclassmen try to push up on you?"

He looked up from his piece of chicken. Teresa giggled.

"I'm joking!" she shrieked.

Sirue made a face and proceeded to tell her about his classes that day. They finished dinner and cleared the table together. It was relaxing to have a normal conversation while they loaded dishes into the dishwasher. No wild mood swings, no accusations, no yelling. They ended up crashing on the couch with a random television show watching them.

Sirue's phone going off jolted them both out of their sleep. Teresa was sprawled out across his body and reached for his phone on the side table. She groggily looked at the caller's name and handed it to him, rolling her eyes and falling back onto his chest.

"Huh?" he said, barely coherent. He put the phone to his ear. "Hey, hello?"

"Wake up," Mara said.

"What – what the hell time is it?"

"Ask Jamie Bond over there, I know she's listening anyway," Mara said dryly.

Sirue yawned and stretched which made Teresa move to the other side of the couch.

"Baby, you should get in bed," he whispered, tapping her hip.

She grumbled and pulled the throw blanket over her body as she pulled herself into a ball against the opposite arm of the couch. Sirue softly rubbed her hip and tried to blink back to his conversation.

"What's up? Is everything okay?"

"Nope."

He rubbed his eyes. The light from the television's screensaver cast a bluish hue across the living room. He squinted to read the time. It was eleven past midnight.

"What's wrong?" he yawned loudly again.

"I'll call you back tomorrow," she answered quietly.

"You woke me up, you better talk."

Sirue heard her let out a small laugh.

"I'm gonna be alone forever, Si."

"No, you're not."

"I am. Tea hates me, too. I can't keep friends. I hate my stupid job. I'm just...," Mara's voice trailed as she sniffed. "And my hormones are fucked up."

Sirue felt for his friend. "Mara. You're healing. Your life has been turned upside down. Give yourself some grace."

She groaned. "That sounds like a fake ass social media inspirational quote."

Now, Sirue chuckled. "Look, *you* called *me* up sounding pitiful, don't—"

"Okay, okay. You're right."

"Why haven't you apologized to Tea for calling her Florence Nightingale yet?"

Mara paused. "She walked away when I tried. But I think we'll both be home tomorrow night. I don't want to call her at work and disturb her. She already hates me enough."

"Wait. You call *me* at work and disturb *me*, though. I ain't Miles, I actually do shit."

Teresa shifted next to him, and he heard Mara laugh.

"Whatever, you like when I bug you," Mara replied, her voice still low.

"I do?"

"Yep." She paused another beat. "I hope she forgives me. I've been such an ass lately."

"She will. And I think once you've mended it with her, things will feel more normal again. You won't feel so overwhelmed."

"Yeah. That's true." Mara yawned. "Thanks, Si. I can go to sleep now."

"Of course you can since I'm wide awake."

She gave another small laugh. "I'm sorry, friend. You need me to stay up?"

"No. Get some sleep. You don't want to be tired when you give her that phony ass apology tomorrow."

"Shut up."

Sirue laughed groggily. "Goodnight."

"Bye, Si."

"You're cleaning again?"

Tea rolled her eyes at Miles' shock and looked directly into her phone screen at him. Her phone was propped against the back of the counter.

"Yes, Miles! It's good to bleach and disinfect the kitchen at least once a week. When's the last time you did yours?"

She unplugged the blender and slid it off the counter while she waited for his response.

"Miles...," she made a face at him.

"I'm thinking!"

Tea laughed and sprayed the counter with her favorite bleach and deodorizing mixture.

"So basically, when Si was there."

"Basically," he laughed in agreement. "Okay, baby, I've been bugging you since your ride home from work."

Tea shrugged. "I'm not complaining," she smiled at him.

He returned the smile and sipped from the water bottle he was holding. They looked at each other for a few seconds. She loved seeing that enamored expression on his face. Miles always looked at her with so much adoration and it gave her chills. She snapped out of her reverie.

"But you're right...I do need to get this done. Talk to you later?"

"Of course," he answered, still giving her the look through the screen.

Tea smiled and waved goodbye, then hung up. She finished wiping down the counters, the doors of the stainless-steel refrigerator, the stovetop, and finally the double sink. She went to grab the broom from the side closet and heard Mara's keys in the front door. She pursed her lips, her feelings still smarting from the other day. She wanted to mention something about her going back to work too early and that she should still be in bed allowing her body to finish healing. But she feared it would come across as too pushy.

Tea focused on sweeping beneath the counters and behind the trash can near the backdoor. Without lifting her head, she heard Mara approaching, tossing her purse on the dining room table. Mara took the dustpan handle from her and helped scoop up the debris.

Tea glanced up and half-smiled at her best friend. When they finished sweeping in silence, she took the handle from Mara and emptied it into the garbage. Mara leaned against the counter and folded her arms. She looked around at the sparkling appliances.

"I'll never understand how you can clean without music," she said quietly.

"Music distracts me – I always end up dancing and never finish cleaning."

"Um, that's the whole point," Mara joked.

"I'm convinced you and Miles are related." They both laughed.

Tea walked to the refrigerator next to Mara and pulled it open, peeking inside. "Hmmm. You hungry?"

Mara didn't answer and she looked over at her.

"I'm sorry, Tea. I really am," Mara said, her hand over her heart. "I hurt your feelings and I'm sorry."

Tea closed the door and hugged her friend. Mara squeezed her hard before letting her go.

"You just wanted to help me, and I was a bitch. It's not like I have people fighting to want to take care of me," Mara said with a tear falling from each eye.

Tea wiped her friend's cheeks with the back of her hand. "I love you and I forgive your mean ass."

Mara smiled. "Your hand smells like bleach and now you just poisoned me, so I guess we're even."

Tea laughed. "Oops, sorry."

They both washed their hands and pulled out leftovers to heat up. Within fifteen minutes, they were at the table eating spaghetti, a salad, and plain write rice that Mara reheated.

"Why is spaghetti always so good the second day?" Mara stabbed at her plate.

"Right?" Tea agreed. "Oh. Guess what Miles asked me?"

Tea recalled the events in her back office at the shop from Sunday, including the beautiful flowers, the delicious food, and the offer to move in with him.

Mara stopped chewing with her fork in midair. "Huh?"

Tea made a face. "I knoooow. I was in shock."

Mara raised her eyebrows and started to absently stab at her lettuce, though her mouth was already full. Tea couldn't quite read her face.

"I told him he's probably just missing Sirue and didn't want to be alone in that house, but he assured me it's because he wants us to move to another level," Tea said, still not sure if she really believed it all her own self.

"Wow. Like, Si *just* left, and we *just* moved in here together," Mara commented, barely loud enough for Tea to hear. "Maybe he should just get a smaller place."

"Yeah," Tea said.

They both studied their plates for the next minute until Mara broke the silence.

"No. I'm not gonna be selfish again," she said, looking across at Tea. "You have my blessing if that's what you want to do. I'll figure out rent and stuff."

Tea gave her a look of panic. "Blessing?!"

"Yeah," Mara said, confused.

"I don't need a blessing! I ain't going nowhere, girl. I told him not until we're married! That's a major step for me, moving into a whole house with him. No way, I'm too …no, we'd need to be married. And I told him we're going to be celibate until then, too."

Mara almost choked on a cucumber. "You said what?"

Tea chuckled. "I'm serious. We decided last week. We're just going to enjoy each other without the sex."

Mara stared at her. "You're for real? And his horny ass agreed?!"

"He did!"

"Yeah, okay, let's see how that's working for y'all by next month. Hell, next week! He can't keep his hands off you, boo." Mara smiled at her friend.

Tea almost blushed. She twirled spaghetti around her fork. "God, I love how much he likes to touch my back, my hands…everything. He's so affectionate."

Mara continued smiling at her.

Tea took a deep breath. "But it's going to work. We'll be on a whole new spiritual level of commitment, ya know?"

Mara made a face of disbelief. "He's probably buying hand towels in bulk as we speak."

Tea giggled and rolled her eyes. "No, he's not. Shut up."

"Watch. Check the recent orders on his phone next time you see him," Mara laughed.

Chapter 47

Mara blasted one of her favorite ratchet rappers in her ears as she pulled into the parking lot of the short office building that housed her job. When she was first hired out of college three years ago, she was excited to join the marketing department in the corporate office of one of the most prestigious department stores in the country. So much had changed in public relations, though, and she knew this was quickly becoming a dead-end position. She wished she could get a promotion.

She also wished again that she had a booming sound system in her car instead of the temperamental static box she called a radio. *One day I'll get a car made in this decade*, she thought to herself as she yanked her earbuds from her ears and stuffed them into her purse. She sighed and threw her head back. She dreaded everything about work lately. She'd been back since Monday and quickly regretted only taking a few weeks off. Her nosy coworkers wanted information that she didn't want to share with them, so they pretty much shunned her and went looking for more office gossip to spread.

Mara preferred the isolation of her cubicle, but it was incredibly mind-numbing to crunch numbers and log advertisement contracts all day. She knew she could help the company triple their ad revenue and improve their public image, but her heart wasn't in it. She also knew she could do the Public Relations Manager's job in her sleep. It was time to finish this master's and realize her potential.

Mara looked out her window at the leaves dancing in swirls around the bases of the trees that lined the building. The wind was picking up and she remembered why this was her favorite time of year. Everything was shifting, shedding its skin. It was time for her to do the same. She'd been putting off her semester project all week, and the deadline to register for spring classes was quickly approaching. She heard Aunt Esther's voice in her head: "If you want something, go get that shit."

She exhaled and grabbed her belongings, then took her newfound energy in to the office. She sped through her day's work tasks within an hour of sitting at her desk and spent the rest of her day consulting with Si during his free time about the spring courses she should choose. With his help, she decided on three classes: Digital Advertising, Entertainment Marketing, and Brand Strategy. It was going to be a challenge juggling four and a half grad credits while working full-time, but she had goals to reach, a degree to finish, and promotions to get.

When Mara got home that evening, she grabbed a snack, then hurried upstairs to change into gym clothes. She hadn't worked out in weeks. Part of her was nervous about how hard she'd push herself, but she was going to heed Tea's advice she shared on the phone a few minutes earlier. She'd ease back into the exercises and call it quits if she experienced any abdominal discomfort. Mara smiled as she brushed her thick hair into a low ponytail. She didn't know what she'd ever do without her best friend.

Walking through Heaven's front doors brought a slight level of panic into her step. So much had changed in her life since the last time she was here, and by the looks of it, things had changed at Heaven's, too. She looked around at the decorations everywhere. The clear holiday lights strung around the circular front desk were a nice touch.

"A little too early for Christmas lights, huh?" a familiar voice asked.

Mara was startled out of her thoughts and saw Pierre waiting for a response.

"Huh? Oh…yeah. It looks nice in here, though." She slid her ID card across the counter.

Pierre grabbed it and gave her a quick once over as he checked her in.

"I haven't seen you in a while," he commented, handing her card back.

"Haven't been here in a while." Mara made a face and slipped her lanyard back into her bag.

"Well, have a good workout," Pierre called after her as she hurried away.

Mara turned and gave him a half-wave and a half-smile. She saw his eyes widen in total surprise before she headed into the secluded area with the more private machines. She found her mid-90s hip hop playlist that always got her hyped up. The elliptical felt like home, and she got into a nice sweat quickly. No abnormal pains, just a good, healthy sweat. After thirty minutes of Diddy and Big, she moved to the open area and sat at one of the arm machines. Fifteen minutes of slow lat pulls and chest presses were enough for her tonight, so she stretched and threw her towel around her neck as she headed back out.

She noticed Pierre trying to busy himself with a stack of papers as she walked past.

"Have a good night, Pierre," she said with a wave.

The wide smile on his face was contagious. "B-bye, bye, Mara," he said shyly.

Sirue loved the rhythm of his new schedule. It had been a few weeks, and not only was he in love with the beautiful autumn colors across campus, but he loved the perks of teaching classes that mattered to the students. They were usually lined up during his office hours, despite his insistence that appointments were mandatory. There were always students who tried to squeeze in between times. He enjoyed fielding questions about the actual content and not just trying to explain what was needed to pass the class.

It was just before seven o'clock when Sirue's day ended. He exhaled and rubbed his eyes. He checked his text messages and saw two from Miles and one from Teresa that he'd missed. Miles was letting him know that since he'd been able to take off work this whole week of Thanksgiving there wouldn't be an issue with getting there early Thursday morning. His next text told him to shut up about his job. Sirue laughed and read Teresa's message that her session had to be pushed back an hour, so she'd pick up dinner for them and get home by eight.

Sirue got home and decided to take a quick shower. In his head he was already devising the menu for later on in the week. He was excited to prepare their humble apartment for his friends. It was a rather spacious one-bedroom, and cozy enough for the five of them to relax and enjoy a delicious meal, and of course, a few games. Miles, Tea, and Mara were planning to get a hotel for a couple of nights, so he didn't have to worry about housing them all in the same space.

The large bathroom with his and her sinks, a jacuzzi-style bathtub, and a separate glass enclosed shower, was easily Sirue's favorite area of the apartment. He hung his bathrobe on the back of the door and walked the few strides to the shower head. While he turned on the water and adjusted the lever to find the perfect temperature, he noticed the wastebasket was pretty full. He made a mental note to dump it when he was done. Sirue turned to step into the shower but did a double take at the items in the trash.

His heart raced.

He looked more closely at the two pregnancy tests that were partially covered with tissues. They were both positive.

Chapter 48

"How much longer? Damn," Mara complained from the backseat. "I need to stretch."

Miles glanced in his rear-view mirror and saw Mara leaning her head back. The luxury sedan he'd rented was much roomier than the previous rental car he picked up during his first visit to Nashville. Mara still managed to nudge the back of his seat repeatedly, mostly on purpose.

"I'm ready for a stretch break, too," Tea joined in from the passenger seat. She rubbed the back of her neck.

"Well, if *some*body wasn't terrified of flying, we would've been at the hotel four hours ago," Miles said evenly, his nerves on edge. This had been the longest ten hours of his life.

"Oh, shut up. I told you I do not fly," Mara rolled her eyes. "Just pull over, for the love of God. My legs hurt! And we need a pee break!"

Miles took the exit for 65 South. "We're almost there, then you can walk and pee all you want. Nobody told you to drink a gallon of water."

"Well, if your cheap ass would turn up the AC, I wouldn't be so damn thirsty! Worried about your stupid gas tank," Mara shot back.

"Gas that you haven't paid one dime for the whole trip!"

"I'll give you your little funky ass ten cents, just pull over, damn! Ew, then you had the nerve to be farting the whole way down here, smelling like death and failure. Sick of this damn car."

"And if I pull over, your ass is getting left!"

"Will y'all stop? Acting like Damien and James," Tea massaged her temples. "How much longer, Miles?"

"About fifteen minutes, baby," he said with as much tenderness as his mood could muster. He reached over and lightly rubbed her leg.

Tea looked over at him. "She said death and failure, though," she laughed at him.

He snatched his hand away, which made her laugh harder.

When he pulled into the Hillerton Suites, they all quickly piled out of the car.

"We made good time," Miles said, heading to the trunk with a loud stretch.

Mara cut him a look while she grabbed her oversized duffle bag.

He laughed. "Why you still mad?"

"Because ten extra minutes wouldn't have killed you." She snatched her small shoulder bag from his hand.

Miles laughed again and shook his head. He grabbed Tea's and his bags, closed the trunk and followed them inside to the lobby to check in.

The elevator doors slowly opened when they reached the third floor and stepped off. Miles trailed behind Mara and Tea as they turned left and walked around a corner to their adjoining rooms. He couldn't keep his eyes off Tea's body and figured it was a good idea of hers to share a room with Mara instead of with him. His imagination had been running wild the entire car ride.

All three of them walked into the room Mara just unlocked with her key card.

"Oooh, it's so spacious in here," she commented and dropped her bags on the large ottoman in the living area. "How is this room bigger than my whole first apartment, though?"

Tea giggled and followed her into the bedroom while Mara used the large, attached bathroom.

"Oh, wow!" Tea plopped down on the huge queen bed closest to the windows. "I'm so tired."

Miles put down both of Tea's bags on the sofa and walked to the kitchenette, checking the contents of the refrigerator. He didn't realize how hungry he was.

"Hey, baby?" he called out, opening the cabinet doors. "You hungry?"

"Yes!" Tea replied from the bedroom.

"Want me to go see what's around here? I can pick something up for us," he yelled back.

"Yes!" he heard Mara yell from the bathroom. "If you would have let us stop somewhere –"

"How you just gonna interject while you peeing?" Miles called back to her.

He headed into the bedroom and saw Tea standing at the window. He walked up behind her and slipped his arms around her waist. Tea leaned her head against his after he bent down to kiss her cheek.

"It's such a beautiful view, huh?" she commented. The distant highway traffic was just beyond an open expanse of land surrounded by full, colorful trees.

"Yes, you are," he kissed her cheek again.

Tea smiled. Miles could feel her body relax into his as she hugged his arms around her even closer.

"Happy Thanksgiving, baby," he whispered.

Tea made a sad face. "I miss the boys. I've never been away from them on Thanksgiving."

"Want to call them? They should be up, right?"

Tea nodded. "If they can smell the food, I'm sure they're up by now."

Miles chuckled and they started to sway slightly together.

He heard Mara open the bathroom door and enter the bedroom space.

"Nuh uh," she said loudly. "Y'all need to take that lovey dovey shit over to your room, Miles."

They both turned around and slowly disentangled themselves. "Always hatin'," Miles joked. Mara rolled her eyes and went to retrieve her bags from the ottoman in the other room.

He took Tea's hand in his and kissed the back of it.

"I'm gonna go find some food," he said quietly to her.

"Okay, we'll start getting ready and I'll call the boys. You told Si we'd be there by noon, right?"

Miles nodded. "All right, see you in a few minutes." He gave her a quick hug and left the bedroom, heading to the door.

"Bring me some bacon biscuits and some kind of hash brown something," Mara said, digging into her duffel bag and pulling out various items of clothes.

Miles paused with his hand on the doorknob. He turned to look at her and noticed she wasn't even looking in his direction. "Ain't offered me a slick nickel, but you got food requests."

"Oh, and some orange juice." She held up a mahogany colored short-sleeved top and laid it on top of the black leggings she put on the couch.

He shook his head and left the room, smiling at his friend, though his mind was already running wild with thoughts of holding Tea again.

Sirue was in the kitchen, staring at the pot of boiling water bubbling out of control. The scene from two days ago kept replaying in his head.

After finding the two pregnancy tests in the wastebasket, he threw his robe back on and walked like a zombie back out into the living room. He sat in silent contemplation and didn't even remember hearing Teresa coming in with bags of Chinese food.

"Hey, honey! I decided on the Kung Pao for you, and I just wanted some lo mein. And don't worry, I got the extra noodles and rolls," she said cheerfully, walking past him and placing the bags carefully onto the dining room table.

From the sofa, Sirue continued to look at the floor, leaning his body forward, his hands clasped. He was quiet as Teresa walked over and stood in front of him.

"Honey," she said softly.

Sirue didn't budge, his breathing remained steady.

Teresa touched the top of his head, then the side of his face. She squatted to get eye-level with him.

"Sirue," she tried again. She covered his hands with hers.

Finally, his gaze met her eyes.

"You're pregnant?"

He could see the shock all over her face, then her expression cycled through about four different emotions.

"How...," she paused. "Shit. I forgot to take that bag out when I left. I'm sorry."

Sirue looked directly into her eyes without responding.

"I wanted to tell you tonight, while we ate."

He continued to look at her.

After a few seconds, Teresa stood up. "Oh my God, say something."

Sirue tried to talk again, but no words came out. She'd had all day, and maybe longer to process the news. He'd only had the last hour. So many thoughts ran through his head at the same time. A baby? An entire human? The money, the bills, their instability…everything flooded in all at once. They'd just started to get settled in a new town, a new state. He was getting accustomed to his new job. They were beginning a new journey within their relationship. A child would disrupt the already shaky balancing act they tried to maintain.

He lowered his head into his hands.

"Well, that's my answer," she mumbled and sulked back into the dining room and sat down.

A few minutes later, Sirue lifted his head and slowly exhaled. He looked over at Teresa sitting at the table. Her back was to him, but he could see her arms were folded and she was staring at the cartons of food in front of her. He stood and walked to stand behind her chair. Sirue leaned down and wrapped his arms around her, snuggling his face into her neck. She tilted her head to the side, and he pecked the soft skin of her shoulder, then on her neck, then on her cheek. He walked around to sit across from her, and he felt her eyes following his movements.

"I've already made up my mind and I'm scheduling a procedure for next week."

Now it was his turn to be in shock. "A…procedure? What kind of procedure, Teresa?"

Her eyes locked on his. "You know what I mean," she said quietly.

Sirue swallowed. He wasn't expecting that declaration so suddenly.

"Wait. Can we…don't you want to talk about it first?" he asked.

"What is there to talk about? You obviously don't want me to keep it," she shrugged, her arms still folded.

Sirue closed his eyes and calmed his breathing.

"Teresa," he said flatly. "You didn't give me time to consider anything. I found out by accident about an hour ago. What do you expect me to say?"

She shrugged again. "So, you want me to keep it?"

"Can we talk about it?" he asked, deliberately much slower this time.

Teresa looked down at the table. "I don't care anymore."

Sirue looked across at her and figured this was upsetting her even more than she was showing. He wondered how she'd been coping today and how much it affected her emotional state. She'd apparently wanted him to be overjoyed with the news and when he didn't immediately express his elation, it flipped a switch inside of her.

"Well, *I* care. We'll figure it out together."

Teresa let a small smile form. Sirue finally smiled, too.

"I've been scared to tell you all day," she admitted.

"Why?"

Teresa made a face. "I know I have my issues, but Sirue...you can be very moody, too."

He nodded. "I'm not the easiest to get along with, I'll admit that."

Teresa sat up, becoming animated. "Like, when you're mad at me, you just stop talking to me. You never really joke around with me. You're so serious all the time. You read your science books more than you interact with me...I could go on."

"Apparently so, damn," Sirue said, sitting back in his chair. "Am I that bad?"

"No," she smiled.

Sirue pondered for a few seconds. "Well, I'm going to do better by you," he said solemnly.

"You are?"

He nodded. "I need to ... express myself more."

"I would love to have a more emotionally available Sirue!" Teresa's eyes widened.

"You're a little too happy about that," Sirue smirked.

They continued to talk over dinner and ended the night cuddled on the sofa in front of the television.

"I don't want to tell anyone," Teresa said, intertwining her fingers in his.

"Okay."

"I'm going to urgent care Friday just to get an idea of how far along I am," she said quietly, neither of them really watching what was on the screen. "Then, we can make a better decision."

"Okay," Sirue repeated. "And I'll be there with you."

He rubbed her arm and kissed the top of her hair. Teresa turned to face him and slid her hands beneath his robe to feel his chest. She kissed all over his warm skin.

"You smell so good," she moaned, sniffing him along his throat.

"I haven't even showered yet," he whispered, getting quickly turned on.

"Well, I want to do something before you do." She reached down to untie his robe and moved her body lower until her knees were on the floor.

Sirue adjusted his position and threw his head back against the sofa. It didn't take much time for her mouth to make him moan.

The knock snapped him out of his memory. He looked at the stove and couldn't remember why he was boiling the water, so he turned off the burner.

Chapter 49

Mara knocked again, harder this time. She was in mid-knock when Sirue yanked the door open.

"It took you long enough," she said, smiling as she reached up to hug him.

"You sounded like the police," he remarked, giving her a warm squeeze.

"You expecting them or something?" She laughed and made her way into his apartment.

"Oh, my goodness, Si!" Tea squealed. "It's beautiful in here!"

She and Mara stepped down into the sunken living room and admired the comfy decorations. The dark gray couch and matching recliner were a perfect complement to the blue-gray mosaic patterned area rug beneath the glass coffee table. As Mara turned, her eyes immediately fell on her favorite painting of the crying mother that was hanging on an accent wall off to the side in a small alcove that served as an office area.

"You like where we put it?" Sirue asked, stepping down into the living room with Miles behind him.

"Yeah," she answered. Mara moved closer to it and folded her arms as she examined it.

"Give us a tour," Tea said, giving Sirue a side hug and leaving her arm around him.

"I mean, I can basically stand in one place and give it to you." He waved his arm in the direction he spoke. "We're standing in the living room, up there where we came in, the bedroom is to the right and the bathroom is straight ahead. It opens from the bedroom and from the hall. Washer and dryer are beside the bathroom. Hmmm, let's see. Mara's in my work-slash-reading area. Dining room is over there, the kitchen is a nice size to the right of the dining room, the patio is over here...that's pretty much it." He shrugged.

Tea playfully slapped his back. "You're all downplaying it. It's so nice and cozy in here. I love it. Especially this wall."

She walked forward and ran her hand along the gray stone-embedded wall that housed the faux fireplace and the large television above the mantle.

"I agree...same thing I told him when I was here. It's pretty lit. And in a good neighborhood, too." Miles went to put the napkins and other bags in the kitchen. Tea went outside to explore the patio, and Sirue followed. He showed her the different sights from his vantage point. There was a park area straight ahead and a lake that gave his apartment complex, The Cottages at Harmony Lake, its name.

Miles started to head through the patio doors to join them but saw Mara still staring at the painting.

"You love that thing, don't you?" He went to stand beside her.

"I really do," she said quietly. Then, "I wonder where the special agent is."

Miles laughed. "You know she ain't gonna be too far away."

They both turned when the bedroom door opened, and Teresa emerged. She was wearing a baggy black, royal blue, and white Skiff University hoodie and black yoga lounge pants. Mara noticed her long hair was neatly brushed into a smooth high bouncy ponytail and she was wearing blue fuzzy slippers. Mara also noticed that her eyes looked like she'd just been crying.

"Hey," she waved to Miles and Mara and stepped down into the living room.

"Hey, Teresa," Miles smiled and met her halfway to give her a quick hug.

Mara nodded her hello and walked to the kitchen at the same time Sirue and Tea came in from outside.

"Well, I don't think the hanging plants would be too much on the other side, if you—"

Tea stopped talking when she saw Teresa. "Hey, girl," she replied to Teresa's hello wave. She embraced her and started telling her about the plant conversation she'd just been having with Sirue.

Mile loudly clapped his hands. "All right, all right, let me see when these games come on today," he said, finding the remote and turning on the television. He sat in the recliner and clicked through several sports channels.

Sirue followed the sounds he heard in the kitchen and saw Mara pulling a foil-wrapped breakfast sandwich from one. He laughed.

"Hold up. I know you smell the food in the oven," he said, peeking in the bag at the rest of her food.

"Bruh, I see a pot with water in it and nothing else on the stove. I'm hungry! You got any juice? I drank mine already."

Sirue grabbed a glass from the cabinet and a carton of tropical fruit punch from the refrigerator. He poured her some and handed her the glass.

"Thanks...hey," she said, looking around. "Is the detective okay?" She looks like y'all had a rough morning." Mara took a sip.

Sirue smirked at her comment. "She's good. Just been nauseous since yesterday."

Mara squinted her eyes. "Nah, I'm not trying to get sick. You know I catch everything."

"I think you'll be okay," he said and put the juice back, then pulled out a huge bowl of washed greens from the bottom shelf of the refrigerator.

"Ooooh, greens?" Mara asked, opening her sandwich.

"Yep. Just these and the rolls left. You're making me hungry with that damn bacon." He looked at her food and Mara tore off a chunk and handed it to him.

Sirue swallowed it, barely chewing. "Mmmm," he groaned, then looked at the sandwich in her hands again.

"Nahhh, man, come on! I haven't even eaten yet!"

"Neither have I!"

"You got all this damn food in the house you could've had. Nope." Mara took a big bite and almost choked on it when she saw Sirue's angry face.

"Greedy *and* selfish," he mumbled, rolling his eyes.

When dinner was finished cooking, Tea and Teresa set the table while Miles and Mara watched the first football broadcast of the day. Sirue brought over his computer chair to the dining room table and told them to turn off the TV so they could all pray over their food. Around the table, they all held hands as Miles blessed the occasion and thanked God for new beginnings and friends who became family. Tea squeezed his hand when he finished, and he kissed the back of hers.

Food was served and the room filled with sounds of laughter and eating. Mara realized that she was scooping her third helping of mashed potatoes while Teresa sat across from her still pushing her original food around her plate. She saw Sirue quietly urging her to eat, and Teresa turning up her nose. They mumbled to each other, and Mara gave them both a once over. Miles interrupted her thoughts.

"I'm so full, damn," he said, leaning back in his chair and patting his stomach. "You threw it down, brother."

"Yeeees," Tea agreed and pushed her plate away.

Mara dropped the mashed potato spoon back into the dish. "So y'all just gonna have me looking like the only hungry one?"

Everyone laughed.

"Go ahead and eat whatever you want," Teresa said with a dismissive wave.

Mara was taken aback by her genuine comment. It was pretty much the only thing she'd said out loud at the table for the past forty minutes.

"Thank you, and I will," Mara said, picking up the spoon again.

Chapter 50

A few minutes later, once the table was cleared, Sirue and Miles moved the chairs to the living room and Teresa went to get a few board games from the hall closet. She came back with BuzzWord, Guesstures, Taboo, and Trivial Pursuit. Everyone agreed to start with Guesstures and decided it would be men versus women. Teresa opted to sit out and busied herself with straightening up in the kitchen. Mara saw Teresa's hand rub her stomach as she walked past her.

Miles turned the game back on, keeping the volume low as they all pitched in to clear the coffee table. Tea decided to go first, and she giggled as she lined her cards up in the timer unit that Miles held for her. He made a face.

"She's not gonna get that one, and definitely not that one," he pointed at her cards.

"Shut up, Miles!" Mara yelled. "Worry about your sorry ass partner over there!"

"Wait! How did I get in this?!" Sirue said, sitting straight up in the recliner.

Tea laughed. "Mara, don't worry, boo. We got this."

When Miles slapped the timer shut, Tea started to act out her first word. She jumped up and down with her fists in front of her.

"Ummm...jackhammer!" Mara screamed.

Tea shook her head and kept jumping, pointing to the imaginary thing in her hands.

"Jump rope? What the hell?" Mara tried again.

The card fell to the floor and both Tea and Mara groaned. Tea acted out her next card. She cupped her hands around her mouth and pretended to yell something, then cupped her hand around her ear as if she was listening to something.

"Echo!" Mara screamed.

Tea pointed at Mara and pumped her fist. She grabbed the card before it fell, then moved on to the next one. When her turn was over, they ended winning a one-point card and a three-point card.

"What the hell was that first jumping one?" Mara asked after giving her partner a high five.

"Clearly it was a pogo stick," Sirue said calmly, standing up to take his turn.

Mara and Tea both sucked her teeth at him.

"*Clearly, it was a pogo stick*," Mara mocked. "With your know-it-all ass."

They all laughed, and Mara went up to hold the device while Sirue picked his cards. He selected the sides of his four cards with the highest possible points. Mara shook her head.

"Okay, go 'head big baller. He ain't gonna get naaaaare one of these words!"

"I have faith in my teammate. Let's go!"

Mara slapped the timer closed and Sirue started to gesture in a downward spiral motion, then blew air out of his mouth. He repeated it again.

"Tornado…oh! Whirlwind!" Miles shouted.

Sirue grabbed the card just before it fell. He acted out the next word my drawing an imaginary line, then pretended to shoot a basket.

"Free throw! Let's goooooo," Miles yelled, clapping his hands.

Sirue grabbed the card and went on to perform the next two words, baker and reflection, just as successfully. Mara and Tea stared at them both with straight faces. Sirue gave Miles a double hand slap as he went to write their score of twelve on the notepad.

"Excuse me," Tea said, bumping the coffee table with her knee as Sirue tried to write.

He laughed. Teresa came in to sit on the couch and watch them continue playing. Near the end of the game, as Miles stood to take his turn, he studied the notepad.

"A'ite, pahht-nah...we only need eleven or more to win," he commented, walking to select his four cards.

"Cake walk," Sirue said flatly as he sat erect in the recliner.

"Ooooh, I hope y'all choke," Tea said, standing up holding the timer unit and rolling her eyes.

"How you gonna root against your own man, though?" Miles said sweetly and leaned in for a kiss on her cheek.

Tea moved away and held out the device for him to drop his cards.

"Don't get distracted, Miles," Sirue said.

Miles nodded. "You right, you right." He arranged his cards in the slots and Tea slammed the timer shut.

He acted out the first three cards and amassed ten points easily. For his last card, he mimed two people talking to each other with his hands, then threw a fishing rod out and pointed to the end of the line. Sirue looked at him intently. Miles repeated the two people talking to each other.

"Argue...fishing...," Sirue thought out loud. "Debate!" He screamed and Miles grabbed the card seconds before it dropped to the floor.

"Oh, my Gooooood," Mara stomped her feet.

"Ughhh," Tea said, and stared angrily at Miles and Sirue as they hollered and bragged.

"Let me see what you got to sip on back here to celebrate our victory," Miles said with a laugh as he stepped over Mara's extended foot that was meant to trip him up.

He headed to the kitchen as Sirue started to pack up the board game.

"Good game, ladies, good ga—"

"Shut up," they both said in unison.

Teresa laughed and started to help Sirue put the pieces back in the box.

"We're gonna get them with Taboo," Tea said, picking up the stray cards all over the floor. "Teresa, do you want to play with us?"

"Uh, I don't think I'm up to y'all's level yet," she said, shaking her head.

Tea smiled. "We'll take it easy on you."

Mara made a face. "I meeeeean...don't go speaking for everybody."

Teresa laughed again. "Nah, it's cool. It's fun just watching how y'all act with each other."

Sirue smiled at her and leaned over to kiss her cheek. She smiled at his kiss and turned to give him a peck on his lips.

Miles came out of the kitchen with five cold bottles of Jose Cuervo. He handed them out and Teresa quickly shook her head when he reached her.

"No thanks, I can't really have...," she glanced at Sirue then back at Miles. "No, thank you."

Miles put the extra bottle down and Mara let her gaze linger on Teresa and Sirue while she opened her drink and sipped it. Her eyes moved from one to the other until she met Sirue's eyes. He quickly averted her stare and clapped his hands.

"All right. Next up, Taboo! Maybe you ladies can redeem yourselves," he said, opening up the game box and taking out the cards, the timer, and the buzzer.

Miles and Tea were having a quiet conversation about something on Miles' phone and Mara squinted at Teresa as she took another sip.

"You feeling okay, Teresa? You've been pretty quiet."

Teresa shrugged. "Not really, if I'm being honest."

Mara noticed her face beginning to look flushed. "What's wrong?"

Sirue glanced up from the game, a look of worry spreading across his face. "You need anything?" he asked her.

Tea and Miles stopped talking and looked over.

"I'm just...I probably just need to get in bed." She stood slowly and dabbed at her forehead with the back of her hand. "I'm sorry, everyone. It was great to see you all."

Sirue followed her to the bedroom and softly closed the door behind them.

Mara crossed one leg over the other and shook it as she took another sip of the white peach margarita. Tea and Miles asked her what happened and as she explained, Sirue emerged from the bedroom.

"Si, does she need me to go get some medicine or something? Does she have a fever?" Tea asked.

He shook his head. "No, she said she's just going to try to get some rest. I'll keep checking in on her, though. She said it's cramps."

Mara looked at him trying to mask his concern. He rubbed the back of his neck and let out a breath.

"Okay, ladies! Winners first?" Miles said, standing up to stretch and crack his fingers.

Tea rolled her eyes. "Here we go again. C'mon, Mara let's kick both their asses!"

Three games and two hours later, Mara was picking up the Trivial Pursuit cards that she'd thrown down after losing.

"You missed some over there," Miles pointed to the corner.

She stood up and paused to stare at him. Everyone laughed.

Miles held up his hands. "Don't be mad 'cause you only got one wedge."

"Shut up," Mara threw a card at him. "You only got two, asshole, and that's because Tea helped you!"

Tea giggled from her position on the floor, leaning against Miles. "I was trying to help you, too!"

Sirue settled back in his recliner and extended the footrests.

"So did y'all have anything specific you wanted to do this weekend?" he asked, flipping the channel to another football game.

"Tomorrow, we want to check out the Andrew Jackson Museum," Tea offered.

"No, *you* wanted to check out the Andrew Jackson Museum," Mara countered. "Miles and I want to go down to Music Row." She went to plop down on the couch, holding a pillow and putting her socked feet on the coffee table.

Sirue lit up. "Oooh, I haven't been to that museum yet," he stated to Tea, disregarding Mara's comment. "You know they renovated his old mansion to look like it did almost two hundred years ago. I was looking at the photos online and they're amazing. The structural resemblance is outstanding."

Miles and Mara both threw their heads back and groaned loudly.

Tea sucked her teeth and slapped Miles' leg. "Well, Si, you and I can go with Teresa and these two can do something else."

Sirue was about to agree but remembered something. "Wait, I'm going with her to an appointment tomorrow, so…we can try for the afternoon? We might be able to get a guided wagon tour, too."

Tea shrugged. "That's perfect, actually." She pulled out her phone and started to make an itinerary.

"I love how they just made plans for us like we ain't even here," Miles said to Mara.

"Like, damn, I see you. You see me?" Mara quipped to Miles.

Sirue laughed. "Well, more up your alley—there's a new lounge bar that opened off campus and we can hit it up tomorrow night after we reconvene."

"Thaaaat's more like it," Mara said.

"As long as it's not all country," Miles added.

"That's not the only type of music they have here." Sirue shook his head. "But that reminds me. There's an African-American Music museum we can check out, too. They have a Roots Theater that I heard is rather amazing."

"Ooh, that sounds fun! Let me add that to our schedule," Tea exclaimed.

Miles smiled at her enthusiasm and rubbed her lower back.

"But, Saturday," Sirue continued, "we are all going to the Adventure Science Center. It's a great facility." He went on to explain their exhibits and attractions. Tea listened with excited interest, while Miles and Mara talked about the game on the screen.

After dessert and another round of drinks, Sirue went to check in on Teresa again. Mara took over his comfy recliner and curled her feet beneath her. He came back within a few minutes and rolled his eyes at his absconded seat. He sat down on the couch, taking another sip of his drink.

"How is she doing?" Mara asked.

"She's...," he started to say something, and Mara noticed him momentarily grappling with his thoughts. "She's still asleep."

He glanced at Mara briefly, then sipped again. Mara nodded her reaction, her eyes returning to the television. Miles had dozed off on the floor next to Tea with his hand on her back as she slept on his torso.

"Weren't they both just awake?" Sirue asked.

Mara chuckled, then yawned. "I guess we do need to be getting back to the hotel. That long ass hot ass car ride was a set up this morning."

Sirue yawned and stretched, then sat back to get comfortable. "Yeah, y'all need some good sleep. Are all of you in a full suite? I know his job paid for everything."

Mara laughed. "He has an adjoining room to ours."

Sirue looked over at her. "Oh, they're not sharing one?"

Mara shook her head, then looked over at the two of them sleeping. "Si," she whispered. "You know they're celibate now. They ain't even doing the slurpy slurp."

Sirue made a face. "I don't need that visual."

"And I can hear your loud ass," Miles said, turning his head to Mara.

"My bad." She bit her lips to keep from laughing.

"It's all right, bro," Sirue interjected. "That's noble, I respect that." He reached over to pat Miles' shoulder. "Just get housekeeping to bring some extra towels in the morning."

Mara busted out with a loud laugh and woke Tea up.

"Fuck all both o' y'all." Miles said as he rubbed Tea's back.

"Huh?" Tea groggily sat up and stretched.

"Nothing, baby, let's get ready to go. Mara's walking back to the hotel."

Chapter 51

The next morning, Miles and Mara hit the hotel gym and although her workout was modified from her usual strenuous sessions, she was still able to work up a lot of sweat. Tea slept until they returned and once everyone was showered and dressed, they located a pancake house and enjoyed a late breakfast together. By one o'clock, Sirue met them in the hotel parking lot without Teresa.

"She's still not feeling well? How'd the appointment go?" Tea asked, concerned.

She was fastening her seatbelt in Sirue's truck, and they'd just waved goodbye to Miles and Mara.

Sirue rubbed his face. "She's still pretty nauseous," he answered, not wanting to fully lie to his dear friend, but still avoiding the whole truth.

"Aw, I'm sorry. We should bring her something back from the gift shop. I hate feeling sick," Tea empathized.

Sirue smiled. "That's a good idea. We'll bring her something nice."

As they toured the Jackson Hermitage Museum, Sirue tried to keep the events from earlier that morning at bay. He truly wanted to enjoy the time hanging out with Tea, but every free moment, he thought about the results of the bloodwork and exam. Teresa was nine and a half weeks pregnant. They talked at length when they returned home about their options and ultimately made a final decision together. Teresa could barely keep anything down, so the thought of walking around a museum didn't sound appealing at all. She just wanted Sirue to lay next to her until she fell asleep, so he held her and then made his way to the hotel. It was close to six when Sirue dropped Tea back off and headed back home to get ready for later.

The Blue Jazz Lounge had a stone and brick façade with large, tinted windows on either side of glass double-doors. There were blue and silver neon lights framing the windows and the words "Blue" and "Jazz" on each door were blinking in sync. As Miles parked, he noticed Sirue's truck.

"Damn, how'd he beat us here?" Miles turned off the radio and checked his goatee in the visor.

"Probably couldn't wait to get away from Miss Germy," Mara said, climbing out of the backseat. She smoothed out her cream and gray color-blocked wide pants set and grabbed her purse before shutting her door.

"Aw, be nice," Tea said and stepped out of the car. She fluffed the back of her pageboy and swept her long bangs to the side. She adjusted her dark blue one-shoulder dress. "I think she's really sick with something."

Mara rolled her eyes. "Yeah, she has something, all right," she mumbled.

Miles got out and beeped the alarm on the car. He walked over to hold Tea's hand.

"You look so damn good," he whispered. It was all he could do to stop looking at the way that fabric held everything in place.

Tea blushed. "I can say the same for you." She admired the gray dress shirt that accentuated his muscular chest and arms. It was tucked perfectly into black slacks.

He kissed her hand, and they followed Mara to the door. Once inside, though the lighting was very dim, Mara noticed Sirue waving them over from a booth on the far right. There were a few empty tables, but for the most part, Mara was surprised at how many people were already there and it was barely nine o'clock. She noticed the long, rectangular bar in the center of the lounge and the spacious dance areas. One area had a low-hanging blue and white lit chandelier with illuminated glass columns. Another had sheer lavender curtains surrounding a wide curved sofa with muted lavender lights shining on the open dance floor. There was a mixture of rhythmic blues and jazz flowing through the speakers and a nice ambience of blue lights around the walls.

"It's kind of crowded to be so early," Mara commented as she slid in the booth beside Sirue.

"Yeah, I think it just opened last week, so everybody's been waiting to get in." He sipped on a blue drink.

"Ooh, what's that?" Tea asked, as she and Miles settled into their side of the booth.

"Looks like a jellyfish shot," Mara answered for him.

"It is and it's damn good," Sirue added.

Miles and Tea looked through the drink and food menus.

"And you couldn't order us a drink?" Mara rolled her eyes, reaching for a menu.

He laughed. "Here," he slid the rest of the drink to her. Mara happily accepted it.

The waitress came over and took everyone's order. When she returned with their drinks, Miles and Tea decided to take theirs to go so they could walk around and admire the different decorations. Mara danced in her seat to the music as she nudged Sirue beside her.

"I really missed y'all," he said thoughtfully.

"We missed you, too." She took another sip of her Aperol spritz.

They talked for a few minutes and watched the people around them. Mara noticed Tea and Miles heading back. "C'mon, let's dance. I look too cute to just be sitting here."

She pulled him out of the booth, and they found a spot near the glass columns just as Miles and Tea arrived.

"Perfect timing," Tea said when she saw the waitress heading their way with a tray of food. She hadn't eaten since brunch earlier that day. The server put the large plate of nachos, cheese, and salsa in the center of the table. Tea took her small plate of burger sliders and made a face.

Miles caught her grimace as he took his plates of fried mozzarella sticks and hot wings.

"I'll be right back with the other orders," the waitress said cheerfully and hurried off.

Tea grabbed one of her napkins and snapped it open with rolled eyes.

"Doesn't look appetizing?" Miles asked her and leaned over to get a closer look at her sliders.

"Not at all," Tea sucked her teeth. The burgers looked much smaller than they did in the menu, and the buns looked dry. "And I was hungry, too."

"I'll get her to take it back and you can pick something else out," he offered.

Tea shrugged. "I guess I should've known we'd just get bar food."

"We'll go find better food after we leave here," Miles said, looking at her. "Want mine?"

Tea smiled and shook her head. Her eyes fell on his beautiful lips, and she leaned over to kiss them.

The waitress arrived a few minutes later with Sirue's and Mara's plates, as well as refills of all the drinks.

"They need to come eat, their food's gonna get cold," Tea said, pulling another loaded nacho from the middle of the table.

Miles nodded with his mouth full of mozzarella.

Tea jumped when her phone notified her of an incoming video call. She looked at it and smiled hard.

"Day!" she said once she accepted the call. She was only able to speak to Damien and James briefly yesterday morning, and they were both too groggy to give her a full conversation.

"Hi, sis," he replied with a wave. Tea waved back, and Miles moved his face into the camera to wave.

"Hi, Miles," he greeted.

From the scenery behind him, Tea saw that Damien was in his bedroom.

"It's kind of late for you to be up, little bro. Is James still awake, too?"

"No, he just fell asleep, but Daddy told me to call you before I go to bed."

Tea was a little stung that her father hadn't called her the day before. "Well, thank you for calling me. I know you're sleepy. Did you have a good Thanksgiving yesterday?" Tea asked.

Damien nodded. "Everything was okay, but I wish you were here to make it more fun."

Tea frowned. "Aw. I'll be home in a few days."

Miles leaned back into the camera's frame. "Yep, and when we get back, I'll show you some new cheats I found for CrossSteel."

Damien's face lit up and they talked for a few more minutes until they all said goodnight.

Tea picked at the nachos and thought about her little brothers. She hoped their day was tension-free. Their father and Anna had a knack for ruining any family function with their non-stop bickering. She got a sense from Damien's demeanor that he and James had to endure it in some form yesterday. Tea knew she served as a buffer for them and was usually successful at keeping the nitpicking and arguing to a minimum, but without her there yesterday, that responsibility fell on Damien. There weren't even any other extended family members who came over, and she was sure it was because no one felt like dealing with the fighting.

Tea was startled when she felt Miles bump her arm.

"You know they were fine yesterday, right?" he asked, wiping his mouth with a napkin.

She nodded and smiled weakly. Before she could respond, Sirue and Mara made their way back to the table. Miles gave Tea a glance and rubbed her leg.

"We'll give them another call in the morning, okay?" Miles suggested.

Tea nodded again and he leaned over to kiss her cheek.

"Y'all just sittin' here eating, not even gonna tell us our food came?" Mara complained as she scooted into the booth.

"Just be glad I didn't eat yours. My sliders look dehydrated," Tea commented.

Sirue looked over at her plate. He motioned for her to give it to him. "They look fine to me," he said as he put her plate of burgers next to his fries and wings. "I mean, realistically, you can't expect restaurant-quality dishes in a place like this. The ambience is more set for drinking and dancing."

Mara rolled her eyes. "Si, first of all, you weren't even over there dancing."

"I was dan—"

"No, you were standing around on your phone." Mara pulled her plate in front of her. "And, anyway, Tea wasn't even saying she wanted something fancy, she just wanted some damn moist burgers." She took a bite of her quesadilla.

He gave her a side-eye as he took a bite of the slider. "Moist *these* buns," he retorted.

They all laughed.

"Bro," Miles almost choked as he tried to swallow.

"Corny ass," Mara laughed, hitting Sirue on the arm.

After about thirty minutes of eating, drinking, and talking, more lounge patrons started to arrive. Tea noticed Sirue had been checking his phone pretty frequently.

"Is Teresa all right?" she asked.

Sirue put his phone back down on the table. She noticed his hesitation.

"She's ...," he began. "Yeah, she's fine."

Mara sipped her drink and glanced over at him before looking at Miles. They both discussed different possible scenarios earlier that day while touring Music Row. Miles put a napkin on his plate and pushed it forward. He looked back at Mara, then scratched the back of his neck. Tea looked at them both and wondered what their subliminal cues were about.

She focused her attention back on Sirue. "Is she still feeling nauseous? It's been two days now, I'm kind of worried about her."

Sirue rubbed a hand over his face twice and leaned back in the booth. He exhaled and glanced around at his friends.

"What's wrong, Si?" Tea asked, worried.

"I probably shouldn't...well...um." He rubbed his temple. "She's...Teresa's pregnant."

Chapter 52

No one said a word. Tea placed her hand over her heart. Miles exhaled. Mara sipped her drink and shook her head lightly.

"Wow. So, how far is she?" Tea wondered.

Sirue cleared his throat. "We found out this morning that she's almost ten weeks now." He recalled to his friends the way he discovered the positive pregnancy tests a few days ago.

"Damn," Miles replied. "How are you feeling about it now? How are both of y'all feeling?"

Sirue shrugged and threw his hands up. "It's still new, you know? We're talking about our options."

"Oh, okay," Miles nodded slowly. "Well, for what it's worth, I'm glad you told us. That's a lot to carry around."

"Exactly," Tea added. "Never feel like you have to deal with things this heavy by yourself. Even if we're hours away, you know we're always here for each other."

Miles reached out his hand and Sirue gave him a slap shake. Tea smiled. She noticed Mara was scrolling on her phone, the straw of her drink resting in her mouth. She knew her friend was probably having mixed emotions, so she didn't press her out about responding. The urge to kick her under the table was still strong, though. She saw that Sirue was also noticing Mara's silent reaction.

"I appreciate y'all. I really do," he looked around the booth.

"You know you're my brother," Miles shrugged and picked up his drink.

"Thanks, man." Sirue gave him a fist dab.

Tea couldn't stop smiling. "We really are all family, huh?" She leaned on Miles' arm.

He turned and kissed the top of her head.

"So…," Sirue yawned and leaned on the table. "Is anyone else ready for bed?"

"Yeah," Miles answered, looking down at Tea. "But we're not–"

Sirue held up a hand. "But you're not going to bed *together*, I know. I don't need details."

Tea shot up in her seat and glared at Miles. She hit his arm. "You told him?"

He laughed and grabbed his arm. "Ouch…no! I didn't say anything. I was going to say, 'But we're not going to the hotel yet, we're getting food first since you're hungry!' *Mara* was the one who told him!"

Tea looked at Mara and now she did kick her under the table. "You told?"

Mara finally looked up from her phone and shrugged. "Huh? About the virgin diaries? It's not that serious." She went back to her phone.

Tea covered her face. "So embarrassing."

"Baby," Miles smiled. He put his hand on her leg, then leaned down to kiss her temple.

Sirue chuckled. "Yeah, it's okay, Big Head. I was going to find out eventually when his right arm bulked up like The Rock's."

Mara giggled at the remark as she swiped through a screen. Tea groaned. Miles gave Sirue a hard look.

"Man, shut up."

Sirue laughed.

"Okay, let's go. I'm hungry for real now," Tea said, urging Miles out of the booth so she could get up.

"Where y'all going?" Mara asked, looking up at them.

"To the Silver Buffet. We found one that's about an hour away," Mile answered. He helped Tea stand up.

"Damn, so I need to call an Uber?"

"Your Uber's sitting right there," he pointed at Sirue.

Mara rolled her eyes and sighed.

"I'll see you later, Mara. And I'll see you tomorrow, Si," Tea said. She leaned down to hug Sirue.

They both watched them leave through the double glass doors. Sirue turned to look at Mara. She looked over at him and flashed a brief smile, then picked up her phone again.

"Mara."

She raised her eyebrows in response, her eyes still focused on her phone.

"What's wrong?" he asked.

She made a face and shook her head, then opened another app.

Sirue nodded slowly and picked up his phone.

Mara rolled her eyes a few seconds later when his text notification popped up on her screen: *You're just going to sit here and not talk to me?*

He leaned over and looked at her phone. "You should reply to that."

Mara put her phone down. "I'm getting a headache. Can you just take me back now?"

Sirue looked at her, tried to read her face, then nodded and moved out of the booth. He waited as Mara scooted out and walked ahead of him out of the lounge.

Once at his truck, she waited for him to beep the doors unlocked and she climbed into the passenger's side. Their ride was silent all the way to the hotel. He parked and got out after she did. Mara turned around, startled at the sound of his door closing.

"You don't have to walk me in, I'm good," she said with a tired smile.

"Yeah, well, it's late and I want to make sure you get to your room." He locked the truck and walked next to her through the parking lot. When they reached the automatic doors, they walked through, and Mara paused.

"I'm here," she said, looking over at Sirue.

"I said to your *room*, stubborn." He glanced down at her as she sighed. They headed past the front desk to the elevators.

"Besides," Sirue continued, "anybody crazy could be in these elevators or on the floors this time of night." He stuffed his hands in his pockets and looked around dramatically.

Mara shook her head and pushed the call button.

When they arrived on her floor, Mara took out her key card and sighed to herself because she knew he would want to come in. Even worse, he would want to *talk* about her reluctance to *talk*.

They entered the suite, and she tossed her purse and key card on the end table of the couch. Sirue looked around.

"Wow. He really went all out, huh?" He tapped on a side door. "That's his room through here?"

Mara nodded. She wasn't in the mood to give a tour. She wanted to sulk. Alone. With the ice cream she stashed in the freezer. She made a face and shrugged.

"Well, I'm gonna go get out of these clothes. Thanks for making sure I got in okay," Mara said dismissively. She headed towards the bedroom but noticed he hadn't moved. She turned around slowly to see Sirue leaning against the wall with his hands in his pants pockets, looking directly at her.

Mara threw her hands up. "What, Si?"

Sirue studied her for a few seconds. "Are you upset because she's pregnant?"

Mara flinched. She felt her eyes stinging.

"Si...I can't, okay?" She held up a hand and turned to walk into the bedroom.

After closing the door, she went to the large dresser. The top drawer housed her night clothes, so she pulled out her gray short-sleeved, oversized night shirt that read *"leave me the EFF alone"* in large black lettering. She took off her pants suit and top, went to the restroom and looked in the huge mirror above the vanity. She couldn't hold the tears back anymore and allowed them to roll as she touched her soft belly. She missed the baby she never met or even knew that she wanted. In her spirit, she knew it was a baby girl. And she knew she would have been called Abigail, her aunt's middle name.

"I'm so sorry I didn't take care of you, Abby," she mouthed and started to cry heavy tears.

Mara wasn't sure how long she'd been standing there crying. She took a few deep breaths and washed her face, then took out her ponytail, letting her thick, natural hair fall in coils to her shoulders. She stared at herself again, blew out a long stream of air, and went to use the toilet.

Back in the bedroom, she slipped the night shirt over her head and craved the cold, smooth taste of cookies and cream ice cream. When she swung open the bedroom door, she jumped when she saw Sirue sitting on the couch, his elbows on his knees. He watched her emerge.

"I thought you left," Mara said quietly.

"You know me better than that."

Mara took a deep breath and stood by the counter in the kitchenette. She looked down at her hands, facing in Sirue's direction. She fought with about ten different sentence starters in her mind but couldn't narrow it down to just one. She felt the stinging behind her eyes again. A tear rolled when she blinked. When she looked back up, Sirue was standing and walking slowly towards her. He stopped a foot away from her.

Mara noticed how he examined her face. She figured she looked atrocious since she just had the ugly cry a few minutes ago. Her voice choked when she tried to talk, so she closed her mouth.

"Can you please talk to me?" Sirue asked softly.

Mara wiped her face. She asked the question she didn't want the answer to. "Is she getting an abortion?"

Sirue looked away briefly, then back at Mara. He nodded slowly.

"Okay," Mara shrugged. "Well," she felt her emotions rising. "I'm glad y'all can just solve your little problem and move the fuck on. Some of us never got that chance."

Her breath caught as she tried to keep the rest of her tears at bay. She moved around Sirue, but not before he held her arm.

"Mara, wait –"

She tugged against his grip. "Let me go," she said calmly.

He let her arm go but stepped in front of her. "Mara, we need –"

"Sirue," Mara interrupted. She closed her eyes and exhaled deeply.

He paused and watched her breathe. When a few seconds passed, he gently rubbed the sides of her arms. The gesture seemed to help at first, but suddenly, Mara yanked herself away from his hands.

"I don't want to talk, okay?" she said through clenched teeth and attempted to step around him.

Sirue slid to his right and blocked her path again. "Mara, I'm not leaving with you this upset. Can we just –"

"I'm not Teresa's punk ass! You need to move the fuck out of my way, for real!" Mara screamed with her fists balled at her sides.

His face was confused as she pushed past him and back into the bedroom, slamming the door.

Chapter 53

Sirue ran his hands over his face, not understanding what just transpired in a matter of seconds. He threw his head back and debated whether to leave and let her cool down. He walked to the bedroom door and listened. Besides the thumping of his heart, Sirue didn't hear a sound. In his mind, he quickly assessed that she was probably fine, just upset. He started to grab his keys from the dining table, then paused in his tracks.

Instead, Sirue took a deep breath and turned to the bedroom door again. He slowly opened it and saw Mara fuming. She was pacing in front of the huge window, punching her fist into her palm. He began approaching her carefully, holding his hands up.

"Mara...," he whispered.

She shook her head, not looking up. "Just leave, Si."

"I'm worried about you, so I can't leave." He stopped walking towards her.

Sirue watched her pace for the next minute, then she turned to face him. Her eyes were swollen, her face was red, and she looked absolutely exhausted. He felt his heart tug.

Mara threw up her hands.

"Si, I'm just being dramatic. Go back home to her. She's probably confused and scared," she said quietly. She turned and looked out of the window and held herself.

"I said I was worried about *you*."

Sirue watched her slightly shake her head, though her back was to him.

He continued. "I just checked on her. She's okay."

Sirue walked to the bed and sat on the edge facing the window. He could see her reflection in the glass before them. He was glad that she'd calmed down, but he knew she was still hurting. He reached forward to lightly pull on her night shirt. Mara turned her head and went to climb onto the edge of the bed beside him, one leg folded beneath her, the other dangling over the side. He looked her over as she busied herself with her hands again.

"I was...more nervous about telling you than the others," Sirue said softly.

"I can't blame you. Look how I reacted," Mara rolled her eyes.

Sirue let out a gentle laugh. "And I knew you would."

He placed a hand on hers and she continued to play with his fingers as she looked down. After some time passed, Mara let out a groan.

"Everything's not about me. I'm so sorry, Si. You're dealing with shit, too." She looked up at him.

"Well, I have to give you a pass on this one, Mara. You've just experienced something very traumatic, and my news triggered you. I should have told you first."

He saw her lip trembling and he squeezed one of her hands. She dropped her head and began sobbing.

"I feel so empty," she said, her body heaving. "She's gone forever."

Sirue felt a lump in his throat. He quickly kicked off his loafers and moved back against the headboard. "Come here," he whispered, lightly pulling her back towards him.

He helped her climb over to him and she settled into a fetal position between his legs, her back partially resting against his raised leg. He wrapped her body in a big embrace, fully encircling his arms around her. Mara's cries alternated between open wails and quiet sobs. He rested his cheek on her hair and rocked her softly until her crying stopped. He heard her sniffling, so he freed one of his arms and reached over to the nightstand. He took the box of tissues and handed them to her. While she blew her nose, he took another tissue and wiped the tears from her eyes and cheeks. When she finished, she snuggled even closer to him and held onto his shirt.

"Hey, Mara," Sirue started. He rubbed her side.

"Hm?" She grabbed onto his shirt a little tighter and sniffled again.

"Um," he cleared his throat. "I...need to ask you something, and it's probably not the right time."

He felt Mara stop breathing. She lifted her head to look at him, her eyes searching his face. "What do you have to ask me?"

Sirue swallowed. "Can you...uh..."

A small, inquisitive grin started to form on Mara's mouth. "Can I...what?"

"Can you please throw away that snot rag?" He made a disgusted face and motioned to her hand that was gripping his shirt.

Mara looked down at the crumpled, wet tissue in her hand and sucked her teeth. She sat up and slapped Sirue's chest.

"What was that for?" he laughed.

"Because I'm all vulnerable and shit." She tossed the tissue onto the floor. "Thought you were gonna ask me to kiss you. Or jerk you off. *Some*thing." She shrugged.

Sirue gave her a blank look. "Really. Why would I even ask you that?"

Mara squinted at him. "You didn't think about it?"

Sirue squinted back. "No."

Mara made a face. "Yes, you did."

"I promise, I didn't."

Mara rolled her eyes and turned around to fully face him, still leaning on his raised leg.

"Why not?" She folded her arms across her chest.

"Because." Sirue smiled.

"Because I'm ugly?" she asked, pouting.

"What?" Sirue was taken aback. "Ugly where?"

Mara shrugged. "I feel like I'm just...very unattractive. Inside and out," she admitted quietly.

Sirue's eyes widened. "You're joking, right? You're so beautiful. Your honesty, your loyalty, your eyes...that little, tiny dimple you get right there when you smile," he reached up and touched the corner of her mouth with the back of his finger. Sirue paused and slowly dropped his hand. "I mean, you're violent as hell, but you're very beautiful, Mara."

Mara smiled. "I'm not violent."

"Mara. You almost fucked me up out there."

She laughed. "My bad."

Sirue gave her a gentle smile. "So, don't refer to yourself as ugly again, okay?"

Mara made a face and rolled her eyes upward.

"I'll take that as a yes," he said quietly.

They looked at each other as their smiles faded. Mara sighed.

"So," she narrowed her eyes at him, "this is usually when friends catch feelings and start to make out."

He nodded. "It is."

"But you don't want to make out?"

Sirue shook his head. He was glad he was so good at keeping his emotions in check.

Mara tilted her head to the side. "Because of Teresa?"

He looked directly at his friend. "Because like you said, you're vulnerable right now. I would never take advantage of you."

Mara smiled. "I love you, Sirue."

"I love you, too, Mara."

His words gave her pause. Memories of Drew's first declaration of love came pouring into her thoughts. Her eyes lingered on Sirue's face as she fought the frown that wanted to form on her lips. Those words meant so much to her and she took them very much to heart. Her eyes stung again.

Sirue pulled his head back a few inches and tried to analyze her expression.

"Are you okay?" he asked.

Mara nodded, then scooted forward and laid with her back against his chest. She played with his hand that rested on his upraised leg. Sirue heard her mumble something.

"Hm?" he asked.

She sighed softly. "I said, I think I just needed to be held."

Sirue leaned down to sniff her hair. "I know."

He reached around her with both arms and rested his hands on her stomach. He felt her body stiffen. She shook her head and gently moved his hands.

"I hate my stomach," she whispered.

"Why?" Sirue asked quietly.

Mara shrugged. "It's empty. It feels so strange."

Sirue slowly placed a hand on her stomach again through the cotton fabric, waiting to gauge her reaction. When she allowed him to continue, he rubbed it in gentle circles. He felt her body relax and heard Mara make soft sounds that he couldn't quite decipher. He swallowed hard and let out a slow breath. As he continued to slowly rub her belly, he tilted his head down and saw a tear streaming down her cheek. He reached up to wipe it away with his free hand, then he smoothed her natural hair back along her hairline. Finally, he took her hand and lightly massaged it with his.

He looked down at their hands and wasn't prepared for the emotion he started to feel. Sirue let out another slow breath and thought about the amazing woman and friend laying on him. He felt blood rushing to areas where her body pressed against his. He knew they could have probably made out and possibly even made love tonight. He also knew that would have been a disaster on so many levels.

Sirue watched intently as his thumb smoothed the back of her soft hand. He wondered how strong he would have been if she really wanted to push for more intimacy. Her entire body felt so soft and warm under his touch.

He felt her stir, and she interrupted his thoughts.

"I don't think we'd work out together, though," Mara said, crossing her ankles.

Sirue looked out at her pretty, pedicured feet. He composed himself quickly, glad she couldn't see his face. "I... can agree with that," he managed to say.

"I mean, you are kind of psycho, so...," Mara shrugged nonchalantly.

"I do *not* agree with that, though."

Mara laughed. They were both quiet for a few moments until she spoke again, her back still on his torso.

"Thank you, Si."

"Of course, Mara," he replied.

He moved his right hand from her stomach and reached up to massage her scalp through her thick hair. He loved the sensation on his fingers as they tenderly roamed through her soft coils. Mara moaned and rested her head back, settling it right beneath his chin. Sirue slightly bent his head to the side and touched her left temple with his cheek, still giving a finger massage to her scalp. She let out a soft moan again and took their entangled left hands and placed them on her stomach. Sirue slid both their hands to the top of her thigh and rested them there, gently squeezing her leg.

He noticed his breaths coming faster and moved his head down until his cheek was against hers. He hoped she couldn't feel his arousal, but there was no way he could contain it now. Thankful for the layers of clothes between them, Sirue lowered his head a little more and sniffed the crook of her neck, then slowly caressed her shoulder with his face.

Mara started to shift again. She moved his hand from her thigh to the mattress and steadied her breathing. She sat up from his torso and Sirue lifted his head. He watched as his hand ran over her hair and down the back of her night shirt. He moved his hand back upwards, then down the length of her arm. His fingers intertwined with hers when he reached her hand.

"Teresa is very lucky, Si," Mara said, still facing away from him. "You should probably go be with her. She needs you."

Sirue sighed. He knew she was right, but he wanted to stay right here and continue to touch her. He didn't respond. Mara scooted forward more and moved his leg out of the way so she could swing hers around over the edge of the bed.

"C'mon," she said with a sad smile, tapping his leg and standing up.

Again, Sirue didn't respond. He looked her over, his tongue pressing against the inside of his cheek. He lightly shook his head.

"Si, c'mon," she reached down and pulled his hand.

Sirue groaned and reluctantly stood from the bed. He slipped his shoes on, still holding on to her fingers. She led him from the bedroom. Even in the dim light, he couldn't help but admire the way her juicy curves moved through the thin fabric of her night shirt. He ran his free hand over his head and behind his neck, trying to get himself together.

When they walked through the living space, he grabbed his keys and they paused at the door. Mara turned and reached up to wrap her arms around his neck. Sirue lowered himself enough to hold her around her waist.

"You're such a sweet teddy bear when you're not grumpy," she said, still hugging him.

Sirue chuckled. She pulled back a little and kissed his cheek. His smile faded and he licked his lips, staring down at hers. She was biting both of hers and also staring at his. Sirue's hands slipped around to her hips, and he squeezed them, his eyes never leaving her mouth.

"Yeah, okay, you gotta go," Mara said quickly, pulling his arms from around her and yanking open the door.

Sirue smiled. He ran his hand over his mouth. "I need to go," he agreed.

Mara patted his back as he walked out of the door. "I need my sleep since you'll be boring us tomorrow at the science center thing."

He laughed and turned around as he walked down the carpeted hall. "It won't be that bad."

She rolled her eyes. "I might get lost on purpose."

Sirue shook his head and called back to her. "Sleep tight, Mara."

He waved as he turned the corner to the elevators. When he was out of her eyesight, he pressed the down button and leaned his forehead on the wall. He placed his hand over his heart until the doors chimed open.

Chapter 54

The parking lot of the Adventure Science Center was half-full by nine o'clock. Miles parked the rental car a few rows from the entrance. He didn't mind the early hour meet-up unlike his passengers.

"Ughhhh," Mara moaned, unfastening her seatbelt from the backseat. "Why so damn early?"

Tea giggled as she pulled her visor down to check her hair. "You always complain about getting up early to do anything but working out."

"That's different. This is early for no damn reason." She looked out of her window at the row of cars in front of them. "And look, he's already here. So pressed."

Tea and Miles looked where she was pointing. Sirue and Teresa climbed out of his truck.

"Aw, I'm glad she's feeling better," Tea commented. She caught Mara's expression in her visor's reflection. She turned to face her. "Mara, don't be mean."

Miles laughed. Mara made a face and held up her hands in surrender. They exited the car and Tea immediately pulled her cardigan closed.

"It's even colder than it was when we left the hotel," she said, waiting for Miles to get to her side before walking. He draped his arm around her and rubbed her arm. She looked behind them as Mara followed a few paces behind.

"You aren't freezing?" She quickly eyed Mara's casual ensemble of leggings and a baggy cream-colored sweater.

Mara shook her head and folded her arms. Before Tea could respond, Sirue approached them while studying something on his phone.

"Good morning, fine people," he greeted, briefly looking up.

"Hey, man. Hey, Teresa. Feeling better?" Miles asked.

Teresa smiled. "So much better. I think I had bad food poisoning or something." She hooked her arm inside of Sirue's.

Tea noticed Sirue's glance at Teresa before looking back on his phone.

"All right," Sirue began. "We can get our day passes there," he pointed in the direction of the entrance gate. "Then, I suggest we start at the visitor's center, which would be right around…there."

"I'm excited. Let's go," Tea said, walking at a quicker pace. She held Miles' hand and ignored the sounds of Mara sucking her teeth behind her.

Once their passes were purchased, they made their way to the visitor's center. Tea and Sirue busied themselves with outlining a general itinerary of activities for the day. They decided on the permanent exhibits first, the traveling train exhibit, the coding and innovation lab, a quick lunch at their sub shop, then the ninety-minute planetarium show in the afternoon. While Sirue and Tea were working on the schedule, Mara, Teresa, and Miles hung around the gift shop area. When they heard the agenda for the day, Mara immediately turned around and asked a nearby employee if the bar was open for day drinking.

After leaving the Sudekum Planetarium, they agreed that they were all impressed with the flight presentations and laser show.

"They have a rotating schedule of planetarium activities throughout the year," Sirue commented as they walked out of the darkened auditorium. He was thumbing through the brochures and leaflets the staff passed out upon their exit.

"Oooh, they do?" Tea rushed to Sirue's side and examined the papers with him.

Mara yawned loudly and rudely, causing Miles to laugh. "So, where are we going tonight?"

Sirue looked up and squinted at Mara. He smirked. "That's a surprise."

Mara threw her hands up, then said to Miles, "Watch, it's gonna be a damn space shuttle launch or some shit."

Miles laughed, then sat on a bench near the planetarium's exit doors. "Don't give him any ideas."

Mara sighed loudly and plopped down on the bench next to him. "I promise, I'll walk back to DC, Si."

He shook his head at her and Miles. "Why do we even hang out with them?" he asked Tea.

"Y'all are terrible," Tea agreed, shaking her head with Sirue.

Teresa smiled. She hooked her arm inside of Sirue's, slightly pulling him away from Tea.

Mara noticed and cut her eyes from Teresa to Sirue.

"Well, at least tell us how to dress. I brought one more good outfit, maybe I can still get a hook-up before we leave," Mara said, crossing her leg and leaning back against the wall behind the bench. She looked directly at Sirue and caught his brief glance up in her direction.

"Yes, your red dress is fire," Tea added, momentarily distracted from the list of museum's attractions in Sirue's hands. She looked over at Miles. "And, sweetie, I have that printed dress you bought for me."

"That dress is beautiful on you," Miles smiled at her.

Tea blew him a kiss and focused back on the brochures.

"Well, yes. I can tell you that much. Some nice, classy attire would work well for tonight," Sirue said, his eyes lingering on Mara's for an extra second. "Okay, guess we should all be getting back to get ready, huh?"

The Island Grove was a reggae-themed spot known for its dual level nightclub and restaurant located in a swanky hotel about thirty minutes outside of Nashville. As they entered the lobby, Sirue explained that he and Teresa attended once after teaching his first week of classes at Skiff by invitation from the natural sciences department chair.

"It's so nice in here. The restaurant area is on the top floor, and the club is on the rooftop," Teresa added as she smoothed her high ponytail. She was wearing a black shawl around her shoulders that covered a loose-fitting black dress.

Mara admired how pretty Teresa looked as they all waited for the elevator. They were all dressed for a nice night on the town. Tea sported the new Asian-inspired wrap dress from Miles, and he was wearing black jeans with a long-sleeved charcoal-colored shirt that Mara had to admit really fit him well. She also admired Sirue's maroon short-sleeved button-down top and black slacks. Mara checked her own form-hugging red dress in the elevator doors' reflection.

"A rooftop? It's like sixty degrees outside," Tea shivered next to Mara in front of the doors. Miles slid behind Tea and started a little groove.

"It'll warm up when we're dancing, gyal."

Mara groaned and everyone else laughed. "Miles, don't start that Jamaican shit again."

"Mi kno dem yah tings, gyal," he said in a heavy accent.

"Miles, is there *any*one in your family even remotely from the islands?" Sirue asked, amused.

The elevator chimed, and the doors opened. They all stepped inside and Sirue pressed the button for the tenth floor.

"Since y'all are so pressed about my heritage," Miles started, smoothing down his shirt, "my Aunt Carrie's half cousin is part Jamaican, in case y'all forgot."

Tea bit her lips to keep from laughing. "But...sweetie, earlier you said it was her half-sister."

Miles looked down at her and shook his head. "It be your own people."

Tea let out a laugh and gave him a side hug. Mara rolled her eyes at her crazy friend and leaned against the back wall of the elevator next to Sirue. He leaned over and slightly nudged her, looking down at her. She nudged him back, looking at the numbers ticking away as they climbed floors.

When they stepped out of the elevator, they were met by a set of double glass doors. Sirue and Miles both held the doors open as the women walked through, and Mara's jaw dropped. The ambience hit her immediately. From the shiny parquet floors, the mixture of gray upholstered couch booths and cushioned white and gray chairs, the white tablecloths and table settings, the low-hanging spherical lanterns placed throughout the spacious dining area, to the large floor-to-ceiling windows with tempered glass that allowed for breathtaking views of the city lights.

"Woooow," Tea said, sharing her sentiment.

Sirue smiled proudly. "Yeah, I figured this location would be more memorable for your last night in town."

"Good choice, bro," Miles agreed.

The tall, loc'd hostess approached the podium and checked her tablet for their reservation. She counted out five menus and led them to a table whose open curved booth faced a large window.

"This is nice, thank you," Mara said to her, scooting across the couched surface. She ended up in the center, with the other ladies on either side. Miles and Sirue capped both ends. The hostess smiled with a nod, then laid the menus in the middle of the table and told them their server would be there shortly.

"This is so perfect," Tea said excitedly. She grabbed her menu but continued to look around the brightly lit restaurant.

Miles saw her enthusiasm and smiled. "Isn't it? Let's take some selfies," he suggested and picked up his phone. He started getting different angles of himself and Tea in different shots.

Mara scooted closer to Teresa. "N'uh uh, don't get me in those. I look horrible, I didn't even check my hair," she joked.

Tea and Miles both laughed and turned the camera away from her direction.

Sirue looked up from his menu and talked across Teresa. "You don't look horrible," he said matter-of-factly, catching Mara's eyes.

She gave him a smile and remembered what he told her last night about talking down on herself. His brows raised a little as he looked directly at her, obviously recalling the conversation, too. There was no trace of a smile on his face. He finally looked back down at his menu. Mara felt her heart thump and found his gesture incredibly sexy.

Teresa cut her eyes at Sirue, then glanced at Mara, looking her over.

"Yeah, you look really pretty. That's a really good color on you." She nodded towards her red dress.

"Thanks, girl." Mara smiled and reached for her menu. She stared blankly at the images and descriptions of the food selections, not understanding why she was still smiling.

When the male waiter appeared, he started the group with beverages then returned to take their dinner orders. They all chose some variation of corn or pea soup as an appetizer and settled on either a jerk chicken or curry goat entrée.

The conversation was fun and light, and everyone finished their plates.

"Good lawd, how are we supposed to go upstairs and dance after this?" Mara groaned, leaning back and wiping her mouth.

"Right, I need a nap," Teresa agreed, tossing her napkin on her plate.

"Where's the restroom?" Tea asked, looking around.

"Um. I think it's down that way," Teresa answered, pointing to their left. "I can show you, I have to go, too."

Miles and Sirue stood and let Tea and Teresa out of the booth.

"Coming?" Tea looked back at Mara as she scooted out.

"Nah, I'm good for now."

"Okay," Tea stood. "Be right back," she smiled at Miles. As he sat back down, they held hands until she walked away.

"Y'all are so damn mushy," Mara joked, making a face.

Miles laughed. "I can't help it, she's amazing."

Sirue leaned back in the booth, looking at his friend. "I'm so happy for y'all. You haven't been able to stop smiling this whole weekend."

"Man, I've never been this happy, for real." Miles put his hand over his heart.

Mara leaned forward on the table and put her chin in her hand. She could see the joy all over his face.

"Like, it's just easy, you know?" Miles added. "Beyond the physical attraction, it's just comfortable."

"Probably because you know each other so well," Mara said.

"Yeah, that's the biggest part. There's no 'feeling each other out' time wasted. I know so much about her –"

"And she already knows everything about you, which says a lot," Sirue interrupted.

Mara chuckled. As Miles and Sirue continued talking, she glanced down at Sirue's phone on the table. His sudoku app was open, so she studied it, making a few moves for him. While talking, Sirue glanced down and smiled at her playing on his phone. *Comfortable.*

"What about you, man? You and Teresa good?" Miles asked, smoothing his goatee.

Sirue shrugged. "It's been a little rough, I can't lie."

"Well, she definitely loosened up a lot around us," Miles commented.

"Yeah, she's been putting in a lot of work on herself. I commend her for that." Sirue nodded.

"Speaking of which, that's what my last journal entry was about," Miles said, getting animated. "The importance of holding your own self accountable before anyone else can."

Mara glanced up at him. "Don't tell me you brought your journal," she said flatly.

Sirue chuckled.

"Maybe if you kept a journal, you wouldn't be so damn mean," Miles retorted.

"Yeah, I would." Mara shrugged and went back to Si's phone.

Miles continued to describe his writing, and a few minutes later, Tea and Teresa were heading back to the table.

"The bathroom was fancy," Tea commented as Miles started to get up.

Before Sirue slid away, he reached under the table and found Mara's pinky with his. He tugged on it gently, then moved out of the booth. Mara smiled to herself.

"We ready to go upstairs?" Sirue asked everyone.

"Yes!" Tea answered.

Teresa smoothed the small creases out of Sirue's dress shirt, then held his hand. With his free hand, he helped Mara from the booth. She adjusted her own clothes once she stood and walked between the couples as they headed to the far end of the restaurant and filed up the stairs that led to the rooftop.

"Y'all do know that the elevators are right over there," Sirue complained as they climbed the metal steps.

The heavy rhythm of the reggae music was the first thing to greet them after they ascended the stairs. The same spherical lanterns from the restaurant lined the perimeter of the roof, but now emitted a dimmer amber glow. The Island Grove's yellow and green logo was prominently located on a large mirror behind the long bar.

"Oooooh, yessss," Tea said, shimmying to the strong beat. She pulled Miles behind her to the main dance floor. They immediately fell into a groove together, with her backside against him as he held her gyrating hips.

"C'mon, this music is infectious," Teresa said to Sirue. She started tugging his arm, and he hesitated. He looked back in Mara's direction. Mara scratched the back of her neck and suddenly felt like a fifth wheel.

"Are you good?" Sirue asked her quietly.

Mara nodded and made a face, waving him off. "Y'all go ahead. I'm gonna check out the bar."

Sirue looked at her for a brief second, then walked off with Teresa.

Mara found an empty stool at the end of the bar. When the bartender sauntered over with his towel over his shoulder, Mara noticed his red-tipped short dreadlocks and the three buttons open on his shirt. She ordered a Cosmopolitan and he winked at her. Mara looked down the length of the bar and admired all the handsome men smiling in the faces of beautiful women. The patrons nearby on the crowded floor were either dancing or mingling. She sighed. This was going to be a long night.

Chapter 55

Sirue followed Teresa's lead to the edge of the main dance floor. When she found an unoccupied spot through the crowd of dancers, she turned and put Sirue's hands on her hips as she draped her arms over his shoulders. Sirue mimicked her swaying rhythm to the reggae dancehall music and studied Teresa's face. He leaned down and whispered in her ear.

"You look very nice tonight," he said.

She turned her head slightly and her lips grazed his cheek as she found his ear. "It took you long enough to give me a compliment."

Sirue pulled back and looked at her. He stopped swaying. "What do you mean it took me long enough?"

"I'm saying…you seem to be looking at everyone *but* me tonight."

Sirue didn't want to fight. He blinked slowly and exhaled. "Teresa."

"Just dance with me," she said, urging him to move to the infectious beats blasting from the speakers.

Sirue obliged, and they started to move again. While his body grooved with hers, his mind was on last night. He squeezed her hips as he remembered giving scalp massages and caressing soft skin. Memories caused a half-smile to form on his lips and Teresa returned a smile.

Instinctively, Sirue turned his head towards the bar to check on his friend. Through the bodies around him on the floor, he could see a gentleman sidling up on a stool next to Mara. Before he could get a better view, he felt Teresa's hand on his cheek, turning his head back to her. They danced for a few more minutes until Sirue's curiosity got the best of him.

"Are you thirsty? I need a drink. I can go grab one for you, too," he offered, nodding his head towards the bar.

Teresa dropped her arms from his shoulders and folded them across her chest. She stared at him hard. "You suddenly need a drink?"

He sighed. "And I want to make sure Mara's okay."

"Of course you do," she conceded.

"I'll be right back," he said, rubbing her arm and walking off. Teresa shook her head and went to sit on a fluffy bench against the wall.

To Mara's right, she smelled the citrus and bergamot fragrance of the man sitting down before she even saw him. Acqua di Gio was one of her favorite scents. He flashed a smile at her as he motioned for the bartender. Mara smiled back, looking over his flawless appearance. Short fade, full beard, toned body beneath a dark-colored turtleneck. A classy fragrance for a classy, sexy ass man.

The bartender arrived with her cocktail, and she took a sip. She listened as Mr. Gio ordered two drinks for himself and his wife. Her eyes dropped down to his hand and his gold wedding band was sitting proudly against his brown skin. Mara rolled her eyes to herself and took a healthy swig from her glass.

When the music changed songs, she swayed in her seat and pulled out her phone, nursing her second cocktail.

"Boo," Sirue said near her ear from behind, making her jump.

She turned to see him smiling. "Boy, you almost got...," she warned.

Sirue laughed and held up his hands. He sat sideways in the vacant stool to her right. He looked at her phone and at her half-empty glass. "You could be doing this in your hotel room, you know."

Mara squinted at him. "Mind your business."

He smiled. "You don't want to get out there and dance? Or go walk around?"

She shrugged. "Maybe after this drink and when I finally beat this dumb ass game." She went back to her phone, noticing Sirue's eyes on her. "You don't have to babysit me."

Sirue continued to look at her for a few more seconds. "I told Teresa I was coming to check on you."

Mara nodded her response, never looking up from sliding the colorful shapes around on her screen. "Y'all having fun?"

"Not really."

Mara gave him a quick glance, then focused back on her game. After a minute passed, Sirue slid his hand over to Mara's phone to tilt it more in his direction so he could watch her play. When his hand grazed hers, she ignored the jolt she felt shooting through her skin. He said something unintelligible just as the song changed and the volume increased in the speakers.

"Huh?" Mara said to him.

Sirue leaned forward and moved his mouth close to her ear. Mara's breathing stopped when she felt the slight contact of his lips on her lobe.

"I said...," he started slowly. "This is your last night here. You should talk to me."

Mara looked down as his thumb rubbed her hand. It reminded her of last night. Her mind was racing.

"Si...um...," she bit her lips.

He slowly retreated, and his thumb stopped touching her. "You should at least come check out the roof," he said.

Mara let out a breath. She turned completely in her stool and faced him. She looked at his face as he looked at hers. She took another sip of her drink and narrowed her eyes.

"Are you attracted to me after last night?" she asked bluntly, leaning closer so he could hear her.

Sirue calmly smiled and also moved closer. "Why do you ask?"

"Answer my question first." She took another sip.

His demeanor changed. His gaze roamed over her body in the red dress and landed back on her eyes. He opened his mouth to speak, but Miles slapped him on the back.

"Here y'all are! We were lookin' for your tall ass," Miles joked.

Tea walked up and put her head on Mara's shoulder. "I'm so damn tired."

She looked down at the glass in Mara's hand. "Oooh, what's that?" She took the drink from her and sipped it.

"You won't like –" Mara began, but Tea had already gagged. "Give me back my Cosmo, girl." She snatched it back.

"Have you seen the view from up here? It's so lit," Miles said, flagging down the bartender.

"C'mon, Mara, you have to see this." Tea hooked her arm in Mara's.

She hurried to grab her phone before Tea pulled her completely off the stool. She paused to take one last long sip of her drink and looked at Sirue, whose eyes hadn't left her once.

Sirue watched them walk away. Miles eyed his friend, then ordered drinks for himself and Tea. He went to occupy the stool Mara just vacated, his back to the bar, elbows resting on it from behind. He looked out on the floor at Tea and Mara, then back at Sirue, who was still watching them.

"So, uh...," Miles started.

Sirue snapped out of his trance and blinked at Miles.

"What's going on with you and Mara? And where's Teresa?" Miles looked at him.

"She's sitting on one of the couches. Shit, I was supposed to be bringing her a drink." Sirue turned and saw the bartender mixing Miles' drinks not too far away and he asked for a double of the same.

"And my other question?" Miles gave him a side-eye.

"I don't know how to answer that one," Sirue said, smoothing his hand over his face.

Miles nodded. He knew his assumptions were right. He noticed a lot of exchanges, verbal and nonverbal, between them both this whole weekend. The glances, the touches when they didn't think anyone was watching. It was strange, but he kept his thoughts to himself. He didn't want to prematurely mention anything to Tea until he spoke to Sirue.

"Well...brother to brother...just be clear with your intentions, man. You know?" Miles said sincerely.

Sirue nodded.

"She deserves your honesty. She talks hard, but you know she also takes things hard."

Sirue nodded again. He looked over at his friend. "Look at you, all wise and shit."

Everyone reconvened around the roof's overlook. Teresa and Mara both shied away from the secured edge, but the others loved the eleven-story high vantage point. They took many pictures and selfies, then found a vacant seating area. The time flew by, and Sirue found it extremely hard not to focus his attention and thoughts on his confusing feelings. He noticed that Mara was also trying to avoid his gaze and seemed lost in her thoughts at different moments.

At about half past one a.m., everyone was pretty much ready to call it a night. Downstairs in the lobby of the hotel, they all stood together.

"What time are you leaving in the morning?" Sirue asked, stuffing his hands into the pockets of his slacks.

Miles yawned. "Actually, in about five hours. We want to get on the road by seven."

"Ugh," Mara groaned.

"And don't drink any water before we leave," he directed to Mara.

"Whatever, we're stopping when I need to pee." She rolled her eyes.

"Pee before we leave!"

"I'm not holding it for ten hours, Miles!"

Tea stood between them. "Y'all, oh my God. We haven't even left yet."

Sirue smiled. "Yeah, y'all need to fly next time."

Miles and Tea both stared daggers at Mara. She shrugged and made a face.

"It was fun having you guys here," Teresa said with a smile.

"Yes, it was. Thank you for spending your holiday with us," Sirue said seriously, looking at his friends.

"You sound like a hotel manager," Tea joked. Everyone laughed, then Tea changed her mood. "I'm gonna miss you so much," she pouted, looking at Sirue.

"Aw, come here, Big Head." He held out his arms and Tea went to hug him. She looked at Teresa, then moved to hug her.

Miles followed suit and gave Sirue a dap, then a hug. "See you soon, brother."

"Yep. Three weeks, actually. Should be up Christmas Eve." Sirue patted Miles' back as he went to hug Teresa.

"Yay!" Tea said, smiling.

Mara looked at Sirue as he walked towards her with his arms extended. She smiled and moved in to wrap her arms around his neck. He squeezed her a little longer than the others and finally released his hold. Mara gave Teresa a half-hug and everyone walked outside.

"All right, I need to get some sleep. See y'all soon. Ready, ladies?" Miles asked, taking Tea's hand.

Sirue watched as they headed to their car, then walked with Teresa to his truck.

When she arrived at their hotel room about thirty minutes later, Mara went straight to the shower, then crawled under her covers. Tea was already snoring in her own bed.

Mara checked her phone and smiled at the text from Sirue.

You really did look amazing in that dress tonight. And to answer your question...no. I was attracted to you even before last night. See you soon.

Chapter 56

The Monday after they returned, Tea made it a point to start early at the shop. She wanted to relieve DeeDee since she held it down for her through the busy Thanksgiving weekend. Her assistant deserved some time off. After pulling the heavy gate partially up, Tea sat at the reception desk and went over the day's clients in the appointment book. She was startled by one of the names.

Tea picked up the phone and dialed the contact number that was given. The woman picked up quickly.

"Hello?"

"Rita? It's Tea!"

"Oh, hey, girl! Good morning, lovely!"

Tea heard the sounds of traffic through the receiver. "I'm sorry to call you back so early, I was just shocked to see you booked with me today."

"I told you I would be coming through. I need you to get this hair right for me, sis. I was glad the woman I spoke to yesterday could squeeze me in so early. I told her we're friends, so that probably bumped me up the line."

Tea laughed. "Benefits of knowing the owner."

"Hey, you know I'm coming from about forty-five minutes away, but I'll be stopping for coffee on my way. Want me to grab you something?"

"No, just get here safely. That 495 traffic is a nightmare."

"You're telling me. I'm about to blast this gospel music so I don't lose my mind. See you soon, girl."

Tea finished her walkthrough of the salon, checking the waiting area, hair stations, dryers, cleanliness of the equipment, and finally went to the back office to sit at her desk. She made a couple of business calls, answered a few emails, and donned her apron. By the time she walked back out to the front, she saw Nikki arrive and she caught Tea up on the events form the past few days at the shop. Nikki went on to help her prep the stations for the first two clients of the day.

When Rita arrived just after eight forty, Tea embraced her friend. She'd always loved Rita's formidable appearance and commented on her powder blue designer jogging set with color coordinated handbag and silver jewelry. As Tea worked on her hair, she told her about her trip to see Sirue in Tennessee and Rita shared how she spent her Thanksgiving week with Sedrick. It was a very welcome conversation, because inspiration hit Tea immediately. She asked Rita for details and also any possible networking contacts. Rita was more than happy to share.

After two hours, Tea's next client was getting a wash from Nikki as she put the finishing touches on Rita's silk press with full, bouncy curls. They hugged their goodbyes and Tea was very impressed with the hundred-dollar tip Rita slipped into her hand as they parted. She watched as Rita thanked Nikki and put a tip in her hand as well. Tea sat in the chair next to her station and pulled out her phone.

Guess what? she texted Miles.

Moments later: *what's up baby?*

you're going to love your Christmas gift

Miles sent a wide-eyed emoji, then: *you already bought it?*

i'm working on it. but you're going to be so happy

i already am baby

Tea smiled and sent him hearts. *awww me too. love you and i'll call you at lunch*

love you back. have a good rest of your morning

Mara wasn't sure if it was a deliberate game of text tag she'd been playing with Sirue since she returned after Thanksgiving, or if it was really due to her focus on her marketing class and his busy teaching schedule. They exchanged a few missed texts to each other all week, which was why she was surprised to receive an instant response from him on Friday night. She called him immediately.

"Damn, you're a hard negro to get in touch with," she said when he answered.

Sirue paused. She heard him sigh. "Yeah, it's been a long week."

"You sound exhausted."

"I am. Work has been...seems like it picked up double-speed for some reason. Or maybe I'm just trying to juggle too much."

Mara didn't like the somber tone in his baritone voice. "What's on your mind, Si?"

She heard him make a sound and she imagined him rubbing his head. "These classes. Life. Teresa. You."

Mara blinked. "Me?"

"You," he repeated flatly.

"The attraction thing?" she asked, her heart beating a little faster.

Sirue was quiet.

"Well, I don't want to be the source of any of your stress," Mara said sadly. She suddenly felt guilty for some reason.

"No, no. I'm sorry it came off like that. You're actually the one thought on that list keeping me sane."

Mara smiled. "Tell me about the other things, then. Maybe it'll help if you talk them out."

Sirue explained the details of his week, including the two arguments he had with Teresa.

"The last one wasn't really an argument, like the kind we used to have. More like...an intense discussion."

Mara sat back on her living room couch and folded a leg beneath her. "About the pregnancy?"

"Yeah," Sirue sighed. "Her procedure is this coming Monday, but she wouldn't talk to me about it beyond that. When I pressed her for a conversation, she ended up telling me she really wanted the abortion because I wouldn't be a good father. In so many words."

Mara's jaw dropped. "That bi—"

"Mara," Sirue interrupted.

"No, Si. No. Her mentally debilitated ass has the nerve to—"

"Mara," he interjected again. "Mara. I probably didn't paraphrase her correctly. She said the same thing about herself being a mother. Said we both weren't capable yet. I have to agree with her."

Mara quietly fumed. There were so many words she had for Teresa, but she could also hear the sadness in Sirue's voice.

"Damn, Si."

"Yeah. So...needless to say, it's been pretty tense." He exhaled.

"I bet." Mara played with the pillow she put on her lap. "That's a lot to deal with at once."

After a few seconds, Sirue broke the silence. "But look. I'm not going to bring you down with all my shit. I'll let you go start your weekend. I know you had a long week, too."

Mara frowned. "I didn't say I had to go."

Sirue let out a short laugh. "Mara, you don't have to babysit me."

"Shut up," she laughed.

They talked for the next hour until Sirue started to fall asleep on the phone. By the time they hung up, Mara had made her way to her bedroom. She laid beneath her comforter and hugged one of her oversized pillows against her body. It was strange to feel this way after talking to Sirue. What had changed? They'd had plenty of conversations throughout their friendship, from the deep to the mundane. Something was different now. The gentle flirting and that sexy voice of his were new, though. Had it always been that hot? Mara felt a sensation moving through her body that she hadn't felt in a long time. She squeezed her thighs and hugged her pillow tighter. The smile she had on her face never left, even during the vivid erotic dream she had about Sirue bending her over outside in the pouring rain.

Chapter 57

Morning came fast, and Mara awoke, realizing she'd have to calm the energy between her legs. Flash scenes of memories flooded into her consciousness. Sirue pressing her body against some alley wall, the side of her face flat against the wet, cold brick. His big, strong hands holding her wrists above her head. His thickness pounding inside her aggressively. Kissing everywhere gently. Mara sighed in her bed. Her own hands searched her body, and she found the sweet release she needed.

After a quick shower and throwing on her workout clothes, Mara pulled her hair into a top ponytail, poofing out her hair. She checked her phone on the way downstairs and was glad that it was only seven thirty. Heaven's would still be rather empty. Tea hadn't even woken up yet. She grabbed a protein bar and two bottles of water from the kitchen then made her way to the gym. Her thoughts were clouded with the physical sensations still radiating through her body. She hoped generating some sweat would help.

Thirty minutes on the treadmill, then thirty minutes on the elliptical. Mara wiped her face and threw her towel over her shoulder. On her way to the weights, she walked past the indoor court and was surprised to see Miles shooting around alone. She made a detour and opened the glass door. He glanced over and smiled when he saw her.

"Hey, you didn't tell me you were coming this morning," he said, casually dribbling between his legs.

Mara tossed her towel on the floor. "Feeling nostalgic for our weekly workouts," she joked, then clapped her hands for the ball.

He passed it to her, and she dribbled it for a quick layup. She retrieved the ball, then dribbled back as Miles played light defense against her. Mara backed into him, faked to her left, then turned to her right and made her shot with his hand in her face. The ball drilled the backboard and fell into the net. Miles rebounded, then tossed the ball to her and they repeated the play a few times until Mara was successfully blocked by Miles' defense.

"Ouch, nice," she said, wiping her forehead.

Miles laughed, then dribbled between his legs as she faced him. "C'mon, let me see what you –"

Mara smacked the ball before it bounced back to his hand and sped to the basket for a layup. Miles stood with his hands in the air.

"So we just foulin' now?"

"Shut up and get the ball," she said, pointing to the ball bouncing away down the court.

"Oh, a'ite," Miles said and jogged after the ball.

They played hard one-on-one for the next twenty minutes, then went to sit on the floor against the wall of the court. Both were breathing hard and wiping their faces and arms with their towels.

"Good game," Mara said, taking a long sip from her water bottle.

Miles gave her a side-eye.

"What? I'm serious," Mara smiled. "You just need to work on your handle a little bit."

Miles stared at her. "Ain't nothing wrong with my handle, thank you."

Mara threw her hands up. "Just sayin'. Trying to help you out." She sipped again.

"I don't need no damn help with my handle."

Mara made a face and looked away. "I meeeean, if you call me beating you off the dribble three times not needing my help, then...," she shrugged.

He stared at her again until she looked back at him. She laughed and he shook his head.

They watched as a few gym members entered the court to shoot around. The three men played for a few minutes before Miles commented. "So, you gonna critique them, too? He just lost the ball."

Mara laughed. "You mad."

Miles playfully hit her with his towel, then wiped his face again. "What's up for today? I think Tea is working open to close."

Mara shrugged. "Probably just cleaning and studying. What about you?"

"Gonna visit my Pops and Aunt Carrie. See how they're doing. It's been a while."

"So, you'll be at the mosque around what time?" Mara asked.

Miles laughed. "Always got jokes."

They both winced simultaneously when one of the players fell from a hard block.

"So...I need to ask you something," Miles continued looking at the court.

"Nah, that was a good block," Mara commented.

Miles chuckled, then looked at her. "No, not that. Something about...well...," Miles took a deep breath, then continued with his question.

Mara listened with rapt attention. When he was finished, she hardly knew what to say.

Sirue sat at the front of his genetics classroom and glanced to his left at the clock above the door.

"Ten minutes remaining," he called out. The students all groaned and started flipping through pages of their final exams with desperation. Sirue absently monitored his students while thoughts of this week raced through his mind. He was grateful that it was Thursday morning, which meant just one more week until he was on a plane heading back to the DMV. He didn't realize how much he needed to be around his friends. He was almost at the end of his rope with his own home life and the change of environment was going to be so helpful. Last night nearly broke him.

Sirue recalled the defeated expression that appeared on Teresa's face when he sat with her on the living room couch, and she turned down the television. He was immediately worried that something was wrong or that she was in some kind of pain, although she'd been recuperating well the past three days post-procedure.

"Are you okay?" he asked.

Teresa shrugged and pulled the throw blanket higher onto her lap. "I'm going back home."

Sirue blinked hard. "What? Where's that coming from?"

"We're over. We tried almost everything." She looked over at him. "You're not in love with me."

Sirue furrowed his eyebrows, trying to understand. "I do love you, Teresa."

"You're not *in love* with me," she repeated.

He sighed and put his head in his hands. Teresa rubbed his back. After a minute of silence, she touched the back of his head.

"You don't have to go," he mumbled into his hands.

Teresa sniffed. "I do. My therapist helped me find one up there. I have to use my energy to work on myself instead of using it to beg you for affection."

Sirue looked over at her from his hands. He felt his throat tighten. "I'm sorry," he said quietly.

"I'm sorry, too."

"Professor Oseon, the timer went off!" A student in the front row interrupted his thoughts.

There were groans from other students who wanted the extra time while their professor daydreamed. Sirue stood and directed his students to come down and submit their exams face down on the front table. After the last student solemnly put his exam down and begged him to have mercy on him, Sirue gathered the papers and placed them in his briefcase. Back in his office upstairs, he sat at his desk and busied himself with organizing the papers and textbooks that covered almost every surface.

His phone flashed on the side of his desk, and he picked up.

"Miles, hey," he answered.

"Hey, man, I hope I'm not disturbing your class."

"No, my last one just ended. About to go find some dinner in a bit, maybe go pick up a Christmas gift I ordered," Sirue said. He leaned back and scratched his head. He didn't really want to rush home and face another hard conversation with Teresa.

"Oh okay. Semester's over, then?" Miles asked.

"One more final tomorrow, then it's a wrap. Oh, I checked earlier, and my plane should get into BWI next Thursday night around nine o'clock."

"I'll be on time," Miles chuckled.

"Because that's Christmas Eve and you know it will be a madhouse," Sirue urged. "I can just get a rental."

Miles laughed again. "I'll be on time. But I called to ask about Teresa. I know she had the, uh, thing a few days ago. How's she doing? How are you doing?"

Sirue sighed. He explained what transpired last night.

"Oh, shit."

"Yeah. It's been...," Sirue ran his hand over his head. "In a way, I guess I knew it was coming. I don't know. Or I've been pushing her away so it *would* happen."

Miles was quiet for a beat. "It's always been complicated with you two, huh?"

"Yeah."

"Damn. Sorry, brother. Don't beat yourself up, though. Figure out your part in it and learn the lesson. Lean on us when you need to."

Sirue nodded. He was impressed with his friend's growth. There was so much he was grateful for within their friendship. "Thanks. Love you, man."

"Of course, love you back, brother." Miles paused. "Uh, look, there's something I need to ask you."

"Sure," Sirue replied. He leaned forward in his chair, not believing what he was hearing.

Chapter 58

Tea looked at the falling snow from the bay window in her living room.

"Mara! Come here!" she called towards the kitchen.

Mara hurried out holding a spatula in one hand and an oven mitt on the other. "What's wrong?" She paused when she saw Tea standing before the wintry scene.

"Look at how pretty the snow is." Tea waved her over.

Mara rolled her eyes as she walked. "Girl, I thought you fell or someth—oooh, it's getting heavier," she commented on the large, fluffy flakes that started to fall at double-speed.

"Yeah." Tea hooked her arm inside of Mara's. "Our first Christmas here in our house and it's snowing."

Mara smiled. She always loved how sentimental Tea was about the holidays. She took over the task of decorating the house for the past week. Almost every inch of the downstairs was adorned with lights, knickknacks, reindeer, oversized ornaments, snow globes, angels, and elves. The seven-foot-tree was to their right, decked out in a mostly red and gold theme.

"It's beautiful," Mara agreed. "Okay, but my pancakes are burning, though."

Tea laughed and pushed her away. She watched the snow fall for a few more minutes until she saw Miles' car pull up into the driveway.

"They're here," she said, clapping her hands.

She rushed to the door and opened it, waving as Sirue and Miles stepped out. They waved back and they both opened the back doors, taking out a multitude of different sized gift bags full of presents.

Tea watched as Sirue made his way up the path first. She smiled at his disgust with the snow as he tried to tighten his scarf and pull his skully farther down his head, all while balancing four large bags. She ushered him inside as she wiped the freshly fallen snow from his coat.

"You act like it's gonna make you melt," she laughed.

He grunted, then smiled. "Hey, Big Head. Merry Christmas," he said warmly, and leaned down to kiss her cheek. Tea hugged him and he entered, putting down his bags. She turned back and saw Miles approaching with four bags full of wrapped gifts.

"Merry Christmas, baby," he said with a huge grin. He kissed her lightly on the mouth and Tea wrapped her arms around his neck.

"Merry Christmas," she said, cheerfully. She took one of the bags as he walked into the living room.

"Oh, wow, it's a winter wonderland in here," Sirue observed, taking off his coat, scarf, and hat.

Tea took them from him and waited for Miles to take off his coat. "Aw, you like it?" she asked Sirue.

"Absolutely. You didn't hold anything back." Sirue walked to the tree and admired all the ornaments.

Tea smiled hard and took Miles' coat. She went to quickly hang them up.

"I'm so glad y'all are here!" She slipped her arm around Miles who leaned down to kiss the top of her head.

Mara stepped out of the kitchen and smiled.

"Merry Christmas!" she said to Miles and Sirue. She went to hug them both and almost didn't want to let go of Sirue, sensing he felt the same way. She stood beside him and leaned her head on his arm.

"It smells like food," Miles said, sniffing the air. "Pancakes, cinnamon rolls, and bacon."

They all looked at him.

"Can I at least set the table?" Mara finally asked.

After Sirue said grace over their meal, everyone started filling their plates. The table was complete with two serving dishes piled high with pancakes, a wide bowl of bacon and sausage, a large carafe of orange juice, a bowl of scrambled eggs, and another serving dish of fried potatoes. By the second round of helpings, just about everyone had slowed down and started to pick at their plates.

"That was delicious," Sirue stated, pouring another refill for his glass.

"Yes! Chef Queden over here threw down," Tea said, smiling at her friend.

Mara nodded. "I did, I did."

"See, you should cook more," Tea suggested.

"Only on holidays in December, sis, and *dassit*!" Mara plucked another sausage link from the bowl in front of her.

Miles reached for two more slices of bacon from the same bowl, then a hefty third spoonful of eggs.

"You said the cinnamon rolls are on the stove, right?" he asked, craning his neck towards the kitchen.

They all laughed.

"I don't know where your food goes," Mara said, shaking her head at him.

"I do," Tea said, winking her eye and picking up a forkful of potatoes.

Sirue and Mara looked at her. "You nasty," Mara smirked.

"And my food is still digesting," Sirue said, making a face.

Miles laughed and looked over at Tea. "Tell 'em, baby."

"Well, to change the subject --," Sirue started

"Thank you!" Mara interjected.

"...I already told Miles, but I wanted to let you two know as well. Teresa and I are officially over. She moved back up here to Maryland to stay with her cousins."

Mara and Tea looked at each other and Sirue.

"What?" Tea asked.

"Wow," Mara mumbled and looked down at her plate.

"Yeah. I think this time, it's really over."

Tea made a face. "I'm sorry, Si." She reached over and touched his arm.

"It's fine. I think it's for the best. I mean, I wish her well, of course. And I hope she can find the happiness she deserves." Sirue glanced across the table at Mara, who was still pushing food around on her plate.

Tea sighed. "You know…things happen for a reason."

Sirue nodded. "I definitely believe that."

"Me, too, really," Mara said, tapping her fork on her plate.

Miles eyed them both and swallowed his last bite of eggs.

"Well," he said, finally pushing his plate away. "Who's ready for presents?"

Chapter 59

Tea sat cross-legged on the floor next to the tree as Sirue stood hunched over, pulling presents out of the gift bags he and Miles brought.

"Okay, these are semi-organized. These are for us," he said, sliding two heavy bags of wrapped gifts towards the coffee table. "The rest are for Aunt Esther and the boys."

He took various sized gifts from the bags and placed them carefully under the tree.

"I guess we all went a little crazy with gifts for Day and James, huh?" Tea asked, loving all the colorfully wrapped presents for the boys.

"But wait...," Mara said, sitting on the couch with her leg drawn beneath her, "we all stuck to our one-gift for each other rule, right?" She motioned to the four of them.

"Ehhh...kind of," Miles commented from the armchair.

"Sort of," Sirue added.

Mara sucked her teeth and Tea giggled. "Well, y'all know I'm broke, so...," Mara shrugged.

"It's not about the amount you spent," Sirue said, finally sitting down beside Mara.

"Yeah, it's about whether or not I can return it for cash," Mara quipped.

"That's not the holiday spirit!" Tea grabbed a candy cane from the tree and threw it at her.

Mara caught it and opened the peppermint treat, breaking off a piece to eat.

"All right, so how do you want to do this?" Sirue leaned forward. "Open them one *present* at a time according to who they're from, or open one *person* at a time according to our proximity to the tree?"

"Really, bro?" Miles threw up his hands.

"Are you serious?" Mara chimed in.

"What?!" Sirue glared at each of them.

"Sirue's right, though –"

"No, Tea, he does this every year," Mara rolled her eyes.

"And we always end up doing it how Tea wants to, anyway," Miles added.

She squinted her eyes at him. "No, we do not."

"Baby," he said, giving her a look.

"Anyway," Tea continued, waving him off. "Okay, let's open them one person at a time."

Miles and Mara made faces at each other, noting that they figured this would be the outcome.

As Tea started to look under the tree, Mara squealed, "Ooooh, me first."

"Guests first," Sirue corrected, straining his neck to get a glance at the gifts Tea started pulling from beneath the back of the tree.

"No. Tea, can you hand me mine, please. Ladies first!"

"Okay, Mara first," Tea said, handing her a small present.

Sirue angrily cut his eyes to Mara but couldn't help but smirk at her joy. She caught his glance and playfully stuck her tongue out at him. She took the present and did a jig in her seat as she ripped open the paper.

"You just tore off the tag, but that's from me by the way," Miles said.

"Oh, my bad," Mara said, continuing to rip the paper off.

Her jaw dropped when she saw the famous logo on the box. "The new SmartWatch 86 Series! Oooh! Thank you!"

She bounced and opened the box. The shiny electronic was her favorite rose gold color for gadgets. "It's so pretty, thank you! I really wanted this!" She reached over and gave Miles a hug.

"You're welcome," he smiled, as she sat back down.

"Here's the next one," Tea said getting Sirue's help to lift the heavy rectangular present. He handed it to her.

"This one is from me," he said proudly. They watched as Mara ripped apart the paper again. She covered her mouth with her hands when she saw the same famous fruit logo, but this time, on a brand-new laptop.

"Whaaaaaat??" Mara said, her eyes immediately welling up as she looked over at Sirue.

He smiled. "For the rest of your grad school journey, and beyond. I know you needed an updated device."

Mara let her tears flow, still covering her mouth. "Si...oh my God. I love it so much. Thank you."

She gently put the box on the coffee table and reached over to hug him, wrapping her arms around his neck. Sirue closed his eyes and rubbed her back.

"You know you're welcome," he said softly.

Mara pulled back and wiped her tears.

"And, this is from me," Tea said, also choked up. She handed Mara a very large gift wrapped perfectly. Sirue helped her give it to Mara.

"Tea...," Mara said, sniffling. "What's this?"

"Open it and see," she smiled.

Mara started crying before she even started tearing the paper off. When she saw the top of the painting, she gasped, and the tears streamed down harder. Sirue helped her pull the painting from the rest of the wrapping paper. It was the same painting that Sirue owned titled "Waiting." The same one she loved getting lost in. Mara sat back and openly wept into her hands. Tea stood and squeezed between her and Sirue, hugging her and sharing tears.

"I love you, girl," Tea said warmly.

"I love you, tooooo," Mara whined, laughing at her own self through the tears.

Tea kissed her forehead and went back to sit near the tree.

Sirue and Miles cleared their throats, playing off the heightened emotions.

"And we've only been through one person so far. This is too emotional!" Miles joked.

"Well, you go next, sir," Tea said, handing him three wrapped presents of varying shapes.

"I'll do that," he said, excitedly. He opened his gift from Sirue first: a collection of moleskine journals with a coordinating set of Monte Carlo red and gold ball point pens. His mouth hung open.

"Wow, man. I'm...," he opened the velvet pen case and admired the pens sitting snug against the fabric-lined interior. "This is perfect. Thank you," he half-stood to reach over and give Sirue a slap handshake.

Next, Miles opened a gift that looked like a shirt box from Mara. He shook the box and squinted over at her.

"Just open it, damn," she said, playfully hitting his leg.

"Okay, okay." Miles pulled the paper off, then opened the shirt box. He lifted a hard-to-find home team basketball jersey from his favorite player. "Woooow. Mara...this is sick!"

"I figure it can help you with your dribble," she said seriously, examining the jersey.

He lowered it and glared at her. "Don't."

She laughed.

"Thank you, Mara. This is nice. Very nice." He reached over to hug her, then placed the jersey carefully back into its box. "And this leaves..." He winked at Tea as he lifted the envelope he'd put on the coffee table.

Tea sat up straight, hardly able to contain her giddy expression.

Miles opened the envelope and it fell from his hands when he took out its contents. Two cruise tickets to Ocho Rios, Jamaica. He stared at them in disbelief, then looked at Tea in disbelief, then back to the tickets.

"Baby," was all he could manage to say.

"They're for March, and there's so much to do there. I printed out 3 versions of their activity schedules that we can look at...," she paused when she saw him staring at the tickets. "Are they okay?"

Miles slowly looked up at her and placed his hand over his heart. He bit his lip and stared into her eyes. "They're perfect. More perfect than you know."

He stood and went to sit beside her on the floor. He embraced her, lifting her slightly, and buried his face in her neck.

Sirue and Mara looked at each other. Mara's eyes widened, and Sirue mouthed, "I know." They watched their friends hug and whisper intimately for the next minute.

"A-*hem*," Sirue finally cleared his throat loudly.

Tea giggled and unwrapped herself from Miles' arms. "Sorry."

Miles kissed her quickly on the mouth and stayed beside her on the floor.

"Si, you're next," Tea said, happily handing him a very heavy wrapped box, a medium-sized present, and an envelope.

He held the envelope and saw it was from Tea. "I'm guessing these are *my* cruise tickets?"

They all laughed.

"They better not be. I didn't get an envelope!" Mara added.

Sirue opened it and immediately smiled. "A season pass to the Adventure Science Center. Tea, this is so thoughtful."

Tea smiled hard. "Yep, when we were there, you kept saying there was so much more you wanted to see, but these two kept rushing you, so…now you can go whenever you want. Up until June, anyway."

Sirue went to hug her and then opened his next present. It was a monogrammed lab coat from Mara. "Dr. Sirue Osean," he read the red script against the crisp white fabric. "Wow. Thank you," he said seriously to Mara.

"You're welcome," she smiled. "I mean, I still don't even know what your PhD is in, but I figured this would work in all of your labs."

Sirue chuckled, then leaned over to give her a tight hug. "Thank you," he whispered again in her ear.

Mara felt a familiar jolt run through her when she felt his breath against her skin. She tried to shake it off as she pulled back from their embrace and gave his arm a light rub.

Next, he reached for the heavy gift from Miles. "This has some weight to it," he commented, tearing off the wrapping paper. "Oooh, nice! Yessss," Sirue said, his eyes wide. He opened the wooden box containing a vintage whiskey decanter set, complete with his initials and various bottles of bourbon and whiskey.

"Ooooooh," Tea said, looking at the beautiful decanter housed in the box.

"Perfect for his drunk ass," Mara joked. Sirue shot her a look.

"Brother. This is just what I needed. Thank you, man. I love this."

"Of course," Miles said, pounding his heart as Sirue did the same.

"We should crack this right on open and put this to use!" Mara reached for the bottle labeled "Martel Blue Swift."

Sirue carefully took it from her hand and placed it back into its box. "Absolutely not."

Mara sucked her teeth. "All you're gonna do is let it sit on your dusty little bar set, anyway."

Miles and Tea laughed.

"Well, let it sit on my dusty bar. You can go drink the champagne we brought," Sirue waved in the direction of the kitchen. He went back to admiring his incredible gift.

Miles rubbed Tea's back. "I think it's time for our cute little elf to open her presents now."

Tea smiled. She reached for a small, wrapped box. "From Mara," she read on the tag. "Ooooh," Tea said as she tore the paper off. She looked at Mara and gave her an emotional pout. "A charm bracelet...I always wanted one and you remembered."

Mara's eyes started to well up again. "Look at the charms I put on, just to start you off."

Tea gingerly lifted the bracelet from its case. She fingered the beautiful heart charm, the tiny hair dryer charm, and the little silver key charm. A tear rolled down her cheek as she looked back up at Mara.

"I have the lock charm on my necklace," she tugged her neckless free from inside her top and lifted it for Tea to see. "You're my sis--," Mara gasped as she tried to talk, her breath catching through the tears. Sirue reached over to rub her back. "...my sister, and I love you for putting up with me. You have the biggest heart and I love you."

Mara wiped her tears and cried as Tea stood up and went to hug her.

"You will always be my sister," Tea cried. They embraced as the guys watched and smiled.

Tea went to sit back down. "Okay, whew! I'm good, I'm good." She waved at her eyes.

Miles leaned over to kiss her on the cheek. He rubbed her leg as she grabbed the next present. She unwrapped it, and her mouth flew open. "Sirue!" She lifted the three framed prints from the box.

He smiled at her. "I remember you looking at them on the walls when we were at that cabaret. You said you needed some for the shop, so...here you go."

Tea sighed and put her hand over her heart. She got up to hug Sirue. "Thank you. I love you."

"You're welcome, Big Head. Love you back," he said endearingly.

She sat down again, and Miles reached behind her to give her a rather large present.

"Ooooh, what's this?" she asked, clapping her hands.

Miles just smiled. He tried to take a few deep breaths inconspicuously.

Tea ripped at the wrapping paper. She saw a large box from a very high-end department store. When she opened the professionally wrapped gift box, her jaw dropped. It was a luxurious pink bathrobe and a very posh home spa set. She noted the designer candles, stones, the plush bath cloths, lotions, body wash, and gourmet chocolates.

"Miiiiiiiiiles, I need this so bad," she cooed. She looked at him.

Miles continued to smile. "You work so hard," he said quietly. "But there's more."

He pointed to the box. Tea was confused but reached inside the box to find a folded sheet of paper. She opened it, and saw a photo of a reclining, heated full body massage chair. The note below was the gift receipt. Her mouth fell open. "Oh my God. You didn't."

"I did. It's getting delivered to the shop tomorrow. It's for your office."

Tea looked over at him and her lips formed a frown. She sniffed and the tears started rolling again. Her arms reached over and hugged him. "I love you. Thank you for always thinking about me," she said quietly.

Miles felt his heart beating outside of his chest and he felt a lump in his throat. He rubbed her back as he held her close. When Tea finally let go, she wiped her face.

"Y'all...," she looked around at them. "We are so blessed to have each other."

Sirue nodded, leaning back and crossing one leg over his knee. "I agree. We really are."

"Like, even if we didn't have these beautiful gifts from each other, there aren't a lot of people who can say they have friends who became family." Tea sniffed. Miles reached over and wrapped his arm around her waist.

"Yeah." Mara said, a tear falling. "I mean...I'm not giving my stuff back, but I feel grateful to have each one of you in my life."

She reached out and held Sirue's hand. He looked down at their hands and rubbed hers with his thumb.

"I love y'all," Miles said.

They all returned the sentiment.

Chapter 60

"Okay, the boys will be here in about an hour or so, I guess we need to get all this paper up," Tea sighed and stood up, gathering the trash.

Miles bit his lips together and stood to help. He glanced over at Sirue and Mara.

"You have any trash bags?" Sirue asked.

"Yeah, in the kitchen. Let me go grab some," Mara answered, getting up and heading to the kitchen.

Sirue began to half-heartedly pick up the torn pieces of wrapping paper trash from around the sofa. "It doesn't take that long to get trash bags," he mumbled after a few seconds as he walked to the kitchen. "Mara! You're just trying to get out of cleaning up!"

"You asked for some damn trash bags, that's what I'm getting!" she yelled back.

Tea shook her head when she heard them fussing at each other in the kitchen. "They argue over everything."

Miles nodded. He stood, looking around at the trash and scratched his head. He couldn't control the pounding in his chest, so he bent back down to start moving their opened gifts into piles. He breathed deeply, trying to conceal his shaking hands.

"That's where we always put them, though!" Mara screamed at Sirue. "Tea! Didn't we just buy that big box of trash bags?"

Tea stood with an armful of wrapping paper. "Yes, it's behind the brooms!"

"We looked in there!" Sirue yelled.

"No, *I* looked in there! You just been in here stressing me out!" Mara corrected. "Tea! Where are they?!"

"Oh, my goodness," Tea dropped the trash and stomped into the kitchen. "Weren't we just saying how much we loved each other?" She walked past them and opened the broom closet. There weren't any trash bags.

She stood with her hands on her hips. "We always put them here," she mumbled to herself and started to look around.

Mara and Sirue both shrugged and opened different cabinets. Tea tapped her chin and glanced at the top of the refrigerator. The big carton of bags was hidden behind two boxes of cereal.

"There they are," she pointed. "Si, can you grab those?"

"Why were they even up there?" she asked Mara as Sirue handed the box to her.

Mara shrugged again. She took the box from Tea and pulled out a bag. "I probably did it while I was slaving away over this stove this morning."

"That's weird," Tea said to herself. She walked back out of the kitchen. "C'mon, y'all, there's not really that much –"

Tea stopped in her tracks when she got to the dining room table and looked into the living room.

Miles was on one knee, holding out a small jewelry box. Her legs went weak. Mara and Sirue followed behind her, grinning.

Miles cleared his throat. He couldn't keep his arms from trembling. "I…um…I know you think I'm too impulsive. But…," he swallowed, attempting to steady his shaking voice. "You are the best decision I have ever made, Tea Racker."

Tea's hand flew to her mouth. She stood in complete shock.

"Will you marry me?" Miles bit both his lips and blinked a tear from his eye.

Tea stared at him through her own tears. She hadn't moved since she saw him.

Mara nudged her back. "You should answer him," she whispered.

"Yes," she finally nodded. "Yes! Yes! Yes!" Tea ran over to Miles, and he stood up to meet her. Tea wrapped her arms around his neck, and he lifted her feet off the floor, spinning her around. He quickly put her down.

"The ring, the ring," he said nervously. He re-opened the box that was in his hand and Tea gasped when she got a close-up look at the gorgeous ring inside. Miles gently took her left hand, noticing both of theirs were shaking. He slowly slipped the ring on her finger and kissed her palm.

"I love you," he said, his voice catching. Tea held the sides of his face as he leaned down.

"I love you," she repeated over and over, kissing his mouth and his chin and back to his mouth again. Miles put his hands on her hips and passionately kissed her back.

Sirue and Mara both wiped tears and put their arms around each other, looking at their friends. Mara rested her head on Sirue's arm.

When Tea finally pulled away from the kiss, she turned around and flashed her ring.

"Look!" she squealed to Mara and Sirue and hurried over to them.

She snatched her hand back when she had a thought. "Wait. Y'all knew about this, didn't you?"

They both nodded. "I mean, our bags are always in the closet," Mara said matter-of-factly.

Tea made a face and lightly slapped them both on the arms.

Miles laughed, feeling extremely relieved. He sat at the table and tenderly pulled Tea over to him. She sat sideways on his lap, and they whispered and kissed as Tea kept examining the reflective jewels on her finger.

Sirue and Mara moved to the living room to finish cleaning up. He looked at Mara a few times, then went to get a small present that he'd tucked near the back of the tree earlier. He handed it to her.

"This is for you," he said quietly.

Mara made a face. She dropped the trash bag and opened the present. It was a thin book titled, You Carried a Miracle. Mara covered her mouth with her hand. She looked up at Sirue.

"Read the inscription," he said softly, helping her turn the cover.

Mara read Sirue's handwriting to herself. *"Remember, there's nothing empty about you."*

She stared at the words as teardrops watered the book. She closed it and read the title again. The book was about coping with the loss of miscarriage. She looked back up at Sirue. The gentleness in his face sent the feeling in her chest into overdrive. She reached up to put her arms around him and Sirue leaned down to wrap his arms around her body. Mara buried her face into his neck and held the back of his head. She wanted to stay there forever. Neither one of them moved.

Miles noticed and tapped Tea's arm. "Hey, baby, look," he whispered.

Tea waved him off and continued studying her ring from different angles.

He chuckled. "Baby," he said again.

Tea looked at him, then looked over at Sirue and Mara, standing in a silent embrace.

"Aww," Tea said, holding her hand over her heart. Then she looked past them out of the window. "And it's still snowing."

She stood up and took Miles' hand. They walked around the couch and stood in front of the window. Miles moved behind Tea and wrapped his arms around her as she held onto them. Mara released her arms from around Sirue and they looked at each other. He wiped her cheeks with his thumbs as Mara held the book to her chest. They turned to walk to the window, holding hands, as they all gazed at the falling snow.

The End...

Acknowledgements

A debut novel is a precious accomplishment for many reasons. I would like to recognize a few people who helped make this part of my dream come true.

To Marmy, Char, Tommy, and Daniel...thank you for the consistent encouragement and suggestions.

To Vicky and Mark, my very first ever beta readers... thank you for your time and valuable feedback. I took it to heart.

To Chelle...thank you for the inspiration.

To Quinten...thank you for being the calm in my stormy mind. That's a full-time job.

To Tatiana...thank you for being my purpose.

To my aunties, nieces, nephews, and cousins... thank you for loving me the way you do.

To everyone who has supported me and cheered me on, you know who you are. Thank you for the hope.

Made in the USA
Middletown, DE
01 May 2022

65093119R00192